Open Season

Alisa Schindler

ISBN: 1976382602

ISBN-13: 978-1976382604

DEDICATION

For all the coaches who dedicate their time, energy and patience,
you're all winners.
And to my husband, Mr. Baseball.

"Little league baseball is a very good thing because it keeps the parents off the streets." – Yogi Berra

ACKNOWLEDGMENTS

This book (and anything I accomplish) could never be done without a host of irreplaceable people. I couldn't have maintained my sanity or my confidence without the steady, loving voice of Pam Gawley in my ear and by my side. My friend, Kara Brodsky, was one of the first to read the book and provide encouragement and feedback, as she does in so many aspects of my life. Alyzia Sands, I can always count on you. Amy Nash, you have the eyes of an eagle and a house that has quickly become one of my son's favorites. Mara Wolman, you are my soul sister, lifelong reader and best friend. My sis-in-law Pam, thank you for being supportive, wonderful and always having my back. Mom, my constant cheerleader, your proofreading is kind of average but your overwhelming enthusiasm and conviction that I am basically perfect is exceptional. My three amazing little leaguers, you are everything - Everything. And to my husband, Bruce, Coach to so many, I hit a homerun when I found you.

To all my Legends teams both old and new, I love sitting and chatting with you, watching and cheering, holding our breath for the pitch, laughing and wincing, shaking our heads with joy or disaster, then folding up our chairs for the next game. You are champions in the trenches and on the sidelines. And to all those beautiful boys we root for, you are the best. Remember this time. Because it is awesome.

i

CHAPTER 1

Rockets (Gold) Team Chat
(Jake, Chris, Landon, Max, Dylan, Balls (Josh), Ryan, Money (Manny), Derek, Tyler, Jimmy, Reggie)

Tyler – Wow!! That game was awesome!!!

Chris – We smoked em!

Reggie – BAM!

Jake – It was a good game

Chris – It was an ass kicking game!

Balls (Josh) – It came down to the wire!

Landon – Wouldn't have if Coach W put Jake in

Balls (Josh) – Bro! STFU!

Ryan – Yeah man, WTF?

Derek – Nah, guys, he's right

Jake – No way, man. U played a great game. We're cool.

Landon – What?! No disrespect, D, but Jakey deserves his fair shake

Reggie – You're an A hole, Lan

Landon – Just speakin' my truth. U all think the same

Money (Manny) – Whatever, dudes. Did we kill it, or what?

Dylan – Killed it

Balls (Josh) – Dead

Money (Manny) – To the stars, Rockets!

Landon – LM(Golden)AO

Balls (Josh) – ROFL

Jimmy – LMGAO!! Yes!!!

Max – Eye roll

Chris - Spring season over! Ready for summer!

Dylan – Got to be in it to win it

Landon – Truth baby!

***

The groundskeeper found him at home plate, lying there on his side as if he had slid in just under the catcher's reach for the score. The championship trophy from the night before rested in the dirt next to his head. He wore his Rockets' uniform, the throwback jersey with their new logo that Deb, the team's general manager, had fought for, pleading to the stodgy and smug men in the FYO (Fort Jefferson Youth Organization) Little League executive committee. Most of them didn't even have kids who played anymore. They just enjoyed the title, the option of a Thursday night meeting with the boys to get out of the house for drinks at Flynn's, and to torture any woman, or man for that matter, but certainly any woman who tried to mess with the status quo. In the end, it had taken Deb three years of common sense mixed with flirtatious smiling and cajoling to get them to agree to a trial with this one jersey where the R in Rockets was enlarged and looked like it was lifting off pristine puffs of smoke.

Now that logo glared up at Donny in the early morning sun. He scratched underneath his cap that covered his balding head with long skinny fingers, blew out a deep breath and whistled low. It looked good, he noted, but it was the only thing since Coach Wayne Savage, FYO executive board member, commissioner of little league baseball and coach of their most elite team, lay sprawled out in the clay and dirt, dead on Field 2, his favorite field.

"Well, this is not good," he said out loud. Donny spent a lot of time alone on the fields commenting to the dewy green grass and the blue skies. He leaned down for a closer inspection, and after concluding that the Coach was indeed dead, Donny sighed and ambled, with no great urgency, back to the golf cart he used to get him round from field to field. He glanced at his walkie-talkie, but there was no one at the field house this early. Joe, FYO's program director, wasn't due in till 9 a.m., the same time that two lacrosse games were set to begin. This had to be dealt with immediately. But who should he call? The police? 911? For a second, he considered Deb, Wayne's right hand but then immediately thought of Faith, his wife.

Donny had witnessed a lot of crazy shit during his thirty plus years working the fields at FYO. The parents fought, the coaches fought, the umpires fought, the teams and the kids fought. Hell, they all fought with each other and plenty of them fought with him as well. There were concussions and injuries. He'd seen coaches, parents and players thrown out, and, in a few instances, banned. There were affairs and scandals. Cat fights and cat calls. But between the drama were amazing dives, catches and plays that could even stop the sentence of the most clueless, chatty mom and bring a whistle of respect from the scouts who occasionally surveyed the talent. Donny had seen it all. But the death of the most recognized coach in town? The coach of FYO's pride, the Rockets, who were crushing it for four years running. Well, that was something else altogether. This was a thing that needed to be handled with kid gloves, not his mangy old mitts.

Making his decision, he picked up his cell and tapped in Joe's number. Joe handled everything. He was the man who would know exactly the right call to make to deal with a situation like this. This was out of his league.

Within nine minutes of the call, two police cars and an ambulance rushed the lot, charging in with urgency, but no sirens screamed; there were only the red and blue twisting lights getting lost in the swelling sun. Donny answered their questions about what time he arrived. 7:45 a.m. And, if he had noticed anything suspicious. "You mean besides the dead coach?" he joked sarcastically. He gave them his name and short history as a native of Fort Jefferson, and star athlete in his day, although it hadn't been his day for over four decades.

Within fifteen minutes, Faith was there, standing by the body dumbstruck. Donny didn't know what to do with pretty little Faith, tears rolling down her apple cheeks, silently sucking in her heaves, her small chest rising and falling. He just kept nodding and tsking, adjusting and readjusting his baseball cap, and finally released his own sigh, one of deep relief when Joe's Bronco truck pulled in five minutes later. "Joe's here, Faith," he soothed. "He's gonna help figure this mess out." Faith barely responded as Donny zoomed off in his cart to greet him.

"You're fucking kidding me," Joe exploded at Donny. "This is a fucking disaster." He didn't wait for Donny's reply and marched out toward the field. He looked down at the body of his friend, well not quite his friend, but a close colleague in the dirty dugout of youth sports. He and Wayne spent hours, days, weeks, and years of their lives arguing and working together, and even occasionally enjoying an early morning run.

Wayne was a pain in his ass, always using him to garner the best times or fields, to make sure the best players were placed on his team despite the infuriation of the other coaches, and to be clean-up crew with outraged parents after he dropped yet another twelve-year-old who wasn't pulling his weight. But even with the occasional controversy and drama, Wayne was a winner. His team was filled with winners, and people liked winners. Certainly, if you're on the winning team. Or aspired to play on the winning team. Wayne's 12U Gold Rockets team ran away with most local tournaments, even on occasion, reaching state levels, which was pretty good for a local town team. But Wayne pushed his team hard, heavy on practices and demanding excellence. He could be tough on the kids and even tougher on the parents. You loved him or hated him, often both.

Just the night before, the Golden Rockets had won the Shore League, typically the last tournament of the spring season, ranking them number one on the North Shore of Long Island for the fourth year in a row. It was a hard earned win, and, as usual, to celebrate there was chest bumping and fist pumping, hooting and hollering along with the pizza and munchkins, although the pizza and munchkins would have been there either way. The players jumped on top of each other with glee while the moms chatted and casually kept an eye on the younger kids. The coaches patted each other on the backs and looked forward to the real celebration later at the bar where they could recap the game and revel in their glory. Other teams' members came by to offer congratulations, and there was enough cheer and food for all. Only occasionally would you hear the random gripe. "Of course he won again, he fixes the teams." Or, "He let my kid go, too much competition for his." But, overall, people played nice. Why not? It was end of season on a warm spring night, and there were munchkins.

"Hey, Faith," Joe said softly, taking the opportunity to put an arm around her fragile shoulders. "Did they tell you what happened?"

"No. They haven't told me anything." She sniffled as they watched the men lift Wayne on the stretcher. "This can't be real," she said as a uniformed cop walked toward her. "It can't be." She looked around helplessly. "He...he has a practice scheduled later..."

"Don't worry about any of it," Joe comforted. "Just go talk with the police and go home and be with your family. Derek and Reggie need you. I'll get it all straightened out."

She nodded as an official looking man, mid-thirties with dark hair and eyes, approached and introduced himself.

"Detective Jonas," he said. "You're Faith Savage, his wife?" Faith nodded. The detective opened his mouth to ask his first question when a loud, red Suburban raged through the gates of Tigers Turf, the official home fields of FYO. Everyone turned as the SUV screeched to a halt diagonally in the center of the parking lot.

The small group of them watched as a tall brunette, slim but athletically built, hurled herself from the vehicle and sprinted up to Field 2. Panting, she reached them, took one glance at the body on the stretcher and fell to the ground, breaking down into loud racking sobs.

From his golf cart by the field house, Donny shook his head and continued tsking.

"Deb," Joe tried, squatting down to her as she hovered over on the grass rocking. "Come on now, girl," he urged. "Get it together." Joe looked at Faith anxiously, but she rolled her eyes and turned her attention back to the detective.

"Drama queen," Faith muttered.

"Deb," Joe said with more force, grabbing her by the shoulders, "you need to get a hold of yourself."

Deb sniffled loudly and wiped her nose in the sleeve of her Lululemon pullover, all of a sudden looking around and realizing her outburst. Slowly, she nodded, but refused Joe's extended hand as she stood and brushed herself off. Her blue eyes turned from liquid to ice, and like that, she was the new picture of control.

"What happened?" she asked, her voice small but accusing.

Joe ignored her tone. It was no secret Deb kind of loved Coach Wayne.

"We don't know anything yet."

Realizing he had nothing to offer her, she sucked up her snot and walked away from him, toward the police and Faith.

"Bitch," Joe muttered and headed back to the field house to start making the calls and writing the email, and preparing for the shit storm that would be his day. "Donny," he yelled as he marched up the stairs to his office. "Make sure the fields are ready for lacrosse by teams' arrival at 8:30 a.m."

Donny shook his head heavily and started up the cart. Just like the show, the games must go on.

The detective, an unobtrusively attractive man with piercing eyes and a poker face, was asking Faith questions that made her even more uncomfortable, a position she didn't think possible since finding out her husband was dead not a half hour before.

"What time did your husband get home last night?

She looked at him uncertainly. She didn't know. She had gone home after helping clean up after the big game and celebration were over, probably around 9 p.m. She was upstairs getting changed for the night when she heard the alarm chimes that accompanied the front door opening. A minute later, Derek and Reggie came up the stairs.

"Hey, Mom," they said, and Reggie gave her a quick hug. "Dad dropped us before going out for the 'coach's meeting.'" He grinned knowingly. They all knew the meeting was at the bar.

She nodded. It was the regular gig—the meetings before to figure out strategy and line up, the meetings after to rehash and re-strategize, the drinks at the bar to celebrate or sulk. The games were just a side bar, a pretense for the men to hang out with their sons but really just reliving their youth alongside them. And since last night's game was a big one, she knew not to expect him back.

"Was your husband home this morning?"

She also had no idea. When she woke up at 7:00 a.m., he was already gone. That wasn't unusual, either. Sometimes, he took an early run. Sometimes, he went to the field to meet with Joe or drop something off, or pick something up. Any excuse to stay connected to the game. There also was the fact that he didn't generally sleep in their bedroom anymore. He used the guest bedroom as his own. They told the kids he snored, which he did, but that wasn't why he slept there as much as he did.

"Has he been acting any differently recently?"

Not that she had realized, but honestly, she could count on one hand the amount of times she saw him these past few weeks. With work, the games, practices, meetings and the nights out at the bar, she had seen Wayne randomly between his rushing in and out of the house, shouting at her to pack a snack bag for them, or find a missing chest guard or cup. So, no, nothing any different than usual.

"Did you kill your husband?"

That one stopped her.

She looked at the detective, who was looking at her with intent brown eyes. What was this young, slightly over-eager man's name? "Excuse me?" she asked. "Detective Jonas, is it? Are you saying that my husband was murdered?"

"Well, Ma'am," he said, and Faith automatically cringed at the term ma'am, "we won't know until we get the official report, but it does look as though he was hit over the head with a blunt object." He turned his attention to two uniformed cops carefully bagging up last night's winning trophy. Faith's eyes followed in understanding and then she noticed the damp patch in the dirt and the small smear of red on home plate.

"Oh my God." She swayed a little; her hundred and ten pound body barely carrying enough weight to keep her grounded.

"What did you just say?" Deb immediately stepped between them, standing almost as tall as Detective Jonas. "What was that? Did you say that Wayne was murdered?" Deb and Detective Jonas met at eye level, and he took a beat to study her short, straight dark hair that cut a sleek line with her chin and the intensity in her red-rimmed blue eyes. She was mid-thirties, about a decade younger than the petite blonde she had just eclipsed.

"Deb, is it?" Detective Jonas sized her up. "And what's your relation to the victim?"

Deb sniffed and stood a little straighter so she was looking down a little on the detective. "I'm the Rocket's team manager and my son, Landon, plays second base."

"And where were you late last night through early morning?"

Deb broke eye contact and looked off to the side and out into the left field. "At home, of course."

"Can anyone corroborate?"

She shrugged. "Well, Landon was home but he was sleeping. He's still sleeping."

"What about your husband?" the detective asked.

"Divorced." Her face pulled in with distaste, like she just sucked a lemon.

"Excuse me." Faith cut in. "But unless there's anything else you need right now, there's a lot of stuff I need to handle today. I want to get home to my boys. Derek and Reggie need to hear this from me before someone texts them."

"Derek and Reggie?" The detective raised a brow. "As in Jeter and Jackson?"

"He loved the Yankees," Faith said flatly, over the annoying question for about a decade already, more amazed that she had already automatically switched to the past tense, 'loved.'

"Of course." The detective pulled a card out of his pocket and handed it to her. "I'll be in touch. And, I'm really sorry for your loss, Mrs. Savage."

"Thank you, Detective. Now, if you'll excuse me." She gave a little snort, maybe of emotion, maybe of distaste, as she brushed past Deb, who shrank just a little. Deb and the detective watched her small frame walk carefully away, stepping through the grass, shrewd enough to know, even under these extreme circumstances, not to walk through the field but around it.

When she was a far enough distance away, Detective Jonas turned to Deb and asked, "Are you and Mrs. Savage friends?"

Deb sniffed and shrugged. "I wouldn't call us friends, but we get along well enough."

"And you're the..." He tapped his pen on his pad. "Team manager, huh? So, what does that entail?"

"Yeah, I'm the team admin, the general manager, Wayne's girl Friday, and Saturday through Thursday as well." She gave a short laugh. "Whatever Wayne needed, whatever the team needed, coordinating tournaments, booking hotels, making reservations for food, ordering uniforms, special belts for special occasions, fundraising, scheduling for practices, emails… what didn't I do, really."

The detective nodded, scribbling away.

"In fact, I have to go speak with Dan and Matt, the assistant coaches, and send out an email to the team, letting them know what happened." Tears welled in her eyes. "I don't know how I'm going to tell them. This is just so awful." Her body slumped, and she convulsed into tears.

Detective Jonas stood a respectable distance from her and watched her shoulders rise and fall. They were surprisingly broad. "I'm sorry," he said. "I can see this is very difficult for you. Why don't you go home. If I have any questions I'll contact you."

Deb nodded. "Fine." She turned to go, walking a few paces, stepping around some goose shit in the grass and continuing on, every so often letting out a loud heave of emotion.

The detective whistled low and slow at her departure. This was turning out to be an doozy of a day.

"You ain't kidding," Donny's voice cut in from behind.

The detective turned and studied the sixty-something-year-old man sitting there, having somehow silently sidled up in his golf cart. He nodded agreeably. "Hey, buddy. I got some more questions for you."

"Yes, sir," Donny said, but he made no move toward the detective and instead waited for him to walk over. Donny had a good thirty years on the man, and although he had been a star basketball player and maintained a wiry frame, his knees were done. Even with the cortisone shots he had been taking, every step was an effort. As he watched the detective walk over, Donny considered how much he wanted to reveal. He had a lot to say. But there was a lot more he wouldn't.

CHAPTER 2

From: Deb Schnitt
To: The Golden Rockets and their Families
(Marie, Rich, Nick, Robin, Barb, Faith, Sean, Nicole)
CC: Coaches Dan Williams and Matt Bidsky
Subject: Private, important and heartbreaking news.

Team. It is with a very heavy heart that I share this disturbing and upsetting news. This morning, our fearless leader, Coach Wayne Savage, was found dead at Tigers Turf. Coach Savage was an inspiration to us all to be the best that we could be. I know he was proud of each and every one of you, and I hope you carry his life lessons with you for all your days. I can't even begin to express my shock and surprise. This is a really bad call from the big guy up above. He totally dropped the ball with this one.

I'm sure there will be more details coming out in the coming days, but please know that we are still a team, will always be a team. I know that Coach W would want us all to stick together and continue to play and win. Because that's what W stands for. Winning. I hope you're up there knocking 'em out of the park, Coach. We'll miss you, and we won't let you down!

I will be communicating with Coach Dan and Coach Matt to discuss how we are going to proceed. I'm sorry to be the bearer of such horrible news. Our hearts and prayers go out to Faith, Derek, and Reggie. When I hear about any funeral details, I will pass them along.

To the stars, Rockets.

Deb

P.S. Of course, practice tonight is canceled.

Coach Dan sat at his kitchen table reading Deb's email. He already knew what had happened, having received a call from both Matt and a Detective Jonas, who was interested in speaking with him. The idea that Wayne was dead was almost unimaginable. His person in life was large. He filled a space both in stature and in personality. The minute Wayne entered a room, the room stopped to acknowledge him, and if they didn't, Wayne made sure that his booming laugh and loud presence overpowered any other action, demanding all the attention.

Dan was used to being his number two, even sometimes bumped to number three. He was the bench whisperer. The quiet force who sat in the dugout and used his low tones and soothing words to either work the kids up or settle them down.

The boys relied on his steady force to balance out the triangle. Coach Savage (or Coach W) charged ahead, driving them hard, but also rewarding them just as hard. Coach Matt, intense and hotheaded but also full of baseball knowledge and sense, who had a way of shouting out words of inspiration that actually inspired. And he was an excellent first base coach.

Wayne and Matt always kept a bit of a distance between themselves and the boys who vacillated between awe and fear. As coaches, they demanded respect and the boys worked hard to prove themselves. In contrast, Dan played it low and on the outside, sitting quietly, keeping the book and maintaining order in the dugout. This had been his role for the last four years, and at times it was frustrating. He knew he could be a stronger driving force on the team, but you could only have so many leaders, besides he enjoyed being more on the inside with the boys. He got used to the boys tentative approaches, their quiet, questioning, "Coach Dan?" as they slid next to him to confide a hurt, seek advice or complain about one of the other players, their parents, or, on rare occasion, one of the other coaches. So even though there were times when his anger flared and he clashed with the big personalities and egos of Wayne or Matt, he quickly got it back under control.

He had his son Jake to think of. He had enough trouble playing catcher, the same position as Wayne's son, and doing a better job of it. It was a regular struggle (for both of them) in humility and patience to get Jake his playing time and his well-earned and deserved credit. Still, he cherished his special place with the boys and on the team. With the pressures of such a competitive atmosphere, the boys naturally drifted to his gentle, soft spoken manner. What would they do now? Those poor boys. They needed him. The team needed him. Faith needed him.

Faith. She was probably a real mess. An image of her popped into his head; her hazel eyes searching, her blonde hair falling loose in her face. She was so small and sexy, and alone now. Like him. His divorce had been final for over two years already. He and his ex, Nicole, had finally come to a place where they could co-parent and coexist, if not in an amicable way, at least not in a hostile one. It had been a battle to get out, and luckily his wife had been as miserable as he was and had an affair. Of course, he was hurt and angry. Who wouldn't be? Coming home to find her in the arms of the contractor who was already raking him over the coals for the bathroom renovations that had taken weeks longer than expected to complete. He was paying for all the extras, but the contractor was the one who was really getting them. It was a real blow to his pride and his pocketbook, and the divorce was even worse.

Now with the passing of years, after having time to process with the assistance of a lot of alcohol, maybe a therapeutic hole or two punched through his bedroom wall and some deep thinking on the matter, he no longer blamed her. He knew they weren't happy and that given the right circumstances, he would have cheated as well. He just never had any real opportunity. Between work, coaching games, the kids, and being generally exhausted, there just wasn't enough time or energy to even consider dabbling, except in fantasy with Faith.

But that was then. Now, he was ready to dabble like crazy. He ran a tired hand through his dark, wavy hair and glanced at the computer screen on his desk at work. 1:37 p.m. The numbers on the marketing report spreadsheet he was analyzing blurred together. Wayne drifted into his brain. His strong features and barrel chest. The way he strode on to a field; his very posture a dare to the opposing team's coach. He was dead. Wayne was dead. It seemed impossible to comprehend, especially when he had just seen him hours before. Those poor boys of his. And Faith. Without thinking, he typed her an email.

From: Dan
To: Faith
Subject: No words

I am so sorry. I don't even know what to say. This is unbelievable. I wanted to come by in person but I thought you might need some alone time to process, and I didn't want to intrude. I'm here for you whenever, whatever you need. Anything, really. Please just let me know.

Not five minutes went by before Dan saw a new message pop up on his screen.

From: Faith
To: Dan

Thank you. No words is right. I am honestly in shock. I can't even form sentences. I promise to let you know if there's anything I need.

He tried to read into it, to find some not so hidden secret plea that would give him an excuse to drop by later, some need, but unfortunately couldn't find any. A little disappointed and not ready to work, Dan zipped off an email to Matt.

From: Dan
To: Matt
Subject: Mind blown

Buddy, is this fucking crazy or what? I am totally... I don't even know. I am in shock! I know we talked, but my brain is churning. I can't stop thinking and wondering what the hell happened. Are you as completely flipped out as I am? Meanwhile, and I know this is going to sound horrible, but what are we going to do with the team? We have a tournament in two weeks. Do we go?

The computer flashed again.

From: Matt
To: Dan

Someone totally popped him. I'm writing up a list of suspects and it's long, dude. And, fuck yeah, we go.

Dan leaned back in his chair, sucking the breath in between his teeth and wondering if he'd be on the list.

***

Rockets Team Chat

(Jake, Chris, Landon, Max, Dylan, Balls (Josh), Ryan, Money (Manny), Derek, Tyler, Jimmy, Reggie)

Balls (Josh) – Holy crap, guys! Did you hear about coach??

Dylan – What?

Josh – He's dead. Dudes, Coach is dead.

Jake – WTF?!

Chris – Shut the hell up!

Money (Manny) – You're making that shit up

Balls (Josh) – I'm not. My dad told me! And then I looked it up!!

Tyler – Googling it!

Balls (Josh) – It's true. Derek, Reggie, I'm so sorry

Max – We're all sorry!

Landon – This is crazy. Does anyone know what happened?

Dylan – Google says 'suspicious circumstances'

Money (Manny) – You mean he was murdered! That is so whack! Maybe he shouldn't have yelled so much.

Jake – Shut up, Money. That's so rude. Derek, Reggie you guys there? I'm so sorry

Money (Manny) – You just want your dad to take it over

Jake – Stop being an asshole

Balls (Josh) – He can't help it

Tyler – Come on, everyone knows Landon's mom is gonna run the team anyway. She's got the power!

Jimmy – Whoop whoop!

Manny – LMAO

Dylan – Choke!

Jake – Guys, just shut up. Derek, you there? We're all really sorry. Reggie? Derek? You there?

***

Dan left work early, grabbing the 3:19 p.m. out of Penn Station, which would pull back into Fort Jefferson by 4:05 p.m.. He wasn't getting anything done anyway and felt the need to be closer to home. Jake had a basketball clinic till 5 p.m., and his daughter Lola was on a play date, so he told his ex that he would stop by the house afterward, maybe have a catch with Jake or take them to an early dinner. He needed to be the one to explain about Coach W to Jake. He couldn't even imagine how he would take the news. They had been part of the team since he was in kindergarten. Hopefully, the school wasn't already buzzing about it. With all the cell phones and the Internet, you couldn't keep anything secret these days.

With a couple of hours to kill and no idea what to do with himself, he decided to head over to Tigers Turf, hoping Joe would be there to commiserate. He parked, emerged from his car, and immediately bumped into Mikey Short, one of the parents on the team and a general psycho, although reasonably likeable when not either screaming from the sidelines at his kid or driving Wayne crazy.

"Hey, Mikey," Dan greeted, shaking his head.

"I can't believe it," Mikey agreed. "I mean, I really can't. I was set to meet him in an hour or so before the practice."

His son, Josh, was one of their star pitchers, a lefty who threw gas with great control while Mikey was one of their star problems. Wayne used to joke especially at games where Josh was really on, that he was picturing his father's face in the catcher's mitt, even suggesting the visualization to Josh who just snorted and laughed.

Mikey was one of those overly invested parents who constantly annoyed him, Wayne and Matt, by second guessing their decisions and not trusting them to do right by his kid. He paced up and down the first base line like a stalker on crack, shouting encouragements, which were more obnoxious, obvious rants—"Josh! You need to pound the zone! Josh! Focus! Stay back!"—to his kid while on the mound and even kept his own pitch count. Wayne had thrown him out of multiple games for being too disruptive.

"I know, I'm still having a hard time believing he's not sitting in the field house right now shooting the shit with Joe."

Mikey leaned in close. A little too close. Mikey was never good with personal space. "So, Danny boy, is it true?"

Dan's lip curled slightly. Only Wayne called him Danny boy. He didn't like it, but he and Wayne had a certain back and forth so from him it was okay. He and Mikey had nothing. Although, if he called attention to it, Mikey would probably call him Danny boy from then on just to be an asshole. He was that guy. Dan played dumb on the question. "What do you mean?"

"You know, about it being a murder." Mikey's eyes were wide, almost googly.

"Oh, yeah," Dan nodded, looking him directly in the eye. "Totally true. You know, I hear you're a suspect."

Mikey blanched and pulled back a little in surprise. Dan gave it three seconds, letting him stew in his anxiety, amused watching him try to find a way through his stammer to come up with a sentence. Poor guy really looked like he swallowed a can of paint thinner. He put him out of his misery. "Relax," he said and gave him a light smack on the shoulder. "I was kidding. Although, you had the look of guilt about you. What were you meeting with Wayne about today, anyway?"

Mikey smiled but was still a bit shaken. "Funny, asshole."

"You probably will be questioned, though. I'm sure we all will, and I would try to do better than you just did."

He laughed, but it was forced. "You just threw me."

"So what were you meeting with Wayne about?" Dan asked again. Wayne hadn't mentioned it to him.

"Ah, it was nothing. No big deal," he said, evasively and then quickly ended their conversation. "I got to run, man. Keep me posted on… well, anything."

Dan watched him go with interest. Everything with Mikey was a big deal. He walked up the steps into the field house on a conversation already in progress, recognizing the voices of Joe and Matt before even stepping in.

Matt was pacing, the way he did when anxious, his long hair pulled back in a ponytail. He had two levels of intensity, hot tempered and chill. It suited him as a pot smoking, craft beer drinking, philosophizing environmental lawyer who almost never wore a suit.

"I'm just saying it's for the good of the team."

Joe's eyes pinched together in tension. "And I'm saying, not today, Matt! We'll figure out what's best for the team soon enough! Oh, Dan, hey."

They both turned. Matt clearly startled but covering fast with a nod. "Hey, man."

Dan nodded back and walked in carefully, like he was entering the lion's den or more accurately the Tiger's. "What are you guys talking about?"

Matt and Joe exchanged a glance.

"We were discussing the future of the Rockets," Matt said, his words lined with just an edge of defensiveness.

"Uh huh." Dan eyed them both. "Wayne isn't even dead a day and you're already applying for the position?"

"Don't give me that shit, Dan," Matt spat. "You're just pissed I beat you to it."

He wasn't completely wrong. Dan had intended to make his pitch for head coach as well. He just thought he'd wait until the dust settled a little. Or at least till after the funeral. Or a day, at least wait a fucking day. Shit. "Yeah, you're right, Matt. You're always right."

Matt sneered and gave a snort. "Hard to argue with that."

"I'm sure you'll find a way," Dan said.

"Guys," Joe cut in, "I know you both want the gig. Let's just let it sit for a while. You can manage together for now, and we'll figure it out. There's no rush."

"Of course," Dan said agreeably. "That's what I figured."

"Yeah, me too," Matt snorted and extended his hand. "May the best coach win."

Dan rolled his eyes and swatted his hand away. "Give me a break."

"Oh," Matt laughed, looking at Joe. "Did you see that? Kind of looks like poor sportsmanship!"

Joe gave Dan a sideways look of understanding. Being FYO's Executive Director in charge of programming and day to day operations, he was used to being surrounded by assholes.

"Hey, you guys want to grab a beer?" Matt asked.

They both shook their heads. "Sorry," Dan said. "I'd love to, but I've got a bunch of shit to do and then I need to go see Jake and Lola. I want to be the one to tell Jake about Wayne.

"I think you're late on that," Matt said. "Manny already called me. There was a group chat. They all know. They know everything with those goddamn phones. In fact, they probably knew even before we did." He chuckled. He was always cracking himself up.

"This new social media world kind of sucks." Dan commented and the other old men in the room nodded their agreement. "Well, as his parent, I still need to talk to him about it unless, of course, there's now an app to replace human interaction."

"Coming soon, I'm sure," Matt joked.

"I'm out too, Matt," Joe said. "Too much to do with all this. But we'll definitely grab that beer soon. There's a lot we need to discuss."

Matt and Dan turned to leave, but Joe stopped them. "Oh, guys, one more thing." They turned back, immediately not trusting Joe's tone or the last minute recollection. "Mikey came in here before, angling to be an assistant coach. You know I've put him off countless times, but now there's actually a need." He put up a hand to stop Matt, whose mouth was already open in protest. "Plus, he came in with a nice-sized donation. I told him I'd talk to you guys about it. So I'm talking and he's going to help the team till we figure—"

"You're fucking kidding me?" Matt cut in, unable to stop himself. "That guy is the worst! He's a hyper neurotic pansy. We had a hard enough time keeping him out of the way when he wasn't wearing a jersey!"

"Matt's right," Dan agreed. "That guy is no good. He's bad for his kid, he's bad for the team, and he's a hundred percent bad for us."

Joe looked back and forth between each of them slowly and chose his words with care. "I hear you," he said nodding. "And you can have him scraping shit off the kids' cleats for all I care but, for now, he will be an assistant coach."

"Fuck!" Matt pushed open the door and stormed out.

"Well that went well," Joe said, his eyes lit in a smile.

"We'll do what we have to do," Dan said. "Don't worry, Matt's a hothead but he'll get over it."

"You were always the reasonable one," Joe said.

"Lot of good that's done me," Dan said lightly, keeping his words as level as the playing ground.

He got outside just in time to see Matt peeling off in his Honda Prius. The man was environmentally conscious after all, although his wife Barb drove around town in an SUV.

Mikey and Donny sat in Donny's golf cart watching him go. The seat next to Donny was always occupied by somebody—a mom whose son forgot his water bottle and needed a quick lift, children angling for a ride, grandparents with difficulty walking or the never-ending stream of coaches, and parents all wanting to shoot the shit or complain about the shit with the all-knowing, wise and tempered eyes and ears of Tigers Turf. Dan walked casually over.

"That man knows how to make an exit," Donny said, his eyes still focused on the exit gates.

"He seemed upset about something," Mikey fished, his stare intense. "Everything okay?"

Dan refused to give anything away. He wasn't going to bond with Mikey over anything. "All good. Just business as usual." He headed toward his car. "See you guys."

His phone rang just as he was pulling up to his house. Not his house, he reminded himself for the millionth time, Nicole's house. Both Jake and Lola were on the lawn; Jake tossing a ball into the pitch back and eight year-old Lola drawing with chalk on the sidewalk. He parked, turned off the engine, and answered. "Hey, Dan, it's me, Deb."

"Hey, Deb. How are you?" He was sure she was a mess.

"Kind of a wreck."

"Yeah. I'm sorry. I know this must be really difficult for you."

"You don't even know the half of it."

He knew much more than half of the half of it, Dan thought grimly, as did half the town. "I'm sorry," he said again. "So what's up. I just pulled up to my ex's to see the kids. Can we talk later?"

"Of course. I just wanted to go over the upcoming practice schedule with you and some details for the tournament in two weeks, and a memorial I've just started to plan for Wayne..." She sniffled a little, and Dan could tell she was crying.

"Deb, you want me to come over after? We can talk."

"I don't know, maybe. I'm not sure. I just keep thinking about yesterday's awesome game. I mean it was yesterday..."

"Yeah, I know," Dan said, although yesterday's game now seemed a lifetime ago. They played the Chiefs, their toughest competitors, a rival club team with a dick coach, Doug, who was always trying to poach their players. He could still see Mikey, biting his cuticles, pacing up and down the line, shouting at Josh on the mound. It was so distracting that at one point Wayne strut over, chest out, anger seeping through his steeled expression of calm. He put an arm around his shoulder and quietly told Mikey to shut the fuck up or he'd throw him the fuck out and pull Josh off the mound. That was the kicker, and it shut him up fast. But the picture in his head that most stuck was a moment right after the win; Wayne beaming, raising one fist to the sky, the other grasping the championship trophy, the boys all circling round jumping.

"Listen, I'll give you a call after and maybe stop by."

"Okay, thanks, Dan."

He hung up, took a breath, then got out of the car, the kids' necks twisting like pups at the sound of the door's slam.

"Dad!" Lola screeched and bounded over, the picture of all things good in the world. Jake. Of course, at twelve, played it way more cool.

"Hey, Dad."

"Hey, guys!" He ruffled both their heads and planted a kiss on top. "What's going on?"

"Mom's inside making dinner. It's baked ziti night!" Lola happily squealed.

Maybe I'm not taking them to dinner, Dan thought. Nicole was unpredictable like that. He'd think they had agreed to something and then she'd unceremoniously change the rules. Even though it had been a few years and they were both in a better place, there was still a wall of divorced resentment between them that sometimes came out in little spiteful bursts, like making a favorite dinner when he planned to take them out. You would think that she was the one who caught him cheating. Still, generally they were good and he tried his best to roll with it. It just made things easier on the kids.

"Sounds delicious," he said. "Can you go tell your mom I'm here?"

Lola smiled happily and skipped back to the house, giving Dan and Jake the moment alone he wanted.

"Hey, buddy, so I wanted to talk to you…"

"Dad, I know about Coach."

"Yeah, I heard you might. I had wanted to tell you myself." Jake shrugged. "I'm sure you have a lot of feelings about what happened."

"Dad. Stop. I'm fine."

"You're fine?"

"I mean, I'm sad and all. I feel bad, but I'm fine."

"Okay," Dan said, giving him some space, "but if you need to talk about it. I'm here."

"I know." They lapsed into silence for a minute. "Dad?" Jake asked tentatively, a wisp of sandy brown hair covering his eyes and any emotion they might hold. "Are you going to take over the team? All the kids are talking about it."

"I don't know what will be, buddy," he answered honestly. "Maybe. I'd like to, but now isn't the time to think about that. Now is the time to think about Wayne and Faith, Derek and Reggie and all they are going through."

"But the team will stay together?" His voice held so much earnest hope, reminding Dan yet again why he was still a coach despite the countless times he wanted to walk, should have walked. His boy loved the game, and he loved his boy.

"The team isn't going anywhere," he promised.

From Matt
To: Deb
CC: Dan
Subject: Taking stock

Okay, let's talk details. What's the upcoming practice schedule? At minimum, we should aim for at least two during the week and one on the weekends. The tourney at Big League Baseball at Yapank is in less than three weeks. Also send out an email to the team about hotel reservations for that weekend so we know what parents are going and what kids are going to have to room with another family. Also, it's a breast cancer tournament. Did we get the pink belts? I know this seems too business as usual considering, but we've got to keep it together and keep going for the team. To the stars Rockets!

From Deb
To: Matt
CC: Dan
Subject: Giving stock

All taken care of, Matt. Reservations made and list of parents attending attached. Practice schedule also attached and belts ordered. I'm working on Wayne's memorial with Joe for next week or the following at TT. I'm ordering special patches for our team. I've attached the logo as well. It's a big W circled with the words Win for Wayne. I'm going to do the best I can for the team, but I'm having a real hard time with business as usual.

From Dan

23

To: Deb and Matt
CC: Joe
Subject: Fresh out of stocks to give

I agree on all fronts. I know it's hard but I think the kids need to keep some sense of normal. Let's schedule a practice tomorrow afternoon. Funeral is in the morning. I think it'll be good for the kids. I'll check with Faith to make sure she's okay with it.

From Joe
To: Dan, Deb and Matt
Subject: ?

Why the hell isn't Mikey on this chain? Was I speaking to myself?

From Dan
To: Faith
Subject: Checking in

Hi there, just checking in because I'm thinking about you and the boys. I know the funeral is tomorrow morning. This is just so surreal.

Also, we were thinking of having a practice tomorrow afternoon for the kids. Thought it would be good for the kids to get out in the fresh air and sweat after such an emotional morning. Your call. We'll wait if you say so. Let me know if you need anything at all.

From Faith
To: Dan
Subject: Thanks

Thanks for checking in. I'm hanging in there. I think the practice is a good idea. It will get the boys out of the house that will be filled with death and old family members. See you tomorrow. I can't believe this is real.

From Matt
To: Deb
Subject: Lock, stock and barrel

Make sure you run everything you schedule by me first. I know Dan and I are going to manage together for a while, but it's better for the team if someone takes the lead. Dan's a great guy and all, but we both know that he lacks the killer instinct that you need to win. Wayne would want it this way. And I know you would want what Wayne would want.

***

"You're kidding me!" Dan sat at Deb's kitchen island, seething. "He's such an asshole."

Deb took a long pull on her beer, then reached her bottle out to tap it to Dan's. "I'll drink to that."

"I can't believe he thinks that's what Wayne would have wanted." Dan hesitated. "Wait, is that what Wayne would have wanted?"

She averted her eyes. "I can only say that Wayne wouldn't have wanted any of it because Wayne wanted to be here, alive and running the team. Wayne didn't talk about who would ever take over for him. He was never stepping down."

Dan conceded the point. He wanted to know what Wayne thought of him, but it was probably better not to. Wayne and Matt had more in common temperament-wise than he and Wayne did, but he always thought that despite their differences, Wayne respected him more. "True," he agreed. He didn't want to put Deb in an awkward position. They were friends, and there was no reason. He changed the subject. "So, how are you doing?"

"Honestly, I'm numb, in total shock and those moments when I'm not, it's worse." Her exhausted and swollen blue eyes pierced him with the depth of their pain. She loved Wayne hard. It made him think about Faith. Faith was his ideal woman even before his divorce from Nicole. He remembered exactly when they first met because she dazzled him right there. It was at Tigers Turf, of course, and their kids were only six years old. He met her with Wayne and the twins, Reggie and Derek. They were a picture perfect family. The boys small and identically adorable in their uniforms but with faces strikingly opposite in feature. Wayne, the epitome of a confident, good looking and amiable jock husband, greeted him with a shit-eating grin and strong handshake. But Faith took his breath away; her smile so warm and genuine, her teeth Colgate white, her body tight and tiny. Her sexy hazel eyes twinkled and teased him right from the start. "Welcome to the big leagues," she said, and he was smitten.

"It'll get better," he said to Deb. It was the standard line. Who knew if it would get better. Who knew what would happen. Who could have guessed that Wayne would be dead. Still, what else was there to say.

"So Mikey, huh?" Deb said. "That sucks."

Dan snorted and took another deep pull from his bottle. "Who says things can't get worse?"

They clinked bottles again.

CHAPTER 3

From: Deb Schnitt
To: The Golden Rockets and their Families
(Marie, Rich, Nick, Robin, Barb, Faith, Sean, Nicole)
CC: Coaches Dan Williams, Matt Bidsky and Mikey Dunn
Subject: Funeral arrangements

Our Lady of Mercy
10 a.m.
Manhasset

The mass and the speakers finally finished and had included a few words from Joe, Matt, who just loved the sound of his own voice, one of Wayne's coworkers and his father, a barrel-chested man who eerily resembled a Wayne that Wayne would never be. It ended with a heartbreaking tribute from the twins, who insisted on trading lines while reading a motivational speech from one of the Rocky movies.

Reggie started, projecting strong and clear. "Our dad's favorite quote from Rocky Balboa says more about him than anything." He passed the paper to Derek, who read much more to his chest than the mourners.

"'You, me, or nobody is gonna hit as hard as life. But it ain't about how hard ya hit." He passed the paper back to Reggie without lifting his head.

"It's about how hard you can get hit and keep moving forward. How much you can take and keep moving forward. That's how winning is done!'" Reggie shouted the last line a bit like Wayne would have, and the crowd gave a light chuckle. He handed the paper to Derek.

"Our dad was a winner. And that's why our team is a winner. And why we're all winners." Reggie finished, smiling painfully with tears rolling down his cheeks. "Thank you, Dad. We love you."

The crowd gave a collective sniffle and then broke into little groups talking amongst themselves. Deb sat off to the side surveying the attenders. Half the town was there. Being a coach for years at FYO meant knowing pretty much everyone and everyone knowing you. Besides coaching the most visible winning team in Fort Jefferson's history, Wayne had his name penned on a few high profile boards and committees—Friends for a Friendly Fort, Friends of Fort Outreach and Fort Beautiful. His Wall Street buddies showed up and so did quite a few coaches from rival teams. Deb even spotted Doug the dick, standing and chatting with some other out of town coaches. She had a vision of Doug from the game the other night. His face hot, his temper hotter as he accused Wayne, not for the first time, of stealing signs. Like he would ever. Wayne didn't need to steal to win, Deb scoffed. Although, they exchanged words over it more than once.

Doug caught her eye and nodded. She looked away. How could he be here and Wayne be gone? The casket at the front of the church was flanked with flowers and trophies. A giant blow up picture of Wayne, her, Dan, Matt and the team stood off to the right, with two boards covered with smaller 8x10, 5x7 and 4x6 prints. Baseball memories filled the space, overlapping the years, with a few pictures of Faith and Wayne and Faith, Wayne and the boys. A large poster board sat off to the side, a headshot of Wayne in his Rockets uniform, not the new one, Deb noted, meant for the boys on the team or whoever to sign and pay their respects. She had suggested the idea, thinking Derek and Reggie might appreciate what their dad had meant to so many kids, but now it just looked cheesy with the kids lining up and signing it like they were at a Bar Mitzvah or some other special occasion party.

She had intended to send out a note telling any boys who may be coming to wear their uniforms out of respect, but it hadn't been necessary. They were all there and all in uniform with the new throw-back jerseys. Deb's eyes welled. The boys looked so beautiful and young, huddling together in this awful place, pretending to be normal and cracking jokes. She watched Josh lightly shove Max and Max shoulder check Jake. They were under a tremendous amount of stress. The practice later was a really good idea. It would unconsciously help them work through all that negative energy, release it out on the fields by working together and working up a good sweat. It was the best tribute to Wayne they could do. It would have made him so proud. Again, her tears pushed up and over her rims and dripped down her face.

She felt a body plop down next to her. Bracing herself for conversation, she wiped her cheeks, plastered a grim smile and turned.

She found Detective Jonas studying her. He reached into his jacket pocket and pulled out a tissue. "Here."

"Thanks." They sat next to each other watching the mill of people. Wayne and Faith's families and friends, neighbors, Dan, Matt, Mikey, Joe, Donny, the whole team and their accompanying parents, other FYO board members and team coaches. Johnny Smith and some of the other lacrosse coaches showed, even though it was well known that lacrosse and baseball had a long time rivalry over field times, and that Wayne sat squarely in the middle of it.

"Nice turnout," Detective Jonas said.

"Well everyone loved Wayne," Deb said, her voice breaking.

"Yeah? Is that right?" Detective Jonas scratched his head. "Cause I feel like I'm meeting a lot of people who didn't like him."

Deb sucked up her emotion and waved her manicured hand, shooing away any annoying thoughts. "Jealous people. So many people were jealous of Wayne."

"Why?" the detective asked, his brown eyes almost innocent in their curiosity.

"Why?" Deb studied at him back, assessing him carefully. "Detective Jonas, right?" The detective nodded. She sat up a little straighter, never dropping her gaze. "Wayne was a winner. Losers don't always like winners, and this town is filled with a lot of sore losers."

After a beat, Detective Jonas asked, "Care to name a few?"

Dan tried to disentangle himself from the team parent circle but couldn't. He had been stuck in their center for over a half an hour, dizzy from their pecking, unmanageable worry. He wanted to speak with Joe and with Deb, and pay his respects to Faith, who looked so lost and fragile he just wanted to pick her up and carry her away, but the parents had so many questions and concerns that he found himself helplessly stuck. Yes, he assured them, the team would go on. Yes, both he and Matt were coaching together for now. Yes, Mikey was joining the coaching staff. Yes, it seemed there was some foul play involved in Wayne's death. No, he didn't know anything. Yes, he would tell them the minute he did. And, yes, practice was today at 4 p.m. The minute he thought he was finished, another parent slid in and asked the same lineup of questions. Escape was impossible.

Faith was in hell. Wayne's overbearing family was crying loudly, demanding her attention and all the patience she had left in the world. These last twenty-four hours were a dream, more accurately, a nightmare. She couldn't believe this new world she lived in, one where she was sitting dressed in black attending her husband's funeral. The future was now a frightening and open landscape that she couldn't even begin to think about. She looked at the time, 11:32 a.m. She didn't know how much more she could take. She really needed a drink.

Matt was stuck talking to Doug the dick who was still being a whiny bitch about losing the game and the fact that they were stealing their signs, which they totally were. "Dude, could you let it go? We're at a funeral. Jeez, show some respect."

"When have you and Wayne ever shown anyone any respect?" Doug challenged.

Matt snapped back. "You want to talk about the playoff game you won last week where you kept delaying the game till time ran out? Real classy move." Matt's voice was no longer in low tones and people turned to stare.

"We learned from the best," Doug spat back.

Matt kept his game face on but moved in closer to Doug. "Man, if you don't take your trash talk out of here, I'm going to throw you out."

Doug paled a little but didn't back down. "Maybe now you guys could get a new coach who tries winning a game without cheating."

That was when Matt punched Doug in the face. The next four minutes were a flurry of arms and fists until both Matt, Doug, and a bunch of spectators found themselves outside of the funeral home.

Matt straightened his sports jacket. "It was time to go, anyway." He chuckled a little and pointed hard at Doug, whose face was red with affront and embarrassment. "You never could just leave it on the field. Amateur." He shook his head in disgust. "Barb! Manny!" he yelled for his wife, who came out shaking her head and his son who was hiding outside with the rest of the younger boys even before the men were ejected. "Time to hustle! See the rest of you boys at TT in a couple of hours!"

Dan stood by the door watching the scene come to its finish, thinking that bizarrely it was almost poetic. Wayne would have loved this battle between Coaches Doug the dick and Matt, fighting for his honor. It was twisted, yet appropriate. He felt a body slide up next to him.

"Hey," Faith said, looking up at him with a small smile.

"Hey," Dan replied, feeling his heart jump to attention. "How're you doing?"

"I could really use a drink," she said.

"Ditto on that."

They stood together, feeling the fresh air on their face.

"Would you mind picking up the boys for the practice," she asked. "I'll have a house full of people for the next few days and it would make it easier."

"Of course. No problem. I'll be there around 3:40 p.m."

"Great." Faith breathed shallow and Dan could almost hear her chest expanding and contracting, the lightness of her. She seemed so delicate, but Dan knew she wasn't. "It was nice, wasn't it? Well, up to the brawl, that is."

Again, Faith's smile pierced him and he nodded in agreement. "Wayne would have loved it, even the brawl, especially the brawl." Faith laughed at that, a beautiful butterfly giggle escaping her pink lips and floating out into the sun. He beamed down at her, pleased to have made her smile, then quickly remembered himself. Wayne was barely dead and he couldn't stop thinking about Faith, although the truth was nothing had changed today that hadn't already been there last week and the week before that. Nothing had changed, and everything had changed.

Faith again put a hand on his arm, immediately burning a hole through the cloth and torching his insides. "Thanks, Dan. You've always been there for me."

If he had anything to do with it he intended to be there a lot more.

***

Rockets Team Chat

(Jake, Chris, Landon, Max, Dylan, Balls (Josh), Ryan, Money (Manny), Derek, Tyler, Jimmy, Reggie)

Money (Manny) – Man, that was a shit show.

Jake – Again Manny? Sensitivity!

Dylan – It was kind of funny.

Balls (Josh) – Coach W would have loved it.

Money (Manny) – That other coach deserved it. He really is a dick.

Chris – I thought it was awful. I couldn't stop bawling.

Jake – Me too.

Jimmy – Like a baby, man

Tyler – Was too much

Landon – Did you guys see the detective dude?

Money (Manny) – Totally, he looked lost, kind of like Dylan in math.

Jake – ROFL!

Jimmy – Zing!

Balls (Josh) – Derek, Reggie? You guys here? We'll see you at practice, k?

Max – Yeah, see you all at practice!

***

When Dan pulled up to Tigers Turf with Derek, Reggie and Jake in tow, Matt already had the kids doing their warmups. He was in full coach mode, shouting out encouragements that often sounded like insults. "Max, that's how you do a push up? Now I understand why you wear pink sneakers... Manny, could you run any slower? I mean, seriously, my grandmother could take you down..." The boys didn't even flinch. Matt's style very much mirrored Wayne's.

"Nice of you guys to join us!" he yelled to Dan as he and the boys walked over. It was 3:55 p.m.

"What are you talking about, it's not even 4 p.m. yet." Did he miss a memo?

"Oh, I might have forgotten to mention, I told the boys' parents that I'd be at the field by 3:30 p.m. if they wanted to drop them early." He chortled, and Dan noticed Mikey in the dugout leaning against the fence grinning. Anger rose from the pit of his stomach into his chest and to his jaw. Dan clenched and unclenched his fists, but he kept his head down and kept walking till he was close enough to whisper in Matt's ear.

"You're an asshole."

Matt jovially patted him on the back. "Aw, ain't no crying in baseball." Dan's sneer stopped Matt's momentum for a beat, then he patted him again. "Come on, dude. I'm just messing with you. Want to hit some flies to the boys?"

"Have Mikey do it," Dan said, refusing to do anything that sounded like Matt was ordering him around. "I'm going to go over the lineup and strategy for the tourney. I'll watch from the dugout."

"Your seat on the bench is still warm," Matt laughed again.

Dan really wanted to punch him but saw the boys watching. He sat down both annoyed and comfortable in the familiar position. Pulling out his clipboard to distract himself, he read over the line up but couldn't focus, and instead just watched the boys dreamily as they fielded pop-ups, threw the ball around and ran bases. They finished practice in the batting cages. By the time the parents came for pick-up, the boys were exhausted, sweaty and done.

Dan kept a wide berth between him, Matt and Mikey, already feeling the collapse of his and Matt's shaky bond that they had shared over the last years with the arrival of Mikey, who was fresh meat and clearly allied with Matt against him. He felt war coming, and he didn't know if he was up to the fight. Rounding the boys, he dropped an uncharacteristically but understandably quiet, Derek and Reggie back at Faith's still bustling house. She gave him a quick wave at the door, long enough to mime a gun to her head with a smile that made his day. He then dropped Jake at Nicole's house, no longer his house, and drove the two miles home. It had been a long day. He was home five minutes before he heard a knock.

"Beer for your thoughts." Matt stood there sporting his best Phish tee shirt and a sideways smile, popping off the top of a Brooklyn Lager and handing it to him as soon as he opened the door. Dan wearily accepted, and Matt followed him in and plopped down on his living room couch.

"What are you doing here?" Dan asked.

"Real nice." Matt laughed.

"It's been a long day."

"Yeah, a crazy day. I still can't wrap my brain around the fact that Wayne is dead. And not just dead, murdered."

"I know exactly how you feel."

"Hey," Matt sat up excitedly. "Want to go over my list of suspects?"

"Why not," Dan shrugged, like it was normal to be discussing potential murder suspects for their late, fellow coach.

"Okay, I've got the obvious ones. Might as well deal with us first."

Dan gave him the go ahead look. "Although, our motive is a bit of a stretch if you ask me. Do we really want this team that bad? Although, you with your… your Faith thing…" Matt cocked a brow and Dan rolled his eyes. "We'll you've certainly got more to gain. And then there's the whole Jake, Derek issue." Dan let it go since there was no point in arguing either his valid point or with Matt in general. He continued. "And speaking of Faith. The neglected wife has got to be up there. I mean Wayne either lived at work or the field, the bar or at Deb's or whoever was his chick of the month. It wasn't like he was even discreet. Then there's Mikey, who hated Wayne for overpitching his son, for not pitching his son, for being a general ass to him, for throwing him out of games. I could go on. Doug the dick had a particular hate for him but so did half the coaches we played. That lacrosse guy Bob Stanley had a particular hard-on for Wayne and was always text stalking him about the fields. Deb is in there, too, of course."

Dan looked at him in surprise. No one loved Wayne like Deb. "Yeah, I know, it seems crazy given how much she loved him, but you know, love like that gets crazy sometimes. And we also both know that even though he was screwing around with her, there's that other chick Wayne was hot on. I don't know her name. Besides, we both know he didn't love Deb and had no intention of leaving Faith, at least not for her." Matt wrapped it up. "So what do you think?"

Dan took a slug of beer. "Not bad. But you forgot that guy from work who Wayne used to brag that when he fired him, he left in a huff threatening to cut off his balls or kill him. And how about Jeff Blum? Remember when Wayne cut Jordan from the team last year and Jeff totally lost it? I mean, really lost it. Every time Jeff passed the field, you could feel him seething while Wayne totally ignored him. I'd kind of want to kill him if I were Jeff too. What he did to his kid was really unacceptable."

"Not if you want to win," Matt said, highlighting the difference between them.

"Jordan was a good first baseman and a decent hitter," Dan argued. "He had a place on the team."

"Yeah, but Chris is better and we don't need two."

Dan fired back. "That's bullshit. Jordan was a useful closer with potential, and he played the outfield well enough. Wayne got rid of him because he didn't like Jeff, which was totally dick. I mean, most of our kids can play other positions. Clearly, we've always had two catchers."

"Yeah, but he wasn't going to cut your kid," Matt said and took a lazy slug on his beer.

"Because Jake is better than Derek?" Dan raised a brow, playing it down but knowing he shouldn't even go there.

Matt guffawed. "No, man, because you were a coach who kept things in check. You have an easy way with the kids, an amazing amount of knowledge from your college baseball days. You're great at strategy, plus you kept the books. He didn't want to lose you. You made him look better."

"Ridiculous," Dan mumbled.

"But true." Matt's eyes twinkled. "I think you gave me another motive to add to your list."

"Awesome."

By the time Matt left, it was after eight. Too early for bed but too late to really do much besides wander his house in circles and go crazy in his own head. If he were home now, back in the home he shared with his kids and Nicole, he would have made Jake go out in the backyard and have a catch with him. Being divorced, he missed stuff like that most—the everyday nothings, like being there to have that catch or see Lola fresh from the shower in her favorite puppy pajamas, to sneak them extra Oreos or test them on spelling homework, and right now to watch Jake more closely while this whole drama was going on. All these tiny, important, irreplaceable moments that make up his children's lives, he had to fit in on weekends and random week nights.

Overall, he was thrilled not to be married to Nicole anymore and the kids seemed to be adjusting fine, but anyone who said freedom didn't come with a price tag was in denial. He understood why some people had to divorce, and all the same, why some people just had to stay. Everything in life was a compromise one way or another.

He sat down on the couch with a peanut butter sandwich and another beer to look over some work that he had blown off and check emails but first called Jake on his cell. That was one good thing about Jake being in middle school, he had his own phone and Dan no longer had to go through the aggravation of calling the house and most likely having to speak with Nicole to get to his kids. Now he at least had a direct line. All hail technology.

"Hey, Dad," Jake answered.

"Hey, buddy. I just thought I'd check in on you. What's going on?"

"Not much. Mom is freaking out that I haven't done my homework yet. I'm supposed to be doing it right now."

"I won't keep you. You need to listen to your mom and do your homework. I just wanted to see how you felt after today. It was kind of crazy."

"Totally. Coach Matt really took that guy to town. He showed him, you don't disrespect Coach W."

Dan sighed. Jake was getting the wrong message here. "Jake, Coach Doug was completely out of line to speak like that at Coach Savage's funeral, but Coach Matt really should have dealt with him in a less physical way. That wasn't okay either. There's a time and place, and that wasn't the time or place for a brawl."

"Maybe sometimes you just have to stick up for things," Jake said, and Dan felt the challenge behind his statement. He didn't have to wonder if he was reading into things because Jake asked, "So, Dad, do you think that now I'll be the main catcher?"

"I don't know, buddy. We're gonna take this team one day at a time. But, yes, you will definitely have more time behind the plate. I guarantee it."

"No big deal," Jake said. "I like Derek. And I don't mind playing outfield. I kind of like it."

"We all like Derek," Dan confirmed. "And there won't be any big changes, certainly not right away. We're going to take it slow and figure things out. Don't worry."

"I'm not worried, Dad."

"Good. So, where's your sister? Is she around to say goodnight?"

"She's already in bed."

"Okay, buddy. Get back to that homework. I'll talk to you tomorrow."

Dan hung up and sighed, emotionally exhausted. He grabbed a bag of chips from the pantry and headed back to the couch with his laptop. The minute he opened his two accounts, one business, one personal, he found a slew of work issues to be dealt with, but he was much more interested in the countless baseball emails. It seemed as though every parent had written and there were chain emails as well. He clicked the first one from Marie and Rich, Max's parents. He liked them both, and Max was a good kid and a damn good third baseman. Both Rich and Marie had an easy manner and a natural good humor. They were good parents who cheered the loudest for their son and the team, but didn't sugar coat Max's short comings. They were a rare breed of involved and easy going, being serious about the game while not taking it too seriously. Maybe it has something to do with the fact that Max was their fourth son. They were pretty seasoned. He read.

From: Rich and Marie
To: Dan
Subject: Just thanks

Dan, Marie and I just want to thank you for always being a steady positive presence for Max and the team. These last days have been a shock, and we are honestly still reeling from the news. I mean, the idea that Wayne is not only dead but was murdered? Well, it's beyond belief. Max is struggling a bit, and we feel safer and better knowing you are there to help. We know that even in this madness, politics as usual continues, and wanted to let you know, subtly, or overtly as it seems, that we are on your team.

Well, that was nice to read Dan thought as he clicked the next email, which he expected he wouldn't like as much. It was from Jeff Blum, the father of Jordan, the guy he and Matt were coincidentally just discussing.

From: Jeff Blum
To: Rockets Gold coaches, Rockets White coaches, Rockets Gold parents, Rockets White parents and Joe
CC: FYO Board of Directors
Subject: Time for a change!

First, let me say that I realize this may come across as a bit of a rant—so I apologize in advance. My sole purpose here is not to rant but to bring awareness to a situation that is need of attention. We all know about the recent tragic events which has rocked our small community. It is a shocking happening and almost impossible to grasp. Almost, because as we all know but probably don't ever want to say, Wayne could make a Buddha master want to kill him. And I know, even as I write this, that you are already up in arms about what I am saying and how disrespectful it may come across but—But, we all know there's truth to it. I have considered greatly whether I should write, have considered it actually for years, but kept finding a reason to keep quiet and keep the status quo. But now that this horrific tragedy has occurred, I feel like we have the opportunity in the coming days, weeks, months, to make something positive happen for the kids and for the community.

I am not writing from emotion, dislike or hatred, although I have felt all those things in the past. Now I am writing about change. Change needs to happen at FYO. People have been whispering for years about the political nepotism, the team stacking, and the bullying that occurs.

The glory of the Gold against a total Whitewash. Why should our children on White have to feel less than? Why should Gold get special privilege to not play by the rules, to add and drop players like M&M's, to have coaching staff that supports these hard lines and hard competitive ways. This is a community program. These are our children, and while I understand that some players are more competitive, I humbly suggest that you reconsider the structure of the baseball program. I have two children who have gone to 'evaluations' each year, and I can pretty much say that the system is rigged. Yup, I said it, and we all know it. The coaches choose who they want and it has often nothing to do with the talent and everything to do with cronyism and keeping an elite team elitist.

I urge you all to please consider the overall welfare of the entire community. I am well aware that I am making enemies right now, but I am also aware that there are many out there like me who have been afraid to speak out and voice their displeasure. Now, I have decided it's time to take a stand and demand change! Let's build a better FYO together!!!

Sincerely,
Jeff Blum

There were twenty-four replies from parents on his team and on the white team. Dan scrolled through them. The tide went both ways, and things were escalating in a very contentious way. Joe had not weighed in yet, but he was going to have to put out something addressing this fast. The natives were growing restless, and Matt's obnoxious quip—"Sore loser"—definitely didn't help things at all.

He moved on, opening up more emails from their teams' parents mostly addressed to him and Matt, relaying their concerns. Then he saw one to him from Deb.

From: Deb
To: Dan
Subject: Shit Show

Holy fuck.

From: Dan
To: Deb
Subject: Shit Storm

That sums it up. There is so much shit flying everywhere. Watch out!

He barely pressed send when his cell rang. Deb. "Hey!" Dan greeted. He was used to random calls from Deb. As the two divorced parents involved in managing the team, they shared a unique bond. It would have been easier for both of them if they would have been attracted to each other. But Dan never thought of Deb that way. She wasn't his 'type' at all and clearly if she was attracted to Wayne, he wasn't hers. "Can you believe what's going on?"

"I can't. I can't believe any of this."

"It's like now that Wayne is gone, the farmers have taken up their pitch forks and are marching the castle." Dan scrolled through more emails while he talked. He found one from Matt to just him.

From: Matt
To: Dan
Subject: Suspects

You were right! Adding Jeff to that list!

Dan smirked regardless of the bad humor. Then he found one from Faith and forgot all about Matt.

From: Faith
To: Dan
Subject: Nightmare

Hi. I was just sitting here all alone in the quiet for the first time in I don't even know how long, feels like forever. The boys are finally in bed and Wayne's family has gone. They all plan on leaving in a couple of days, thank God. Hopefully, I can hold on till then. There's really not enough alcohol in the house. I feel like I'm living in a dream state, and nothing seems real. I'm just floating along, trying not to think or feel or deal with this new reality. Just having someone that I can reach out to helps me remember I can still breathe when my breath becomes heaves and starts to choke me. There I go. I've said too much. I don't want to scare you away, my friend, by showing off all my crazy in one email. Just thanks for trying and for being decent. We'll talk when the dust settles.

Dan reread the email, looking for hidden meanings, getting lost in the intimacy of her words and the fact that she chose to write to him. He was stuck on the friend part. Did she have to specifically categorize him as her friend like that? Maybe she did. Her husband was barely gone a minute, what did he expect, Faith to proclaim her love for him? To acknowledge that they had been dancing this dance for years already?

"Dan? Are you listening to me? Dan?" Deb's voice broke Dan from Faith's spell.

"Sorry, I got distracted by an email. What were you saying?"

Deb exhaled in annoyance. "I was saying that Detective Jonas just made an impromptu visit here! He freaked me out a little. Asking a bunch of questions about, you know, stuff."

Dan did know, but he and Deb never really talked about her relationship with Wayne. It was one of those topics they just skirted around. Dan liked Deb and didn't want to judge her. Not that he really could, considering his own emotional indiscretions and that one other time that he tried hard not to think about or it would consume him. He pushed the thought away, he would think about it later when he was alone in bed. "So what did he say?"

"He wanted to know about Wayne and me. He started asking specifics!"

"What did you say?"

"I was kind of evasive, and he kept looking at me like are you sure you don't want to share a little bit more! And I did want to but then I freaked out and didn't! I got all defensive and totally looked like I was hiding something, which I was, and shit, it's not like enough people don't know we slept together!"

She sounded manic, cracked up on grief, stress and probably alcohol. "Deb, calm down. I'm sure you can fix this. I mean, it's not like you killed him."

"Please," she snorted. "He's the one who killed me. Every day he killed a little piece of my heart and then he'd bring me back to life, only to kill me again." That was quite a revelation Dan thought in the quiet that followed. "He was asking about you too," Deb said when she recovered a bit. That got Dan's attention.

"Yeah, what about?"

"Mostly your relationship with Wayne. And your relationship with Faith." Again they sat in the quiet.

"We definitely should have just slept together and made this all easier." Dan joked, trying to lighten things up.

"I got no immediate plans," Deb said.

Rockets Team Chat
(Jake, Chris, Landon, Max, Dylan, Balls (Josh), Ryan, Money (Manny), Tyler, Jimmy) Derek and Reggie – Off Chat

Dylan – Dudes, was Coach totally murdered?!

Balls (Josh) – They don't have detectives when you die of old age

Chris – Duh!

Jake – It's freaking crazy man

Chris – I'm seriously like "??????????"

Tyler – I got no words

Money (Manny) – My parents put me in therapy!

Landon – You're gonna find me in the waiting room.

Balls (Josh) – I have no idea how to talk to Reggie and Derek

Ryan – Totally awkward.

Max – Derek is all F'd up.

Jake – His dad was M U R D E R E D

Jimmy – Yeah, cut him slack

Dylan – Who do you guys think did it?

Money (Manny) – Could be anyone

Max – What do you mean? Everyone loved him

Landon – Dude, half the town hated him.

Money (Manny) – It's true. He could be a total dick

Balls (Josh) – This is so messed up

Max – Totally

Chris – Doesn't seem real

Dylan – And life goes on

Jake – The world doesn't even stop

Landon – And neither does baseball

From: Barb
To: Marie and Robin
Subject: Shaking head

Is it just me or does no one seem to think it's crazy that Wayne is not only dead but murdered!!!

From: Robin
To: Marie and Barb

I think people are in shock. It just doesn't seem real.

From: Marie
To: Barb and Robin

I feel so bad for Faith and the boys. Awful.

From: Barb
To: Marie and Robin

Should we bring over food?

From: Marie
To: Robin & Barb

Count me in for a casserole.

From: Robin
To: Barb and Marie

I'm in for lasagna.

From: Barb
To: Marie and Robin

Great. I'll see if anyone else wants to contribute.

From: Marie
To: Robin
Subject: World gone mad

What was with that scene today at the funeral? That's what the kids need to see? Isn't enough that their coach has been murdered. Do we need their other coach to go to jail for assault?

From: Robin
To: Marie
Subject: Speechless

Barb must want to kill him.

CHAPTER 4
(Wayne's last opening day)

"Ah! A beautiful baseball morning!" Wayne stood in his running shorts and moisture wicking tee shirt at his open front door, inhaling the early June air deeply. "This weather is perfect," he said to himself and strode out to retrieve the paper. Later it would be a little too warm but right now it was sixty-four degrees, optimal temperature for a run.

It was 5:15 a.m., and, as usual, he had beaten the sun to morning. He liked to start the day winning, and he couldn't think of a better way to begin than being one step ahead of the brightest star in the sky. By 5:45 a.m., he'd be out running. Today he was meeting Joe to do their usual five mile loop, then he'd take a quick shower before racing off to catch the 7:17 a.m. train to Penn Station and be at his trading desk by 8:30 a.m. Not as early as many of his colleagues, but acceptable. He was in a position of control, had been for some time. He did his time when he was in his twenties and thirties, named one of the youngest vice presidents at Goldman Sachs. He had never been any good at bowing to authority or taking orders. He was a natural leader and people followed him.

Today was going to be a great day, he thought. Today was the day the Golden Rockets would win their fourth end of spring season tournament and beat out Doug the dick. Again. He had it all planned out… the line-up, the strategy, the celebration afterward.

He lightly jogged the quarter of mile to meet Joe at their usual meeting spot and saw him coming from the opposite direction. When they ran, they always met at exactly the same time and started on their path with the barest of nods. Often they ran for a while in silence, but today Wayne felt something more than early morning solitude behind it. Joe had something brewing, and he was building up to it; his pace stronger than usual, his expression set, the tension steaming off of him.

"You're on quite a tear there, old man," Wayne said. Joe puffed next to him but stayed silent. He was about a decade older than Wayne but in great shape. "Nothing yet?" he asked every half mile or so.

They were in the final stretch of their run before Joe let it out. "You're padding FYO's accounts with extras for your team."

"What are you talking about?"

"You know what I'm talking about, Wayne. The new throwback jerseys this year? The matching hats? Who paid for them? FYO or your team?"

"It's pennies. Not a big deal."

"I have to account for those pennies! You're making me look like an asshole who can't run his own organization! I have enough problems with you stealing field times from other teams, dropping players, and strutting around like you own the joint. This is a whole new level. This is…" Joe pulled up short, panting, and taking a second to catch his breath. His breathing was rapid and his eyes wild. "This is a fucking felony!"

"Whoa!" Wayne stopped, leaning over placing his hands on his knees and breathing heavily. "Hang on there. You're really blowing this way out of proportion. Are you still just mad because I decided to do the team's winter workouts with Pro-Sports instead of your connection at Scouters?"

"Really, Wayne? Really? That's where you're going? You think I'm so petty?" Joe shook his head. "I've put up with a lot of shit from you over the years, Wayne. A lot of shit. And this is how you repay me?"

"You need to cool down, Joe. I can see you're upset." Wayne moved toward Joe, smiling.

"I'm beyond upset, Wayne. I'm done." He started running in the other direction toward home. "There's going to be some serious changes, Wayne, and you're not going to like them." He started running off.

"Joe, come on! Don't go away mad. Joe!" he called after him, but Joe was already out of ear shot, or ignoring him. Wayne shrugged and took a slow jog home, checking his Sunnto GPS running watch appreciatively. It may not have been their best conversation, but it was one of their fastest times. He should piss Joe off more often.

He strutted into his house in a slightly less optimistic mood than he had walked out an hour ago, but he had no time to wallow.

"How was your run?" Faith asked, moving between the fridge and the food closets, putting together lunches for the boys, already in work mode.

"You're up early," Wayne said, nudging her aside at the fridge to grab a bottle of water.

"I didn't sleep well last night. And I have to meet Nikky from the club early. I'm helping her organize the Back to School initiative this year."

Wayne barely nodded. He wasn't actually listening.

"So tonight's the big game, huh? Six o'clock, right? I assume you'll be home early?" Faith asked.

"I'll be home by the time school is out. I want to get them to the field for a little BP before the team's practice."

It was standard for teams to arrive an hour before game time for warming up, but with Wayne, he liked to be there at least an hour and a half before to work out his boys. Luckily, the game was at TT and not the opposing team's field, which was much more of a schlepp than the five minute ride over to their town field.

"Excited, huh?" Faith asked.

Wayne didn't answer. He sucked down his water and flipped through the sports section. Faith watched him with tempered annoyance. Having been married to Wayne for fourteen years, she was a seasoned player and knew she wasn't a starter anymore. She didn't even know if she was second string.

In the past, she demanded his attention, made herself known, put in an effort, cried a lot, but she had finally arrived at a different place these last few years, a more accepting place. She was no longer interested in fighting, not for his attention or him. Faith had moved past her anger and resentment into apathy with a side of rebellion. More and more, she fantasized about a new life and being free, about being with a man who treasured and preferred her company to the sweaty, gruff past-their-prime men he spent his leisure time with at the fields and bars. And, of course, the other women.

"Hey, bring over a cooler filled with Gatorade for the team when you come."

Faith sighed. "So while I have you, I just wanted to remind you that I am going out tomorrow night. I told you, remember? And you're going to be home for the boys, right?"

Wayne lifted his head and looked at her. Seeing her opening, Faith opened her mouth to continue, to tell him about *Unorthodox*, the book they were discussing at book club and how Lucy, who was hosting, had already planned out a theme complete with mini bagels and lox and Babka. She was excited for the night and to discuss this book and the author who found the courage to escape a life where she felt boxed in and incapable of independent thought. Faith's privileged existence was a far stretch from the alien and mysterious sect in Orthodox Judaism, but Faith felt a fluttering of kinship to those feelings of being trapped.

"Make sure to get to the field on time," Wayne said. "I'm starting Reggie on the mound."

Faith shut her mouth, all thoughts of her book club gone. "Really?" she asked carefully. "You think that's a good idea?"

"Just for the opening inning. He'll be fine."

Faith nodded, knowing that there was no reason to argue, that he wouldn't change his mind and they would just waste ugly words and start the day sour. Reggie, of course, would be fine and he also would not. He was used to his father putting him in these pressure situations for the mere fact that he hated them. He had a decent arm, but the pressure of pitching was a struggle for him and he wanted no part of it. Wayne found that to be the best reason to throw him as any. That was how you dealt with your inadequacies. You hit them head on, even if you threw up from nerves, even if you cried, even if you were four, or eight or now twelve years old. No matter, it was all the more reason. Facing your fears was how you overcame them, according to Wayne, who didn't have to sit at night with one of their children dry heaving his anxiety into a paper bag.

"Does he know?" she asked.

Wayne closed the paper. "He will soon enough. I'm going up to shower." He walked out without another word. Faith took a deep calming breath, then finished up with the lunches and started making a quick couple of eggs for the boys' breakfast. They would be down any minute, and she wanted them to start off the day on a good note. Someone should.

She envied Wayne's morning runs. It gave him a release of energy and stress that Faith only found in a bottle of wine. She wished she liked exercise. She had so many friends who ran, took kickboxing, or did yoga. She tried everything from Bar Method to spin, but she hated all of it. The only true way Faith wanted to exert herself and get sweaty was by having sex, but there hadn't been any of that in longer than she cared to remember.

She stopped scrambling the eggs and considered the last time she and

Wayne had sex; quickly remembered and resumed scrambling. It was that one night the year before, after the FYO dinner where he was honored as a standout coach and contributor to the Fort Jefferson community. It had been a good night and they were both drunk. Wayne was so high on himself that he forgot that he didn't do that anymore, at least not with her. Not that she was interested. She had lost any desire for him years back and more recently any interest in even caring about it.

The boys wandered in gorgeous and sleepy. Their dog, Yogi, padded in after them. Faith hugged both boys and gave Yogi a good scratch behind the ears. He was old and partially blind. She and Wayne got him as a pup the year they married, having passed him on the street by Union Square in the city during an "Adopt-A-Pet" effort. He was small and sweet, licking her on the face, and immediately claiming her heart. Fifteen years later, it was about the end of the line for their sweet Shepard Spaniel mutt and ironically for her marriage.

"Egg sandwiches are up," she said to the boys, placing a plate in front of them. "Now you guys just have to get up." She smiled at their young, maturing faces—Derek, dark-haired and eyed, smart and serious, and Reggie, more fair, both in looks and personality. "You guys excited for tonight's game?" Faith placed a dish of food on the floor for Yogi. Reggie shrugged and Derek ignored her, too busy concentrating on his phone. "Phone down, Derek," she lightly scolded. "You know the rule." Derek gave her a grudging sneer but put his cell away.

"I was just starting a group text for the team!" he said. "We're gonna kick ass tonight!"

Faith gave him a warning brow but smiled. They were such good boys. "Just have fun."

"And win!" Wayne added, stomping in and grabbing the sandwich off of Reggie's plate and helping himself to a bite.

"I have more," Faith said lightly, trying to hide her disapproval. It was not a big deal but after a while, the 'take whatever you want' attitude of his grated heavily on her nerves.

"I'm good. Boys, let's hustle!"

The boys gathered their stuff. They had morning down to a science at the Savage house. Backpacks were always packed the night before, breakfast waiting when they came down, and if for some reason it wasn't, a granola bar quickly substituted, then Wayne dropped them at school on the way to his train. Generally, it ran like clockwork and they made adjustments for early morning extra help or intramurals or what have you, when necessary.

With a quick hug to their mother, they followed their father out.

"Faith!" Wayne yelled, and she startled at his tone but waited for him to toss her a goodbye. "Yogi shit the floor." Then the door slammed, and Faith felt its bang reverberating through her. At least she was alone. Yogi pandered up to her, his nose nudging her leg. Well, not completely alone. "Guess it's just me and you." She bent down to give him a good scruff. "I hear you left me a little present in the hallway." She grabbed some Clorox wipes and a plastic bag. "Come on, let's see."

After she had re-gifted Yogi's offering to the garbage in the garage, Faith relaxed at her kitchen island with a cup of coffee. She really didn't need to rush. She wasn't meeting Nikky for over an hour. She didn't even know why she told Wayne that was the reason she was up early. Truth was she couldn't sleep. A lot of stuff had been spinning around in her brain lately, her crappy marriage not the least of them. But was she willing to do something about it? To make such a momentous step into the unknown when her life was overall pretty okay. She had two great kids. Friends. She lived in a beautiful house with a pool and a yard as big as a baseball field. She could have almost anything she wanted. Except love and happiness, she thought sourly. To distract herself she went to her computer to check her emails. She found one from Dan and her spirits immediately lifted.

From: Dan
To: Faith
Subject: Dumb jokes make girls smile

What do you call a grizzly with no teeth?

From: Faith
To: Dan
Subject: Smiling already

Tell me.

From: Dan
To: Faith
Subject: Drumroll

A gummy bear

From: Faith

To: Dan
Subject: Eye roll

You're right. That was terrible. Stick with… wait, what is it that you best at again?

From: Dan
To: Faith
Subject: Too bad you're married.

Everything

Faith's skin flushed. She loved playing with Dan. Their flirting was so easy and natural. Right from their first hello so many years back, she felt it. A connection. That special chemistry you only feel with very few people. She used to have it with Wayne. At least she thought she did. She could hardly remember anymore, it was so long ago. Now it was Dan's attention that often got her through the bad days—filled a need in her to feel wanted, not just needed. He made her feel special and desired, and she knew that she did the same for him. That he probably thought of her when he was alone at night. At least she hoped he did.

She stepped away from the computer even though it was begging her to write back. He was begging her to, but it was time for a break. That was the way it worked, they flirted, came right up to that invisible line, then retreated back to their corners. It was a dance that kept them spinning.

Wayne sat on the 7:17 a.m. to Penn in the eighth car on the outside of a two seat row, four rows from the door. His briefcase rested on the seat next to him, and he scrolled through his emails looking up every few seconds to say hello or wave to all the people he knew passing through. The Fort Jefferson line was the first (or last stop) of the train, so it was possible to know basically everyone on it. Especially if you're a community man, like he was.

"Hey, Wayne," Bob, a lacrosse coach from town, greeted. "Great game last week!"

"Thanks," he responded. "Heard your boys have been sweeping the tournaments."

Mark Wilson, a neighbor, passed by next with a big smile. "We gonna go all the way tonight?" he asked. He had two young girls but loved hearing about the Golden Rockets and occasionally stopped by a game just to watch.

"You know it," Wayne said.

Erika, a local lacrosse mom and head of PTA, took a moment to stop, resting a pink manicured hand on his shoulder. "Wayne, I just wanted to thank you and your boys again for helping out with our school carnival fundraiser."

"Anytime, Erika, happy to help out."

"I'm going to call you again," she warned, teasing.

"I'll be waiting."

Cory Russo suggested he and Faith wanted to catch dinner one of these nights. Shane Miller asked if he'd take a look at his younger son's swing. Harry Chin wanted to know if he could recommend a good -2 drop baseball bat for his eleven-year-old, and Warren Reynolds wished him luck tonight.

Right before the final door closed and the train departed, a body slid in to the seat next to him and Wayne simultaneously lifted his briefcase and half stood to let him pass.

"I see your time management skills are still killer," Wayne commented.

"Nice tie," Matt said, pointing to Wayne's stylish Salvatore Ferragamo.

"Not a nice tie," Wayne said, pointing to Matt's wacky bow tie.

Matt's face opened into a broad smile, his style ranged between eclectic and grunge. "You're just pissed you can't pull it off."

"Oh, I'd like to pull it off," Wayne quipped good naturedly. "I'll bet Barb does as well. How does she let you walk out looking like that?"

Matt snorted. "Ha! Woman's got to pick her battles. The tie doesn't even register." The formalities concluded, Matt transitioned to the real reason they sat side by side every morning—to discuss, analyze, and dissect baseball. They generally began with whatever major league game was played the night before and then moved on to the Rockets. Today, the only thing on their minds was their game. "So we ready for tonight?" Matt asked.

"You know it."

"We good with the line up?"

"I think we settled it the other night when we met," Wayne said.

"So we're keeping Jake in the outfield?"

Wayne nodded. "We'll start Derek as catcher and see how it goes. We can sub Jake in in the second half or if Derek seems to be struggling."

"Sounds fair," Matt said. "You think Dan will be okay with it? You didn't really play Jake much in the playoffs either."

"You know Danny boy isn't one to make waves. He goes with the flow."

Matt nodded. "Yeah, Dan's a good guy. A little soft, but he knows his shit. Speaking of making waves, how about that Mikey?"

Wayne's nostrils flared. "That guy is a roach under my shoes. How many times is he going to ask to help coach. Doesn't he have any pride? I can barely stand him pacing the sidelines counting his kids' pitches and freaking out over any advice I give him. I said we're good countless times and what does he do? He goes to Joe. And now Joe's up my ass."

"Asshole!" Matt agreed.

"Complete."

Wayne craned his neck and looked around the train, then lowered his voice to a whisper. "And get this. He says to me out of nowhere, 'I heard you and Deb have this thing going on and wouldn't it be a shame if people started to talk."

"He did not."

"So I said, yeah it would be a shame since it isn't true and are you fucking threatening me, Mikey?" So he backs way off and says, 'No way, never. I just know how people talk.' So I get real close and I say, 'I totally do. In fact, I've been hearing a lot about how you have a real hard-on for the white team and you're fucking Coach Blum and the two of you are looking to start a new team, not white or gold, but rainbow.'"

"Fucking brilliant," Matt said and then after a beat changed the subject. "So how are we looking for summer?"

This started a whole dissection of the summer tournaments and competition that lasted right up to the moment they pulled into Penn. There was never enough time in the day to talk about baseball.

CHAPTER 5

Gold ribbons started appearing all over town. They hung around trees and stop signs, parking meters, and lamp posts. Facebook posts somberly shared their images, sometimes next to a picture of Wayne in his uniform or Wayne with the team, accruing dozens, sometimes hundreds, of sad emoji face likes and RIP comments, many baseball themed like, 'Hope you're playing in that big field in the sky,' 'Forever on that field of dreams,' 'Bad call,' and 'Now you're truly home.'

Deb busied herself pouring all her energies into planning the upcoming memorial. She ordered the special patches and gold belts for the team. She hoped to use all the picture posters from the funeral. It seemed a waste to make up more when those were already done and perfect, but she hadn't successfully been able to confirm that Faith would supply them. She made that first call, but the reception on the other end was so chilly it made her shake with nerves.

"Hey, Faith, it's Deb," she said, even though was sure Faith knew exactly who it was before answering. Faith didn't reply. After a beat of awkward silence, Deb found her voice through her nerves. "So how are you?"

"I'm about to hang up is how I am," she replied.

"Okay," Deb charged forward, realizing the small talk wasn't at all small or working. "So I was hoping we could use the pictures from the funeral for Wayne's memorial at Tigers Turf next week."

"That hope is a killer, isn't it," Faith said and hung up on her.

Over the years, she and Faith maintained a cool tolerance of each other—the wife and the baseball wife. Deb never knew how much Faith knew or didn't know about them. Wayne never wanted to discuss his and Faith's relationship with her. In fact, he never wanted to discuss anything relating to any future together. She pressed, she did. She wasn't proud of herself, but after years of waiting on the sidelines hoping she found herself becoming more insistent. She knew it had put Wayne off. That their last months or so were filled with tension, that she probably even drove him further into the arms of what's her name and made her seem even more appealing. Wayne still came and went, same as usual, although not quite as often, not demanding but expecting as always that she would be there waiting to do his bidding. And she was. And here she was now, even after he's dead, still trying to please him. She couldn't find the nerve to call Faith back. Instead, she emailed Dan.

To: Dan
From: Deb
Subject: Memorial

Can you ask Faith if we can use the pictures from Wayne's funeral?

From: Dan
To: Deb
Subject: Not in my job description

Why can't you?

From: Deb
To: Dan
Subject: Duh

Just do it.

Dan pulled into Tigers Turf ready for their 2 p.m. practice. He dragged his bucket of balls from the trunk and headed over to Field 2, where he appeared to be the first to have arrived. He dropped the bag and his clipboard in the dugout and checked the time on his phone. 1:47 p.m.. Stretching, he took a moment to appreciate the quiet of the beautiful June day and looked around. Jeff Blum's White team was out practicing over on Field 3 and the younger 10U teams all occupied fields 1, 4, 5, and 6. He focused on the White team and assessed the talent. They didn't look terrible. He watched the third baseman make a throw that bounced before it reached Jordan at first. Okay, not great.

Out of the corner of his vision, he saw Donny's almost emaciated, erect frame driving in his cart toward him with someone riding shotgun, the only way you could ride in the two-seater. He cursed his forty-year-old eyes that no longer saw distance as well but kept his gaze on them till the blurry face came into focus. Detective Jonas.

The cart came to a stop right in front of him.

"Detective," Dan greeted. "Working Saturdays, huh. I guess murder investigation is a twenty-four hour gig. How's it going?"

"It's coming along," the detective said. "Slowly, but at some point all the pieces will fit. So, do you mind if I ask you a few questions?"

"Not at all," Dan agreed. "The boys should be here any minute for practice, but of course."

The detective got out of the cart and nodded to Donny who took off without a word. "So, I just need to get a few details in order here. First, do you have an alibi for the night of Wayne's death?"

"An alibi? Am I a suspect?"

The detective weighed his words. "At this point, we're not ruling anyone out, but we're trying to. So?" He looked at him expectantly.

"Well, I guess not really. I live alone since the divorce. The kids were at Nicole's that night. I was with Wayne up to a certain point. We all went out for drinks at Flynn's Tavern after the game to celebrate."

"And what time did you leave Flynn's?"

"Oh, I'd say around 11 p.m. or so."

"Did anyone see you leave?"

"Well, Wayne…" He realized that probably wasn't helpful. "Let me think a minute. Deb was definitely there. And Matt, Mikey, and Jeff Blum were out and so was Johnny and Joe. We were all outside of the bar."

"Why did you guys leave the bar?" the detective asked slowly, but a dangerous curiosity lined his voice.

Dan sighed, then admitted what he knew the detective already knew. "Wayne had words with that lacrosse guy, Johnny Smith. They got into a fight in Flynn's. I got in the middle of them and tried to break it up, and we were all thrown out. The brawl continued a bit outside and then Wayne and I had words. I was angry but I didn't want to argue in front of an audience, especially since Wayne was totally drunk, so I left."

"What was your argument about," the detective asked calmly.

"Between Johnny and Wayne?" he asked.

"No, between you and Wayne."

Dan looked out to the parking lot and saw boys on the team being dropped off and heading over toward the field. He saw Matt's car pull in and park as well. He was bringing Jake, Landon, and Manny since they were all coming together straight from some kid's birthday party. "A few things," Dan said hurriedly. "I don't really want to get into it now because the team is coming and my kid. Can we meet later tonight?"

"Of course," the detective agreed. "Want me to come by your house later?"

"Actually, can we do it tomorrow after I drop my kids back at my ex's. It's my weekend, and we're supposed to go to dinner and a movie tonight. Come over tomorrow. Around five o'clock good?"

"See you then." The detective turned and stepped right back into the cart that sat idle waiting for him; Donny somehow arriving at exactly the right moment. As they were about to pull away the detective casually threw out the standard, but no less disturbing, warning. "And, of course, you know not to leave town please."

Dan nodded, mute, and watched them drive off, heading straight to Field 3 and Jeff Blum.

"Hey, dude, looking a little peaked." Matt laughed, giving him a hearty slap on the back. "Was that the detective?"

"Yup," Dan said. "Cages first?" he asked.

"Nah, let's finish with the cages. I think they really need to work on bunting defense. They were totally sloppy last game. We got lucky."

"Agreed. Here comes assistant Coach Mikey." Dan mocked him lightly and nodded to where Mikey and his son Josh were walking up the field toward them.

"So we're not going to talk about the detective?" Matt asked.

"Nope."

"Okay, Coach," Matt said agreeably, eyes sparkling like a fox. "Let's play ball."

After practice, Dan and Jake picked Lola up from her friend's house and went to dinner at Bare Burger, a local, organic, upscale burger joint. Since the warmer weather had arrived, Bare Burger opened their restaurant storefront so that customers were sitting outside even when they were inside. Even though the service was questionable, it was one of their favorite places for dinner.

Dan always let the kids choose the restaurants they ate at and was happy that both Jake and Lola were adventurous with their eating and willing to try new things. They loved going for sushi as much they loved ribs, Chinese takeout, or pizza. But tonight, Bare Burger was the clear winner. The kids loved their eclectic menu: panko chicken tenders for Lola and grass fed beef with avocado and bacon for both Dan and Jake.

They all loved the crispy sweet potato fries and Oreo milkshakes, and devoured every last bite and slurp.

They caught a 7:30 p.m. showing of the new remake of The Never Ending Story, which was surprisingly awesome. By 10 p.m., the kids were all tucked in their beds. Dan let out a long exhausted breath, popped open a beer and his computer to check emails. His eye immediately focused in on one from Faith. It was sent only seven minutes before.

To: Dan
From: Faith
Subject: Not easy

I'm sorry. I hope I'm not bothering you. I am just sitting here alone. The boys are in bed and there's so much for me to do, but I can't do anything. I feel paralyzed. I'm supposed to speak with lawyers and attorneys, figure out my finances and all that. I don't have any idea what we have and don't have. Wayne handled all of that and anytime I asked he told me not to worry, that we were covered. I feel like such a dumb housewife, skipping along, shopping, and sitting out by my pool like some prima donna. So now I'm just drinking by myself and beating myself up. I'm kind of a master at that.

I had a difficult conversation with Derek and Reggie, who both seem like they're in shock or they have no emotions, so I'm going with shock. I'm hoping they're talking with each other. They have that twin thing that I never quite understood. They certainly aren't confiding in me. They tell me they're fine, but they're too silent. I've made them both appointments with a therapist.

You must think I'm crazy going on like this. But just writing it out helps and at least I know it's going to a friend who I trust. I'm sorry to be so serious, and I hope it's okay. I know we're usually much lighter, sarcastic, and playful.

Did I mention that detective came by today, asking me a bunch of questions about my marriage? He asked about you as well.

Anyway, thanks for listening. Or reading. Or whatever. I'm going to go now before I say something inappropriate. I'm emotional, and nothing good can come of me working on my third glass of wine. Even this email is suspect.

Dan leaned back and reread, his heart aching. All he wanted to do was go to her and hold her, and keep her safe. But, of course, this wasn't the right time for them, not even a week since her husband died, was found dead. He corrected himself. Murdered. It could only look bad for him to have a romantic relationship with the victim's widow. He probably shouldn't even be exchanging emails with her. He didn't care.

To: Faith
From: Dan
Subject: Thank you

First, thank you for trusting me enough to write. I am happy that you feel comfortable shar...

Dan stopped, deleted, and stared at the screen. He took a deep pull on his beer and started over, typing quickly and pushing send before he could change his mind.

To: Faith
From: Dan
Subject: Cheers

Faith, there is nothing you can say that I don't want to hear—your feelings, your hurt, your struggling, whatever you need... I'm sitting here also drinking alone and thinking of you. Here's to being inappropriate.

Thirty seconds later, her message popped up but the subject area was empty so he had no clue as to her train of thought. He just had to open it and see. Taking a deep breath, he clicked it open.

To: Dan
From: Faith
Subject:

First smile of my day. Thank you.

He breathed and smiled back at the screen, happy.

***

Rockets Team Chat

(Jake, Chris, Landon, Max, Dylan, Balls (Josh), Ryan, Money (Manny), Derek, Tyler, Jimmy, Reggie)

Chris – Anyone up?

Jake – Here.

Tyler – Here

Josh – Check

Money (Manny) – Wasssuppp!

Jimmy – Holla!

Jake – Good practice today

Landon – Except watching Coach Mikey trying to hit us bunts!

Money (Manny) – Epic fail!

Chris – Aw, give him a break. It was his first day, he was nervous.

Landon – Poor little new coachie

Jake – ROFL

Josh – Real nice guys

Landon – We're just messing with u

Josh – It's cool

Chris – You guys think we're gonna wind up staying a team?

Jake – My dad says so

Landon – Your dad always says nice things. Manny what does your dad say?

Josh - Guffaw!!!

Chris – Bahaha!!!

Money (Manny) – He says, yo mama!

Landon – Not funny dude

Money (Manny) – What??!

Landon – Leave my mother out of it

Money (Manny) – I was kidding

Jake – I think he was kidding

Landon – I'm out

Money (Manny) – Whad I do?

Josh – Leave it, it's late.

Jake - He'll come round

Chris – Drama! Nite all!

The next day, Dan dropped the kids back at Nicole's around 4 p.m., stopped to pick up his dry cleaning, and got back to his house around 4:30 p.m. in anticipation of the detective's five o'clock arrival, but when he pulled into his driveway he found the detective already waiting on his stoop.

"Detective," he said as he stepped from the car. "You're early."

The detective stood and brushed off his trousers. "Yeah, well, my last interview ended abruptly, so here I am."

Dan raised a brow, intrigued. "Anyone I know?" He fiddled with his keys, finally finding the right one and opening the door.

"A detective never tells." He smiled and followed Dan inside. "Nice place you got here," he commented, looking around.

"Thanks. It works for us. I needed to stay in town after the divorce for the kids. It's important to me to be close. It's been an adjustment, but now it's working. We're all at a good place." Dan threw his keys on the kitchen counter, opened the fridge, and took out two waters. He handed one to the detective. "So, you've got some questions. Shoot."

"Tell me about the argument."

"It wasn't that big of a deal. It was over a coaching call Wayne made during the game that day to not put my son in to catch."

"Is your son the catcher?"

"Best on the team."

"So who did he use?"

"His son."

"I see."

"Wayne was drunk and just saying stupid shit. I usually let it go, but it just got under my skin."

"Well, I could understand why it would. Your son plays second fiddle to his son when he's clearly better while you play second fiddle to his father when you think you're clearly better. Is that right?"

Dan chuckled uneasily. "When you put it like that it doesn't sound so good. But, yeah. I guess that's right."

"It also doesn't sound so good that there are some rumors around regarding you and Mrs. Savage."

Dan stopped smiling. "What rumors?"

The detective shrugged. "Mostly that you are in love with her."

Dan looked at the detective who looked back at him carefully. After an extended silence, Dan looked away. "I don't know what you're talking about."

More silence except for the sound of the detective's pen tapping on his pad. "Are you sure about that?"

"Yeah. I'm sure. We're good friends."

"That's all?"

"That's all."

The detective put his pen down, looking disappointed. "Okay, but you know how to reach me if you want to reconsider your statement."

Dan's cell rang, breaking the tension. "Excuse me a minute." He walked out of the room leaving the detective alone in the kitchen. Detective Jonas immediately picked up Dan's water bottle and left his in its place.

"We're done for now," the detective called out, and Dan reemerged with the phone to his ear.

He put up a finger to wait. "Okay, I'll look for it. No problem." He hung up. "It was my ex," he explained. "One of my kids left a book they need for school."

"Not a problem," he said. "I'll be in touch." He headed out the door with Dan following, stopped and held up his bottle. "And thanks for the water."

After the detective left, Dan looked in Lola's bedroom, found her book lost in the covers of her bed, then grabbed his keys and left the house. Without thinking things through, he drove off in the opposite direction of his old house, deciding to make a pit stop along the way.

After ten seconds, the detective started his car and followed.

Dan pulled up to Faith's house and let the car idle for a moment while he gathered his courage. He wasn't sure if she would even want to see him. It was easy trading emails back and forth. There was a physical wall of distance even with the intimacy of their exchanges. It was safe. This was not safe. For many reasons.

He shut the engine, took one last breath, got out and walked quickly to her door. He stood there a moment and then rang the bell. He should have called or texted and given her a heads up. She might not even be home. It was probably better if she wasn't. But then he heard the lock turn and the door slowly opened.

She stood before him, blonde hair in a messy bun on top of her head, pink tank top and denim shorts. She looked a little worn and definitely tired but when she saw him, she at first looked surprised and then gave him a warm smile that melted his anxiety away.

"Hi," he said. "Funny running into you here."

She cast her eyes down, still smiling. "Yeah. What a coincidence."

Shaking his head, the detective watched Dan walk into her house.

"Do you want a drink?" Faith asked. "I just made myself one." She shrugged a little self-consciously. "I know I'm drinking too much, but I'm having a real tough time getting through without it. I know it's not good, but I'm giving myself a pass this month. And, hey, it is after five and the boys are out till later."

"You don't have to make any excuses for me. I get it. What are you drinking?"

"Vodka lemonade. I didn't have anywhere to go so I was sitting out back by the pool pretending to read but really just staring off into space."

"Can I join you?"

Faith hesitated but only for a moment. "Sure." She pulled the vodka from her cabinet and fixed him a drink. They walked with their drinks into the yard and sat down, each on a lounge chair.

"Your yard is beautiful," Dan said, admiring the lush greenery that surrounded them and the in-ground pool with a cascading waterfall. A hot tub sat off to one side next to a bluestone patio with a bar, fire pit and a BBQ big enough to feed a baseball team. It was an oasis.

Faith nodded. "It is special. I spend an awful lot of time out here. It calms me." They lapsed into silence, appreciating the late afternoon June day in this near perfect setting. "So," Faith started, "to what do I owe the pleasure."

"Besides it just being a pleasure to see me?" Dan teased.

"Of course." Faith smiled but Dan could tell she was trying not to engage. It was more than understandable.

"Well, a few things." He paused. "A lot of things really."

She sipped her drink. "Let's start with one."

"Okay, here's an easy one. Deb has asked me to pick up Wayne's picture boards from the funeral to use at the memorial next week. Is that okay?"

"I love how she asked you to ask me," Faith said in a tone that clearly indicated that she didn't love it.

"I'm sorry," Dan said.

Faith waved it off. "Not your fault. I'm just struggling a little and Deb is the last person I want to do anything for."

"I get it."

"I know you do," Faith said pointedly.

"Okay!" Dan let out a loud breath and tugged at the collar of his tee shirt. "It's getting a little hot out here."

Faith laughed. "Sorry. Too intense. Of course, I'll give you the boards." She smiled up at him. "What else can I do for you?"

Dan raised a brow suggestively.

Faith smacked him in the arm. "Seriously."

Dan raised a brow again.

"Stop it." She giggled.

"Okay," Dan said, happy for her to seem so much lighter than when he first arrived but turned more solemn. "How about telling me how you are? Seriously."

Faith sighed. "I'm not great. I'm worried about the boys. I'm worried about the future. I'm sad." She stopped talking, tears sliding down her face. "I mean, I know Wayne wasn't a good husband in many ways and our marriage was shot, but he was good in many ways too. And I did love him once. We had a long history and children together. The idea

that he was murdered? The idea that he is no longer here on earth…"
She stopped speaking because she was crying too much.

Dan moved to her lounge chair and wrapped her in his embrace. "Shhh…" he soothed. "I'm sorry this happened to you. To Wayne. I'm sorry for a lot of things. But it's going to be okay. You're going to be okay."

She cried a little more, her small shoulders shaking in their grief, but he held tight until finally she regained control and quieted. She looked up at him, tears staining her face, her hazel eyes soft and vulnerable. The air around them stilled and all Dan could see was her face so close to his, her lips wet and lush, her eyes filled with pain and longing. She closed her eyes, and he bent his head down toward hers at the same moment she tilted hers up toward his. Their lips barely touched, igniting a storm of desire in them both. The doorbell rang.

Startled, they immediately pulled back, like teens whose parents had just walked in.

"Shit." Faith jumped up, brushing the tears from her eyes. She looked nervously at Dan and headed back into the house toward the front door.

Dan followed. "Who is it?" he asked as she peered out the side window.

"Detective Jonas."

"Shit."

"Yeah," Faith agreed. "Okay. I'm going to open up. Ready?"

Dan opened his hands in a helpless gesture. There was no ready, there was only what it was.

"Here goes." She opened the door. Detective Jonas looked at them. They looked at Detective Jonas.

"Do you want to change your statement," he asked Dan.

Dan snorted but shook his head. "No. I told you we are friends. Are you following me?"

"No. Well, actually yes, I just did," he admitted. "But you made it very easy."

"Because I'm not doing anything wrong. I wanted to see how she was doing, and I needed to pick up some picture boards for Wayne's memorial."

Detective Jonas turned to Faith. "Is that right?"

Faith gulped and nodded. She managed an extremely convincing, "Yeah."

"And you're not sleeping together." He threw it out, taking them both by surprise. Dan looked shocked. Faith looked horrified.

"No," they both said at the same time.

Detective Jonas nodded. "Okay. I believe you. Doesn't mean a jury will but at the moment I do."

"What do you mean by that?" Dan asked.

He shrugged. "Just not so subtly letting you know that you are one of our prime suspects."

"That's ridiculous," Dan stammered. Faith looked at Dan wide eyed. "I did not kill Wayne!" He looked directly into her eyes, the ones that melted him only minutes ago and he watched hers retreat a bit.

He looked desperately at the detective. "You can't be serious."

"Sorry to say I am."

"This is so ridiculous." He ran his hand through his mass of wavy dark hair, flustered. "I can't. I don't know what to say." Then he thought of something. "Well, I hope I'm not the only one." He looked hard at the detective.

"You're not the only one," he said.

He was still shaking his head in distress when Faith brought him three large picture boards. "Thanks," he mumbled, not looking at her, afraid to see her eyes filled with anything but affection for him. She opened the front door, and Dan handed two of the boards to the detective. "Would you mind giving me a hand and taking these out to my trunk?" He clicked a button on his keys and the trunk of his car popped open.

"Sure." Detective Jonas took them from him and walked out, giving them a moment alone.

The minute he was out the door, Dan turned to her. "Faith, I hope you know that there's absolutely no truth to that."

"I know," she said, but her voice was small.

"Faith," he said, sounding stronger, almost desperate. "Please believe me. I would never hurt you. I would never hurt Wayne. I don't hurt people. I'm generally the one being hurt."

Faith nodded. "I know. I do. He just shocked me, that's all. I know you would never hurt Wayne or anyone. But..." She lowered her voice to a whisper. "What just happened can't happen again. I'm a mess. The timing just isn't right."

"The timing is terrible," Dan agreed with a small smile and reached a hand out to cradle her face. She leaned into him and their eyes met. All at once their connection started releasing an electrical current between them.

"Shit," she said. Her mouth going dry and watering at the same time. He took a step closer so that their bodies lined up, heat radiating. She reached up and put her arms around his neck and rested her head against his chest. His heart beat hard against hers. If she looked up, he would kiss her. There was no way to stop it. But she didn't look up and they stood there locked together, luxuriating in their closeness, in their need for each other that was undeniable but there was no choice but to deny. Dan kissed her hair and whispered, "I don't care about the timing." Faith hugged him to her even more tightly.

"Uh hem." The detective cleared his throat, and they reluctantly moved away from each other.

"Thank you for the boards," Dan said. "I'll bring them down to Tigers Turf."

"Of course."

"I'll talk to you later," he said. "If you need me, you know where to find me."

She smiled non-committal.

"Dan?" the detective asked as he walked out the door. "I forgot, I have one more question." Dan looked at him expectantly. "What size shoe are you?"

"Usually ten and a half." The detective nodded and scribbled in his pad. "Is that good or bad?" Dan asked uncertainly.

"I'll let you know," the detective said, then turned away from him to address Faith. "Mrs. Savage, I have something I need to ask you as well since I'm already here, if that's okay"

She nodded and raised a hand to Dan like she was saying goodbye to her knight in shining armor, who was also a suspect to murder. Now, it was just her and the detective. She braced herself, unsure why the man who was supposed to be helping made her nervous.

"Do you have a bathroom I could use?" the detective asked.

"Down the hall to the left," Faith directed.

"This is a beautiful house. Beautiful." He looked around at the wide open front hallway and whistled. "I'll only be a moment." He stopped along the way at every open doorway to gaze inside. "Beautiful." Faith heard him say at least a half dozen times.

"Where are you from?" Faith asked when he returned almost ten minutes later. She had almost gone down and knocked on the bathroom door to check on him, but that would have been weird and she actually appreciated the small reprieve. It had given her a moment to collect herself a bit. In the past hour, she had gone from crying to almost kissing Dan to his being considered a prime suspect in Wayne's death back to almost kissing. The feelings were all too much, the sadness, the confusion, the anxiety, but mostly the overwhelming rush of desire that was so strong that it blocked out all the others. It was something she had never experienced before. At least not since the last time Dan had kissed her. Her attraction to him was a tornado that she now was almost powerless to stop. They had kept it at bay for years, as of course they should have, occasionally allowing some release to the buildup of their natural chemistry by letting it seep out safely in flirty banter.

Recently, it had become overwhelming and she could no longer deny it, even though she knew it was wrong or at least that the timing was wrong. But her need for comfort was not wrong, and the gaping hole inside her that compelled her to him could not be wrong. Unless, of course, he killed her husband. She sighed, she wasn't prepared for any of this shit.

"I'm from Fort Jefferson," he answered. "I'm a local."

"Oh." Faith was surprised. He seemed so out of his element in the grandness of her home, which was not even close to one of the nicest homes she knew in the area. They stood there in her kitchen, not saying anything. The drink that Faith had discarded when the detective interrupted her and Dan was calling her name. "So, what did you want to ask me?" she asked, trying not to sound impatient, reminding herself that this man was here to help. Still, she felt claustrophobic and anxious and wanted some alone time before the boys got home.

"Oh, I just wanted to know if I could use the bathroom. Thank you," he said. "I'll show myself out." Faith watched baffled as he walked out. "I'll be in touch," he called back to her, and she heard the door click closed.

CHAPTER 6

"I got the boards from Faith," Dan said the next evening on the phone with Deb.

"Yeah. Great." Deb sounded distant, only half paying attention. You'd think she didn't just call him.

"So we have practice tomorrow?" he confirmed. "Six o'clock, right? Did you send an email out to the team?"

"Yeah."

"Deb, what's up? You're somewhere else."

"Sorry. I'm just checking emails, and I'm reading through this one from Joe. It's about the new uniforms. Apparently, our team owes him $2,744.53."

"What? Why?"

"Yeah, I'm trying to work through it here myself. It says that Wayne used funds from FYO, and the team needs to pay it back."

"Send it to me," Dan said. Thirty seconds later, he got it and read as they sat on the phone with each other breathing.

"Dan, what exactly does this mean? And how did this happen?"

"I'm not sure," Dan said, already considering the possibilities, none of them good. Still, he reassured Deb. "Don't worry about it. I'll speak with Joe."

"Thanks."

"You okay, Deb?" Dan asked, concerned. It couldn't be easy being the mistress of the deceased.

"I've been better," she conceded.

"Is there anything I can do?" Dan asked.

"Nah, it's nice of you to ask though. No one asks me how I'm doing." Deb heard the anger in her voice and changed the subject. "In other news, Mikey has been up my ass like I'm his own personal secretary. 'Deb, when's the next practice? Deb, can you get me a room for the next tournament? Deb, do you keep a record for the stats on the kids?'" She tried to mimic Mikey's voice.

"Hey," Dan interrupted. "Why did Mikey ask for the stats on the boys?"

"I don't know. I didn't ask. Besides, you're the one who keeps the books. I told him so and that maybe Matt, and, of course, Wayne had a copy."

"Deb, I got to go. I don't have time to deal with Mikey. I'm gonna call Joe. I'll get back to you."

Dan hung up. All of a sudden, he had a headache. There was so much shit spinning around in there, he couldn't keep his thoughts straight. If he didn't keep moving forward, he would get stuck. He picked the phone back up and dialed Joe. "Joe! What's happening? It's Dan."

"Hey, Dan," Joe grumbled. "How's it going?"

"I was just checking on a bill Deb just forwarded me from you. One for almost three grand? Can you tell me what it's for?"

"Uniform stuff," Joe said gruffly.

"What kind of uniform stuff? The team paid for their uniforms already."

"Yeah, well, Wayne left some outstanding bills, and FYO isn't going to pick up the tab."

"Joe, is there something you're not telling me? Wait..." Something clicked in Dan's head. "Is this about thing you alluded to at the bar the night Wayne was..." He couldn't say it. "That night," he finally just said.

Joe avoided the question. "None of that makes any difference now. I'm just telling you that you need to get it paid. That's all. Wayne's not here to clean up this mess, so the Rockets need to clean it up. I'm not taking the fall."

"And what do I tell the parents?"

"Just say there was a billing error and they owe approximately two hundred plus dollars per family."

"Shit. I don't know if that's gonna fly."

"Make it fly," Joe said and hung up.

Dan's headache was getting worse. He went to his medicine cabinet and rummaged through till he found a bottle of Advil and popped three pills. Then he called Matt. Lately, he spent both his days at work and his evenings dealing with baseball or Wayne. He thought that the team consumed his life before Wayne's death, now it was his life.

Matt picked up on the third ring. "Yello!"

Dan rolled his eyes. "Hey, it's me. We need to talk about—"

"Ha!" Matt's voice continued. "Gotcha! I'm not here right now but leave a message." The phone beeped. Dan had an urge to smash the phone repeatedly on his coffee table. Instead, he spoke through grated teeth. "Matt, it's Dan. Call me."

He should call Mikey but decided he'd been tortured enough. He could talk to him tomorrow at practice. He picked up the phone and dialed the number he shouldn't. Then hung up. He was a murder suspect for her husband. He was emotional and overwhelmed and couldn't stop thinking about her. Nothing good could happen from speaking with her tonight. He picked the phone back up and called Jake.

"Hey, buddy," he said when Jake answered. He felt the tension in him dissipate just a little.

"Hey, Dad."

"How are you doing?"

"Good."

"How's school?"

"Good."

"Hey how are Derek and Reggie doing? Have you spoken with them?"

Dan could almost see Jake shrugging. "They're different lately. They don't really hang out or talk much."

"Yeah. I can imagine." Dan kicked off his shoes and closed his eyes. "But don't give up on them, okay. They're going through a tough time."

"Okay, Dad. See you tomorrow at practice. Bye."

That was how twelve year olds hung up when they had enough of a conversation. At the moment, Dan appreciated it. He unbuttoned his shirt, stripped off his slacks, and laid them carefully over the chair in his room. He took a long hot shower thinking about Faith, then fell into bed to sleep. It was barely ten o'clock, and he was out.

Sean stood out by the fence at Field 2 waiting for him to walk up, excited to see him. "Hey, Dan! How are you?" Sean was Chris' dad and one of the nicest guys on the team. Like Mikey, he always wanted to be a coach, help coach, and somehow get in the dugout. Unlike Mikey, he wasn't an annoying asshole. He was a genuine nice guy who loved being part of the team.

"Hey, Sean. I'm good. Excited to get a good practice in today."

"It's a great night," Sean agreed, puttering around him. "So how's everything going? How's the team? Is there anything I can do to help out?"

Dan stopped unpacking his gear to stretch a bit and look at Sean. He was so earnest in his hope to help, to wear the Rockets jersey to mix it up with the team. "You play any sports when you were younger," Dan asked him.

Sean shook his head, already demurring. "Nah, not really. I wrestled in high school a bit, played a little soccer."

"That's cool," Dan said.

"Well, we all can't be star athletes like you!" Sean gushed a little and Dan marveled. He didn't say it sarcastically. He actually meant it.

"It was a long time ago."

"Yeah, but you were the real deal. A pitcher for a Division I school."

"That was a long time ago."

"You still know your stuff. I mean you're always throwing to the kids and you still swing the bat great. And look at you. You're in great shape!"

Dan smiled. "You looking for a date, Sean? Cause you know I'm available."

Sean laughed embarrassed. "I'm just saying, you know."

"Yeah, thanks, Sean." He decided to toss him a bone. It was the least he could do for the guy. "Hey, you think you could help me out? I'm going to pitch to the kids. Can you maybe get behind the plate and call 'em?"

Sean stuttered for a moment with excitement. "Yeah, totally. Thanks Dan." He bounded off with new pup excitement. Dan heaved up the ball bag to walk over to the mound.

Mikey walked up to him. "Matt called me to say he was running late and may not even make it."

"No problem. I'm going to throw to the kids and then we'll just run some plays and see how it goes. You want to go over the book and see if we've got our line-up right?"

Mikey eyed him. The book was a guarded document. It was never just handed to him. "Yeah?" he asked.

"Sure," Dan said agreeably. "Just go over the kids hitting stats and make sure we're not overestimating anyone or underestimating anyone. Sometimes we forget to do it and just get used to doing what we're doing, but when we check, we can see if someone we didn't realize is struggling or if someone's on base percentage has really taken a leap. It's good to know."

"Thanks," Mikey said, still a little shocked. "Wayne never would have given me this."

"Yeah," Dan said. "But I'm not Wayne.

Practice ran smoother than any they had since Wayne's death and even before that. After feeling so overwhelmed the day before, Dan had woken up in the morning with new resolve. He was just going to go on with life the best he could. He wasn't going to run from the detective, Matt, Mikey, the team, or Faith. He was going to be him, a decent dad, a decent coach, and a decent person and hope it all fell into place.

The hours spent in the low, early evening sun working on infield outfield, first and third situations and run downs got the kids fired up in a good way. They all sweat and focused, and looked more like a team than they had in a long while.

By eight o'clock, the parents were there to pick up their exhausted children. Matt had shown up at the end of practice but stayed off to the sides. Besides belting out an unnecessary comment when his kid bobbled a ball, he remained uninvolved and let Dan finish out what he started. Both Mikey and Sean turned out to be surprisingly decent assistants, and at least half the kids thanked him at the end of practice with actual eye contact.

There was only one 'almost incident' toward the end when Landon shouted, "This is like the best practice we ever had, Coach!" The whole team's ears perked with attention, and both Derek and Reggie visibly stiffened. Dan couldn't be certain, but something in Landon's demeanor looked as if it was an intended slight.

Dan quickly shut down the situation. "That's just because your head is finally in the game, Landon. Now go collect some of those outfield balls. Chris, Jake and Josh, go help him." Then he called Derek over to catch off to the side while Reggie threw some practice pitches to him. Crises averted.

Dan thanked Sean and Mikey for their assistance. "No, thank you," Sean said, beaming. "Great practice. Thanks for letting me be a part of it."

He chatted a little with each of the parents if they came up to the field, but most of the kids just ran to meet them at their cars in the parking lot. He saw Faith's car pull up and caught a glimpse of her profile and ponytail as Reggie and Derek jumped in and they left.

Deb walked up. It was a nice night and she hadn't taken her car. Often Deb and Landon walked to and from the field since their house was only a few blocks from it.

"Hey," she greeted them and lingered, making small talk until all the kids were gone and it was only her, Dan, Matt, and Mikey. They stood there for a couple of minutes, the boys goofing around on the field, Dan, Deb and Matt all waiting for Mikey to leave. When it became clear he wasn't, they got down to a little after practice business.

Matt began. "So, Jeff approached me about having a little scrimmage on Saturday morning. I think it's a good idea."

"I agree," Dan said. "The boys are itching to play, and it'll be a fun, friendly competition."

"If you say so," Matt snorted.

Dan ignored him. "Deb, set it up?"

"On it. I'll coordinate with Jeff."

"You know, I've been watching White. They're looking pretty good," Mikey added.

"If you say so," Matt snorted again.

Dan hesitated a minute, then exchanged a glance with Deb.

"What?" Matt asked.

"So I don't know if you guys know," Dan said, "but we have a little situation."

"Are you talking about the money?" Matt asked, and Dan nodded.

"What money?" Mikey asked.

The other three sighed and Matt filled him in, sort of. "It seems there was a snafu somewhere on our team's accounting. Long story short, our team owes a couple of grand back to FYO."

"Shit," Mikey said. "How the fuck did that happen?"

"Good question," Dan said, "but doesn't matter. It happened, and now it's in our hands and we're responsible."

"So what do we do?" he asked.

"I was thinking about that last night," Deb said. "I think there's a way we can maybe slide this in under the radar without any attention. Do you think we can have a bake sale or something like that, maybe at the memorial, to raise money for something to honor Wayne?"

"You mean like him not being remembered for embezzling money from a not-for-profit organization for kids?" Matt snorted.

Deb rolled her eyes while Mikey's bugged out. Dan smacked Matt on the arm, but he only laughed. "Whatever, yeah, Deb. I think that's a great idea."

"How about a bench?" Dan suggested. "You know for the

spectators. We can have it engraved."

"I love that idea," Deb said. "It's perfect. The team will be excited to rally around something for Wayne and maybe, hopefully, we'll raise enough money to secure the memory of him."

"And his reputation," Matt added.

The plan set and agreed upon, they all called their kids over and disbanded. "You guys want a ride?" Dan asked Deb and Landon who were walking back to their house.

Deb shook her head. "It's a nice night. We're good." She put an arm around Landon, who shrugged her off. "Just some quality time for me and my boy." She shook her head at Dan in exasperation but just followed alongside her son.

"Okay, talk tomorrow. Good practice, Landon," Dan called to him and then drove off.

Deb and Landon ambled slowly toward home. It was 8:10 p.m. and the sun hadn't yet completely disappeared for its night rest, leaving the sky a dark purplish gray but with enough light to easily guide them on their five minute walk. "So practice was good?" she asked her son.

"Uh huh."

A standard response. "How's everyone doing?" she pressed. Deb didn't mention it to Dan, only to her friend Liza who lived over in NJ, but she was worried about Landon. He had been moody and difficult for a while now. She chocked it up to twelve-year-old hormones, but in her gut she knew that it had a lot more to do with Wayne's death and what went on that night than she wanted to admit. Although, it certainly didn't help that his asshole father had been an asshole about his visits, disappointing him on more than a couple of occasions. She really should be more up his ass about it, but she had avoided dealing and now was overwhelmed with just keeping it together.

"Fine."

"How are you doing?" she pushed gently, hoping he wouldn't close down.

"Fine."

"Are you honey?" she asked. "Because you've got me a little worried lately. You're not eating much, and I hear you up late at night and early morning. Are you even sleeping?"

He shrugged.

"You want to talk about it?"

Landon shrugged again.

Deb tried to make the small opening he gave her just a little bit wider. "Can I talk a little?"

"Free country."

Deb let out some air. "Okay, yeah. So a lot has gone on lately. And I'm certainly feeling kind of a mess about everything. I mean, I know your dad has been really distracted with work and hasn't been around much. I hope you know he loves you so much and sometimes adults just get caught up in work and crap that really doesn't matter. He'll show up on Saturday."

"That would be cool," Landon said, and Deb's heart did a little cheer. They were almost at their house. Deb took what little time she had left of his attention and tried to make use of it.

"And then there's Coach Wayne dying. That can't be easy on you, either. He had such a big part of our lives." Landon seemed to retreat. "I know that last night was ugly, really ugly, but he thought of you like a son. All the boys on the team were like—"

Deb didn't finish her sentence because the look of pure rage on Landon's face stopped her. "A son?" he stammered, his face flushed pink with emotion. "He had two sons, and believe me I wouldn't want to be one of them! He was an asshole, Mom! And I don't even think he was a good coach. I don't care that he's dead. I didn't even like him! You're the one who liked him!"

Deb stood speechless and fumbled with her keys to open the door. The minute she did, Landon pushed past her up to his room. He slammed his door, and Deb jerked physically from the sound. She was divorced with a dead married lover and almost no girlfriends. She held down a decent job in pharmaceutical sales and made a nice salary, but she wrapped her whole life around her son's baseball team—the administration, the politics, the planning, the games, the practices, and the coaches. They hung out together at bars and went away to tournaments. They strategized and socialized. They were her friends, but were they really? Without the team, what did they really have? And without Wayne, what did she really have? Her life was fucked up, and she was alone. Standing at the bottom of the stairs with the front door hanging open and her son's door shut up tight, she couldn't stop shaking.

From: Deb Schnitt
To: The Golden Rockets and their Families

CC: Coaches Dan Williams, Matt Bidsky and Mikey Dunn, Joe Costa
Subject: Let's Bake!

Rockets, the coaches and I have discussed a way that we can memorialize the memory of our beloved Coach Savage. We were thinking about purchasing a spectator bench for Field 2 (of course) and having it engraved. We are planning a string of bake sales—first one at the scrimmage this Saturday!—leading up to the memorial event next Saturday! Hopefully after a week full of sales at TT, we'll be set! Barb, can't wait to get my paws on one of your fabulous brownies! Come on, team, let's get those ovens heated up!!

To the star, Rockets!

***

Rockets Team Chat
(Jake, Chris, Landon, Max, Dylan, Balls (Josh), Ryan, Money (Manny), Derek, Tyler, Jimmy, Reggie)

Ryan – Another bake sale? Seriously?

Tyler - Gag

Money (Manny) – My mom is already baking brownies

Chris – Down for that!

Money (Manny) – It's a cool idea

Chris – Yeah. I hear we're looking to buy coach a bench or something

Reggie – My dad would've liked that

Jake – Reg!

Chris – Dude!

Balls (Josh) – It's a nice idea.

Jake – How you doin' man?

Reggie – Hangin' in there

Money (Manny) – Don't worry, we'll catch you if you fall

Reggie – Thanks, guys

Ryan – Was a great practice today

Jimmy – Tyler's slow as ass

Tyler – STFU man!

Balls (Josh) – Right? It felt really good

Reggie – Your dad was awesome, Jake

Jake – Thanks, Reg, he learned from the best

Reggie – Thanks for saying that, man

Money (Manny) – Where's Lando at? It's not like him to dis a chat.

Chris – LANDO!!!?

***

It was 2:34 a.m., and Dan heard his phone buzz, alerting him to a new message. What the hell, he thought, grabbing it. It wasn't like he was sleeping, anyway. He scrolled his emails. It was from Faith. He sat up, his heart beating.

From: Faith
To: Dan
Subject: Hindsight is 20/20

I couldn't sleep. My brain is going a mile a minute thinking about

Wayne and what happened. How someone out there wanted to hurt him. And then did. Although, I could think of a lot of people who certainly held a grudge. Once I started compiling, the list was a lot longer than I thought.

I'm thinking about you a lot too. I know I shouldn't be, and I probably shouldn't be telling you this for so many reasons. One, because I'm a recent widow who is so emotionally messed up that there is no way she should be getting involved with anyone. Second, because the detective came by again today to ask a few questions and to let me know that I'm a prime suspect as well, so I guess you're in good company. Apparently, the spouse is always a prime suspect and especially one whose husband brazenly cheats on her, who is left alone on a regular basis and ignored, and who flirts shamelessly with assistant coaches. On paper, I'm not looking too good either.

So, yeah, I'm thinking about you. I can't help it. With all the stress my brain needs a happy thing to focus on and—no pressure (ha!)—but it's kind of you and the vodkas I've been drinking too much of lately. So here I am just rambling to you inappropriately in the wee hours of the morning. I'd say, stay away from this one. Nothing but trouble here.

From: Dan
To: Faith
Subject: Looking for trouble

I think about that kiss all the time.

From: Faith
To: Dan

I do too.

From: Dan
To: Faith

Damn, I wish you were here with me right now.

From: Faith
To: Dan

I do too.

Faith shut off her phone. She couldn't take any more. It was too much, but at the same time, it was exactly what she needed. Thank God she had Dan. Focusing on him was the only thing that kept her from going crazy. That and the boys. At least Reggie talked to her about his feelings. She'd sit by his bed at night, tickling his back and listening as he poured his heart out in his haphazard pre-teen style, randomly interspersing the daily grind with heavy thoughts. In a five minute span, he might cry about missing his dad, gloat over a test he nailed in Latin and plead for the new LeBron sneakers he desperately needed. It all came out. Derek was another story. He bottled things up, and Faith was never convinced that when he said he was 'fine' that he meant it. How could he be? She tried making special time for each of the boys. "Let's go to dinner, just you and me," she'd say to Derek, but he continued to put her off. She had him seeing a therapist, both boys actually were, but so far Derek remained a clam. So she mothered around him, making his favorite foods, hugging him to annoyance and generally pestering him with her well-meaning attempts at connection. She just wanted him to open up to someone, but unfortunately he had also backed away from his friends as well. At least he had Reggie who told her not to worry, but who listens to twelve year olds.

The only thing Derek did ask of her, which at first took her by surprise yet shouldn't have, was permission to quit the team. Her first impulses were mixed. She worried about him leaving something that he was a part of for so long, especially in the midst of all this upheaval and now that he had isolated himself so, but even though she wasn't thrilled with the timing, she was okay with his decision. Derek hadn't been happy playing ball for some time, but with Wayne it hadn't mattered. You played, watched, talked, lived baseball in the Savage house, end of story. Faith understood Derek's feelings better than anyone. She was not only over baseball, she was over watching Derek play a sport that he wasn't excited about. If he wanted to quit, she supported him.

Out of respect for Wayne, what she knew he would have wanted, she cautioned him to wait a little, that it wasn't wise making such a big decision so soon after a traumatic event but Derek was resolute, and she could only respect his decision. He said he would wait till after the memorial the next week before telling the team, and she agreed. It was probably for the best. Derek had needed a break from the game for a long time. It wasn't the first time he had asked to quit. It was just a shame that only now he was finally allowed to.

CHAPTER 7
(Wayne rounds the bases)

Derek really, really, really didn't want to catch for the championship game. He wanted Jake to catch. Jake was a better catcher. He deserved the position much more than he did, but every time he told his dad it was like talking to a thick brick. Sometimes he just wanted to throw the brick at his head.

"But, Dad," he whined over the phone, "it's not fair. You've had me in for most of the playoffs too. It's Jake's turn. I'm happier in the outfield."

"Kid, how many times do I have to tell you that it's not about fair. Life isn't fair. You got to take your opportunities and make your opportunities."

"But he deserves it," Derek said, his voice defeated. He wanted to add that that he didn't want the opportunity, that him wanting it for him wasn't the same thing, but instead he gave up. It wasn't like he was going to win. His dad didn't like being argued with unless he was the one doing the arguing.

"Jake's a good kid and you're right, he's a good catcher but he has plenty of opportunities. And I'm not worried about him. He's not my son. Case closed."

Not for the first time, Derek was kind of wishing that he wasn't his son. Wayne took his silence as submission.

"Listen, I'm wrapping up my day now and getting out of here. I'll be on the 3:38. Tell Reggie to be dressed and ready for when I get home. We'll head right over to TT for some BP and practice before the team even arrives. Remind your mom to pack us sandwiches and snacks. And not to forget the Gatorade. And tell her to—wait, is she there? Let me talk to her."

"Sure, Dad," Derek grumbled, feeling like his words and feelings meant nothing to his father. Might as well hand him off to mom, talking to him was a waste anyway. He heard nothing and only liked hearing himself talk.

"Chin up, boy!" Wayne boomed. "Tonight is going to be fun."

"Whatever, Dad. I've got homework to do." He handed Faith the phone. "Here. Dad wants to talk to you."

Faith put down the knife she was using to cut up an apple for Reggie and gave Derek her sad face, pouting out her lip in empathy. Derek rolled his eyes, took his loose leaf binder, and walked out of the room.

"Hey," Faith said, cradling the phone into her shoulder so she could continue cutting up the apple. "What's up?"

"I just wanted to remind you about the Gatorade for the team. And if you could get my shorts and game jersey up from the laundry rack. I'll be on the 3:48, so make sure the boys are ready to go when I walk in. And have a cooler with sandwiches and snacks."

"On it, Coach." Faith rolled her eyes at the familiar list of requests, looking a lot like Derek had only a minute before.

"You don't have to be snarky. I was just reminding you."

"You're right. Sometimes reminders help. I guess I should have reminded you it was our anniversary last week."

She knew she shouldn't have said it. It wasn't worth the trouble it was going to cause, but sometimes she just couldn't help herself. Four times this past week alone, he had taken a ridiculously early train home for baseball practices or games, but, as always, on a day that was supposed to be about her, he not only didn't take an early train, he took a later one than usual. Apparently, if you leave early all the time, you've got to catch up sometime. Sometime was always her time. She knew it. It had been that way for years. She was numb to it on most levels, didn't even care. They had somehow managed to maintain a marriage where they came together on certain points like the kids and baseball games for the kids and certain social functions, generally baseball related where they needed to be a couple, but by and large they lived separately together. She had her boys, her friends, her books, her house and her alcohol. He had his work, his running, his board position at FYO, his coaches meetings and politics, his practices and workouts, his beloved Yankees, and his bar nights out mainly at Flynn's, the local Irish pub. She had to hand it to him. The man had a lot on his plate. Too bad she wasn't even a side dish. He already had a few of those as well.

"Really, Faith? Now? Championship day? You're going there now? You're too much. I got to go or I'll miss the train."

"Okay, you're righ—" she started to say but never finished the sentence. He had hung up without a goodbye. Faith took a deep calming breath and admitted to herself that he was right. Her timing sucked. But sometimes even though she had made a semi-comfortable peace with their arrangement, on a deep level it nagged at her that this was her life. That she was compromising so much for her pretty house. But, of course, that wasn't all it. There were the boys to think of, and being alone wasn't all it was cracked up to be. She had seen divorce up close countless times. And, it generally wasn't for the better.

Wayne hung up, frustrated. Did she really need to pull that shit now? He grabbed his briefcase and headed for the door. If he missed the train he was going to kill her.

Luckily, there was no need. He made the train without even a minute to spare, sliding into the doors just as they were about to close. His face trickled sweat from his buzz cut down the side of his cheek. He could only be thankful that the car he sat in was air conditioned, and, of course, given the odd mid-week time that there was only a person or two in it.

The train just started to pull out when he felt a hand on his shoulder. "Why Mr. Savage, funny running into you again." Erika's pink manicured nails caressed his shoulder gently. "Mind if I sit with you?" she asked, raising an already arched brow and sliding into the seat next to him. "I have a feeling things are coming up that we need to talk about."

Wayne looked at her and grinned. "Things certainly have come up recently, Erika, that need your attention. Let me show you what we're working with." He placed her hand on his extended crotch. "Do you think you could help me out?"

"Oh, Mr. Savage." Erika pretended shock and playfully pulled her hand back to cover her mouth in surprise. "You do seem to have a very big problem."

"Unfortunately, I do." He placed her hand back between his legs. "It will require all of your attention I'm afraid."

She began rubbing him surreptitiously. "Well, you were so helpful with the carnival that I feel like it's the least I could do. I mean what kind of person would I be to leave you in such dire straits?"

Wayne craned his neck around the car. There was no one near them. "Thank you, Erika. I knew I could count on you, and I promise to heartily repay this kindness."

"Oh, I know you will," she said, then unzipped his fly and blew him away.

"Will I see you later?" she asked, fixing her lipstick as the train pulled into the Fort Jefferson station.

"I'm going to try," Wayne said. "It would probably be late since the game won't be over till eight, then there's the after game festivities, then I have to go to the bar with the other coaches to celebrate."

"Celebrate? Oh you are a cocky bastard." She laughed.

"What you love about me."

"You got that right." She placed a hand back between his legs and pat gently. "See you later, you big cocky bastard." She grabbed her bag and left. Wayne waited thirty seconds and followed, walking past her to his car without a glance.

He stormed through his door invigorated, like a man on a mission, like a winner. Erika did that for him. She had a way about her that made him feel like an animal. A tiger. A beast on the prowl. She made him feel fucking awesome. "Boys!" he called out. "Where are you?" He dropped his bag on the floor, right next to the cooler Faith had left for him along with a case of Blue Gatorade and a case of red Gatorade. He was taking off his shoes when Derek and Reggie came from kitchen to greet him.

"Hi, Dad," they said in unison. They were ready to go like he expected, except the expression on Derek's face. That was not a ready to go face. He ignored it and tried to let his enthusiasm infect them.

"Come on! Let's see some energy! Are you guys ready to kick ass?!!!" he bellowed.

"Yeah," they repeated with a little more gusto.

"That's it?! Come on!!! Are you ready to kill it?!" He was screaming now, a little over the top even for him, but he could see the magic happening. Even Derek was smiling.

"We're ready to kill it!!!" they screamed back.

"Good," Wayne said, beaming, using his normal voice. "I'm going up to take a quick shower and change. We're leaving in five minutes"

They were out the door in less than ten minutes. In preparation for the crazy day, Wayne had already packed all their gear in the trunk that morning before his run with Joe. He didn't want to worry about forgetting anything or being rushed. The conversation with Joe weighed on him. He didn't like Joe's attitude or his insinuations, but he also knew that he hadn't handled things correctly and needed to fix it. They buckled their seatbelts as Wayne pulled out of the driveway. "Boys, we've got one stop to make," he said. "Then it's a straight path to victory!"

CHAPTER 8

From: Deb
To: Joe
CC: Matt, Dan, Mikey
Subject: Payback

Joe, we expect to have the funds to repay any outstanding charges made in the Rockets' name back to FYO by Saturday. We are also hoping to raise enough money to cover the costs of a bench that we can place on the side of Field 2 in Wayne's honor.

See you at the scrimmage!

At 7:45 a.m., Matt, Dan and Mikey got their gear and their kids out of their cars and headed toward Field 2 for some warmups. The rest of the team was to report by eight. As they trudged, fueling their early morning energy with the warmth of the sun, they saw Jeff and his assistant coaches Rick and Dave heading out toward Field 3 to get ready for their own practice drills; their children also dragging behind.

No one loved early weekend games, but once they were all up and going it was good. Scheduling the games out in the mornings so that it didn't interrupt the entire day was accepted in general parental consensus as the actions of a considerate coach, although the young players definitely would disagree.

Dan gave a wave over to Jeff and the other coaches, then decided to walk over to say hello. "I'll be right back," he said to Matt and Mikey.

"Conspiring with the enemy?" Matt asked, dragging a bucket of balls with one hand and gripping his stainless steel coffee mug in the other.

"Remember, this is a friendly game," Dan warned, wishing he remembered to get himself a cup of coffee. No doubt Barb had handed it to Matt before he left. Barb was a good woman.

"Hey, Jeff." Dan extended his hand to shake. "Beautiful day we got here."

"Perfect for baseball."

"Looking forward to a good fun game. I heard your team is looking pretty good," Dan said. He always liked Jeff. Despite his momentarily loss of sanity when he sent that email around, he was a good guy. He felt horrible how Wayne had treated him and his son, but at the time he didn't feel like he was in a position to do anything.

"We're improving. Jordan is starting to pitch now as well."

"Nice," Dan said, grinning. "A real threat. Glad to hear it. We'll see you in about an hour over on Field 5."

"Hey, Dan," Jeff called after him, and Dan turned. "I was wondering if maybe you'd consider giving Jordan some pointers some time. You were always so great with him."

Dan smiled. "I'd be happy too. Anytime."

By 8:45 a.m., Tigers Turf was already shifting into high gear. There were two other baseball scrimmages for younger teams, and a lacrosse practice getting ready to start. Deb gave a salute from the center of the complex where she was busy with Barb setting up the table with treats to sell for their bake sale.

Jeff had requested they play on a neutral field so they were playing today on Field 5. Unlike Fields 1 and 6 which were Turf, there was no physical difference between Field 2, 3, 4 or 5 but mentally Field 2 was considered the Gold Rockets field just like Field 3 was considered White's home turf. Field 5 was neutral and Rockets Gold and White were all settled in their dugouts and ready to begin by the time the umps arrived.

Parents, grandparents and siblings lined the fences, half of them sitting in the bleachers and the other half unfolding sport chairs to get even closer to the action. Parents who couldn't sit still paced up and down, unable to control their excitement.

"Play ball!" the Ump shouted.

A boy named Noah emerged from White's dugout, and from behind the plate, Jake yelled, "Balls in!" and the team in the field responded, "Coming down!" The game was about to start. Josh was starting pitcher and Jake was catching. He would have been anyway, but Derek had asked to play outfield, which made it easier.

"Hey, Dan," Sean greeted. "Sorry to interrupt. I just got some extra coffees for anyone. Interested?" He produced a cardboard tray from Dunkin Donuts with four hot coffees. Dan immediately grabbed one. "Sean, you're a lifesaver. Thank you."

"Oh, it's no problem, Coach," he said. "Happy to be of assistance."

"Hey, you want to really be of assistance?" Dan asked, knowing full well Sean salivated at any opportunity to help.

"Of course." He nodded enthusiastically, kind of like a bobble head.

"Would you keep the pitch count?" He handed over the device.

"Yeah, sure. Thanks, Dan!"

Dan smiled, watching him walk back behind the fence to watch the game, holding the counter like it was a prized possession. Why had they never given Sean this job? It was so easy, and it made him really feel part of the team. That was what they all wanted from the experience, to be included. He realized that Wayne had created an exclusive club and you were either in or out. That wasn't the way he would run his team.

He looked over to Mikey, who had always kept his own secret count on his kid regardless. Mikey too, had been an outsider, forced through Wayne's obsessive control to take his own sort of control. Maybe he wasn't such a neurotic asshole. Maybe he just wanted to be involved on the team with his kid. "Hey, Mikey," Dan said. "I hope you don't mind, but I gave Sean the counter."

Mikey nodded. He and Sean were sideline buddies. Up until a little over a week ago, the idea that Sean would keep count and Mikey would be in the dugout was just plain ridiculous, but now it felt right. "That's cool, Dan. I'm cool with it."

Josh threw the first pitch, a strike.

Dan took a sip of warm coffee, letting it seep through his system giving him an extra buzz of energy. Josh threw another strike. He looked around at the parents. Mikey was watching his boy intently. Matt stood at the gateway between the dugout and the field assessing every move and the position of every player. "Reggie, come in a little!" "Jimmy, two steps over!" "Landon? Where's your Rockets' hat?"

Max's dad, Rich, caught his eye and raised an identical cup of Dunkin Donuts coffee at him in salute. He saw Faith standing by the bleachers talking with Marie and Dylan's mom, Robyn. She glanced over at him and smiled. His heart stopped just as the Ump called strike three.

Dan appreciated this moment when everything felt like it was coming together. The team was suddenly starting to feel like the team that he always wanted. Maybe there was a chance for him and Faith. Then he looked over and found another set of eyes on his. Detective Jonas.

The game became tied in the sixth inning when Jeff's son Jordan smacked an inside pitch from Reggie over the fence for an amazing homeroom with guys on first and third. Both sets of coaches agreed to continue till the win. It was a tense couple of innings, both sides at the edge of their seats with every catch, every pitch, every out. It was so exciting and fun and both teams and their spectators were wonderful sports, applauding a diving catch by Landon and a pick off from the catcher to Dylan at second. The other team had their moments as well and all the parents cheered. The game ended when Manny knocked in the winning run with a line drive out of reach of the third baseman.

It was a town scrimmage, all the boys and their parents were friends, and the White team congratulated the Gold, while the Gold team thanked the White for a good game. Dan and Jeff shook hands.

"Great game. Congratulations," Jeff said.

"It was a great game. Your boys looked really good out there. And Jordan has got great fundamentals. I'm happy to work with him."

"Thanks, Dan. This has been a real pleasure." Their silence acknowledged the fact that not only would it never have happened with Wayne, but that it certainly wouldn't have been a pleasure.

"Hey," Dan changed the subject. "I saw your youngest out there selling some cake for us. That kid could be in commercials with that face and all the crazy hair. I'll bet he made us a small fortune."

Jeff smiled his thanks when Matt cut in. "Great game, Jeff! I thought it was going to be blowout."

Dan translated. "That's Matt's way of saying, he's impressed."

Matt gave a hearty laugh. "Yes, Jeff. That's what I was saying."

They all patted each other on the back, traded compliments, and tentatively scheduled another scrimmage. Everyone played nice, and the boys from both teams mingled and horsed around a bit. They all bought brownies, Rice Krispy treats, and chocolate chip cookies.

Dan looked around for the detective. All throughout the game he had intermittently glanced over, finding him absorbed in the competition. On one occasion, he found him over by the first base line deep in conversation with Joe. It was a lot to take in. It was even more to ignore, but he tried his best to keep focused. Amazingly, he, Matt and

Mikey did a pretty good job balancing the coaching. Matt coached third, Dan coached first, and Mikey did the book in the dugout. They agreed on the lineup and even when it was time to pull Josh and relieve him with Reggie. It was a perfect game on a perfect morning, except for the obvious.

Now that the game was done, it seemed the detective had gone. The parents had mostly finished their chatting and started rounding up their kids as well.

"It seems like everything went pretty well today," Deb said, sidling up next to Dan as he packed up his stuff in the dugout.

"It really did," he agreed. "How was the bake sale?"

"We did great. I didn't do the official count yet since Faith and Marie are still over there trying to sell the last bits of overpriced sugar to the souped-up children and their parents, but I'll bet we easily made over $500. Well on our way. We're going to hit the train station on Wednesday during rush hour. That should be good for some cash."

"Perfect. Wouldn't it be amazing if we got out of this mess unscathed?"

"It would be," Deb said, and both of them were thinking their own thoughts. "Hey, I invited whoever was around over to my house for pizza and whatever, if Jake's allowed."

"Sure. Fine by me."

"Okay, I'm going to get the cashiers box from the table, drive home, and let the boys walk.

"Hey, why don't you let me get the cashiers box. I'll drop it back to you when I pick up Jake." Deb gave a sideways glance at Faith working the table and slid her eyes back to him knowingly. "Sure. I'll take any excuse not to interact with Faith, just like you'll take any excuse to."

"Whatever." He ignored her comment. "So, did you see the detective?"

She nodded. "Briefly. He bought a brownie and a cookie, and asked me a bunch of random questions about the team and my involvement." She shrugged. "He's a funny one."

"You can say that again." Deb opened her mouth. "But don't," Dan advised.

She smiled and walked off. "See you in a couple of hours."

Dan walked over to the table where Faith stood cleaning up alone. TT had cleared out. The younger teams games had ended hours before and so had the lacrosse practice. Now that their game was over and the Gold and White teams were heading out, the fields were almost empty.

"Excuse me, miss. Do you have anything sweet and delicious?"

Faith turned around and smiled shyly. "Well, there's some melted chocolate chip cookies and some squished cupcakes. I can slip them to you on the sly." She handed him a piece of cookie.

He ignored it and leaned in to whisper in her ear. "There's something else I want much more." He felt her tremble.

She looked up into his eyes, and Dan felt the strength of their attraction. Of her desire. "Come home with me," he whispered.

"Dad!" Jake yelled coming toward them from across the field. Dan stepped back, putting an appropriate distance between them. "I'm going to go to Landon's, okay? All the guys are going."

"Okay, buddy. Be good, and I'll pick you up in a little bit." Jake gave him a quick smile and then bolted off toward the group of boys already leaving the field.

"Are Derek and Reggie going?" Dan asked.

"Just for an hour," Faith said softly. "We have stuff we need to do." She watched him carefully with eyes like a predator who was also prey.

Dan moved back around the table to be closer to her and slid a hand around her waist under her tee shirt. Her skin burned where he touched it. "I could make good use of that hour," he said, wanting her so bad it physically hurt. She looked around and saw no one. They were alone at Tiger Turf. She moved closer to him so that their bodies lined up. Her chest pushed into his. Her groin rubbed up against the hardness that was more than obvious through his sport shorts. He groaned.

"It's not a good time," she said softly but he couldn't hear, could only see her pink lips open, begging him to kiss her. He pulled her up to him with one arm and placed the other under her chin lifting her to him. She opened her eyes and looked directly into his.

"Please," she said so softly he couldn't tell if she was begging him to kiss her or begging him not to. It didn't matter. She didn't even know what she was saying. She was lost to the heat from their bodies, their closeness and need, his hardness rubbing against her making every inch of her body pulse with desperation. She was on fire. She wanted him to push her against the fence and fuck her so bad. She wanted him more than she wanted anything in her life. In this moment, nothing else mattered. Nothing. Her body was both tense and slack with need. It was possible she was drooling. She didn't even know her own name.

"I'm going to kiss you." He nuzzled her cheek and her neck. He bit her earlobe. She was powerless, lost. He could do anything to her, and she only hoped he would. In all her life, she had never felt even an ounce of this desperation and hunger. She waited for that impossibly long moment until he reached her mouth and then bit her bottom lip as well. She sighed with relief as their lips, tongues and mouths came together, touching, probing, first lightly then with such intensity and longing that Faith thought she might faint. She didn't think she could wait another second to have him.

"We need to get out of here," Dan said, his voice throaty with desire.

It was then that they broke apart and looked around. Their entire interaction they were beyond caring, consumed with each other, but now slowly, they returned to earth and they realized how public they were and the risk they had taken. Thankfully, Tiger's Turf truly had cleared out. No one was around, and they breathed easier.

Dan seriously considered grabbing her again and taking her behind the field house. He knew she would comply but decided against it for the obvious reason that it wasn't a wise idea and for the more romantic reason that for the first time they were together, he didn't want it to be here. He wanted her in his bed, and he wanted her there for a long time.

"Wow." Faith shook her head softly. "Wow." In all her life she had never felt anything as intense as their connection.

"I'll take that cookie now," he said. She handed him a baggie and took one for herself. They both held it in their hands but made no move to open it or eat, and instead continued looking at each other carefully. "Can we do that again soon?" she asked shyly.

He moved closer and slid a hand briefly underneath the waistband of her shorts, grabbed her by them and pulled her to him, breathing hard in her ear. "Try to stop me."

She couldn't wait.

From across the field Donny watched their entire interaction, shaking his head with disapproval and tsking.

CHAPTER 9

From: Robin
To: Detective Jonas
Subject: Murder

Detective,

I've called the precinct to speak with you numerous times but have been put off. (Just so you know, Detective Roberts has a bit of an attitude.) I was the small redhead who approached you at the scrimmage. You said it wasn't a good time to talk but then I saw you on the bake sale line buying brownies and cookies. By the way, I made those cookies. I hope you liked them.
I'm hoping I don't seem like too much of a pest, but I think I speak for the whole Rockets team when I ask if there has been any new information on who killed Wayne? I for certain would like to be assured that neither my family nor my child—or anyone on the team. Or the whole community for that matter!—is in danger. I think that it is only fair for the police to be a little more communicative. We are talking about murder.

Sincerely,
Robin Peterson

From: Detective Jonas
To: Robin

Mrs. Peterson,

Firstly, I want you to know that I spoke with Detective Roberts. He is sorry that his tone may have offended, but he gently suggests that calling a police station more than a half dozen times in a short period of time may lead to some slight aggravation. I do apologize that he has not appropriately satisfied your request for more information but as we are in the middle of a murder investigation, the dissemination of information is quite specific. Please know that we feel as though this was a one off incident and do not feel as though there is any danger to anyone else on the team or in the community. Thank you for your concern and rest assured we are hard at work trying to get to the bottom of this very serious matter.

Detective Jonas

P.S. Your cookie was delicious. Thank you.

When Dan arrived to pick up Jake a couple of hours later, he found Deb sitting at the table, her head in her hands. He placed the cashiers box gently down on the table. "Deb?" he asked, pulling up a chair next to her.

Deb picked up her head and Dan almost wished she'd put it back down. Her eyes were swollen and a bit bloodshot, the crystal blue washed over from her tears, her face ruddy and damp, her always stylish dark hair slightly disheveled. This could not be the same woman from just a few hours ago, organizing the bake sale and bantering with him smugly.

"I just can't anymore," Deb cried. It was more of a wail from a dying animal. Dan looked around for the kids concerned. "Oh, don't worry. They're in the basement, souped-up on X-box. Most of them have gone now anyway. It's just Landon, Jake, and Chris."

Dan placed a comforting hand on her shoulder. "Has something happened?" he asked and regretted it the minute he said it. The faded blue of her eyes immediately brightened.

"Has something happened?" She pushed back from her seat and stood up. Her voice was dangerously near hysteria.

"Deb, Deb," he soothed, rising as well. "I know. Come here." He took her in hug and she let him, heaving hard, her broad shoulders moving up and down in rhythm. Deb was almost as tall as he was. It was strange to hold her. In all their years of being friends they had never had this intimacy. "You're going to be okay."

She pulled back, her eyes probing his. "Am I?"

"Yes," Dan assured her. "Absolutely."

She sucked up her snot and her breath and withdrew from Dan's embrace, collapsing back in the chair. She seemed marginally more in control. "I'm so alone," she said. "I just don't know if I can do it anymore."

Dan sat back down too and pulled his chair closer. "Deb, I know we never talked about it, but I'm going to give you some honesty."

She eyed at him skeptically. "Is it going to make me more miserable than I already am?"

"I hope not," he said with just the hint of a smile. "I'm going for motivational here."

"Might as well give it a shot."

"Okay, here goes." He exhaled and plowed forward. "So, of course, I'm not saying that Wayne being dead is a good thing." At the sight of her widened stare, he emphasized, "I am not saying that." He had her attention, so he chose his words carefully. "But, you have been entangled in a 'situation' with Wayne for some time and I don't think it was to your benefit. You deserve to be a priority, to be number one in your relationship. Right now, it's time for a fresh start for you."

"You knew about Erika?" Deb asked point blank, making Dan cringe. They had never even openly discussed the fact that she was having an affair with Wayne, this was a whole new level of boundaries they were crashing through, and Dan wasn't quite sure he wanted to go there. He remained silent. "You knew about Erika!" she accused, tears pouring from her eyes.

"Deb! Stop it!" He looked her dead in the eyes. "This has nothing to do with Erika. Wayne was not right for you and you know it. It meant much more to you than to him and you know it. You have to get yourself together. It's time to move on."

She cried for a minute more before she got herself back under control. "You're right. You're right." She looked at him. "Did everyone know?"

Dan shrugged. "Wayne wasn't shy about sharing, but I think it was reasonably under wraps. I really don't know. I didn't discuss it."

They sat in silence for a few minutes until Deb laughed. "So, should we count how much money we made so far to memorialize that asshole?"

They raised $717 which was impressive for a morning's work. They did bump the usual fundraising prices up by at least a buck, so a brownie that they normally sold for two dollars, they charged three, or in a few instances, whatever the person had. It was a fundraiser, after all. People were generous and many gave more than the price or told them to keep the change. Wayne had coached many kids over the years and was almost an institution at FYO, most people were happy to contribute.

Sean arrived to pick up Chris, and Dan took that as his time to exit as well and called for Jake. "Deb, I was thinking," he said as the kids stomped up the stairs. "We should set up a team meeting and have a talk with the kids and their parents."

"I think that's a really good idea, Coach." Sean always called him "Coach."

"I agree," Deb said, back in business mode. "The boys need to be able to ask any questions they may have and the parents too. How about tomorrow evening. No one generally does all that much on a Sunday. I'll put out an email."

"Sounds good. You can invite them all to my house around five. I'll get some pizza. It should only be for an hour or so."

"On it, Coach," Deb said, looking alert and so much improved from when he first walked in.

Dan took her aside. "Listen, if it's too much for you. It's fine. I can send out the email. I can even organize the baking thing for Wednesday or whatever."

"Please, you could not."

Dan laughed. "You're right! I'd probably ask Robin or Barb to do it!"

"I am so not that easily replaced." She sniffed but there was no more snot, just huffy smugness.

Dan winked. "You know it, boss."

Faith sat on her couch with Derek and Reggie watching Eddie Murphy's *Coming to America*. The movie was still a classic, she thought, even though she was only half paying attention. The boys were into it, though, tuned in and zoned out, subconsciously eating their own buckets of popcorn while she sat curled up with her own snack, a vodka and club. She sipped leisurely, often closing her eyes dreamily. She was reliving her encounter with Dan at Tigers Turf, every juicy, sexy bit of it. She had been doing it all day. In fact, she had spent the entire day reeling from their encounter and still was not over it, nor did she want to be.

Wayne barged into her brain uninvited. He always was so pushy, but he was her husband so he had right to be there. For better and for worse, they had been married and had two children and a life together or at least the general appearance of one. They worked with each other, she could say that at least. Wayne did his part supporting her and his family. They lived an upscale life on the North Shore of Long Island and it took a lot of hard work to maintain their status. She absolutely appreciated that. And she appreciated the time he devoted to his sons. No father made more time for his boys than Wayne. Unfortunately, at times, it may have been too much, but that was Wayne—too much. Too much competitiveness, too much testosterone, too much pride and vanity. He was always in it to win it.

Except with her. He hadn't wanted to win her over in years. Not that she wanted him. She couldn't say who lost interest in who and when it happened. She remembered being angry and disappointed for a long while for Wayne not being the husband she expected, for not making time to cherish their connection but then somewhere along the way, so long ago she couldn't even place it, she stopped being angry. She just let it go, and when she did, she let him go, and they became partners instead of lovers. They shared the house, the boys, a life, but they didn't share any love; if anything, each subtly (and at times overtly) resented the other for being there. Yet, they were dependent on each other to make each day run smoothly. To mess with that and disrupt her boys' lives always seemed like more work than it was worth.

She didn't think he would leave her, although at times she wished he would, but she didn't think so. He prided himself on being a family man of the community. Still, it could've happened. She heard he was hot and heavy with this new flame, Erika Stanley. Poor Deb, she thought and then took it back. Deb got what she deserved.

It was funny that since Wayne's death, she spent more time thinking about him than she had in years. They did the morning dance together, the school functions and baseball, but besides her responsibilities to him—make dinner, pick up the dry cleaning, go to the bank or whatever, he never entered her mind. Dan, on the other hand, had lived there in a sexy bubble that floated all around her, just waiting to be popped.

Her phone buzzed, and she automatically checked her messages. It was from Deb to the team. She looked up to the ceiling for strength. Just because she had no longer been sleeping with her husband didn't mean she was going to like the woman who was. Correction, women.

From: Deb
To: The Golden Rockets and their Families
CC: Coaches Dan, Matt and Mikey
Subject: Team Meeting tomorrow

The coaches would like to gather everyone together so that we can all sit down and talk about the recent events. It would be nice for as many of you to show as possible. It is mandatory for the team. 5 p.m. Coach Dan's house. It won't be a long meeting. Any problems or issues let me know. We'll work it out. There will be pizza and munchkins. So no excuses.

To the stars, Rockets!

It was a good idea, Faith thought, and got up from the couch and headed into the kitchen. She dialed Dan's number. He answered on the first ring.

"Hey," he said, his smile brightening his words. "What a nice surprise."

"I just got the email about the meeting tomorrow."

"Yeah, we thought it was a good idea. Some of the boys seem to be struggling. It would be nice to give them a safe outlet to talk and ask questions."

"I'm a little worried for my boys particularly," she said. "Some of those questions may be difficult."

Dan was silent. "I hadn't thought about that. I promise to be very vigilant and sensitive. We have the email Robin sent around to everyone where the detective assures her that no one is in any danger. That should alleviate some fears, but we'll just have to be on top of the conversation. And if any of the kids have questions that they're not comfortable sharing—or that we're not comfortable answering in a group setting, we'll make ourselves available for private discussions. How about that?"

"You're a good man," Faith said. "Really."

"Who is going to do very bad things to you."

Faith felt his words tingle through every part of her body.

***

Erika Stanley teetered into Detective Jonas' office on kitten heels, clutching a Tory Burch bag. Her lips were soft pink, but her mouth was dirty.

"Detective," she greeted. "I know you called and said that you would see me tomorrow, but I was in the neighborhood and thought I should introduce myself." She held out a delicate hand, nails bubble gum pink. "Erika Stanley. I was sleeping with Wayne Savage."

Detective Jonas didn't blink. He had practiced and mastered the ability to control his facial emotion long ago. He looked at her casually with brown eyes displaying just the right amount of interest. "Yes, Erika. I'm glad you came by and saved me a trip." He clasped her hand and shook, but she didn't let go as quickly as he did.

"You have a nice firm handshake," she said.

"Yeah, well I shake a lot of hands." He gestured to the empty seat.

"Oh. I'm sure you do." He flustered her a little. She had been hoping to throw him off guard by surprising him at his office and by the way she usually threw men off just by being herself, but he was tough and she liked it. She sat down, somehow managing to do so in her pencil thin, tight skirt. "So do you want to interrogate me or should I just tell you what I know?"

Detective Jonas didn't say anything but continued assessing at her. After an extended silence, he finally said, "Let's start with what you think I want to hear." She looked startled by him. "I'm waiting, Mrs. Stanley. Please tell me what you know."

Again, he caught her unaware and she shifted in her seat uncomfortably. Erika liked holding the cards. She didn't like not being in control. "Well, I wanted to tell you about the special relationship that Wayne and I shared and how jealous Deb Schnitt was that he was no longer interested in her. She was completely obsessed with him."

"I see," the detective said. "And were you 'obsessed' with him as well?"

Erika guffawed. "God no. But he had a really big cock." She hoped to see a little shock in his face but was disappointed. He was really getting under her skin.

"Good to know," Detective Jonas said and wrote something on his pad. "So how long were the two of you sleeping together?"

She pursed her lips and shrugged. "Couple of months or so."

"And what about Mrs. Savage?"

"What about her?"

"Was she aware of you and her husband?"

"I'm pretty sure. It was one of those non secret secrets."

"Did you want Wayne to leave Faith?" he asked.

"What? And trade my Bobby for Wayne? No chance. Sure he was good for a roll, but Bobby is my bread and butter if you know what I mean."

"I do know what you mean, thank you."

"Plus, you know lacrosse guys, their sticks ain't bad either." She winked at him. "Anyway, I just wanted you to know that he and Deb got into it that night. Wayne called me afterward and wanted me to pick him up but I was like, no way asshole. Good luck to you."

"I see. And what about your husband, Bob. What did he think about you and Wayne?"

She gave a cute little half shrug. "I can't say. He pretended not to know."

"But he did know."

"I never told him."

An extended silence followed while the detective seemed hard at thought. "Mrs. Stanley, what is your husband's shoe size?"

"He's an eleven and a half, a more than a respectable size." She winked. "Why?"

"Just one of those police details," he said a bit evasively. He didn't need to explain about the partial sneaker print found at the scene. Bob's foot size wasn't a match, anyhow.

"Playing detective, huh?"

"Being detective," he said. "Now, I appreciate you coming in. I'll contact you if I have any further questions and you can let your husband know I'll be in touch with him as well."

"Oh, you want to talk to Bobby?

"Is that a problem?" Detective Jonas asked, his eyes alert.

"No. I just—" She seemed to struggle a bit for words. "I just hoped not to involve him. Bob doesn't like when I... attract negative attention."

"Sorry, can't help that now." She looked disappointed but maybe not. She was an interesting bird. From his seat, he watched her maneuver her body, using mostly her arms to bring herself to her feet. "One more question," the detective said. "How do you even get that skirt on?

"Wouldn't you rather know how to get it off?" she asked with another wink and then teetered out satisfied. She finally got a good one in.

Detective Jonas watched the back of her tight ass disappear and finally allowed a smile to lift his lips. Mrs. Stanley had given him another potential suspect or two, and a very nice hard-on.

***

Matt arrived at Dan's a few minutes early, carrying a tray of Barb's brownies and a six pack of beer. Dan took two bottles out, popped the caps off and handed one back to Matt. He put the rest in the fridge. They clinked bottles and each took a slug.

"Good stuff," Dan said appreciatively of the Lager.

"I'm hooked." They took another drink.

"This is a good idea," Matt said and uncharacteristically said no more.

"Thanks."

"So, how are you doing?" Matt asked. "Things have been, what's the word, let's just say, totally fucked up."

"That about says it," Dan agreed and took another sip.

"Are you worried about being a suspect?"

Dan swallowed and placed his beer down. "I'm trying not to."

"So did you do it?" Matt asked, and Dan stared at him. "Don't kill me for asking." He laughed hard and put his hands up in a don't shoot motion.

"You're such an ass."

"I'm kidding!" He cocked a brow. "But people are starting to talk. And you know what happens when the whisper train pulls out of the station."

"People are starting to talk?" Dan asked, a little shocked.

"Dude, starting? Did you just move here? There are no secrets in the suburbs."

Dan's expression soured. "Great."

"Well, if it's any consolation, Barb says the circles it's traveling in are still pretty contained.

"Let's just talk about something else." The doorbell rang and like dogs they both turned toward the sound. "Well, I guess that's as good a subject changer as any."

"Hey," Matt called out as Dan headed to the door. "Would you mind if I brought a kid down to consider for the team? He hasn't played FYO yet, but he's damn good."

"Sure, why not." Dan shrugged and opened the door. The team rolled in like an old Peanuts cartoon, all legs and arms and kicked up dust tumbling by. "And they've arrived."

The room was full of bodies, both parents and preteen boys all sitting around Dan's living room eating pizza off paper plates and talking. Dan, Matt, and Mikey sat at the front.

"Everyone." Dan called them to attention. "I just want to thank you all for coming, especially on such short notice. But we thought it was important to get together. A lot has happened in a short amount of time, and we just wanted to let you know that we understand that this has been a very difficult time. It has been for all of us. But we are a team and we plan to stick together. Boys, it's important that you are there for your teammates. You need each other now. No one else will really understand what you are going through. Of course, your parents are available at any time to answer any questions or just to talk, and so are we. So, that being said, does anyone have any questions? And trust me, no question is too stupid. This is a safe space."

He looked around at all the wide eyes of the team, some intently focused on him and some already checked out. His eyes fell on Faith, looking serious, sitting between her boys. She wore a khaki tank top, making her hazel eyes glimmer green, and her blonde hair fell softly to her shoulders. He lingered on her an extra beat and watched her blush lightly and cast her eyes down. It took a supreme effort to take his eyes off of her.

Finally, Chris raised a hand. "Are they going to find out who did it?"

"Good question, and we hope so. The detective has assured us that it is their top priority. He has also assured us that none of us are in any danger."

"What about the team?" Rich, Max's dad, asked.

"Right now the team is as it is. As you know, Mikey is aboard and Matt and I are sharing duties. And I have to say doing surprisingly well." A light chuckle lifted the room.

"For now." Matt cut in and Dan paused, to control his annoyance, then agreed.

Landon's hand shot up. "Is there more pizza?" he asked and the room cracked up.

"Okay, I get it. I know it's tough to talk about. If no one wants to say anything, it's okay. Just hang out and if you want a private moment with me or any of the coaches, just say so." It was almost as if he could feel the kids relax. "Fine. You are released children. Come find me if you want me."

The boys all went outside on the back lawn to play manhunt while the parents all refilled their drinks.

"So you guys have any questions?" Dan asked the adults who all looked at one another a little nervously. "Okay, fine," he said. "I get it. Clearly you know I'm a suspect, but I did not kill Wayne. The police are just investigating every avenue. I'm happy to step down if any one of you are uncomfortable."

No one said anything but finally Matt stood up. "I think you should step down." All around the room jaws dropped. "I'm kidding! Sheesh! You guys really need more alcohol."

Faith stood. She looked nervous and spoke in a small voice. "I want to tell you guys something because I want you to understand how wide the net is cast. I'm a suspect as well. There are a lot of suspects." A brief glance passed between her and Dan. Mikey's nostrils flared. Deb looked off to the side as she generally did anytime Faith had the floor.

"I'm just speaking for myself," Rich said, "but Marie and I fully support you, Dan."

"Here, here!" Sean chimed in.

"We're behind you!" they all said. Dan appreciated their support and really hoped they meant it.

"Hey, Faith," he said once the room had started conversing about things other than murder. "Can you come here a minute. I want to show you something."

She looked around hesitantly, like she was being called into the principal's office. "Sure." She followed him down the hall into the small office off to the side. The minute they were in, he pushed her up against the door and pressed his body to hers. She responded immediately and put her arms around his neck bringing her lips to his. She sighed into him, and all the stress in her body relaxed while the tension between them intensified.

"Thanks," he said when they broke apart. "You didn't have to do that."

"What?" She giggled. "Kiss you?"

"No, tell them about your being a suspect. You didn't need."

"I wanted them to know, to understand how it works. You know I bet there are more suspects in there than just us. Wayne had trouble with a few of them."

He nodded. "Yeah, I know."

"We've got to get back out there."

"Yeah, I know," he said, holding her up against the wall and kissing her softly. "Just one more minute."

No one batted a lash when they reemerged in the main room. The parents were all casually hanging around and noshing, broken into small circles of conversation. He joined Matt, Rich, and Marie. "Thanks for having my back," he said to Rich.

"You've always had ours," Marie replied.

"But I was thinking, maybe I should step off for a bit. I don't want anyone to feel uncomfortable, and maybe some parents do and aren't saying so."

"Let's ask them," Matt said, picking up a spoon from the table and clinking his bottle. "Can I have everyone's attention please," he said grandly, and all the parents looked up. Barb, Matt's wife, who had come late with their younger daughter, covered her eyes, pretending fear of her husband taking the stage. "We've been talking over here, and now that the kids are out of the room, we want to know really how you feel about Dan being a suspect and still being an active coach. I know I joked before but should he continue or step down for now? Really. Don't be polite."

The room was silent for a minute while everyone gulped their drink and the lump in their throat uncomfortably.

"I'm going to leave the room," Dan said. "I get it. It's cool. I'll check on the boys."

After he walked out, Matt continued. "So what do we think?

After a beat, Rich spoke up. "I'm with Dan. I completely trust him."

"I agree," Marie said. "He's such a good person. There is no way he did that."

"I trust Dan completely," Sean piped in.

Matt cut in. "You all know I would be more than thrilled to take over as head coach, but it's not because I think Dan is a danger to the kids in any way."

"That's not saying that you don't think he killed Wayne," Robin, Dylan's mom, pointed out.

"You're right," Matt said. "I'm saying I don't think he's a danger. Jury is still out on the rest. I mean a lot of us were there in the bar that night..." He let the statement hang in the air.

Deb jumped in. "That's ridiculous. Dan did not kill anyone. Maybe you did because you wanted to be head coach so bad."

Matt took a casual drink of his beer, and shrugged, unoffended. "Pretty flimsy motive, don't you think? Maybe you did in a jealous rage."

Deb turned beat red and looked about to kill him.

"Okay." Barb stood up and took control. "Everyone settle. This is not helping. Who would like Dan to continue on coaching? Show of hands." Around the room, all hands went up showing their support. Only Dylan's parents wavered. "Robin? Nick? What are you thinking?"

They didn't get to answer, Josh charged into the room. "Come quick! They're fighting!" Immediately everyone was on their feet running to the door.

Outside on the lawn was mayhem. Dan stood in the center trying to separate a mess of boys, some of whom who were screaming and some who stood close to the action but enough steps away not to become entangled. At the center of the ring were Landon and Derek still trying to get at one another, even though Dan pulled Landon off and Reggie held back his brother.

The parents all swooped in, and Faith ran right to her son and demanded his attention. "Derek!" she yelled right in his line of vision. She wasn't much over five feet and Derek was already her height. "Step away, now!" Almost immediately he stopped struggling.

The aggression left his body but not the anger. "You're a piece of shit," he yelled to Landon.

"Yeah," Landon spat, struggling against Dan, ignoring Deb's pleas to stop. "Well, you're the son of a piece of shit."

That got both Derek and Reggie going and it took the assistance of Matt, Mikey, and Rich to keep the boys apart.

Once the boys were calm and contained, Dan took Deb, Landon, Faith, Derek and Reggie in one room to talk while Matt and Mikey spoke with the rest of the boys and their parents.

"What the hell happened out there, guys?" Dan asked, trying to keep the frustration out of his voice. No one answered.

"Landon? Want to tell me what happened?" Landon continued staring down at his hands.

"Derek? Reg?"

"Come on, boys," Faith encouraged.

Reggie spoke. "We finished manhunt and were just tossing around the football, playing a little touch, and Landon came from the side and just rammed into Derek."

"What a wuss," Landon snorted. "It was nothing."

"It was a dick move, Landon," Reggie yelled.

"Landon?" Deb asked, angry filling her voice.

"Fine," Landon said defensively. "I'm sorry!" Then he softened just a little. "I'm sorry, Derek."

Derek nodded but wouldn't meet his eye. "Sure man, whatever."

Deb, Faith and Dan exchanged a glance. At least Dan exchanged glances with both of them. Deb and Faith didn't look at one another.

"Boys," Dan said. "I know there's a lot of built up anger about things, anger that you may at times divert to the wrong person because it has to come out. I get how that can happen, but we can't let it. Stuff like this will rip us apart and we need to stick together. I want you to get things out but in a way that helps not hurts. Come on, I love you guys. You're good boys. This is a really rough time. I know you're struggling, but we're going to get through it." Derek looked like he wanted to say something but decided against it. They all looked wiped and defeated. "Let's shake hands, okay?"

They stood, and Derek and Landon and Derek and Reggie shook. Neither looked at the other. "Okay, acceptable for now. Group hug!" Dan wrapped them all and pulled Deb and Faith in as well. "We're a team, okay. I don't want to see this shit again. You hear me?" They all held together. "Do you hear me?" he repeated.

"Yes, Coach," they said.

Dan gave them one last squeeze, and allowed his hand to find Faith's ass and give that a quick squeeze as well. She tried not to squeak in her surprise. "Good." He released them and gave an exhausted smile. "Now let's all eat Barb's brownies so everyone can get the hell out of my house."

He sat alone on his couch. Jake and Lola finally in bed, hopefully sleeping and popped the cap off his second bottle of Matt's Brooklyn Lager. He hadn't even had a chance to finish the first with all the crazy. After order was restored and everyone had finally left, Dan had asked Jake what had happened. Jake relayed the same basic story except he added that for a while now there had been a building tension between Derek and Landon. They constantly had words with each other and seemed always on the verge of a fight. Dan couldn't ignore the words Landon had shouted back at Derek about Wayne. There was obviously something going on here and given the parents and their activities, it seemed possible that the children knew more than the parents would like. Matt's words came back to him. 'There are no secrets.' It couldn't be truer.

Both Deb and Faith emailed him simultaneously. He opened Deb's first, savoring Faith.

From: Deb
To: Dan
Subject: Thanks

I don't know what to say, but thank you.

From: Dan
To: Deb

You're welcome. Get some sleep. We'll talk tomorrow.

Taking a second to settle into the couch comfortably, he took a drink of his beer and clicked open Faith's email.

From: Faith
To: Dan
Subject: Call AA

Well that didn't go completely as expected or hoped. I mean it was good to get everyone together and talk. And I feel really supported by everyone, especially Marie and Barb. (They're really wonderful.) But wow. That last bit really threw me. I tried to get more info out of my boys but they stayed quiet for the rest of the night, even going to bed early. I don't blame them. All this emotional crap is so exhausting.

Anyway, the reason I was writing tonight—beside the obvious, that I've clearly become an email stalker and need to write to you—is that I wanted to tell you before anyone else that Derek is quitting the team. I know what you're going to say, but don't bother. He's been done for a while, and now he really is done. It has nothing to do with tonight. I meant to tell you for a few days now but never got the chance. Anyway, he'll finish out the week, meaning he'll go to the bake sale fundraiser at the train Wednesday and, of course, go to the memorial but that's it. We've talked about it, and I respect his decision. He said he'd tell the team on Saturday. I just wanted to give you a heads up. I hoped to tell you in person, but unfortunately there really hasn't been any time for us to talk. Not that I'm complaining about the kiss. If you ask me at the moment talking is mostly overrated.

Okay, I'm going to bed. Wish you were with me.

From: Dan
To: Faith

I am going to have to reread and process everything you have just said here tomorrow because now I'm just imagining you in bed.

Rockets Team Chat
(Jake, Chris, Max, Dylan, Balls (Josh), Ryan, Money (Manny), Tyler, Jimmy) Derek, Reggie & Landon – Off Chat

Balls (Josh) – Anyone awake?

Jimmy – Total insomnia over here!

Chris – Who could sleep after tonight!

Jake – That was freaking crazy man

Chris – Like it wasn't insane enough to have team Rockets group therapy

Tyler – Or a dead coach…

Money (Manny) – Landon's been out of control lately

Balls (Josh) – He's been talking a lot of smack

Ryan – Kind of acting dickish

Max – Like shit isn't awkward enuff

Jake – My dad almost lost it tonight

Money (Manny) – Nah, he was cool

Max – Yeah, Jake, we know the rumor's not true

Money (Manny) – My dad is way more a killer than your dad

Balls (Josh) – That is so messed up, Money!

Max – LMAO

Chris – Your golden ass!

Jimmy – That's right. LMGAO!

Ryan – Better than a white ass!

Max – Ha!

Balls (Josh) – White played a good game, right?

Money (Manny) – I was impressed.

Jake – Hey, where's Dylan?

Max – Dude's out!

Chris – His mom gave him warm milk and a cookie and put him to bed.

Ryan – LOL

Jake – I'm out now too.

Balls (Josh) – zzzzzzzz

CHAPTER 10
(Wayne's Up to Bat)

Tigers Turf shined in the glow of June's late afternoon sun. There were a few games set to begin at 6 p.m., but 12U's game featuring the Fort Jefferson Golden Rockets vs. The Williston City Chiefs for the Nassau county spring (NCS) championship was the main event. Moms and Dads jockeyed for position, dropping their bags on blankets or opening sport chairs all along the first and third base lines for the best field views. The bleachers didn't have an inch of bench to spare; covered end to end with enthusiastic grandparents, parents and friends, some ready to cheer and others just interested in appreciating a beautiful day among friends. Coolers continually opened and shut, overstocked with snacks, drinks, and possibly dinner while the line for the snack bar remained steady, always good for a blue Slushie and a soft pretzel, which was especially useful in keeping the non-playing siblings happy. Kids as young as three ran around the complex, comfortable as if it were their own backyards, which for many of them it almost could be for the amount of time they spent there. So many of these 'baseball' families spent the majority of their leisure time here season after season, year after year, playing both intramurals and travel, games and practices. The dads bringing their kids down to hit in cages when a random hour presented itself, and filling in the off-season with football, either tackle or flag.

It seemed as though half the town was present and Wayne felt a great pride swell in him. Or it could have been because he had just seen Erika pass through, picking up her younger son from practice. Either way, he was thick with emotion on this beautiful day. They hadn't even started yet, but they were going to win. There was no question. And Derek would play catcher, regardless of what he thought he wanted, regardless of the words over it that he just had with Faith, regardless that Dan's kid was better. Derek had potential to be a great catcher. The kid just needed some confidence and a push.

He walked into the dugout to check in with Dan and Matt and go over the line-up. He had Josh and Chris pitching with Reggie in the pen in case they got into trouble. Jake was their lead-off hitter, then Derek, Landon and Manny, followed by Reggie, Max, Josh, Chris and Tyler. If Reggie wasn't his kid he probably would have been batting behind Chris, but the difference between them was marginal. It added to a smattering of random griping from the peanut gallery, but it wasn't a game changer. The real heat would come from Ryan and Dylan's parents because, as he often did with games of real magnitude, he had decided to only bat nine and stick with their strongest line-up.

"All right, Rockets, huddle in!" Wayne yelled and the team spit out their seeds and moved in closer. "We've worked hard to get to this spot right now. You're well trained, and now we are going to take the win. Take it like we own it. Take it like they never had a chance. And we're going to show no mercy. Because the Rockets rock. You rock. Now it's time to rock and roll! All in on three."

The boys laid their hands in the center and chanted together. "One. Two. Three. Rockets!"

Wayne went out to shake hands with the coach of the Chiefs. "Good luck, Coach," he said to Doug, smirking just a bit. "Maybe this'll be your year, but I wouldn't count on it." He smiled, showing off his pearly whites before turning away.

"Dick," both Doug and Wayne muttered to themselves as they walked back to their own dugouts.

Wayne stood at the open area dividing the dugout and the field and chewed on sunflower seeds, so immersed in the game that he sometimes forgot to spit out the shells.

He didn't notice Deb watching him as much as she watched her son or the game. He didn't notice Dan fuming when he never took out Derek as catcher to put Jake in, especially after Derek botched a major play at the plate and then another one. He didn't notice Joe giving him the eye or Sean handing out iced coffees to Barb and Faith. He didn't notice the dozens of fans watching and whispering about him, intimidated and intrigued. He didn't notice Jeff Blum's disgust or Matt's respect of his coaching. He didn't notice Donny sitting off to the side in his cart watching or Rich and Marie sitting in the bleachers under an umbrella to shield them from the sun. He didn't notice Mikey pacing up and down the first base line like a maniac, hopping and shouting at Jake. Until he did notice and then he calmly went over and told him to shut the fuck up.

What he did notice was every move his guys made. When Reggie played too far out or Landon dropped his shoulder. He saw how Manny always took the perfect lead to steal, and Josh could tune his father out on the mound and relax under pressure. And after a bit, he noticed that Coach Doug only put on signs when a play was happening, and pretty soon Wayne figured out what those signs were and reacted accordingly.

It was a close game. Doug may be a dick but his team was top notch, and the game was neck and neck for the run of it, especially when Derek fucked up the play at the plate that second time to put the game in a tie. But in the end, they pulled through with a suicide squeeze. Jake was on third and Wayne gave Landon, arguably their best hitter, the bunt sign. The minute he did, Jake took off and scored. It was genius and beautiful, and they were victorious.

Then the team was on him, jumping and hooting until they lined up for the end of game handshake, which they all did respectfully. Last in line was Doug. When he put his hand out, about to say, 'Better luck next year,' Doug surprisingly didn't take it. "You're a poor sportsman and a fucking cheater," he hissed low in his ear.

Wayne was surprised but just smiled and hissed right back, "And you're a fucking sore loser."

He followed the boys, who resumed their hooting and hollering and skipped, cartwheeled and tumbled over each other to the outfield for his wrap-up speech.

"Boys!" he boomed, feeling larger than life. Feeling like the fucking winner that he was. "You made me so proud. You should be damn proud of yourselves! You grabbed victory by the balls. Your bats were on fire, you were focused and prepared. This is where hard work pays off. I know I ride you hard. I expect a lot. But that's why you're on this team because each and every one of you is special and talented. You're winners. And don't you forget it. Now, let's go get our Goddamn trophies! All in on three."

"One. Two. Three. Rockets!" They cheered and continued rolling all over each other like puppies.

"Good game, Coach," Matt said and shook Wayne's hand. "There were some stellar plays. I think our team really produced out there. Sure there were some snafus—Manny's bat was a little weak, Max lost that ball in center and Chris way overthrew that play to first, but overall it was a damn good showing."

"Thanks, man." Wayne smacked him on the back. "What say you, Dan? Awful subdued over there."

Dan's eyes were unreadable slits. "Good game, Coach."

"Are you pissed because I didn't use Jake?" Wayne asked, clearly a challenge to his voice.

"I think it was a bad call for our team," Dan said, using all his patience not to engage. "It put us in a difficult spot, unnecessarily."

"Good thing, I'm the head coach here. And I'd say it all turned out pretty damn good."

Dan walked away from them.

"Leave it alone," Matt said to Wayne. "He'll get past it. He always does."

"Such a Dan downer," Wayne laughed. "Ain't gonna spoil our party. It's trophy time."

They all went up for the ceremony, where Wayne handed each kid his trophy—a three foot high tiered monstrosity topped with a golden batter. "See," he said, "they already knew Gold was gonna take it."

After all the trophies were distributed, he, Matt and Dan stood for ceremonial pictures, letting all the families snap away until the formal poses dissolved along with the kids patience into candid ones. Beautiful pictures of youth sports in all its glory with Wayne standing in the center, his trophy raised in triumph and the boys beaming and jumping around him.

"God, this thing is heavy." Wayne laughed and brought it down. "You guys are the best," he said to the team and pointed to the parents, then pounded his chest in a show of strength and love.

Deb ate it up, Matt was all in, and Dan tried not to roll his eyes. The minute the pictures were done, he separated himself from the pack. Barb and Marie started opening boxes of pizza and breaking out Munchkins. He needed a minute to cool down. The idea that Wayne would keep Derek in the entire time and not give Jake his turn behind the plate was so disrespectful to both his son's talent and him, his assistant coach and semi-friend, that it was hard for him to take and he took a lot to stay with Jake on this team.

It wasn't easy being the most knowledgeable person in the dugout and not being heard, or worse, being completely disregarded, but he wasn't easily rattled and reminded himself that this wasn't about him. He didn't need to be head coach to fuel his ego like Wayne did. Not that he wouldn't love the job, but he was just a divorced dad trying to stay involved with his kid. A long time ago, he decided to pretty much take whatever Wayne could throw, but to disregard his son? That was a whole other story.

He walked behind the snack bar to have a minute to calm himself when Faith walked past. "Hey, pretty lady," he smiled, already almost forgetting how stressed he was the minute before.

She smiled genuine and sexy. "Good game, huh?"

"Yup, I'm enjoying the spoils of victory over here."

Faith looked perplexed, realizing that he was standing alone away from all the action. "What are you doing over here?"

"Waiting for you to walk by." He liked flirting with Faith. He liked it too much.

She smiled at him again, clearly flirting back. "Well, here I am, you lucky guy. You caught me on my way to my car to sneak out of here."

"I'm feeling luckier already." All of a sudden he was feeling very unlucky. How did Wayne get this girl? How was he head coach? How did he allow him to get away with not playing his son at a position he was clearly better at.

"Yup, I'm a lucky charm." Faith said brightly, still playing and not realizing the change in Dan.

"Magically delicious," he said softly, but he must have sounded a little too serious and sad.

She looked at him funny. "Are you okay?" she asked and took a couple of steps toward him. "Dan?"

She was so close he could smell the strawberry scent of her hair, could feel the heat from her small body. He could touch her if he wanted to and then he did, raising his hand her face and cupping her cheek in his palm gently. Her misty hazel eyes probed his questioningly, and he looked into them and saw little flecks of green, gold and brown. And excitement. Just a flicker, but it was there. Before he could think, he pulled her closer to him and kissed her deep and sexy, filled with lust and longing. She responded immediately, pressing her body to his, kissing him back fully, losing herself in the feel of his hard body on hers, his hands in her hair and his mouth consuming hers.

Until she pulled back in shock, covering her mouth with her hand. "What just happened?" she asked baffled and quickly looked around.

"I don't know," he said. "I'm sorry. I really shouldn't have done that."

"You really shouldn't have," she said, turned, and walked off.

It seemed like forever before she got to her car and found her breath. She sat and concentrated on inhaling and exhaling, reeling from what Dan just did. What she just did.

Her cell rang startling her. It was Wayne.

"Hey, where'd ya go?" he asked, more like an accusation. "Barb asked me if you were going to help clean up after, and I said yes."

She felt a small surge of annoyance, but it was dull compared to everything else she was feeling. "I just left something in the car," she said. "I'll be back in a few minutes."

"Okay good." Now he was distracted. He had interrupted his celebrating to find his missing wife for Barb's clean-up crew and was ready to go back to the revelry surrounding him. She expected him to hang up on her but he said, "Oh, and Reggie wants to know if you have his phone."

"I do." She heard him start to speak to Matt and another man in the background, exchanging a few lines and laughing loudly before coming back to her.

"Great." He hung up without saying anything more. She sat there holding the phone to her ear blankly.

A million conflicting thoughts crashed together in her head, but one rose above the others, leaving her shaky, dazed and electrified. It was the best kiss she had ever experienced in her whole plain Jane life.

Back against the wall of the snack bar, Dan was thinking the same.

CHAPTER 11

Deb woke Monday morning and found Detective Jonas at her door when she almost tripped over him sitting on her stoop, to collect the paper that he was already reading.

"Holy shit," she said. "You can't startle someone like that before they've had their coffee."

The detective allowed a small grin. "Sorry about that. I was in the neighborhood." He handed her the paper.

"You were in the neighborhood? The whole town is the neighborhood, Detective. It's 7 a.m." She stood to her full height; at five-foot-eleven, she was almost an inch taller than the detective.

"I know, I know. I'm sorry. When I can't sleep, it's better for me to just get on with it, you know." He lifted a small to-go cup from Dunkin. "I'm already on number two."

"Come in, I guess, but I really don't have that much time. I've got a full load of appointments today with doctors to see, scattered all over the island.

"Right, pharmaceutical sales. I won't keep you long," he said, following her in.

Landon sat at the kitchen table scoffing down a bowl of Frosted Mini Wheats® while absorbed in a YouTube video on his phone. He stopped his spoon midway to his lips when the detective walked in, eyeing him warily. "What's he doing here?"

"Landon." Deb used her quiet warning voice. "The detective just has a few questions."

"Whatever," Landon said and grabbed his backpack from the floor.

"I got to go catch the bus."

"Okay, honey. Have a good day. I won't be home till around five today, so just let yourself in. You know what to do."

"Yeah, I know what to do, Mom. I've been doing it since Dad left."

Deb looked stricken. "Well, that was kind of unnecessary."

Landon shrugged. "Just saying the truth. "Bye." He walked out.

"Bye," she called after him forlornly, looking much smaller than she had only minutes before.

"Teenagers," the detective said, shaking his head.

Deb sighed, went to her Keurig and made herself a cup of coffee. "He's just thirteen. Can you imagine what I'm going to deal with when he is a full-fledged teen?"

"I can't."

"He's had such a hard time. His father left and turned out to be pretty crappy in the divorced dad department. It hasn't been easy on him. And now Wayne is dead and he's fighting with his friends, and you're here."

The detective watched her carefully, waiting as the Keurig dripped its final drops into her cup. She picked up her coffee, closed her eyes, and inhaled the smell deeply before taking a nice satisfying sip.

"Better?" the detective asked.

"So much better." She pushed her dark, nearly black hair out of her way, letting her sharp blue eyes look back at him over the rim of her mug. "Now why are you here?"

He nodded. "I don't want to waste your time. I know you're busy and have a lot going on, but I need some clarification. And I wanted to give you this opportunity to clear things up." He raised his brow expectantly.

"Yes, fine. You're right. I wasn't completely forthcoming." She placed the mug down on the counter but kept her hands locked around it, anchoring her with its familiarity, constancy and warmth. "Wayne and I have been having." She corrected herself. "Had been having an affair for almost two years."

"Yup." The detective nodded. She wasn't telling him anything he didn't know. "And…"

"And it was awesome," she said dreamily. "Well, kind of. I did truly love him."

"Why kind of?"

"Well, there was the obvious problem that he was married, which unfortunately wasn't much of a problem for him. And, of course, I was extremely uncomfortable being around Faith on a semi-regular basis.

Again, not a problem for him." Her eyes fluttered as she blinked back tears. "But the real problem. The real problem was that he didn't love me. Or maybe he just didn't love me enough. Not to leave his wife. Or to keep from having other…" Her face scrunched like she swallowed a lemon as she struggled to find the right words. "Extra relationships."

"So you knew about Erika?"

"Yeah, I knew about Erika. And about Dena before her, and Lizzie before her." She was back in control now, sipping her coffee and chatting easily, like they were discussing the weather.

"And you were okay with that? With him using you like that?"

The casual chitchat was over. Deb's face steeled, and her eyes hardened as well. "Wayne wasn't using me. We were a team, and I understood him. I know he was flawed, deeply flawed, but it was all part of his magnetism, his competitiveness, his drive to succeed and conquer. And no, I wasn't okay with the other women, but he always came back to me because I knew him better than he even knew himself."

"So you were waiting Erika out?"

She nodded. "I know it sounds pathetic, but I loved him. It's my only defense. When you're in love, you do very stupid things."

His look said he knew that far better than she did. "So did you do anything particularly stupid you think you should share on the night of Wayne's death?"

Deb bit her lip, considering.

"Trust me, it's better for you to share with me, especially things I may already know than for me find out or think you're hiding something from me."

"We may have had an argument," Deb admitted.

"May have?" the detective asked pointedly.

Deb held his gaze. "He came here, we argued, and he stormed off."

"Around what time would that be?"

"Maybe around midnight?"

"And what did you argue about?"

She paused. "Erika. Now if that's all, I've got to get going. I'm going to be late now as it is."

"Of course, thank you. You've been most helpful." They walked out together, and she locked the door behind them.

"So how's the case going?" she asked, now feeling more comfortable that the interrogation was behind her and they were out in the fresh air. "Any leads?"

Detective Jonas shook his head. "Almost too many to follow."

***

Dan parked his car and trotted across the street to Dunkin Donuts to purchase a cup of coffee before catching the train to work like he did almost every morning. He slowed, noticing something different about Main Street. It was like Christmas in June; every pole on the street wrapped in gold ribbons. There was a giant banner hanging that read, "To the Stars, Wayne" and cited the information for this Saturday's memorial service. Dan was torn between appreciation and disgust.

His phone dinged a text, distracting him. It was from Matt.

"Are you seeing this? Wayne is fucking loving this, wherever he is."

"No shit. I hear they're renaming the town, Fort Wayne"

Matt chuckled. "Classic. You taking the 7:47?"

Another text came through. This one from Faith. "I'm home alone." He wrote back to Matt. "Late train today. Catch you later."

Quickly, he turned and headed back to his car, typing to Faith as he walked. "Not for long."

Seven minutes later, she opened the door and he stood before her, all man, all desire, staring her down like he wanted to consume her. She stepped back slowly as he made his way in, closing the door behind them. For a second, they stood in the silent open hallway, enjoying the anticipation, heightening the excitement. Years of flirting and untapped, forbidden chemistry danced between them, but there was nothing in their way now. He moved toward her, keeping his eyes locked on hers. She held his stare. He was so close she could feel the heat rising from his chest, feel his breath closing in on her mouth. She raised her hand, reaching out to touch him, desperately needing to feel his body, yet inching away instinctually, whirling in desire, needing a wall to hold her up. He met her there and held her against it, pressing himself to her. She sighed with desire, aching with need. He had his hands in her hair, on her face, running down the length of her body. She wanted to rip off her clothes and his, and she stroked the hardness of his upper body then the hardness lower. They both groaned and she pressed herself against him, tipping her head back and allowing him to place fluttering kisses down her neck, on her breasts over her tank top. She felt weak enough to pass out, literally thought she might but then he lifted her up off her feet.

"Where?" he asked, lowering his head and nipping at the cloth covering her breast.

"Upstairs," she managed, though her voice was so husky she had no idea who she was. He carried her up the steps like Scarlett O'Hara, then laid her gently on the soft white bed in her bedroom.

Dan looked around what was clearly her bedroom, the one she shared with Wayne, then looked at her for a moment questioningly.

"Don't even think about it," she said, pulling him down to her. "This is my bedroom. All mine." He nodded and focused back on her laying there beneath him, flushed pink as her tank top that he was about to take off.

They took their time with each other. They hadn't waited this long to rush things and making each other wait intensified their pleasure. Dan kissed and touched and appreciated her entire body and she did the same for him. He was more muscular and beautiful than she imagined and when he finally entered her, she came almost immediately, and he quickly followed.

"Wow," he said.

"Wow," she agreed. "We should have done that years ago."

Dan smiled but shook his head. Of course, he had wanted her from day one but back then they were both married. Then he was divorced but she was married, although it had been a very loose definition.

"Better now." He hadn't wanted Wayne to be dead, but he could admit that he wouldn't have minded him out of the picture. He was an arrogant, vain, son of a bitch. "Now I don't have to share you. Now you can be mine."

She loved the sound of that and rolled over to caress his chest. "You're very sexy," she said, unable to keep her hands off him. He really was such a good looking man, she thought, rugged and athletic with wavy brown hair falling appealingly over his goldish green eyes. It was amazing that some girl hadn't snapped him up. After years of feeling dead inside, her body hummed with electricity. The feeling was all consuming.

"Oh, I'm sexy?" he laughed, his face breaking open into a broad, mischievous and traffic stopping grin.

Laying in her bed naked, he may have been the sexiest thing Faith had seen in her whole life.

Then he stopped smiling and looked at her seriously. "And you're beautiful." It felt so good to feel this good; to smile, to lay satisfied with a woman he cared about. These last weeks had been so emotionally stressful. He finally felt at peace. "I am so happy at this moment. I don't ever want to go back to the real world."

"Don't worry. I'm not sending you back," she said, and he leaned over and kissed her, so soft and then so deep that she felt her body fluster and flutter with need. She glanced down and noticed he felt exactly the same.

***

Detective Jonas swiveled in his chair to stare at the corkboard he had set up on the wall behind his desk. If his father was alive, he would have loved this case, he thought. An old jock who played basketball and baseball with Donny throughout high school, he had spent years gently forcing him to play sports when really all he loved were the puzzles of robotics, chess club, and Legos. His father's love of sports and his perpetual disinterest remained a light nagging chasm between them. This was a case they would have bonded over.

The amount of solid suspects in this case was more than any other case Jonas had ever worked. Love him or hate him, Wayne Savage certainly left an impression.

Dan, Faith, Bob, Deb and Mikey topped the list as the group of people with the most motive and opportunity, although he was about to cross Mikey off the list. He had just finished questioning him in the conference room. The man made Robin Williams seem catatonic. He could barely sit in the seat to answer; his legs shook up and down, his fingers tapped the chair's edge, he sat forward, he sat back, his eyes darted every which way. If ever there was someone in need of a Xanax, it was this man.

When the story broke, a private investigator who Jonas knew had disclosed that someone was paying him to take pictures of his victim and one of his mistresses. It turned out that person was Mikey.

All Jonas needed to do was let on to Mikey that he knew he was blackmailing Wayne, and Mikey broke like a stick of uncooked spaghetti. Mikey told him they were set to meet the morning after the game. He had planned to use the pictures to secure a spot on the coaching staff.

He almost broke down and cried when Jonas had confronted him, blubbering that he didn't mean any real harm, that he wasn't really going to do it. It was just that Wayne never listened to him and he was so frustrated, he said. He had wanted some leverage. Luckily for Mikey, it had never happened and he had a pretty solid alibi for the night of Wayne's death. His wife Carol claimed that he had arrived home at around 10:45 p.m.. They opened a bag of chips and binge watched a few episodes of Friday Night Lights. His neighbor from across the street, out walking the dog, verified that she had seen him pull up at around that time and go into the house. When Jonas had snuck in a question about the FNL episodes he watched that night, Mikey actually looked excited to tell him, in way too much detail, what was going on in their show. Definitely not the guy.

He was ready to cross off Faith as well. She was too small to be any match for Wayne unless she hired someone to do it, and there was no evidence suggesting that. Besides, even though Wayne was a runaround, he had been for years, it didn't make any sense why she would all of a sudden care enough to kill him.

Old Donny, Joe, Matt, Jeff Blum, Johnny Smith, all the parents on the Rockets and Doug (who actually was kind of a dick) had all been interviewed as people of interest, some more than once. There were a few solid grudges and light motives, but they mostly served to double check facts and fill in blanks. None of them added up to the full picture.

He looked at the rest of the names—their alibis or lack of, some with multiple motives and opportunity. They were all there for a reason, and Detective Jonas kept fishing through the evidence and floating different theories and hypothesis, but one name kept bobbing to the top.

CHAPTER 12

From: Matt
To: Dan and Mikey
CC: Deb
Subject: Fresh meat

Dan, I mentioned to you a few days ago about a kid I met who lives in town but has never played for FYO before. Apparently, he was into soccer or some bullshit sport like that. Anyway, I have him set to come down to practice with the team on Saturday after the memorial. His name is Carlos. And from what I've seen, we want this boy.

From: Dan
To: Matt and Mikey
CC: Deb

I've got the red carpet ready to roll.

From: Mikey
To: Matt
Subject: Carlos

Did you tell Dan the kid's a catcher?

From: Matt

To: Mikey

Working on it.

On Wednesday, the boys all met at TT at 4 p.m. for a quick practice before heading over to catch a few of the trains coming in from Penn and do some serious brownie selling to raise money for Wayne.

For the first time, Mikey was running the practice along with Sean because both Dan and Matt were running late. They were excited with their new responsibilities and, being nervous energy kind of guys to begin with, had the kids bouncing along with them up and down the fields.

By the time Dan showed up, he just watched amused. It was more of a circus than a practice, but all the kids were laughing and having a good time. Even Landon, who had clearly been having a difficult time lately, was more relaxed. True to Faith's word, Derek hadn't shown. She said she would drop him at the train station at around 5:30 p.m. to sell and help raise money with the team.

At about five o'clock, Matt stormed out of the field house, his ponytail flapping behind him. Dan looked up at him in surprise. "Hey, I didn't know you were here?" he said, and Matt turned on him.

"I didn't know I needed to tell you my schedule, Coach," he snapped, clearly not in as good a mood as the rest of the team. "And what the hell kind of practice is this?" he shouted, and the boys who were cheering on Reggie in the middle of a mock run down between Max and Dylan all stopped and went silent. "That is the sloppiest display I have ever seen. You weren't even running in the baseline?! I'm embarrassed by what I'm seeing here. Practice isn't a joke. And if memory serves, Reggie, the last time you were in an actual rundown you got tagged." He swiveled at the sound of giggles and narrowed his vision on Landon. "You didn't do so hot on your last rundown either, funny boy." He turned to them all. "Ten laps. All of you. It's time to take things a little more seriously."

The boys grumbled under their breath but got busy running off the last bits of their energy. Matt headed over to Dan, Sean, and Mikey. Dan put his hands up in surrender. "Bad day, Coach?"

Matt wasn't amused. "Come on, Dan. What the fuck? This isn't a practice. It's an exercise in reinforcing bad habits."

"Whoa, Matt, you're getting a little carried away. The practice was fine. Not as serious maybe, but the boys had fun. And right now, what's important is that they're bonding and feeling like a team."

"Maybe that's what you think, Dan, but you were always soft. That's why you spent all the time warming the bench." Matt stared him down.

Mikey and Sean stood like children watching the coaches argue, horrified to be standing there, terrified to say anything and get in the middle.

Dan took a step forward. "Watch it, Matt."

"Or what?" Matt sneered. "You'll kill me?"

"No. But..." Dan clocked Matt, knocking him to the ground.

Sean and Mikey's mouths fell to the floor along with Matt. The team stopped running to gape. Jeff Blum and his team on Field 3 all looked over. Donny, of course, saw it all.

Matt sat on the grass rubbing his jaw. Dan extended his hand to help him up and Matt took it. "Nice right you got there."

"You had the perfect mouth for it."

"You got me," Matt said, almost smiling as if maybe Dan had knocked some sense into him.

"Don't make me do that again."

Matt smirked, back to his smug self. "Can't promise. Sometimes my charm requires special attention."

Practice being officially over, Dan, Matt, Sean and Mikey drove the boys up to the train where Barb and Deb already had a table set up with goodies.

"What happened to you?" Barb asked the minute she saw Matt's swollen cheek.

"I got hit by a wild one," he said jovially, glancing at Dan, eyes twinkling.

"You probably deserved it," she said but fussed around him and insisted on running across the street to the pizza place and getting a bag of ice.

Starting with the first train's arrival at 5:47 p.m., the boys hit the ground running, fanning out all over the station and giving the hard sell to every unfortunate passenger just trying to get home after a long day's work.

They got a surprise bonus when a thin blonde woman with tight clothes and very high heels walked over to their table.

"This is for Coach Wayne?" she asked Max, who was sitting at the table. He nodded.

"Was he a good coach?" she asked, looking over the display of cookies, brownies, and treats.

"The best," Chris piped in.

"Well then, I'll take a brownie and a cookie," she said.

"That'll be five dollars," Chris announced.

The woman reached into her Marc Jacobs purse and handed him a hundred dollar bill. "Keep the change," she said, catching Deb's eye and winking before she teetered away.

Max and Chris looked at each other wide eyed and gleeful. "That lady gave us a hundred bucks!" they chanted to anyone who would listen. It took all Deb's control not to take her dirty money and shove it back in her face.

During the twenty minutes between train times, the kids goofed around but when each train pulled in they went to work. The plan was to wrap it up after the 7:01 pulled in at 7:40 but the boys begged to stay longer and they relented, bringing over boxes of pizza from Frank's. It was a few blocks out of the way considering there were three perfectly acceptable pizza places within a block, but the boys insisted it was the best. Since the parents couldn't argue the point, Sean and Mikey took a run over. They finally left the station after the 7:27 pulled in at 8:04. By 8:30 p.m., all the boys and parents were home in their respective houses, exhausted.

From: Dan
To: Faith
Subject: Stood up

I was hoping I'd see you

From: Faith
To: Dan
Subject: Never

I know. Derek didn't want to go. Can I interest you in Friday night? I have two boys sleeping out and nothing to do...

From: Dan
To: Faith
Subject: Hallelujah

My house. I'll be home by 7 p.m. The door will be unlocked. I expect you to be there. And don't expect me to let you leave.

From: Robin
To: Barb, Marie, Faith, Deb, Nicole
Subject: Sheesh

With all the practices and bake sales, when is my kid ever supposed
to do his homework or study?

From: Barb
To: Robin, Marie, Faith, Deb, Nicole

What? Don't tell me baseball isn't your first priority? Don't let that
cat out of the bag.

From: Robin
To: Barb, Marie, Faith, Deb, Nicole

I was kind of being serious.

From: Barb
To: Marie
Subject: LOL

Well, meow.

From: Deb
To: The Golden Rockets and their Families
CC: Coaches Dan, Matt and Mikey
Subject: FUN raising

Are you ready crew? Because this is amazing. We raised $1,570.50.
Ask me if that's the final number? Go ahead? Okay, I'll just tell you. No!
That is not the final number. Combine that with the $717 dollars from
the other day and we have a grand total of $2,287.50. You guys are
awesome!!! Thank you bakers!! Thank you sellers!! Thank you all!!!

From: Deb
To: Dan, Matt & Mikey
Subject: Now what?

If we have to have another bake sale on Friday, I may kill myself. We are still down about $500 and that's not even taking into consideration the bench we are actually supposed to be raising this money for.

From: Matt
To: Dan, Mikey & Deb

I hate to suggest but can we 'borrow' from the funds we raised from the Super Bowl and March Madness pools for Cooperstown?

From: Deb
To: Matt, Dan & Mikey

No can do. Already tied up in special swag (hoodies, duffle and trading pins) for team and family and sibling spectator tee-shirts.

From: Matt
To: Dan, Mikey and Deb

Let me talk to Joe. Maybe I can get him to agree to half now and we'll have another bake sale in a couple of weeks. How much are the benches?

From: Deb
To: Matt, Dan and Mikey

I have them priced between $500 and $1,000 depending. I'll see if I can do better. Unless one of you has any carpentry skills?

From: Matt
To: Joe
Subject: Outstanding issues

Hey, sorry about today. I know I lost my cool. You know I'm just frustrated with everything. I mean, how long do I need to share the team, man. I don't know if you can tell but I don't play that nice with others. I've been trying, but the team is mine. So give it to me. Please. (That's me trying)

Also, we've raised a little over two grand toward the bill so far. Can we give you that and pay off the last 700 or so?

From: Joe
To: Matt
Subject: Just issues

First on the coaching, you'll have to wait, like I said, for the board to meet next week. And second, no. And I am sorry about that, but we close out the books end of month and it all needs to add up. I'm not looking like an incompetent or a thief because Wayne was an incompetent thief.

From: Matt
To: Dan, Deb and Mikey
Subject: No Go

Joe said books close end of month and they need full amount. Dan, do you want to split the rest with me. We'll be doing a lot of continued fundraising for Cooperstown. If we recoup, we recoup, if not, it is what it is...

From: Dan
To: Matt, Deb, and Mikey
Subject: Yes

Let's just move on.

From Mikey
To: Dan, Matt and Deb

Count me in to split as well

From: Matt
To: Mikey, Dan and Deb

Welcome to the team! LOL!

From: Barb
To: Marie
Subject: Loose cannon?

Apparently, Dan punched Matt in the face at practice today.

From: Marie
To: Barb

Don't take this the wrong way but... what did he do. ;)

From: Barb
To: Marie

I know. I know. He probably deserved it, but still... a red flag, no? Maybe?

From: Deb
To: Dan
Subject: So....

So you had a brawl on the field? Care to share?

From: Dan
To: Deb

Nope

From: Robin
To: Nicole
Subject: Dan

I know we don't really speak much, but I just wanted to check in to get your take on Dan. I hope I'm not overstepping here, but it's been a crazy couple of weeks. I mean Wayne is dead, Dan is a suspect, and now I hear he sucker punched Matt at TT? Is he okay? I'm just concerned for the kids. I want everyone to be safe.

From: Nicole
To: Robin
Subject: Overstepping

Dan is fine. You... questionable.

Rockets Team Chat
(Jake, Chris, Landon, Max, Dylan, Balls (Josh), Ryan, Money (Manny), Derek, Tyler, Jimmy, Reggie)

Derek – Hey, guys

Jimmy – Dude!

Tyler - Where you been?

Chris – Long time no chat

Reggie – Bro!

Derek – Sorry I missed the bake sale. Appreciate you guys doing that.

Jake – All good

Chris – It was awesome

Balls (Josh) – Sorry you missed

Derek – So I wanted to tell you guys, I'm quitting the team

Tyler – What?!

Balls (Josh) – Dude. STFU!

Ryan – Yeah, man, WTF?

Reggie – It's ok, guys

Derek – It's time. I'm done.

Jake – Really, man? This isn't cause of us, is it? U know we're cool.

Derek – I know. Not u. Me.

Derek – I don't want to play anymore

Balls (Josh) – What about Cooperstown, man!!!?

Derek - Shrug

Money (Manny) – Jeez! I take a shower and miss everything.

Money (Manny) – I'm gonna miss u

Derek – Thx man

Balls (Josh) – We'll still hang out

Reggie – Of course!

Max – Once a Rocket…

Dylan - Always a Rocket!

Josh – U're going to memorial tomorrow, right?

Derek – Of course. Final showing in uniform

Chris – Selfies!

From: Mikey
To: Matt
Subject: Catcher position

Josh just told me Derek is quitting the team. Guess that's one less catcher you need to worry about benching.

From: Matt
To: Mikey

Manny just told me. Carlos ready to play. You'll see him in action tomorrow. He's a beast.

Texts between Landon and Chris

L: Good riddance.

C: Dude. Come on.

L: Seriously. He was holding the team back.

C: Whatever.

Texts between Landon and Jake

L: Dude! You're in

J: Yeah, but I feel bad

L: STFU girl! You the man

J: LMGAO

Texts between Landon and Manny

L: Buh buy, Felicia

M: My dad says he's got a hot new catcher coming down tomorrow

L: Shit. Jake ain't gonna be happy about that

CHAPTER 13

It was 6:57 p.m. when Dan walked through his front door Friday night. Turning the knob gently, he pushed and found it unlocked, just as he had left it when he went to work that morning. He placed his keys gently on the counter. His senses alert to the quiet, he looked for signs of her but found none. Maybe she had not come after all, he thought for a second, but, of course, she had. Her car was parked in his driveway.

Then he smelled it, the enticing aroma of food cooking filling his house making it feel warmer and cozier, more like a home. She stood there, leaning up against the doorframe, having emerged from the kitchen. Her silk pink pajama shirt had only one button fastened at her chest, leaving the rest to hang open revealing tiny pink panties and shapely legs. She took a little sip from the glass in her hands without ever moving her eyes from him.

"Hi, honey, welcome home," she said, walking toward him and handing him the cup. "I made you a drink. Dinner's almost ready."

It was all so sexy. She was so sexy. He took a gulp of the drink, then placed it down next to his keys. "Good, because I'm very hungry."

The hint of a smile lit her lips but then his hands moved under her shirt around her body, pulling her close and the smile disappeared with his kiss, replaced by a desperate longing.

"Thank God it's Friday," she said as he lifted her up, and she wrapped her legs around his waist.

He carried her into the den and she undressed him, opening his shirt one button at a time and kissing him all the way down to the button of his chinos until she fell to her knees and continued removing his clothes. She loved every inch of him, reveling in the sensuality and joy of getting and giving pleasure that she had forgotten.

They made love on the floor on a soft plush throw blanket, rolling around blissfully. Afterward, spent and satisfied, Faith dipped her head to his, panting. He kissed her softly, and from seemingly nowhere Faith felt emotion and tears rise within her and fall down her cheeks.

"Faith?" Dan asked quietly, looking at her concerned.

"It's almost too much," she whispered and placed her head down on his shoulder while he put his arms more tightly around her in an embrace. They stayed like that, locked together in every way, not wanting to break their emotional and physical connection. Finally, Faith lifted her head, sniffled a little, and pushed back the emotion that had flooded her; the sadness over her recent loss mixed with these wondrous new feelings and the guilt and confusion that came along with it. She pushed it all aside and gave his a small playful smile. "I hope dinner's not ruined."

"Don't worry," he gently joked. "Dessert was awesome."

"So I'm not Betty Croker," she admitted as they ate her offerings of chicken cutlets, pasta and sautéed broccoli. "But I make a good drink." She raised her glass to him and he returned the gesture.

"You're good at much more than that," Dan said and winked at her. "And you're too hard on yourself. This is delicious."

Faith blushed just a little, pleased with both compliments. She had gotten used to living in a house where no one mentioned or appreciated anything she did. It was just her job to do it. "Well then, wait till you see what I made for dessert," she said.

"More dessert?" He raised his brow suggestively.

She smiled at him. She couldn't help it. He charmed her, she was ridiculously attracted to him, and he made her laugh. "Listen," she said getting a little serious. "I don't know exactly what we're doing. I mean, of course the timing is terrible and I just want to warn you that even though I look like I've got it all together..." She stopped and laughed at his expression of disbelief. "Real funny. You know what I mean. I just want you to know that I may break out into tears now and then and seem a little crazy, but it's not because I'm not so happy in this moment right now. Part of it is because I am. You know... I'm just a little overwhelmed." Emotion once again started to bubble inside her. Her eyes welled and threatened to pour over. "See?" She laughed at the mess that was her and her life.

He left his seat and went to her. "I understand. I do. I can't imagine how difficult these past weeks have been."

"You've made it easier." She looked at him meaningfully, and he tenderly brushed a strand of hair away from her face.

"I'm glad."

They washed the dishes together, making out a little, laughing and having an impromptu soap bubble fight. Afterward, they sat in the den under the throw blanket, sharing a bowl of popcorn and watching, *When Harry Met Sally*. When it was over, they went up to Dan's bed, made love again, then fell into a deep, comfortable sleep.

In the morning, Dan woke to the smell of eggs cooking. He could really get used to this, he thought, stretching his lean, muscled body out leisurely. He took a quick shower, walked downstairs and found Faith at the stove already dressed. He wrapped his arms around her from behind and kissed her neck. "I wanted to wake up with you in my bed," he said. She turned in his arms and they kissed.

"Good morning," she said.

"I can still bring you back up there," he growled.

She shook her head. "It's time for me to go. We have the memorial today, and I have to pick up the boys and make sure they're ready."

"Yeah, I know. I'm just not ready to let you go." He nuzzled her neck. "This has been..."

"Perfect." Faith completed his sentence. "I'll work on setting up more sleepovers for the boys." They stayed locked together, letting the heat from their connection automatically pull each other in closer.

"Are you sure we can't go back upstairs?" He nibbled at her ear and started working his way around.

Faith gave herself up for a moment to be swept away, feeling the strength of his body and his need pressing against her. Inhaling his scent deeply, she sighed, then pulled back. "No can do, mister." Her voice sounded throaty, almost like her grandmother's used to, except hers was because of a thirty-year smoking habit. "Come on, sit down, I made coffee and a tomato and cheese omelet. And you have to try my special lemon bars that we never ate last night."

They played house for the next half an hour until Faith had to leave to pick up the boys and Dan had to get ready to go to the field. The memorial was set to begin at 10 a.m., and the Rockets had a practice session directly following.

"I'll see you there," he said at the door, really not wanting to go to the memorial or anywhere, just wanting them both to stay in this bubble where there were no kids and no dead husbands, no murder investigation or baseball. Just them.

"Okay." She lifted up on her tippy toes and lightly kissed his lips.

He grabbed her closer and kissed her more deeply, suddenly afraid to let her go. Every kiss with her was a gift that he still couldn't believe was real. He searched her eyes and found warmth, happiness, and excitement.

"Okay," he agreed, releasing her. He didn't trust himself to say anything more, realizing he was almost as emotionally overwhelmed as she was; standing by the door watching her walk to her car, a bounce in her step that matched her ponytail. She blew him a kiss as she opened the door and got in. He caught it and held it to his heart. Could this really work out, he wondered in amazement, but stopped himself. He didn't want to jinx it by even thinking it.

By 9:45 a.m., you couldn't find a spot at Tigers Turf. The cars lined the perimeter and were double parked, blocking each other in. It seemed half the town showed up to honor Wayne.

Strung along the fences, held up by gold ribbons were banners highlighting the Rockets' winning tournaments from over the years. The big ones like, Williamsport District 28 Champions 2014, 2015, 2016, and the awesome and surprising win at Williamsport State Champions, 2016. A dozen other exciting tournament banners were displayed, from local wins at Hicksville and Big League Baseball to special travel tourneys like Sports at the Beach in Rehoboth, Delaware, and Cal Ripken's in Aberdeen.

In the center of Field 2, set around the pitcher's mound, the poster boards covered with pictures of Wayne and the team from his funeral were proudly displayed behind a standup microphone. The entire Rockets team stood off to one side, standing up straight and proud wearing the throwback jerseys from their last winning tournament and Wayne's last day alive. The special W patches that Deb had ordered adorned their shoulder sleeves and their new gold memorial belts were fastened around their waists. On the other side, also in uniform, stood Joe, Matt and Dan, and after some back and forth, Mikey.

The National Anthem started playing through the speakers and anyone sitting rose to their feet, turned toward the flag flying high on the pole by the field house and placed a hand over their hearts. Dan looked out into the crowd and recognized almost every face he saw... all the parents from the team, some grandparents, even Nicole, who was an infrequent spectator, had shown. He saw Erika, Wayne's last fling, standing in her signature kitten heels and lanky, hobbled Donny holding his cap to his chest, the only time he revealed his balding head. Deb stood near Jeff Blum and his family. Dan noticed Jeff's adorable, wild-haired boy sitting at the ground by his feet playing with dirt. Faith was flanked between Sean and Marie, looking beautiful and fragile but with an expression of determined strength. His heart leapt seeing her and then it raced. Standing not too far to the left of her stood Detective Jonas along with two uniformed police officers, and they were looking directly at him.

Dan began to sweat. It was already near seventy degrees with a strong sun. The song ended and Joe took the mic, thanking everyone for coming, giving condolences to Faith, his boys and his family and speaking for a moment about Wayne's commitment to the game and to his team. Matt said a few words, cracking jokes about Wayne's 'winning temperament' but ultimately expressing what an honor it had been to be part of his team and learn from the best. He was grateful and privileged to have known him and swore to continue his winning ways with the Golden Rockets. He would never be Wayne, he said, "but as Wayne never tired of reminding us, he taught us well and we weren't allowed to let him down. I'm the coach who won't let him down, either."

It was such blatant self-promotion and yet the crowd cheered. By the time it was Dan's turn, he thought he might pass out. Detective Jonas hadn't removed his eyes from him and with the sun, he was feeling dizzy. Still, he stood in front of the mic and addressed the crowd.

"I just want to say how sorry I am to be here for this occasion. That we should lose someone so vital to the community and so important to his family is nothing short of a tragedy. I've coached with Wayne for many years. Our styles are different and we haven't always agreed, but we were a team. And on a team you respect one another. And I respected Wayne. No one gave more of himself to this game and to his boys than Wayne. He showed up like no one I know has ever shown up—for every practice, for every game, for indoor workouts, outdoor workouts, for the pizza parties, the meetings and board meetings, the coaches meetings, travel meetings, and parent meetings. From the bake sales to championships games, Wayne was all in. He was great coach, a vibrant member of the community and a great dad, which above everything else makes him a true winner."

Dan finished and quickly moved aside for the team, who were already nervously pushing forward, standing together shoulder to shoulder in front of the crowd. Like at the funeral, Derek and Reggie stood before the mic.

Reggie's voice shook when he said, "Dad, you did so much for us.

We're going to try to make you proud. Not just in baseball but always."

Derek stepped to the mic, tears pouring from his face. "We love you, and we miss you very much."

The entire team stepped back, looking even younger than their twelve and thirteen years. The crowd gave a collective heave of emotion. The song, *Take Me Out to the Ball Game* played, concluding the ceremony. Everyone started to depart, wiping their eyes and shaking their heads over the shame of it all.

Dan saw his team and the parents all hugging their children and each other. He saw Faith between both her boys and saw the circle of parents who surrounded them. He heard Matt's booming voice rallying the boys off to the side, telling them to keep their chins up, that they would work out their anger and energy with a tough practice. He saw everything surreally in his peripheral vision but remained glued to where he stood. He knew what was coming. He knew it right at the start of the ceremony and he knew it now as they made their way toward him, parting the crowds with their uniforms of authority and a power of curiosity that could part rivers.

"Dan Williams," Detective Jonas said, and even with the hundreds of people talking, crying, hugging; the kids starting to throw around a ball and the younger ones now free to race and giggle, it was as though a hush fell over the fields. "You're under arrest for the murder of Wayne Savage."

Dan looked up at the detective and met his eyes. He saw seriousness and conviction, but he also saw softness. "I didn't do it," he said but knew it didn't matter.

The detective nodded solemnly. "That's up to the evidence to say and a jury." He started reading him his rights.

As if in slow motion, he looked around and saw the horrified faces of every person he knew, people he loved and people who trusted him. He noticed funny little things—Deb putting on dark sunglasses, Marie covering her mouth with her hand, Landon staring, wearing a special tournament hat instead of his official Rockets hat, Donny scratching his head under his cap and tsking.

He lifted his hands for the police officers just as his son Jake and daughter Lola rushed over, clinging to him.

"Dad!" Jake cried. "This isn't true, is it?" He was no longer twelve. He was six-year-old Jake, nervous and scared, like he used to be of monsters under his bed after they saw Monsters, Inc.

"Daddy," Lola wailed.

Nicole rushed over and gently pulled her children aside. "Dan?" she questioned, looking at him directly. They had had a difficult divorce and a strained relationship and barely spoke anymore.

"It's not true," he said and held her intent scrutiny.

After a beat, Nicole pulled back and nodded confidently. "Okay." She turned to her children, kneeled and went back and forth between them, looking each of them dead in the eye. "Listen to me, both of you, because this is important. Your dad is a wonderful, good man. You know it. This is a terrible mistake. Don't worry, we'll fix it. It's going to be okay." Both Jake and Lola nodded mutely, completely shell-shocked. Nicole pulled them closely to her.

"Thank you," Dan mouthed to her, never loving her more in their whole marriage than he did at this moment.

"I'll get you an attorney," she said. "Don't worry."

He almost smiled at that but couldn't muster it as he watched his hysterical children being led away right before he was. Dan's heart broke. It couldn't be more awful but then he looked up and saw Faith, and it was. She stared at him as he started to walk away with the detectives and the police. She didn't look angry; she looked devastated, which was almost worse. His broken heart shattered, he turned away from her and from everyone. The last thing he saw as he made the slow march from the fields to a squad car was a glimpse of Jeff's dirt stained, cherub-faced, wild-haired boy watching him, waving bye-bye to him as he went.

CHAPTER 14

Dan sat slouched in his chair in the small, dimly lit room. It was cool, just past comfortable with gray walls, a gray floor and a standard issue gray table. It was almost exactly like you would see on television, Dan thought. He hadn't spoken much since he was taken into custody. He listened and responded when appropriate, but the rest of the time waited stone-faced and cold, fitting in perfectly with the room.

When he arrived at the precinct, an officer asked him to empty his pockets of all personal possessions, which he did. He signed for them and then followed another officer to a seat where he gave standard information about himself, got fingerprinted and photographed. He was told he would be arraigned in the morning before they put him in this cliché interrogation room where he had sat for about an hour, he guessed, because he no longer had a watch or a phone, before Detective Jonas joined him.

"Can I get you something to drink?" the detective asked.

"I'd like a water," Dan said, sounding hoarse. His throat had dried over hours ago from nerves and clogged up emotion.

The detective made a gesture and immediately the door opened and a cop handed him a bottle, which he handed to Dan. "Thanks." He opened it and guzzled half its contents.

"I was hoping we wouldn't be meeting like this," the detective said. "You seemed like a good guy."

Dan had seen this play before on countless shows; a detective trying to soften up the perp and get him to trust him, get him to think he was on his side. But Detective Jonas had arrested him. He was clearly not on his side. He didn't respond.

The detective gave a little snort. "Okay, so are we not talking now?"

"I'm waiting for my attorney."

"Sure," the detective said. "Of course. That's your right, but I thought we could talk a little, just us, before all the red tape gets involved."

It was Dan's turn to snort. "Just us and the people watching behind the screen?"

"Yeah," the detective agreed. "Just us and them."

"Of course." Dan smirked. It was without humor.

"Why don't I give you a rundown of where you're at with us, and you could let us know if you want to fill in any blanks. Fair?"

Dan shrugged. Nothing was fair.

"Well you know you have been arrested for the murder of Wayne Savage. We have testimony that has you exchanging heated words on the night in question. We also found your DNA under three of Mr. Savage's fingernails, which indicate that you were engaged in a physical altercation. You were one of the last people witnessed to have seen Mr. Savage that evening. You are having an obvious love affair with his wife and harbored a smoldering resentment toward Wayne for being condescending to you as a coach when you are clearly more experienced, and for passing over your son when he is clearly more talented. You were the last person Wayne called that night. Your shoe size matches a print we found that morning on Field 2. And, lastly, you have no alibi for the night in question. I think that's about it."

"That's all true, but I didn't kill Wayne."

"Then who did?"

"I'm not the police. You must have other leads?"

"Yeah. But none add up with motive, opportunity, and forensics like you do."

"Sounds like you got yourself a triple, but I'm telling you, there's a homerun out there, and it's not me."

The detective leaned back in his chair with his hands behind his head and growled. "Baseball guys."

The faded gold ribbons around town started to fray and fly loose in the breeze until finally they started to disappear altogether. It was the whispers that did it. The hushed voices running all through the neighborhood about Dan.

'I heard he wanted to be head coach so bad, he killed him.'

'I heard he was sleeping with Wayne's wife.'

'I heard Wayne was sleeping with the woman who managed his baseball team.'

'I heard he was sleeping with Erika Stanley."

'I heard that too.'

'I heard Dan was volatile, always getting into fistfights.'

'I heard his wife left him.'

'I heard he was a real asshole.'

Everyone knew something and even if they didn't, they heard something through someone about something, and you can be assured it was good inside information. Totally legit. There was so much drama that was almost too much for one town to handle. No one could talk about anything else. No one cared about so and so's bar mitzvah or so and so's affair. No one cared about who had plastic surgery or who had put on weight. It was all focused around one delicious scandal that had twists and turns, murder, sex, betrayal, love, and sports. You could not make up a better story, and just like any good page turner, it kept getting better and better.

Less than a week after the memorial and Dan's arrest, Joe sat in a shit storm of fallback. A dozen parents were hassling him to make sure that the background checks for all the coaches were up to date. Another dozen were calling daily just to hear a reassuring voice that their child was safe and it was all under control as if control in life were at all possible. The lacrosse coaches had begun a steady, rising force of pressure on him to grant them more field time. They claimed that baseball had overtaken FYO, and it was time for a change.

For years, Wayne's strength on the board kept lacrosse in line; battling them over preferred fields and field time, allocating them to the crappy times and the crappy fields. Since baseball had a stronger presence in Fort Jefferson, they kept lacrosse at bay, and Joe, being a baseball guy, had allowed Wayne to bully them. But without Wayne, the gates had opened and now everyone was fighting for fields. He had just gotten off the phone with Bob Stanley, the commissioner of Lacrosse, who was amiably hassling him to find better field times for one of his teams this weekend. Joe, of course, ensured him that he would look into it. The whole dance was exhausting, and he was out of fucks to give.

As if on cue, Matt barged into his office, belly first, shit eating grin second. "Hey, Joe, I'm here to make your day."

Joe sneered. "What do you want, Matt?"

"Oh, you sweet talker," Matt said. "You know I'm your man now, right? With Wayne and Dan gone. It's just you and me."

The FYO board had held an emergency meeting at Flynn's Tavern the night it all went down, and Matt was officially crowned head coach for the golden Rockets. No one debated the issue, and no one cared to. Securing Matt as head coach was a necessary course of action. Plus beer.

"And Jeff, Rick, Gabe, Ron..." Joe said, listing a string of FYO baseball coaches, but Matt cut him off.

"Yeah, yeah. But you don't want to have a beer with those guys. Come on."

"Fine, Clint." Joe gave in. "Tell me, how are you going to make my day because unless someone's about to blow me under my desk, I think it's pretty much a goner."

"Come on outside with me," Matt encouraged. "You'll see."

Joe grumbled but got up from his desk and followed him out to Field 2 where the Rockets were practicing.

Joe noticed immediately. "Who's the new kid?"

Matt smiled smugly. "Carlos. Our new ringer."

They watched his pop time from behind the plate, whaling the ball down to Dylan on second, catching Tyler as he tried to steal.

"Wow." Joe admired. "A fucking hose."

"I know. You should see him swing. We took him to this past week's tourney. I'm telling you, winning teams are made with players like Carlos."

"You already are a winning team," Joe pointed out.

"Yeah, but this is going to be *my* winning team."

As they watched the boy move, Joe really did feel better. There was something magical about the fields, the innocence of boys playing America's national pastime and beauty of raw talent.

"So a catcher, huh?" Joe said evenly, after a few minutes of silent appreciation. "Where does that leave Dan's boy?"

Neither of them looked at the other, keeping their eyes on the field. "No worse off than he was with Wayne at the helm," Matt maintained. "Jake's a good kid. He'll be fine. At least Carlos legitimately merits the position."

"I don't know if he'll see it that way. Or if Dan will."

"All's fair in love and baseball," Matt said coolly, giving Joe a sideways glance.

"Even if it ain't fair, huh?" Joe responded flatly. "So, any word on Dan?"

Matt shook his head. "I'm not in the know."

Joe looked at him with surprise. "Have you spoken with Nicole?"

"Nah."

"I thought you guys were friends?" Joe asked.

"Sure, we're friends," Matt agreed. "But Wayne was *friends* with him too. I've just taken over the team he wanted and replaced his son's position. I think it's best to keep my distance." He gave a chuckle amused with himself.

Joe turned away, disgusted. He always tried to play by the rules, although it wasn't always easy or possible. He didn't approve of poor sportsmanship, especially from a smug asshole. He had checked in with Nicole a few days back just to see if there was anything he could do for her or the kids. Or for Dan, who at the moment was being held at the Nassau County Correctional Facility. He still didn't believe Dan did it. He had been questioned by the detective as well as a possible suspect, especially after a witness had come forward claiming to have seen him and Wayne in a heated argument the morning of his death. Joe had come clean about the skimming—which the detective had called embezzling—and the position Wayne had put him in. He believed in being completely forthright, although he was happy that none of it had leaked out, which reminded him there were only two days left in June. "So where are we on the check? Time's running out."

"I know. I'll have it you by tomorrow."

"You'd better," Joe warned. "And make sure you got that kid's papers filed with FYO or he won't be on your roster for long."

"You got it, boss." Matt saluted, then turned his attention back to his team. "Okay, boys," he yelled, "let's get over to those cages and get some swings in."

***

Dan sat on the cot in his cell. It had been exactly one week since the game changing arrest where his life had officially gone from bliss to complete shit. He had been arrested and arraigned, booked on murder, and denied bail. Nicole had, as promised, secured a fierce criminal attorney named Louis Grand.

Louis won him over immediately with a strong handshake and a stronger presence. Standing about a head taller than Dan and a solid fifty pounds heavier, Louis was someone who demanded attention. He had a sharp eye and a sharper tongue, and Dan felt good having him in his corner. He trusted his confidence and experience, even when Louis had admitted that it would be a tough case. The prosecution had amassed enough circumstantial evidence and a motive that, while weak, was certainly motive enough.

They would just need to chip away at every piece of it while simultaneously presenting other possible suspects for the jury to consider. Thankfully, there were plenty of those. Subpoenas were going out next week. Dan knew that however unpopular he was now, it was about to get worse.

Since his incarceration, he had received an outpouring of both support and hate mail. The hate mail was outweighing the support at a rate of about three to one. The majority of the letters he received were from people he didn't even know. The angry mail had the same general theme—how dare he take the life of such an honorable man, create such heartache and havoc for his family and community for such base selfishness. 'What kind of a psycho kills someone to coach a team?' Letter after letter asked him to explain himself. 'You have no balls!' someone wrote, to try to steal both a man's wife and his position. All of a sudden, he was the poster boy for everything ugly about competitiveness and what was wrong with youth sports and America.

There were letters of support as well. A few from people in his town who he didn't know well but had some interaction—one of Lola's friends' parents, a neighbor of his, the father of a kid whose swing he helped improve. Maria and Rich had written to him. Kind words refusing to believe he had anything to do with any of it. Sean had written as well along with Jeff Blum, which he truly appreciated. But the majority of support came from women he didn't know, who apparently decided he was too attractive to really be bad. They enclosed pictures of themselves and promised to keep up his spirits as pen pals with a suggestion to more. Each smiling, trying too hard to be sexy, face looking out at him made Dan more sad than the last. So many lonely people in the world.

Of course, the real surprise was the people who hadn't reached out. Deb for one. He couldn't believe that Deb, of all people, would desert him. They had been allies and friends. The idea that she could turn on him truly hurt. Matt was less hurtful because he was Matt but still upsetting. Despite their competitive and snarky banter, he had always considered Matt a friend. Of course, the person he had not heard from and the one who most concerned him was Faith. He had written to her three times already, swearing his innocence and devotion, begging her to come see him. He was allowed two visitors, each for an hour, once a week. Nicole had come with Jake and Lola yesterday, thank God. He had been going out of his mind with worry for them. They had been noticeably awkward and scared walking into the strange cold room with tables and chairs set up, but when they saw him they ran and jumped into his arms. He hugged them fiercely to him, afraid to put them down, afraid to let go. Just, so afraid. It wasn't until Lola reprimanded, "Daddy, you're squishing me!" that he softened his hold, but he couldn't let go until he commanded his eyes to stop watering.

They spent the hour huddled together. Lola on his lap, knee to knee with Jake, catching up on their week, trying to be upbeat and talk about normal things. From Jake, he heard about Matt's new official head coach role on the team and the new player he brought in. Dan tried to put a positive spin on it but he wanted to kill Matt, which considering, wasn't a very good testament to his character. Lola lightened the mood describing the end of year pool party at her friend Lexi's that she went to where they had a contest who could cannonball the best. She had them all laughing as she reenacted every one of her friends jumps. Too soon, it was time to go and it was almost unbearable. Lola gave him a picture she made to keep with him, and Nicole, who had sat at another table to give him time and space alone with the kids, came over and handed him a few photographs.

He was honestly close to crying again. "I really can't thank you enough," he said. Nicole, who he had virtually cut out almost all but necessary communication with up until last week, had turned out to be the biggest surprise of them all.

"Don't," she said taking him by the shoulders and forcing him to look her directly in the eye. "I know we've had our issues but I know who you are, and you are a good person. I'll be here to do whatever I can. And I promise to bring the kids every week until it's over. Okay? And it'll be over soon. I know it." He looked away, but she forced his attention back by pinching him. "Okay?" She smiled.

"Okay." He tried on a small smile, but it didn't really fit. "Have you heard from anyone? Deb?" He wanted to ask about Faith but didn't.

"Only Joe," she said. "And Marie brought over a bottle of wine and a lasagna."

"Not Deb, huh?" he said sadly, deeply disappointed in his old friend for so many reasons.

"Time," the correction officer interrupted, startling them all a little. The kids looked to him, terrified.

"It's okay," he soothed, getting down low and hugging them to him. "Mommy will bring you to see me next week." He winked. "I'm just going to be sitting right here waiting to see you guys again."

"Daddy, I miss you," Lola said.

"I miss you too, baby. Bring me another picture next week, okay?"

"I'll make you a good one," she promised.

"And, Jake, for now just keep your head focused and play your game."

"I haven't felt like going lately," he said. "I'm not sure when I will."

"Take your time. You don't need to. When you're ready, you'll play. Right now, you have a more important job. You've got to look after your sister and your mom."

"Okay, Dad," he said shyly but stood a little straighter. See you next week."

That was yesterday, and the hole in his heart was still a gaping wound. He tried not to hope too much that Faith would come, but he couldn't help it. Hope was all he had left, but what he needed was Faith.

***

Faith shook her head and threw down the paper in disgust. The headlines kept coming. It was a figurative field day for so many editors who lived for this shit. Day after day, they feasted.

'Lots of crying in baseball'

'Killer Coach'

'Youth Sports is Murder!'

'The Killing Season'

"Little League goes to the Big House"

It was open season, and Dan was the target. So far, she had escaped relatively unscathed. Their connection had yet to come out, but she had no illusions. It would and then she would be the woman cheating with her dead husband's killer. She couldn't even imagine what the headlines would be for that and what it would do to her boys.

She worried for them constantly, but she couldn't stop thinking about Dan, either. How alone he must feel, how broken. Her brain told her to stay away from him, that it would only be worse if she didn't, but her heart, oh, how it wept. She tried to steel herself. She told herself over and over that she really didn't know him or what he was capable of. But she remembered the softness in his eyes and the way he kissed her, and she couldn't make herself believe it. She picked up the last letter she had received from him and reread it for the hundredth time, her eyes blurring into tears. It was only three lines.

I didn't do it. Have faith in me. Please come.
You mean everything.
Dan

She couldn't stop crying. But she couldn't go.

Rockets Team Chat
(Chris, Landon, Max, Dylan, Balls (Josh), Ryan, Money (Manny), Tyler, Jimmy, Reggie, Carlos) Jake – Off chat

Tyler – Officially welcome to the team, Carlos!

Chris – Yeah, dude, now that you're on the chat it's official!

Reggie – You're a Golden Rocket! How's it feel?

Carlos – I'm over the moon

Jimmy - ROFL

Landon – Funny dude

Balls (Josh) – You've got it going on. I'm lovin' throwing to your glove

Ryan – You guys are good together

Money (Manny) – Aw! Such a cute couple

Chris – Jake's gonna be jealous!

Balls (Josh) – Shit. Don't I know it.

Carlos – I don't wanna make no waves

Jimmy – Ain't you, man. It's the situation

Money (Manny) – And it sucks

Balls (Josh) – Anyone know when's Jake coming back?

Landon – My mom said when things cool down a bit.

Ryan – Poor Jake

Reggie – Uh, excuse me.

Ryan – Shit. Sorry, Reg

Reggie – No offense taken. I know what you meant.

Tyler – Yeah, we don't need no stinkin' Jake!

Jimmy – Bad blood

Reggie – No guys. That's not what I'm saying.

Tyler, Jimmy, Balls (Josh), Ryan, Money (Manny) – Carlos! Carlos! Carlos!

CHAPTER 15
(Wayne's last round)

Flynn's Tavern was packed end to end with drunk people. It was almost midnight and no one looked even remotely ready to leave, not that anyone was rushing anyone. At Flynn's, the light was always on and the long bar was never short on spirits or spirit. It was the official FYO drinking and meeting joint, and many of the baseball guys had taken it over as their own private bar while the lacrosse guys tended to centralize at O'Hare's, another local pub at the other end of Main Street. Tonight, however, it was all mix and mingle. The lacrosse guys had just come from a tournament over in Manhasset, and the Golden Rockets' had taken the championship title for the fourth consecutive year. It was a good night for FYO sports, and the crowd was apple cheeked and rowdy, singing songs, and having one too many.

"Another round?" Wayne called out to Charlie, a bartender who had worked at Flynn's since he was sixteen and was now pushing sixty. Charlie looked over questioningly to Matt, Deb, and Dan, who stood next to him.

"Charlie," Wayne slurred a bit, offended. "I don't need their permission. Hit me again!"

"You're the coach," Charlie said, eyeing the group and pulling out a bottle of vodka, and mixing it with tonic. He went heavy on the tonic.

"Hey, congratulations on today, man!" a stocky man with a short crop of hair bellowed, patting Wayne hard on the back. Dan recognized him as Johnny Smith, a lacrosse dad known for his big mouth.

"Thanks, Johnny."

"Yeah, must be something about those magic fields you never let us use."

Wayne laughed, not picking up his aggressive tone. "What can I say, you backed the wrong sport, buddy."

"I'm out of here," Dan said to Deb, having had more than enough already and seeing this headed in a bad direction. "I'm not going to get into a fight for him."

Deb looked anxiously back and forth between the two men sparring and pleaded with Dan. "Don't go yet. He's really drunk."

Johnny placed an hand on Wayne's arm. "Maybe you'd consider sharing a bit. You know, sharing is caring."

Wayne looked at Johnny with new eyes. "Fuck off my arm, man." He lurched upright, and Johnny backed off but not much.

"Easy man," Johnny taunted, "you know baseball's not a contact sport. Don't want to mess with lacrosse." The two men circled each other like cocks in a cage.

Deb tugged at Dan. The situation was getting out of hand really fast. Dan stood up. "Guys, let's not do this. We've all been drinking a lot. We can discuss this tomorrow. It's a been a good night, let's not ruin it."

Johnny jumped all over that. "Yeah, Wayne, your mom here says it's time to go home."

Wayne sneered. "Fuck yourself, Johnny."

"No, fuck yourself, Wayne."

"No need, man. Erika's got me covered. You know lacrosse wives, they like a big stick."

Johnny shoved Wayne. Wayne shoved Johnny. Dan placed himself dead center and tried to keep them apart. Johnny's fist nearly hit his face. Wayne ripped at Dan's arm trying to grab at Johnny.

"Guys!" Charlie intervened, grabbing them both, surprisingly strong for a seemingly smaller and older man. "Not in my bar! Take it outside." Two younger beefier men appeared and took over, showing Wayne, Johnny and Dan the door.

Outside with Johnny and Wayne, Dan was disgusted. He was furious at Wayne from the game and from years of build-up. He was furious that he was here right now trying to protect him from an ass beating when he just wanted to beat the shit out of him himself.

"I'm out," Johnny said, apparently losing steam in the open night air. "You're just an asshole, Wayne. It wouldn't kill you to be a little more magnanimous."

"I didn't know lacrosse guys used such big words!" Wayne yelled after him. "Thought your brains were all scrambled from being knocked around."

"I'm out too." Dan started walking away.

"Go ahead. That's what you do, Danny boy, right? You walk away. Come on. I know you're pissed at me. Why don't you just man up and say it!"

Dan took a deep breath and turned around. "You're drunk, Wayne."

"And you're a pussy. Can't even stand up to me for your own kid." Wayne spat on the ground. He had barely picked his head back up when Dan lunged at him.

Deb, Matt, Joe and a few others poured out of the bar. Deb screamed. "Matt! Make them stop!"

They rolled around on the sidewalk, trading punches but not really landing anything solid.

"I'm quitting the team," Dan yelled. "I'm taking Jake and I'm out, you narcissistic arrogant asshole!" Matt and Joe pulled him away. "I'm done! Clean up your own shit."

"Calm, Dan," Matt said. "Serious. I've never seen you so riled. I kind of like it." Dan cut his eyes to him and gave him a dirty look. Matt laughed. "Nice. I like this side of you Dan."

"Just leave it alone, Matt. I am over it all. I'm done."

"It'll be fine tomorrow. It's been a long night. You know how he gets when he drinks."

"I don't think I care anymore."

Deb now had Wayne on the a bench and was talking low and soothingly into his ear. He looked sloppy. She looked like a snake circling her venom infected prey.

"Just sleep on it," Matt said confidently. "No need to make any snap decisions. It's not like he'll remember any of this in the morning, anyway."

Joe walked over. "Matt's right. In fact, there will probably be some big changes on your team soon. I'd suggest you ride it out."

That got their attention. Matt and Dan looked at Joe curiously. "What are you saying?" Dan asked.

"I'm saying that Wayne may have gotten himself in over his head this time." Matt opened his mouth, but Joe put up a warning hand and stopped him. "For now, that's all I'm saying."

He walked away, leaving Dan and Matt completely intrigued.

"What do you think that was all about?" Matt asked, but Dan didn't even get a chance to answer. Deb appeared, distraught and asking for help, although from her it was more like a demand.

"Can you help me get Wayne into my car? There's no way he can drive. I'm going to take him home." Both Dan and Matt exchanged a glance.

Matt looked at Deb with a smirk. "Whose home?" he asked.

"Just help me," she said, annoyed.

Dan begged off and let Matt and Joe help Wayne to Deb's car. He had helped enough for one day.

"Where's my trophy!" Wayne yelled, stopping half way to the car and refusing to budge.

After some back and forth between them, Joe called over to Jeff Blum, who had been standing outside, and asked him to run back into the bar and get his trophy. Jeff clearly didn't appreciate the job but went anyway. The faster Wayne got his trophy and left, the faster they would all be rewarded.

CHAPTER 16

"Landon!" Deb yelled up the stairs. "I left your uniform down here so you can be ready for when Matt picks you up later for tonight's practice, but I can't find your hat or your water bottle. I have to go. You're going to have to find them yourself." Landon didn't respond. Having an almost thirteen-year-old was so much fun, Deb thought sarcastically. "There's some turkey in the fridge if you get hungry." Still no response. "Do you need money?" she asked knowingly, and immediately heard heavy feet stomping. She sighed. Yup. That always did it.

"Yeah, Mom. I could use some cash." He stood at the top of the step, looking down on her. He looked older, Deb thought. He no longer had the face of a boy. Could he have grown since only last week? She heard that trauma could age you. Had he been traumatized? I'm going to leave ten dollars on the counter. Are you planning on going anywhere?

"I might meet Max or Carlos and walk for pizza or something. I don't know.

School was officially out, and her boy had officially nothing to do for the summer. Thankfully, there were a few of the other boys on the team who also had nothing to do, so at least they could do nothing together. Hopefully, nothing didn't mean trouble.

"Okay. I'll be home in time to pick you up from practice."

He shrugged indifferently, a gesture now as familiar as his smile used to be. "No biggie. I can walk if you're not."

"Okay." She smiled at him. They had gotten over a really rough patch these last weeks and now finally felt as though they were on the other side. Or at least closer to the other side. Progress was progress, Deb kept reminding herself. "Just keep your phone with you and check in please." He gave her a thumbs up with just a touch of attitude. Progress.

She left her house, taking a moment in the car to prepare herself for the day. Every day, every hour, every minute, she waited for it to become easier, but so far it had only gotten harder. There was too much that had happened and too much to come. Today would be yet another challenging day. She had a full workload ahead—a few of the main doctors who wrote for her needed a little encouragement to continue writing her company's drugs. She had at least three lunches set to be dropped off at their offices. She scheduled them for 11:45 a.m., 12:45 p.m. and 1:30 p.m, so she could arrive with each, remind the doctors and staff how much they loved her and her company's pharmaceuticals, drop off a few promotional goodies, then pop off to the next office.

It was going to be exhausting, but she was used to that. What really had her on edge was her first meeting of the day with Faith, who had called the night before suggesting they meet. Deb had been almost too stunned to speak. There was zero love between them and Faith had never, in all the years she was sleeping with her husband, called her house or asked to meet with her. Why now? Her curiosity almost supplanted her terror. Deb had stuttered before finally managing to spit out one word. "Okay."

"See you at nine," Faith had said and hung up.

Now, even with her hands secured to the steering wheel, they shook as she drove the five minutes to the Blue Finn book store where Faith had requested they meet. Blue Finn, located at the bottom of Main Street, was at the hub, if not the hub, of lower Fort Jefferson. It bustled up against the Sound along with a few other quaint, throwback antique, knickknack and specialty shops and restaurants, some of which seemed more in the business of being a charming part of the community than being a business.

Deb walked into Blue Finn's stiff and anxious, every move of her head too quick, like a cat alert to an attack. The store was part book shop, part eclectic toy store, part cafe. Books and accessories, from stationary to quirky jewelry, poured from every shelf. There were tables still displaying gifts for graduates and dads, and a camp area with funky pens and pillows, tie-die backpacks and gear for care packages for a child away for the summer.

She walked down two steps to the cafe and found Faith sitting at a table sipping a cup of coffee that they sold along with other light items and treats. At night, the area showcased local talent, live music, authors doing book signings and readings or maybe an open mic night.

As soon as Deb entered the room, Faith looked up and met her eye. There was no greeting of hello, no hint of a smile, just a straight dead stare. Deb instinctually arched her back and walked over.

"Hi," she said and placed her bag over the back of the chair. Faith raised a brow slightly, her invitation to sit. "So, how are you?" Deb asked because being around Faith made her babble. She was typically the cool imposing force with her height and attitude, but Faith humbled her. She had been Wayne's wife. She was just the woman who wanted to be his wife.

Faith ignored Deb's question. She would never have a genuine conversation with the woman, so what was the point of pretending. She got right to the point. "I have something for you," she said and reached into her bag. She pulled a cashier's check out of her wallet and handed it to her. It was made out to FYO for $2,744.53.

It was the lost money that needed to be paid back to Joe by the next day. With Dan gone, the responsibility fell on Matt and Mikey to split. Unfortunately, Mikey had mentioned the issue to Sean who had mentioned it to Nick and like that, word spread around the team.

Deb thought that when this happened, the team would automatically rally and each family would make up the difference that they owed, but it didn't work out like that. The team was split between just paying back the money for Wayne and going to Faith to ask for it. Like Robin had said, Wayne was responsible for the mess and his family should be the one to clean it up. So far, no one had been able to work up the nerve to approach her mostly because the other half of the team was fighting to keep the whole thing under wraps and wanted to spare her any more heartache.

"So…" Deb started, but Faith stopped her.

She had so much to say to this woman, had actually imagined a show down with her countless times, but now that she was sitting across from her, instead of looking forward to having it out, she itched to get away from her. All those years sitting on the sidelines, festering with resentment, waiting for the right moment to call her out and shame her, and she didn't want to talk about Wayne or any of it. She just wanted to find out what she needed to know. At the moment, the rest didn't matter.

"Forget it. We're not here to chit chat. I think this belongs to you guys. I found it last week in Wayne's wallet but then I forgot about it. I guess he meant to give it to you himself but never got the chance."

Deb took the check. "Yes, thank you. We have been looking for this."

Faith nodded. "I figured it was important. I'm sorry I sat on it."

"You have a lot on your mind," Deb reasoned.

"I do." Faith pursed her lips, ready to delve forward. She'd had enough of this awkward conversation. The check was just an excuse.

She certainly could have dropped it to Joe at FYO or even to Matt. The real reason behind seeing Deb was solely to ask about Dan. "As I'm sure you do as well." It was the closest Faith could come to acknowledging her pain over Wayne's death.

Deb's eyes softened and she tightened her lips, trying to secure that no emotion would leak out. "Yeah, thanks. I do," she admitted. They sat for a beat in silence but then the air surrounding them became too intimate for either of them.

"So, I was wondering about Dan," Faith asked. "How is he holding up?"

Deb shook her head in a harsh gesture and a glaze of anger coated her eyes. "I have no idea, and I don't care," she said.

Faith sat back, surprised. "Oh, I thought you guys were close?"

"Before I found out he killed Wayne?" Her lip curled in disgust.

"You really think he killed Wayne?" Faith was floored. If there was anyone she thought would be on Dan's side, it would be Deb. He had always been a good friend to her.

"Evidence doesn't lie."

"It doesn't always tell the whole truth, either," Faith challenged.

Deb's eyes steeled, realizing that no matter what, she and Faith would always be on opposite sides. "You were his wife," she accused.

"You were his friend," she shot back. "He needs his friends right now."

Deb scoffed. "Friends like that could kill you."

Faith was besides herself with anger. She felt close to rage. How could she believe Dan capable of doing something like that? "You're exactly the horrible person I thought you were," she hissed. "I am so embarrassed that my husband had anything to do with you!" She stood to leave. Now she was shaking.

Deb abruptly stood as well and grabbed her bag from the back of the chair almost knocking the chair to floor. "Well, now I know why he did. He certainly had no loyalty in his own home!" She swung around and this time did knock the chair over in her attempt to escape.

They stared each other down for a last beat before Deb stormed out of the store.

Deflated, Faith sat back down for a minute to calm her nerves. She was too rattled to walk, too rattled to think. She was so sad. Her children were sad. Wayne was dead. Dan was in prison. Tears ran down her face that she hadn't even realized she had been crying. She wiped them away, but they kept coming with no sign of stopping. Finally, she just accepted the moment, relieved that no one besides the coffee guy was there to witness, and put her head in her hands until control returned to her.

***

Deb felt emotionally ambushed by Faith. In this one regard, she expected Faith as her ally not her enemy. How could she abandon her husband's memory and stand behind Dan, the person who killed him? She knew Dan had been crazy for Faith, but she had no idea it went both ways. Or maybe Faith was just crazy. She straightened down her dress, pulled out a pair of dark sunglasses and headed to her car. She had a long day of work to get through, a check for Joe to drop at Tigers Turf and some plans to make. If Faith wasn't going to be the woman who stood behind Wayne, then she certainly would be.

***

Faith drove home, her mind racing. It was true, she admitted to herself. She had been worried about publicly supporting Dan, about what people would say if she stood behind him. She intentionally set up to meet with someone she had been avoiding for years just to hear a little news about him. She had been wrong on both accounts. At the next light, she pulled out her cell and found Nicole's number and pressed send. She answered on the first ring.

"Hi, Faith," she said. She obviously had her number programmed into her phone. "How are you doing?"

"I'm hanging from a thread. You?"

Nicole laughed. "Yep. I'm kind of shitty myself."

Faith and Nicole never had much of a relationship. Faith was the coach's wife and extremely present. She showed up at all the games and many of the practices, often with Gatorades and cookies. She traveled with the team to most tournaments and participated in fundraising and social events. Faith knew that Nicole had an affair years back and that she and Dan went through a difficult divorce. At some point, everyone winds up knowing everything on a team that spends as much time together on the bleachers as the Rockets did. A comment here, an overheard conversation there. It all comes out.

Nicole showed up randomly but always maintained a distance, possibly to protect herself from the critical eyes and gossip or just because she had a lot going on and spending half her life on a field was not on her agenda. Now Faith could respect both, but over the years she had engaged in occasional cattiness at her expense. At the time, she and Barb had thought that Nicole should participate and show up more. It was wrong to judge her, especially since they routinely gave Carol, Mikey's wife, a pass and Ryan and Tyler's parents both worked odd hours and rarely came to anything.

Considering that more than half the time, Faith had wished she were elsewhere, she really should have known better. She never gave Nicole a chance, possibly because she was too busy flirting with her husband. Hopefully, it was all water under the bridge because, right now, Faith appreciated her easy laugh.

"It's been quite a month," Faith agreed.

"So, are you friend or foe?" Nicole asked straight out. "I just want to know what I'm dealing with here." She didn't sound aggressive or defensive, just curious. "For you, I could understand either way."

"Friend," Faith said quietly. "Good friend."

"I'm really glad to hear that," Nicole said. "I've been kind of fascinated that so many people have turned on him. That they've just decided that he's guilty and have completely ignored that he has spent years being a wonderful coach and neighbor and friend and dad. I'm the *terrible* ex-wife, and I'm shocked."

"I am too."

"It's been awful for him. I've brought the kids there twice now to see him, and it's heartbreaking. "

Faith couldn't stand it anymore. "Nicole, can I please have his lawyer's number? I need to get on the list to see him."

"You got it, honey. I'll text it to you."

The minute Faith got home, she dropped her bag and reached for the phone. Her heart skipping beats, she waited as it rang. "Louis Grand," his voice boomed, throwing Faith off even more. She had expected to reach a secretary or something.

"Oh, hi." She sounded like a little girl. She cleared her throat and stood up a little straighter, possibly hitting five-foot-two. "I'm Faith Savage, and I was hoping—"

"Faith Savage," Louis repeated. "As in Wayne Savage's wife?"

"Yes, that's me."

"Well, hello, Mrs. Savage." Faith absolutely imagined him leaning back in his chair and putting his feet up. He might even be smoking a cigar.

"Hi," she said again, suddenly feel more nervous than less.

"It's funny," Louis said. "I was going to come speak to you myself. I'm glad you called me. But first, what can I do for you?"

"I wanted to be put on the jail list to visit Dan."

There was an extended silence that went for so long that Faith was about to ask if he was still there but then he spoke.

"I'm not sure that's a good idea, Mrs. Savage."

She wasn't expecting that. "What? What do you mean?"

"Well, think about it if you are a juror. How does it look if the wife of the dead husband is visiting the accused, especially since there is some talk of an affair between the two. It might add to motive, don't you think?"

"Oh." Faith didn't know what to say.

"It's my hope to keep you off the stands. I don't know if I will be able to. The prosecution might call you, but you know a lot of Wayne's secrets as well so even though you can't testify against Wayne, the fact that your marriage wasn't happy might keep him from using you as a character witness."

"But I can't see Dan?" The idea of seeing him had significantly boosted her spirits, but now she felt the darkness seeping back in.

"I'm afraid not. It's not in his best interest. I know it's not much of a consolation, but I am going to need to see you."

She hung up miserable, with a date to meet with Louis early next week to answer some questions. How was she going to get through this? How was he?

***

Dan sat in his cell alone, thinking about Faith. He thought about kissing her and making love to her. He thought about their last night together, watching a movie and laughing, having breakfast together in the morning. He imagined their first kiss over and over. So sudden, so surprising, so sexy. He thought about her sweet face and soft skin. The smell of her hair. The twinkle in her eyes. The way her body moved. The way her hair fell into her face when she tilted her head and smiled at him. The way he loved her. The only thing he didn't think about, couldn't think about, was that she hadn't come.

***

Faith waited impatiently for her boys to come home. She needed a distraction from herself and her brain, and the boys were the only thing good and positive to focus on. Derek walked in the door first, having hung out most of the day with a friend at their pool. "Hey." She tried to stop him from immediately running up to his room.

"Hey, Mom," he called without stopping. "I need to change."

There was always a reason for him not to talk with her but she couldn't argue, he was in a swim suit. "Okay, but we're going to pick up Reggie from practice in a half hour and go out to dinner. So just be ready."

Thankfully, he seemed okay with that plan since he didn't give her a hard time. He actually didn't say a word back, but Faith was working with the 'no news is good news' approach.

Ten minutes later, he came down without Faith having to ask him twice, which she totally appreciated. Little things like that created big stress levels for no reason.

When they arrived at TT, Reggie was already in the parking lot waiting. He jumped right in the car. "Hey," she asked. "How was practice?"

He shrugged. His expression much more mirroring Derek's frown then his own typical smile. She didn't have time to question him further because Matt was at her window.

"Hey there, how are you?" He chuckled. "Forget it, don't answer that. Stupid question."

Faith just stared at him blankly. She really had nothing to say to this man. Thankfully, Matt was the kind of guy who didn't need an active participant in a conversation. He was good with just having an audience.

"So, I wanted to thank you. Deb told me that you found the check. You really saved us."

"Of course." She waited for him to get to the point. Finally, he did.

"So you know that tourney is less than a week away over at Big League and you haven't responded about Reg going." Matt looked into the back seat. "Oh, hey, Derek."

"Hey, Coach," Derek said.

"I'm sorry," Faith said. "I did see that, but I've been really busy. I'm honestly not sure. Let me think about it, and I promise I'll let you know later."

"Sure, sure, but the sooner the better. I may have to borrow a player from Jeff."

"Okay." All Faith wanted was to step on the gas and pull away. She didn't care if his head was in the window. All of a sudden, she had a visceral negative reaction to his face.

"So, I hear you and Deb had some words." Faith shouldn't have been surprised but she was. Matt leaned in a little closer and Faith automatically leaned away. "You should know, she's kind of fired up about it."

Faith felt her fight or flight defenses kick into high gear. "I don't really want to talk about that," she said sharply.

"Of course, of course. I get it. I'll let you go." He pulled back, and Faith immediately put the car into gear. The last thing she heard before she pulled away was his mocking voice. "Say hi to Dan."

"Mom, are you okay?" Reggie asked when they had driven for a minute in silence.

"Yeah, honey," I'm fine." Faith worked to control the tension in her voice. "Where should we eat? How about Mashburger?"

"Sure, Mom, sounds good," they agreed, and the silence again filled the car.

At Mash, an upscale fast food burger joint, they ordered burgers and mash fries and the boys ordered milkshakes. Faith watched Derek scoff his food down in his typical manner barely breathing between bites while Reggie, who was typically a more picky eater, worked extra slowly.

"Reg, is it okay?" Faith asked. Her own burger sat in front of her, barely touched. She wanted to eat it but couldn't get it down with all the butterflies that were swirling like a tornado in her stomach.

"It's fine, Ma."

"So, listen, I was thinking, if it's okay with you..." She was hedging, beating around the bush, afraid he was going to freak out. "But I was thinking that maybe you wouldn't go to the tournament next weekend. Unless you really want. I mean, it's ultimately up to you but I can't go and I think I'd prefer if you stayed near home." It was a mouthful but she got it out and waited for him to give her a hard time.

He didn't looked at her and kept his eyes on his food. "Sure," he said nonchalantly. "It's fine."

"Because if you really want then—"

"I said it's fine, Ma."

"Okay, I just wanted you to—"

"Ma!" Now Derek interrupted. "He said, it's fine."

She sat back and let it alone, allowing them to eat in peace. Faith couldn't be certain, but it seemed like Reggie returned to his food with a little extra vigor as if some of his own butterflies had flown away.

They talked a little about school, mainly Faith asking questions and the boys grunting, and also about their feelings, which was basically also a bunch of grunting. Both lines of questions ultimately led to the boys rolling their eyes but good naturedly.

"Mom, we're okay," Derek assured her. "Really." Reggie still looked a little distracted. It was unsettling since until now, she had been more worried about Derek than Reggie.

"Really?" she asked, eyeing them both carefully. "Because you can tell me anything and I will hear you and do my best to help. No question, no judgement." They looked at her amused. "Okay fine," she conceded, "maybe some questions but you know what I mean."

The meal lightened up even more and they kidded a little with each other. Faith actually felt relaxed enough to eat half her burger. On the way out, the boys ran into friends from school and went to chat with them for a minute while the kid's mom, someone Faith knew vaguely through other people, came over to say hello. The woman's pulled back hair only made her blue eyes appear unnaturally wide with curiosity and Faith was immediately on guard. She didn't even know the woman's name.

"So I'm sorry for your loss," she said immediately. "I know we don't know each other well, but, of course, I heard."

"Thanks." She looked off to the side to find the boys, hoping to escape.

"So," the woman continued. "This whole case against that coach. It's crazy, right? I mean, are you like stunned? I mean, you know him, right? I heard he has a real bad temper. At least you're going to get some justice here." She looked at Faith greedily as if she had stumbled upon a lost treasure and was about to bask in its riches.

Faith looked over at the boys again who didn't notice. "If you'll excuse me," she said and walked away, abandoning the woman and the awkward conversation.

The woman looked back at a table where three other women sat watching her and shrugged, an amused smirk on her lips. Her friends returned her crafty, hungry expression. Their eyes followed Faith all the way out while their fingers hurriedly typed, already reporting the encounter through their cell phones.

CHAPTER 17

Chicken cutlets or tacos. Nicole debated looking at both options in her fridge. Tacos or chicken cutlets. Or maybe just go out for a slice. It was a nice night and cooking and cleaning felt like a hassle. She looked again in the fridge. Tacos, she decided.

The loud crashing sound of glass breaking stopped all thoughts in Nicole's brain, and she ran toward the noise to find out what the commotion was. Her front living room window was broken, and shattered glass glistened dangerously across the floor. How did that happen, she wondered naively, looking around. She went to the front door and opened it, scanning the block. Nothing seemed out of the ordinary. She went back to the living room to assess the damage and that was when she saw it, rolled over by the corner near the couch. A baseball.

She walked to it slowly, bent down, and picked it up. It was a ball from Tigers Turf, clearly stamped with the FYO emblem, although the words written in black sharpie obscured it a little. It said, 'Jake You're Out!' She handled the ball carefully, like it was a glass figure, studying it in her hands fascinated before hurling it at the wall.

First, she called the police, explaining who she was and what had happened. She gave her address, and they said they would be over to file a report. Next, she called Dan's attorney, Louise Grand, and told him. Then she called Joe over at FYO. It took all her patience not to freak out on him but he responded with appropriate outrage, which slightly tempered her fury. She considered calling Robert, her boyfriend, but they were still relatively new and she didn't know if their relationship could handle any more crisis. Her re-involvement with Dan had been a lot for him to take, was still a lot for him to take, and she didn't want to burden him with any more shit. At least, not right now.

She called her mom instead and after they hashed and rehashed, she called Michelle, one of her few true friends. Nicole had been surprised by the number of friends who turned out to not really be friends. Who said stupid things or just dropped her. When she saw it happing to Dan, she was outraged but didn't think it would happen to her, although she wasn't surprised by anything anymore. She had thick skin left over from their messy divorce. Not only did she care less than most people, she expected less. Still, she was disgusted by people's reaction and lack of faith and loyalty, by their willingness to embrace rumor and innuendo and not trust the people that they knew for years. She didn't want these people as friends. And it was good to see their true colors, as dark as they were.

After cleaning the glass on the floor, she called the window guy and then took a few pictures of the offending ball before stashing it in a safe place. As she waited for the police to come, so relieved that the kids were out with friends, she agonized whether or not to tell Dan at their visit the next day.

Sitting in the common room at the prison, she still couldn't decide. She sat a couple of tables away from Dan and the kids, exactly as she had the previous two times to give them their privacy. Dan had lost weight, and although his face lit up at the sight of their kids, an overwhelming sadness shadowed his features. As naturally good looking as he was, he looked beaten when all she had ever really known him to be was strong. And decent. She had been the one who really fucked up their marriage. He was generally easy, wanting nothing more than to hang out with his kids and be a good dad. He made a good living and was a kind and reasonably supportive husband. Far from perfect, of course. They had very different ideas of what a good time would be; him wanting to sit on the couch with her and the kids, watch a movie and eat popcorn, and her wanting to go out and socialize, maybe listen to some music and have a few drinks. He agreed on occasion but wasn't really into it at all, which left her going out more and more without him.

Unfortunately, the more you go out without your partner, the more you open up the door to other partners and that was kind of what happened. She met someone along the way who spoke to her as person, was truly interested in her and her thoughts, and who she seemed to connect with first mentally and then physically.

Of course, it wasn't all her fault. It wasn't as simple as she liked going out and he liked staying in; they had stopped communicating and stopped making an effort, which turned the smaller problems into bigger ones. They bickered over nonsense because neither of them were happy. Petty, ugly snipes. Passive aggressive digs. By the end, they could barely look at each other. She shouldn't have cheated, but she hadn't been happy and at the time those feelings owned her.

Now that it was over and they were past the hurt and anger, she knew that even if it may not have all been for the best, especially where the kids were concerned, it was okay. The kids were fine, and she had learned a lot about herself and what she really wanted in a partner. She saw the possibility of a real future with Robert.

Both she and Dan and made such progress this last year and seemed to be headed in a good direction. Until this. This was a hurricane on a clear blue day. There was no warning siren or preparation for it, but no matter what they had been through or what was coming, she resolved to be there for Dan. She owed it to him and to their kids whom, at the moment, were both sitting on his lap. It was comical seeing lanky, almost teen-aged Jake on one knee, clearly content being bopped up and down as Dan horsed around with them a bit. They were all so clingy of each other. Leaving had gotten a little better but that was difficult to see as well. How they were all adapting to this new reality.

When there was about ten minutes left in their hour, Nicole walked over and the kids went over to the table she had just vacated so she and Dan could take a few minute to talk. She sat down and grabbed his hand with concern. "You look awful."

"Too much going out and partying," he lightly joked. The room was heavy enough.

She snorted a little. "Yeah, I know how it is."

"So give me the word from the outside," he asked. "What's been going on?"

Nicole filled him in on how she thought the kids were doing and the mood around town. Before she could stop herself, she told him about the ball through the window. The look on his face was murderous. He abruptly stood and paced but there was nowhere to go.

"Fuck!" he muttered under his breath, aware that his kids were so close by.

Nicole waited him out. She couldn't imagine how powerless he felt in this moment, for the world to be against him and his family and for him to be stuck and unable to safeguard them. "I know. But I called the police, Louis and Joe. Obviously, he's not going back to that team." Dan ran a last hand through his hair and sat back down. She could see the visible effort it took for him to remain calm.

"Obviously. I just can't believe someone did that. Who would take out their frustration on a kid?"

"Most likely another kid," Nicole reasoned.

Dan thought for a moment. "You're probably right." He sighed, deep and heavy, like the bags under his eyes.

"Don't worry." She stopped and amended. "Try not to worry. We're okay. Jake and Lola are okay. We can handle it, and we'll do whatever we have to do. Right now, they don't even know about it."

The guard signaled that their time was nearly up.

"Anything else going on?" Dan asked wearily.

"Faith called me," she said and watched Dan visibly perk.

"Yeah?" he asked, trying not to look too interested and failing. "What for?"

"She wanted to know about how you were doing and seemed really interested in coming to see you."

He seemed to take that in, literally sucking up the air around him. He nodded but the light in his eyes had dimmed. "Apparently, not interested enough," he said and then their time was up.

***

Rockets Team Chat
(Chris, Landon, Max, Dylan, Balls (Josh), Ryan, Money (Manny), Jimmy, Reggie, Carlos)

Dylan – Did you hear about Jake?

Money (Manny) – I heard he quit the team

Reggie – Uh, I wouldn't say that he just quit the team

Landon – Maybe he decided he just didn't like us

Ryan – Maybe he just didn't like you

Max – Zing!

Dylan – You're both talking smack

Balls (Josh) – I feel really bad

Tyler – His choice

Chris – Um, I heard someone threw a ball threw his window

Jimmy – Bye, Felicia!

Ryan – Sensitivity alert

Chris – That's serious shit

Carlos – Who's up for the tourney this weekend!!

Jimmy – Psyched AF

Dylan – Woot! Woot!

***

Faith settled herself on the bleachers, putting a large bag next to her to discourage unwanted chumminess, not that she was feeling any love, more cool nods and fearful hesitation. It was the first game she was attending since the spring tournament championship and the night of Wayne's death and she tried not to pay attention to the stares. It wasn't easy. She felt the eyes of the entire complex on her.

It was a scrimmage with a local team before the weekend tournament that Reggie would not be attending. After being a presence on the fields for her boys for so many years, Faith felt bad not showing up at least every once in a while to support Reggie, especially with all that was going on. He never put any pressure on her but it didn't matter, she put it on herself. She just hoped to get through this and get home without any drama.

She spent as much time as she could looking down to her phone using it as another deterrent to the outside world. On the sly, she scanned the crowd. It was a light spectator day, but, of course, Deb sat in her sports chair over by the fence next to Robin, who was known to sit and watch the game blankly, saying almost nothing for two hours, seeming asleep but when something happened, jumping from her chair and cheering wildly. Faith remembered the first time she had sat near her. Robin was so quiet, Faith forgot she was even there until her son got a big hit at the plate and she screamed and flew into the air. Startled,

Faith jumped and dropped her coffee. From then on, she made sure not to sit too close.

Mikey and Matt were, of course, busy with the game and Sean sat on the bleacher near her keeping the book. Another woman and man who she didn't know also sat in sport chairs near first base. Faith assumed they were Carlos' parents.

She checked her cell. There was at least another hour left to the game. When she looked up, Sean had moved closer to her.

"Hey there," he said as solicitously as he could. "I just wanted to say hi. How are you doing?" he asked. "I was surprised not to see you at the meeting last night."

Faith looked at him clueless. "What meeting?"

"Last night's meeting at Deb's about what happened. Terrible."

"What happened?" Faith asked, unable to imagine anything more terrible could happen than what was already going on.

"What? You don't know?" Sean seemed stunned.

"Please tell me, Sean. I can't handle any more anticipation of awful."

"Sure. Of course. No one got hurt or anything. It was about the other day, someone threw a baseball into Nicole's window with a threatening note to Jake that said basically, you're off the team."

"You're kidding."

"I can't believe you didn't know."

Faith's brain was churning. "Can I see the email?" she asked, and Sean handed her his cell. It was, of course, from Deb and sent out to the team, minus her and Nicole. She tried not to seem too incensed. "I'm not on the list."

"Huh," Sean said. "Must have been an oversight or something." He was really a sweet man, never believing anyone could really do wrong.

"Yeah. I'm sure," Faith agreed. "Can you tell me what I missed?" As Sean filled her in, she caught Deb giving her the eye. She gave it right back.

When the game ended, she waited patiently for the team to wrap up and head out so she could speak with Matt without an audience. Finally, most everyone was gone and she asked Reggie to wait for her in the car.

Reggie hesitated. "Mom, everything all right?"

"No," she said. "It's not. Now get in the car." Reggie took the keys and did as she asked. She approached Matt talking with Manny and asked to speak with him alone.

Matt gave his son the nod. "Outta here, kid. Give us a moment. Why don't you go see if Reggie wants to have a catch."

"We're not going to be here very long," Faith warned as he headed off. Faith looked at Matt and sucked up a deep breath, trying to get her bouncing heart to calm down. It was no use. She felt lightheaded from all the blood that was pumping through her system. "Matt, I hear you had a meeting last night that I wasn't invited to."

"Oh, yeah. That was a last minute decision. Deb thought maybe it would be better if you weren't. You know, with the possibility that Reggie was the culprit. And with all the talk about you and Dan."

Matt just blew her mind on both counts. She started to shake. "First, what do you mean, Reggie was the culprit?"

"Well, he did have the biggest motive."

"What? Are you playing detective now? Are you kidding me?"

"I asked him about it, but he denied it. But, of course, that's to be expected."

"You talked to my son about this without consulting me?" Her blood was pumping so hard she could feel it in her chest, her eyes and her head. "And then had a team meeting without me present so that everyone could confirm in their heads that Reggie did it?!"

"Faith, I was just trying to look out for you guys," Matt said diplomatically. "I didn't think Wayne would want you in that position."

"What do you know about what Wayne wanted? You've been gunning for his job from day one!"

Matt had the sense to look apologetic. "This wasn't how I wanted to get it."

"Regardless." Faith sniffed, believing none of his excuses. They weren't trying to protect them, he and Deb wanted Reggie to take the fall. "And what do you mean about me and Dan?"

Matt's demeanor lightened. Now here was a topic he reveled. "I mean, come on, it's no secret how Dan coveted you from afar." He teased, and she wanted to throw up.

"What, Matt? Just say it."

"So you're supporting him?" He looked at her like that meant more than he was saying and that she knew exactly what he meant.

"Yeah, so what? We're friends."

"How close?" he asked, his brow raised suggestively.

"Fuck you."

"Sounds pretty close." Matt laughed.

Faith couldn't take it anymore. She stormed off but stopped and turned back around. He had already gone back to putting his shit in his bag, like the conversation didn't even merit a thoughtful pause.

"Matt, Reggie is not playing for the Rockets anymore. We are done." Then she continued her hurried walk back to Reggie and the car. She needed to get the hell off these fields before she passed out, threw up, or cried. One, if not all, of those seemed inevitable.

She didn't even have to call for Reggie who sat on the steps of the field house talking with Manny. He saw her and ran over. Within seconds, they were in the car and took off out of Tigers Turf without looking back.

Once she got home, she broke the news to Reggie that she had pulled him off the team. She couldn't speak in the car. The audacity of both Deb and Matt horrified her as did their casual lack of loyalty to Dan. She knew that her feelings for Dan tainted her perspective, but she still refused to believe that she would ever think Dan capable of such an act. Reggie took it all way better than she expected.

"It's fine, Mom. Honestly, I was thinking about quitting."

"Really?" she asked. Reggie always loved baseball, much more than Derek ever had.

"Since Dad died, it's gotten kind of ugly and just doesn't feel like a team anymore. Or at least not a team that I want to be a part of."

He sounded so mature. Faith was sure there was a lot he wasn't saying. "I get that. But you know, just because we're quitting this team doesn't mean you have to quit baseball. Let's just take a break. You can play with your school, and we'll see if you want to join a new travel team at some point."

"That sounds good, Mom. Now, I'm going to go find Derek and see if he wants to bike ride to the park. Some kids I know are shooting hoops."

"Okay." She smiled for the first time that day. "But you're not hungry? Let me make you something quick."

"Sure, Ma, make me a sandwich while I change."

She pulled him in for a hug, and he hugged her back. On the verge of tears, she pushed him away, sniffling and smiling. "Go, before I drip all over you."

While she was making a couple of peanut butter Nutella® sandwiches, she called Nicole.

"Hey, Faith!" Nicole greeted. "How are you?"

"I'm calling to ask you that question." There was something about Nicole that Faith immediately connected with. It was amazing to discover since they had literally known each other for years but mainly stayed on opposite sides of the fence, figuratively, of course.

"Things have been better," she said.

"Yeah, I just heard. I'm so sorry that happened. It's disgusting."

"I haven't told Jake and I'm really just blindly, against all reason, hoping he never finds out."

"I hope so too." In the pause, Faith decided to go out on a limb. "Hey, do you want to go out later and maybe grab a drink? I know I could use one."

Nicole's response was immediate. "Why, Faith, I thought you'd never ask."

They met at Hara, a local upscale sushi joint that had the freshest, most delectable fish in town and yet was never really crowded. Tonight, it was the not crowded part that was most appealing. Leaving the safety and privacy of their houses was getting more and more difficult for both of them.

Faith arrived first and waited nervously at a small table off to the side for Nicole to arrive. She ordered herself a glass of wine and sipped slowly, hoping that meeting Nicole wasn't a bad idea. Five minutes later, she walked through the door, surveyed the restaurant, found her and smiled genuinely. She walked over and they did an awkward hug.

"Oh my god, I totally feel like we're on a first date." Nicole laughed and placed her bag down on the empty chair next to her.

"Me too!" Faith agreed with relief, immediately feeling comfortable.

"It's weird that I feel like I've just met you and yet we've known each other forever," Nicole said, summing up exactly how Faith felt.

"Wine?" Faith asked. "It's Sauvignon Blanc. I'm sorry I started without you. You know, first date jitters."

"Yes, please," Nicole replied, signaling the waiter, pointing to Faith's wine and then to herself and giving a thumbs up. He brought one over and they clinked glasses. "It is funny, but we really never got to know each other. Baseball was Dan's thing, and we were in a difficult place for a long time. I definitely stayed on the outside. I didn't understand all the crazy surrounding it all. I mean they're kids, and back then they were little kids."

"For me, it was, of course, totally Wayne's thing, admittedly to a very not normal level, but somehow I became the First Lady. He expected me to, but I can't blame him. I took the role and ran with it. In the beginning I really liked it, and even in the end I still generally liked it—usually."

Nicole gave a little choke on the wine she was drinking. "What did you like about it? Have a numb butt from sitting on a hard bleacher for hours? In the cold? Maybe in the rain? The laundry? The balls, bags, hats, and crap everywhere? The practices? The whining? The 'where's my cup?' The schlepping in rush hour to play over on the South Shore? The crazy parents screaming at their kid to just 'hit the ball'? The crazy parents who think their kid is some kind of superstar? The crazy parents who—"

Faith put her hands up in mock defense. "Okay, okay. I know, believe me, I get it. And, yeah, there's a lot of crazy out there. It's kind of a fascinating study on human nature. But there's also something beautiful about sitting with other team parents on nice sky blue day, overlooking a perfect green field and watching your kids play, especially when they're really on and making their plays and looking and feeling so proud of themselves. They smack that ball and their whole body and spirit lights up. They run, we cheer. There's no better thing to see."

"Oh, you've drank the Kool-Aid."

Faith tipped her glass to her before taking another sip. "You have no idea how much Kool-Aid I've drank." The waiter made his way over to take their orders.

"But the crazy parents?" Nicole pressed. "Come on, so many of them are lunatics, screaming, pacing, wild eyed and so over intense and involved, it borders on, well, crazy."

"Yup. I know every one of those parents."

"And we haven't even mentioned those crazy coaches..." Nicole winked at her.

"I think we know a few of those too."

They ordered food and sat talking like old friends. The conversation flowed naturally. There was so much to discuss besides the team and having been married to coaches. There was the insanity that was happening in both their lives, that from an outside perspective should have them across enemy lines—the widow of the dead coach and the supportive ex-wife of the accused. It was all too twisted, dark, and a little incestuous. But instead of creating divisions, it connected them. The truth was they were a perfect match. Neither had many close friends and both were allies of Dan. They had kids the same age, all of whom were going through something unique and horrible. No one could truly understand but each other. They had finished eating and sat lingering over their second glasses of wine.

"This has been really nice," Faith said. "I'm so glad I asked you out."

"Yeah, you've been a great date. And speaking of dates," Nicole started, deciding to delve into a topic they had avoided so far. "I was wondering if you were going to go see Dan. I think he'd really appreciate seeing you. Although, I do understand that it's a difficult thing for you given the situation. I don't blame you for not going. People will definitely talk."

Faith's face fell. "I know. And, honestly, what people would say did bother me a bit but that was for a hot minute. I'm over it. I called Louis and told him to put me on the list, but he advised me not to go. He said that the idea that we were…" She stopped, blushing, but Nicole just rolled her eyes and gestured for her to continue. "The idea that we were involved would add credibility to motive. He said the prosecution would see it in the log and would use it against him." She looked miserable. "I really can't imagine what he's thinking, and I really don't know what to do."

Nicole nodded. "Yeah. I get it. But I'll tell him. Knowing that you want to will make a huge difference for him. Almost everyone has dropped him."

Faith shook her head miserably. "I really can't believe that."

"I know."

"So you want to elaborate a little on 'involved'?" Nicole asked, raising her brow comically.

"Well," Faith said coyly. "I kind of like him."

"I think he kind of likes you too." She said it seriously, and Faith felt the truth that she already knew.

"I was wondering," Faith asked shyly, pulling an envelope from her bag. "Do you think you could give this to him."

Nicole snatched from her hand. "Just like high school. I love it."

"I figured that if it came to him unofficially, on the sly, I could sneak it in."

"You can count on me."

"I'm counting on it," Faith said and downed the last drops of her glass.

Detective Jonas sat in his office looking over the report that had been dropped on his desk on Nicole, Dan's ex-wife, regarding a recent threat and act of vandalism. Normally, this would get filed in another department but because it had a link to the Savage Murder investigation, it came to him.

He flipped through it. It was standard but would get under people's skins, especially since it required talking about their children and asking them some difficult questions. He blew out a bunch of air and glanced to the other side of his desk at the Savage folder, thick with potential suspects, ultimately boiling down to the one. One that he was confident about and thought would yield a conviction yet still had some nagging doubts. If the prosecution hadn't pressed his captain so hard, he may have had the extra time to absolve himself of those doubts. But unfortunately, there was town pressure and the DA's office took the case from him the moment it seemed there was enough evidence to convict. It was an unfortunate part of the job, especially for someone who didn't like loose ends.

There had been plenty in this case, and now resting on top of the bloated file was a box which had arrived at the precinct for him earlier this morning. It dangled in front of him as loose and sexy as that Erika Stanley woman.

Inside the box was a hat, a Rockets baseball cap, sized Youth Large with the name Schnitt written in black Sharpie on the inside rim. The note read, "Found this the morning of Wayne Savage's murder near Field 2. I know it wasn't there the night before because I was the one who cleaned up and closed up. I know I should have given it to you sooner. At first, I didn't think much of it but then I did but still hesitated. I don't know why. I'm sorry."—Donny

With the case officially closed on Wayne Savage, it was a lucky break that someone was stupid enough to send that baseball through Nicole Williams' window. It gave him a reason to get back in there and shake things up just a little. He wanted those loose ends tied tight. His needed to pay a visit to young Landon Schnitt.

CHAPTER 18
(Wayne – Stopped at Third)

Deb glanced skittishly over at Wayne, his head resting back, mouth a little slack. He looked relaxed and almost peaceful, if he weren't actually piss drunk in the passenger seat of her car. She couldn't decide whether to drop him off at home, deposit him on the doorstep for Faith, or to take him to her house. She wanted to take him to her house. She loved having him in her bed and under her control, especially like this. He'd almost be at her mercy. She could strip him down and have her way with him. She could make him his favorite hangover shake and eggs in the morning. It had been almost a month since they had been together, since he went cuckoo for Cocoa Puffs® over Erika and wanted almost nothing to do with her. But Deb knew he didn't mean it. Erika was an infatuation that would wear off and then he'd be completely hers again. Or almost completely hers. That was it. She decided to take him to her house. It had been too long and she needed to remind him why he should love her.

"Home." Wayne mumbled, eyes closed, the giant winning trophy sticking out obscenely from his lap.

"Of course, baby, mama's gonna take good care of you."

Pulling into her driveway, she shut down the car, got out and went around to the passenger side. When she opened the door, he nearly fell over on to her. "Okay, I've got you," she said and swung his dead arm over her shoulder trying to heave him from the car. He stood shakily, using Deb for support, his other hand still grasping his trophy. They walked slowly across her front lawn toward her house but then he stopped midway.

"Wait." He looked around seemingly for the first time and realized where they were. "What are we doing here?"

Deb turned into him and pressed herself to him. She whispered hotly in his ear. "I've missed you, baby. I want to show you how much." She nipped at his ear and to her relief, joy and satisfaction, he grabbed her roughly, stroking her ass and pushing his hardness against her. Even shitfaced, Wayne never had a problem getting it up. "Yeah, that's what I want," she cooed, rubbing him through his pants. "Come on, let's get inside." She tried to usher him along but instead he knocked her off her feet, and she stumbled to the grass. He stumbled on top of her, groping and kissing her sloppily. "Not here!" Deb laughed, enjoying his attention but still trying to push him off so they could get inside.

"Yes, here," he demanded gruffly, refusing to budge.

As he mauled her, she seriously considered it. His hands moved up her shirt, roughly caressing. It was after midnight. No one was out or up. His hands spread open her legs. It was almost pitch black. His hands went to push down his shorts. It was easy with the elastic waistband.

"Are you kidding me?!" Landon screamed, and a light went on in the house across the street.

"Landon!" Deb cried, shoving Wayne from her. He rolled lazily off.

"What are you doing? You are pathetic!" he yelled. Five minutes before, he had been happily alone in his room, listening to music and smoking a cigarette out the window, the same thing he did most nights until this shit show rolled in like drunk teenagers on their front lawn.

Since his dad left, his mom had gone all desperate and glommed onto Wayne who treated her like shit. For two years, he used her and she let him. She didn't just let him, she encouraged him. She was disgusting. He hated her.

"Get up!" he screamed with all the frustration and sadness of a thirteen-year-old boy. Another light on block went on.

"Landon," Deb said anxiously, standing up shakily to her feet. "Please calm down."

Landon looked at her with disgust. "Worried about what the neighbors will think? Why isn't he worried about that? He's the married one."

Wayne still sat on the ground, trying to tuck in his shirt, like it mattered, and pushing down his hair. "Son, I know you're upset here, but..."

"Don't you call me son. You're not my father. You're my coach and you suck. Did you hear me, you suck! You both suck!"

"I hear you," Deb said, moving toward him, trying to calm him. "I hear you. Let's talk about it."

"I don't want to talk to you. You're a slut! And everyone knows it. The whole team knows it!"

Wayne was finally on his feet and decided to take some control. He was the coach, after all. "Listen, that's not okay. You cannot speak to your mother like that. You need to apologize right now, young man!"

"That's funny. I am done taking orders from you. I am done with all of this."

They all stood out there on the lawn in silence, two disheveled adults and one boy/man in long shorts, a slightly too small tee shirt and his Rockets baseball cap, assessing at each other and deciding their next move.

Wayne took shook his head. "Sorry, Deb. This is not my problem. I'm out." He picked up the trophy from the grass, turned, and started walking down the block.

"Not your problem is right!" Landon yelled. "We have never been your problem. You don't give a shit about anyone but yourself!" Landon suddenly realized he was wearing his Rockets cap. He took it off and flung it at Wayne. It landed in the grass by his feet. Wayne stopped and turned. He didn't say anything but slowly bent down, brushed it off and picked it up. "I'll just keep this cap with me till you're ready to apologize. To me and to your mother." Then he turned again, clutching his trophy and the cap and lumbered down the street.

For a second, Deb thought about going after him. He was drunk and on foot, but looking at her poor distraught boy, she immediately thought better of it. Wayne had his cell. He was grown man, he would be fine. She started walking back toward the house.

"Come on," she encouraged Landon, wearily smiling just a little to let him know it was okay, that she wasn't angry. She passed him standing there on the lawn, knowing better than to invade his space and try to touch him. "Let's go eat some cake."

After a moment, he followed her in.

CHAPTER 19

At the end of their visit right before their time was up, Nicole handed Dan a few new pictures that Lola had drawn. "I really like her," she whispered. Dan's eyes raised with curiosity, and he looked down at the colorful creations Lola had created. "The third one is my favorite." She smiled at him and patted his arm affectionately. "Kids, come on. Time to go. Come hug, Daddy." They swarmed his body and for a minute he roughed them up lovingly. Then he stood as he had for weeks now watching them go, taking his heart but fortifying his spirit.

The guard took him back to his cell where he sat on his cot holding Lola's pictures. He looked at the first one. It was clearly a picture of Daddy, Jake and Lola, outside in front of a house. There were rainbows in the sky and all over the grass as well, like colorful lollipop flowers. The second picture was just a little girl with dark hair and pigtails like her own and a purple dog, at least he thought it was a dog. It could have been a dwarfed horse. Next to the picture of the little girl she wrote, I love u. And next to the dog she wrote, I want a dog. He chuckled. Very subtle, Lola. The third picture was similar to the first. It was him and the kids, but this time the dog was there, and for some reason in this version he had a tiny head but apparently had put on about a hundred pounds. At least he was smiling. He moved to the fourth one, clearly Lola and him eating ice cream. Probably how he put on that hundred pounds. He went back to the third one that Nicole had referenced and studied it. He flipped it over to the other side and found a letter taped to the back.

Dan,

I wish I could be there in person. I really do, but I have been *advised* that it is not in your best interest for me to come. And I don't want to do anything to make things worse for you. Please know that I am thinking about you constantly. That you have opened up my heart in a way that I didn't think possible anymore. I can't wait to see you and feel you and have you in my arms. I know I'm being so corny. I know! But these words are all I have to let you know how desperate I am to have you with me again. Have hope. You already have Faith. xoxo

Dan wiped some wetness from his eyes. Tough guys don't cry.

The next Wednesday morning, Matt opened his door wearing his robe and nothing underneath. He lingered in the fresh new day, stretched, scratched his stomach and leaned down to grab the paper. When he stood back up a young man had invaded his space. "Matt Bidsky?" he asked.

"Yeah."

He handed him an envelope. "You've been served."

The man found Joe at the field house, where he always was, sitting at his desk. Mikey was also easily located at Tigers Turf. Johnny Smith was drinking at O'Hare's while Doug the dick was in his office, preparing a presentation for his boss. Erika was home having a specialized, energetic 'workout' with Raj, her longtime personal trainer, and her husband Bob was doing bench presses at the gym. He caught Deb just coming home from work.

"What's this?" she asked as he handed it to her.

"I'm just the messenger," he said and walked off.

She opened it while standing on her doorstep. She couldn't even wait to get inside. 'The United States District court vs. Dan Williams. You are commanded to appear in the U.S District court at the date, time and place indicated to testify in this criminal case...' "Shit," she said. "Just shit."

"Something the matter?"

Startled, Deb flung around. "Oh my god, Detective! You scared the daylights out of me."

Detective Jonas almost smiled. "Sorry about that. Whatcha got there?" he asked.

"It's a subpoena for Dan's trial," she said.

"From the prosecution or the defense."

Deb studied the paper. "The defense."

"Hmmm..." the detective said, considering.

"Care to elaborate?" Deb asked, sarcastically.

"Not really," the detective said, "but I'd be prepared for the possibility of it getting a little ugly."

"Great. Looking forward to that." She opened her front door and gestured for him to enter."

"Thanks," he said, walking past. "This won't take long. By the way, is Landon here?"

"Landon? No. Why?"

"Just a couple of questions." He looked around, like a detective. "So do you know around when he'll be home?"

Deb became evasive. "Yeah, I don't really know. It's summer, and I'm not sure."

"Uh huh." Detective Jonas eyed her. "You know, I'm going to talk to him one way or another. It's better to do it friendly, you know?"

"So what do you want to talk to him about?" They both turned at the sound of the door opening. In walked Landon.

"Hey, Ma!" he called out and walked in to the kitchen, stopping immediately when he saw the detective sitting there. He looked ready to bolt.

"Hi, Landon," he said. "We were just talking about you."

"Oh, yeah?" he asked, walking to the fridge and grabbing the juice. "What about?"

"Well a few things," he started. "First, there was a report filed, as I'm sure you know, about a ball being thrown through Nicole Williams window with a threatening message for Jake."

Landon took a long slug of juice from the bottle. "Yeah, so?"

"So what do you know about it?"

He shrugged. "Just what you just said."

"Any idea who would do something like that?" He looked at him through veiled lids.

"I dunno, maybe Reggie? You know, makes sense with his Dad and all."

"Yeah, that does makes sense Landon." Deb piped in and Detective Jonas frowned at her.

"So you know nothing about it?" he pressed.

Landon went game face. "Nah, man."

The detective stood. "Okay, if you say so, but I have a feeling I'll be back. Don't worry, I'll show myself out." He started walking and stopped. "Oh, I forgot. Landon, any chance you can you tell me what happened to your Rockets baseball cap?" Landon went white at the question. "Are you okay, Landon? All of a sudden you don't look so good."

"I lost it," he stammered. "I don't know where it is."

"Oh, that's funny," the detective smirked, "because I do."

From: Deb
To: Matt and Mikey
Subject: Subpoena

Did you guys get one?

From: Mikey
To: Matt and Deb

Yup. Heard a bunch of people did. Joe got served at the field same time I did.

From: Matt
To: Deb and Mikey

Yup. I'm not surprised, but it's all from the defense, which surprises me.

From: Deb
To: Matt and Mikey

I don't think I can take any more surprises.

From: Matt
To: Deb and Mikey

Fasten your seatbelts!

Rockets Team Chat
(Chris, Landon, Max, Dylan, Balls (Josh), Ryan, Money (Manny), Tyler, Jimmy, Carlos)

Carlos – Did you hear Coach Matt picked up two new guys?

Jimmy – For the team or just tomorrow's tourney?

Landon – Team. Unless they fuck up the tourney.

Tyler – Then they're out

Balls (Josh) – I think it's a pitcher who can catch and a centerfielder.

Ryan – We totally need more pitchers.

Money (Manny) – Poor tired Josh

Tyler – And someone to replace Reg

Chris – So much new blood!

Money (Manny) – So… did anyone have the detective show up and question them?

Balls (Josh), Chris, Landon, Max, Dylan, Ryan, Tyler, Jimmy, Carlos – Yes!!!

Tyler – Was shittin' my pants

Dylan – Did anyone say anything?

Landon – No one knows anything, so there's nothing to say.

Landon – Right?

Landon – Right?!

Balls (Josh) – Of course. Right.

Carlos – This is a crazy team

Jimmy – Don't nobody mess with the Rockets!

Money (Manny) – Bet your golden ass!

They sat in the bleachers sweating. It was the fourth of July weekend, and for the Golden Rockets that meant spending two nights at the

Holiday Inn in Yaphank out east in Long Island and three days at the Big League Baseball complex for their first summer tournament weekend. They were on their second game of day two, crushing their game last night but getting crushed this morning. This game at 2 p.m., in the dead heat, could go either way. They were up a run in the fourth, but both teams were dragging. It wasn't their best showing, but the two new kids, Benji and Sam, boys who had been playing club teams, were clearly talented players. They would be a big help at Cooperstown.

The parents weren't looking too good, either. Barb wiped the sweat from her brow with a cool rag she took out from her cooler. Marie and Rich sat a little distance from the group in the far corner using their umbrella to shield them from the beating sun. Deb wore a hat and oversized Gucci sunglasses. She was applying sunblock to her arms and keeping cool with non-stop iced teas and by occasionally using a spray fan that misted water on her. Sean dripped on the play book while Nick and Robin argued over who forgot Dylan's Gatorade, which, of course, wasn't a big deal since they could just buy Gatorade at the snack bar. Carlos' parents were in conversation with the parents of Benji and Sam, the newcomers to the team, forming their own little new clique huddle. Jeff Blum sat there as well because Matt asked to borrow his son Jordan when not only Reggie bailed out but Ryan came down with a stomach virus and had to drop. Matt was irritated watching his team drag, and Mikey was bouncing around being even more irritating.

The game wasn't exciting, which meant that all the parents had to do between occasional glances to the field, shaking their heads at the lackluster performance was snack and talk. With the heat, most of the snacking was liquid and the talk was far from substantive as well.

"So you all had the police come by to question the boys?" Marie leaned in to ask, and they all nodded.

"I'm still reeling from it," Robin said. "Not that I think he should have stayed on the team." Marie looked at her like she was crazy. "I'm not saying I condone what happened," she quickly amended. "I'm just saying that it was time for Jake to leave."

"It really wasn't good for the team," Barb agreed. "I think the whole thing made the boys uncomfortable and awkward with each other. You can't play with people you don't trust."

"And why wouldn't they trust Jake?" Marie asked, incredulous. "We're talking about a sweet twelve-year-old."

"Well, come on." Robin gave her a sour look. "Think of the havoc his family has caused and the impact to the team and the boys."

"I'm not getting it," Marie said and pulled away, back under the protective shield of her umbrella with her husband.

"How could the boys act comfortable around a boy whose father murdered their coach!" Robin said, more strongly.

"I understand what you're saying, Marie," Deb placated, "and no one is saying that what happened was okay. It most certainly wasn't okay. But I think we're just agreeing over here that maybe the outcome was for the best. That maybe it was time for Jake to leave the team anyway given the circumstances." Robin and Barb nodded in agreement.

Jeff, clearly not a team member, just a visiting eavesdropper on the bleacher, wasn't going to get involved but he looked over at Marie and Rich sympathetically, catching their eye, and shaking his head in disbelief.

"It was a shame that Reggie left, though," Deb said. "I think Wayne would be sad to think that now neither of his boys are on his team."

"Well, it's kind of not his team anymore," Barb said with just a hint of defensiveness. "So much has changed."

"True," Robin said sadly.

"So are we all going to see each other in court next week?" Deb asked.

"Looks that way," Barb said.

"I'd like the boys all there to support Wayne."

"Of course," Robin agreed.

"We'll be there," Sean said.

"But what about supporting Dan?" Marie asked and the women stared at her emotionless.

"I support Dan," Sean said, but it was a useless sentiment and everyone ignored him. He was supportive of everyone, which meant he also supported no one. He swayed whichever way the group told him to sway yet harbored no hard or strong feelings. So he would stand for Wayne but would probably wave to Dan and give him an encouraging thumbs up.

"I don't think it's right to have the boys attend a murder trial of one of their former coaches. I think it's confusing for them, uncomfortable, and very inappropriate," Marie said. "None of this is black and white, and the kids are not mature enough to understand."

Deb shrugged. "Your choice, of course. You're the parent. But Max may be the only one who doesn't show up with his team. I'm just saying. How's that going to feel for him?"

Marie leaned back and whispered to Rich. "Should we expect a ball through our window next?"

Deb sat in the stands for the last two days talking and acting like she wasn't about to fall to pieces, like baseball had any meaning any more or any of this mattered. How she managed to sit there casually, she really had no idea. They had an appointment set up for first thing Monday morning with a New York bigwig criminal attorney who was highly recommended through her cousin, a lawyer big in personal injury, who knew about those kind of people and those kinds of things. If only all they had to worry about was a ball thrown through a window. Criminal mischief? Vandalism? Peanuts. They could deal with that, but where they sat was much more frightening.

After the detective dropped his bomb, she had looked from Landon to Detective Jonas confused.

"What are you saying?" she asked, feeling the danger of his simple question.

"I'm just asking Landon about his Rockets hat. Where it is? It's a straight forward question." He eyed Landon. His boyish tan face depleted of color.

Deb turned to Landon, who seemed about to crumple and cry but then she suddenly remembered. "Wayne had it!" In her fear for her son, she practically shouted, then stammered on anxiously. "Right, Landon? Remember? Landon took a step back with the wide, terrified, accepting eyes of a deer in the headlights. "Yes! I remember," Deb continued. "When we were all fighting here before Wayne left, he took the hat with him!" She was panting from the exertion of telling the story, from the fight or flight adrenaline pumping thru her body. As white as Landon was, she was hot pink flushed with the passion of protecting her son.

"And why would he take Landon's hat?" the detective asked, looking directly at Landon.

Deb opened her mouth, but Landon's voice came out, small and unnatural. "I was angry, and I threw it at him."

"Okay, son, why were you angry?"

Deb tripped over herself to respond. "He, he found us on the lawn, Wayne and me, and was upset so he took off his Rockets cap that he was wearing and threw it at him. Wayne picked it up and left."

The detective took a long pause. "So that's the story, Landon? Do you want to speak for yourself? Is what your mother saying correct?"

Landon opened his mouth, but the words that may or may not have come out were replaced by Deb's. "Yes, that's what happened. I was there. That's the whole story. That's it." The detective looked at Landon for confirmation, but Deb shook her head. "Landon will not say another word."

"Okay then, fine," Detective Jonas said. "Just one more question and then I'm leaving. It's an easy one." Deb eyed him warily. "What size shoe does Landon wear?"

Deb remained tightlipped.

"It's not something that you can hide, Ms. Schnitt. You might as well tell me."

After an extended staring game where Deb realized there was no escaping the fact or what it meant, she answered. "Ten and a half."

The detective nodded knowingly and checked off the box in his head. "I wouldn't leave town," he said flatly.

The minute the door closed behind him, Deb turned to Landon. "That is it, right? I totally remember. That's it!" She was now near hysterical, pacing, not even looking at Landon. "I've got calls to make! Don't you worry. This is nothing," she reassured him, her address book already open and phone in hand. "Go on to your room," she had said, wanting to be calm but knowing she was shrill and manic. "I'm gonna make sure everything is okay!" Landon slunk away, his face the tight mask of a tortured soul.

Since then, they had barely spoken about it. Deb tried a few times to open the door, but Landon was now closed up tight. They couldn't see an attorney till Monday anyway, so the tournament provided a great distraction for them both. He was playing like shit, but who cared? He had friends around and things to do. It was better than sitting home and not looking at each other, driving each other crazy. Nothing could be done this weekend, anyway. The constant chatter on the bleachers half the time helped as a diversion to her own brain, but the other half of the time almost drove her to murder. Her nerves were raw, but it was better being here than being alone with nothing to focus on. Here, at least there was baseball business to attend to. No matter what, the game must go on.

From: Deb
CC: Matt and Mikey
To: Rockets team and their families
Subject: Court and other important news

Please come to support the memory of Coach W. All team players should wear their gold memorial belts and special tribute hats. I have placed an order for the design of the memorial patches to be made into pins as well for the parents and siblings and any supporters who show up. The trial starts next Monday with any number of people taking the stand throughout the week. Show up one day or all. Any details or changes, I promise to update.

Also, congratulations on today's win! It was a tough game out there in the heat—for the fans too! But you guys pulled it together and showed them what our Rockets are made of! We have the first playoff game tomorrow at 8 a.m. Team to report at 7 a.m. We will coordinate rides for parents who don't want to go early.

And, lastly, I have made reservations for tonight at ChaCha's. We will meet in the lobby at seven o'clock and walk over. Early curfew tonight boys. Coach's orders. Lights out at ten.

To the stars, Rockets!

Louis Grand sat on one couch in Faith's living room, his hulking body taking up half the sofa while Faith sat looking almost childlike in comparison on the other. Both held cups of coffee in front of them. At the moment, Faith had spoken with the prosecution requesting not to be put on the stand, using Wayne's infidelities as an excuse not to testify to his character. Louis could put her on the stand but like everything in this case, nothing was cut and dry.

"So how do things look?" Faith asked.

Louis, being the privileged confident of Dan, knew exactly how he felt about Faith and now speaking with Faith understood exactly how she felt about him. It was good to know, and if they hadn't slept together she would have been a strong character witness in Dan's favor. He was still considering using her, though. They hadn't engaged in the affair during their marriage. It made a big difference, but the impression it left on the jury that they were involved now could be negative. It was risky. He would play it by ear. But they had picked a jury he was comfortable with, and the trial started this week. It was go time.

"It's a tough one," he said. "Hard to gauge. They have a strong case, but it's mainly circumstantial. We just need to knock it down peg by peg, and we can. There are explanations for all of it. And then we need to slowly layer other suspects for the jury to consider. There are quite a few. All we need is reasonable doubt."

"Okay. So you think Dan has a chance?" Faith asked nervously.

"He does, but I may need your help." He leaned forward. "I'm not sure if I will, but if it comes down to it, I may have to use you as a character witness for Dan and against Wayne. It won't be easy because if I put you up the prosecution will attack you and everyone will also know about you and Dan."

Faith had thought a lot about the way people talked and how much she cared. Being the subject of scorn was never easy, but she could take it. She worried for her boys and didn't want to subject them to anything more than they were already going through. "I'm not worried about me. I'm worried about my sons."

"If it comes down to it, we can keep them from being in court that day."

"I actually don't want them in court at all," Faith said. "This whole case is going to be ugly all around, whether it's about me and Dan or Wayne's infidelities. I can't put my boys in that position. Although, I know they'll find out what goes on at trial anyway. People talk too much. Still, I've decided to send them to my parents' upstate for as long as the trial goes on. Regardless of how much I believe in Dan, and my children support him as well, they may not have as easy a time if they think I'm involved with him. Even worse, if kids start teasing them."

"I understand. Let's see how it goes. So is there anything you can tell me that you think may help? You were a presence on the team for years. You know all the players. Tell me about the dynamics, and don't leave anything out. I'll decide if anything is important or not."

Faith spent the next forty-five minutes talking about the team and everyone on it. Detailing the power struggles, the kids who Wayne had cut over the years. The parents who took it extra hard. The crazy fans. The coaches from other organizations who he fought with. The coaches within FYO who he fought with. Wayne was a divisive guy, and there were a lot of unhappy people both on his team and off it. She spoke of Matt's competitiveness, the calculation in his eye and obvious desire to be top dog. She spoke of the disrespectful way Wayne treated Mikey and, of course, Deb's obsessive love.

"And what about Dan?" Louis asked, jotting things down. "What are they going to say about Dan?"

Faith thought about it. Dan was always the steady force in the dugout. He was balanced and fair, rarely raising his voice. "He took a lot shit from Wayne," she said. "I think Wayne tested him even more than the others but in a different way. Dan was real competition for Wayne.

Mikey was someone to humiliate, Matt was a protégé who was very similar in style to him, but Dan was his real competition. He was the most experienced in the dugout, and the boys all respected him. They turned to him for support and words of wisdom or when they were struggling on the mound or at the plate. Dan balanced out the team. Wayne needed him, and Wayne didn't like to need anyone. It was partly why he didn't play Jake as much as he should have. It was a power thing because he could be kind of an asshole, but really it was to show Dan who was boss."

"Okay, thanks," Louis said when they had finished talking. "That was helpful." He opened his briefcase to put some files back in and pulled out an envelope. "From Dan," he said, handing it to her.

She took it carefully. "Thank you."

"He wasn't happy with me telling you not to visit. It's the least I can do. Feel free to give me any correspondence. I'll make sure he gets it. It's better from me than Nicole. I'm safer." He picked up his bag and held out his hand to shake. "See you Monday."

They shook, and she followed him to the door. "I'm really nervous about the whole thing," Faith admitted. "I just can't believe this is real life."

"No one ever can," he said.

When the door was closed tight and she was alone again, she sat back down on the couch holding the envelope tenderly. She couldn't wait to read it but didn't want to rush. Slowly and carefully she worked the flap open and pulled out a piece of folded lined paper. She opened it up and first took note of Dan's handwriting, small and neat. She touched his words then read.

Faith,

I am sitting in my cell on my cot alone, like I do most of the day, thinking. There's really nothing much to do here but pass my days lost in my own head. I think about my life and my kids, my marriage and my failures as a person, a husband and a father. I think about the things I've done wrong, and I think about the things I think I've done right, and how I can do better. And I think about you. Endlessly, I think about you. I see you there in my mind, and I smile and all of this falls away. I wish I could stay in that dream state where there is only you and me. (Okay, maybe there's beer too.) I know it all seems fast. I mean we've only just really discovered each other but it feels as though it has been there for years, that we were slowly getting to know each other, laughing, teasing and flirting. Right from the first, you mesmerized me and even though I know you are probably in a very weird place given everything, I hope that we somehow survive this nightmare to give us a real chance. That's what I dream about. Us. And the possibility that we could exist and be happy. That and a cheeseburger and fries. Damn. My mouth is watering at the thought of you both. Please write.

Dan

Faith held the letter to her chest and let the tears pour. How did she get to this place where her husband of so many years was dead and she was falling for the person accused of killing him? She was a tangle of emotion. She wasn't even sure who or what she was crying for. Both, she realized. Poor Wayne, who had so much drive and energy. And testosterone. She laughed through her sob. His exploits were as sad as her lack of them. They spent years in an unhappy but comfortable marriage resenting each other but still carrying on. What a waste. What a mistake. Wayne shouldn't have to be dead for her to be happy. He should have had the chance to be happy too. She sniffled up her emotions. There was no sense in crying now or looking back at what they should have done. There was only the present. Tomorrow could be a big fuck you. Faith planned to live and be happy regardless what people thought. When Derek and Reggie came home, she planned to have a long talk with them. She wanted them to know what was going on before leaving them upstate with her parents. She wanted them to have the drive to think on it and the two days with her away from all this to talk it through. It was getting late and she needed to pack, who knew how long they would be there, but that could wait a bit. Right now she just wanted to write back to Dan.

CHAPTER 20
(Wayne Makes a Play for the Plate)

Wayne wobbled down the street cursing. How did that just happen? One minute he's at Flynn's having a brawl with that lacrosse asshole, Johnny Smith, and the next minute he's on Deb's lawn about to fuck her but then Landon came out and what a shit show. Although, it was far from the first time Landon had caught him and his mom in a compromising position. The boy knew what was going on. Had known for years. Not that he should but he did, and this was bad. He wasn't even supposed to fucking be there. He didn't want to be screwing around with Deb. He wanted to be screwing around with Erika. Erika. He fumbled around in his pocket, struggling to produce his phone, then dropped it to the sidewalk. When he bent down to pick it up he lost his balance and almost fell managing to semi catch himself with a hedge on the side of someone's house. "Shit!" He pushed his way out of it, picked up the phone, stumbled to the curb and sat, exhaling loudly. He found Erika's number and dialed. She picked up on the second ring.

"Hello, sugar, I thought I'd hear from you earlier."

"Sorry, babe. The celebration went longer than expected and then there was a fight with Johnny Smith and I wound up—"

She cut him off. "Lacrosse Johnny?"

"Yeah."

"Well, shit. Why are ya fighting with Johnny?"

"I forgot him and your husband are tight."

"As a pair of titties."

Wayne chuckled. "Babe, will you come pick me up?"

"I don't know. It's late. Bobby'll be home from his carousing soon."

"Come on. I'll make it worth your while." He tried to sound suggestive but bordered on incoherent.

"Well," she said considering, "where are you?"

"I'm by Deb's house. She lives right by Tigers Turf."

"Well what the fuck you doing there?" Erika asked, clearly annoyed.

"Long story. Just pick me up."

There was a long pause before Erika spoke, her voice light but clear and dismissive. "You know what, sugar. I've changed my mind. I'm real tired. You have a good night now." She hung up on him.

"Shit!"

He threw his phone down and then realized how stupid that was and picked it up to see a long crack going down the center. Luckily, he was still too drunk to care. He thought for a minute, found Dan's number in his phone and dialed. It went to voicemail. "Dannn," he slurred. "Listen I know we got into a little fight before, but you know I was just messing with you. I was all stirred up and shouldn't have said some of that shit. Deb took me to her lair to have her way with me, but I'm walking to TT. I need a ride come. Can ya get me? Come on, man, come pick me." Freaking pussy wasn't answering his phone on purpose, Wayne thought.

Using all his strength, he lifted himself up off the ground and started walking, dragging the long heavy trophy and making his way to Tigers Turf. He was pretty sure Dan would show up to rescue him.

"Cake?" Deb asked Landon when they were both inside, pulling open the box with a half-eaten apple pie from the fridge. She placed it on the island and grabbed two forks, and started eating straight from the box. She placed a forkful in her mouth. "It's good."

He didn't answer but he did think about it for a minute, just letting the resentment and anger go, giving in and just eating cake.

"I know your angry," Deb said. "And you have every right to be. Your dad left and—"

That set him immediately off. "This is not about Dad!" he screamed. "This is about you! You being too desperate to realize that he just uses you. And you want to be used. It's disgusting. You're disgusting, and he's disgusting!" He stormed out of the kitchen and stomped up the stairs.

Deb slowly gulped down her pie, but she still had a lump in her throat.

In his room, Landon paced for the fifteen minutes it took for Deb to come up the stairs and knock on his door, for him to tell her to go away and for her to sigh loudly and shuffle down the hallway to her room. After he heard the click of her door close, he quietly snuck out of his room, padded down the stairs, and out the front door into the sticky cool evening. He would find Wayne. The only place he could think where he could be was Tigers Turf, so he headed in that direction. He didn't know what he planned to say, but he knew for certain that Wayne was never going to use his mom again.

CHAPTER 21

After his conversation with the Schnitts, Detective Jonas itched from head to toe. All those loose ends lightly brushing against every part of him, tickling him, torturing him. He couldn't rest. How had he missed this giant piece of the puzzle? He knew that there had been some altercation between Deb and Wayne that night, but he hadn't probed deep enough and now this hat had tipped a can of worms into his lap. He remembered that first day asking Deb about her alibi. She said she had been home with her son, who was there sleeping. Landon wasn't just a new piece, he was a whole new puzzle with a size ten and a half shoe, and Deb lied from the beginning.

He started with the basics: casing the neighborhood the way he should have weeks before, knocking on doors old school, and what he discovered was no small thing. Wayne and Deb's argument was more of a blow up. Almost the entire block had heard something and a few had witnessed it, peering through windows at the show on the front lawn.

"It was better than any soap opera," an older lady across the street, a Mrs. Chloe Damsky, stated, chortling. "The man and woman were all over each other like a couple of horny teens. But then the real teen came out and started screaming profanities and reprimanding them. I don't know how, but my Bailey slept through the whole thing, but he can't even hear when he's awake."

"What a scene!" said Mara Jackson, a small curly-haired woman who opened the door holding a bowl of ice cream in one hand and restraining two big dogs with the other. "The guy was clearly drunk. And Deb was clearly out of her mind to let all that go down on the front lawn." She shook her head compassionately. "That poor kid. He's really struggled since his father left."

"The guy fell into my hedges and crushed my hydrangeas," said Addy Cohn, the neighbor three houses down. "He was loud and talking to himself but by the time I came out, I didn't see him. I just caught a glimpse of the back of the kid, Lando, or whatever his name is, a house or two down, following."

Detective Jonas' practiced blank brown eyes sparkled. He couldn't help it. He not only had a motive, a hat, and a matching sized footprint, he had found a potential witness.

In the dugout, Matt analyzed his team. It was eighty degrees and sunny, and they were dragging bad. He didn't blame them. Conditions out there were tough, yet he was still making a mental list of their strengths and failures to go over with them at a later time. Max got picked off because he took too big of a lead. Dylan was lazy and didn't get a jump on anything hit to left. Josh was all over the place on the mound. Jimmy had to control his over-anxiousness at the plate and, at times, Manny was still reaching. Benji and Sam, the new kids, were gonna be game changers for the team. Good fundamentals. Strong at the plate. Good arms. Carlos had brought new energy to the team in this last month as well.

These new boys were going to give the current boys a run for their money. A little competition was good for the blood. They were getting lazy. They weren't babies anymore. They were at the end of their official little league careers. Soon, he would be speaking with the parents about who he would be continuing with as they moved forward in solely a travel capacity playing on the big 60/90 field. It was put up or shut up, get moving or get out. He wanted a winning team, and he wasn't shy about hurting feelings to get there.

He looked over to the stands and the men and women he had sat through years of games with. Some would go on with him and some would be left behind. He glanced at Mikey, bug-eyed and intense. He hadn't been as bad as he'd expected, but he wasn't good enough either. It was nothing personal. It was just baseball. He wouldn't think about any of that till after Cooperstown next month. He had just started planting the seeds. There was some time to weed out the weak and focus on the strong. He had already started. He thought about Wayne and his vision for the team, and knew he would be proud. The winning Golden Rockets were his legacy, even if his sons no longer played. That was just a small matter. Wayne would be forever remembered with this team.

Deb came home on Sunday, the Rockets having placed second in the tournament, which considering their lackluster performance was actually pretty good. She was so happy to be back. It had been extremely stressful staying focused and maintaining normal back and forth conversations with so much going on in her brain. She and Landon shared another silent car ride home and when they got to the house he walked in and went straight to his room.

"Landon," she called out to him. "Maybe we should talk." But he just continued up the stairs, ignoring her. This couldn't go on. She was on her last nerve. The doorbell rang, startling her. She stood fearfully. Lately, people at her door brought nothing but bad news. She looked through the side window relieved. It was only Chloe, the older woman from across the street.

"Hi, Deb," she greeted, smiling broadly, showing off lipstick stained teeth.

"Hey, Chloe." It was strange to have her at her door. The only other time had been a few years ago after her husband had left. She came with a casserole. Deb looked down.

"I made something for you," Chloe said and produced a covered deep dish. "It's lasagna."

Deb took the dish from her outstretched hands, looking perplexed. "Thanks, Chloe. That was very nice of you." She made a move to go back inside.

"I figured you were going through a tough time with the whole business on the lawn a month or so ago and then the police coming round this weekend."

Deb stopped. "The police were around this weekend?"

Chloe shook her head emphatically, and strangely Deb fixated on her fluff of white hair that never moved. "Oh, yes, a very nice detective man asking questions about that night."

Deb looked back and forth, up and down her block. Her eyes darting around nervously. "Yes, well thank you so much. That was very kind of you. I'll return the dish to you when we're done." She gave a quick wave and shut the door on Chloe's smiling face.

Deb leaned up against the door, holding the dish and releasing her breath. The doorbell rang again.

Full of adrenaline, she flipped around and quickly opened it. "Chloe, thank you but it's not a good—"

She stopped. A young man she didn't know stood before her, but she did recognize the envelope in his hand and cringed. "Are you Deb Schnitt?" he asked, and she nodded weakly. He handed her the envelope. "You are being served as a parent or guardian of Landon Schnitt." He walked away, and Deb opened the envelope for confirmation. Landon was required to appear in court as well. She crumpled it up and threw it down, then jumped up and down on it, screaming. From across the street Chloe just watched, shaking her head.

Monday morning, Deb and Landon sat in the waiting area of Wynn and Silver, highly regarded Criminal Defense Attorneys, waiting for their 10 a.m. appointment with Howard (How we Win!) Wynn. The office was an intimidating space, modern and cool, with sleek slate gray walls, black leather chairs and couches, chrome metals used for side tables and fixtures, and funky urban art screaming from the walls. They looked around and then down at their laps silently. Deb put a hand on Landon's leg and was so happy when he didn't brush her off.

A twenty- something-year-old woman walked over to greet them, her tight bun pulling at her smile and outstretched a hand first to Deb and then to Landon, who quickly stood up. "Hello, I'm Maryann, Mr. Wynn's assistant. He's ready to see you now."

She turned, and Deb and Landon followed her down a hall to a massive office space with walls of glass. She gave a quick knock at the side of the open door. Howard, "Call me Howie," looked up from the work he was looking at on his desk. He stood, all five foot five feet of him, and walked around to greet them. "Hello, come in. Sit."

They shook hands, and he gestured them to one of the two black couches. Deb and Landon sat side by side, stiffly. Deb wore a summer dress and now her legs were sticking to the furniture and making a sucking sound whenever she moved. She tried not to move.

"I've been reading over your information, and I spoke with a few people, including the district attorney's office and Jean Gibbs, the prosecutor. I've also got a call in to Louis, the defense attorney. We go back a long way. It's an interesting case, a lot of open ends." He looked at his watch. "And it's just started. Deb, I see that you've been subpoenaed and Landon has as well. I'd like to hear everything from you from the beginning. Pretend I know nothing. Tell me why you're here and what I can do for you."

Deb looked uncomfortable. "Landon, could you please step into the hall for a few minutes." It wasn't a question. Thankfully, he was too traumatized to give her any attitude and just walked out.

Without her son's presence, Deb explained her dysfunctional back and forth adulterous relationship with Wayne leading up to the events on the lawn.

Howie remained blank-faced throughout and when she was done, called Landon back into the room.

He began slowly, but once he started talking, once he gave voice to all the inside turmoil he had been shutting away and not dealing with, he was like a locomotive, picking up steam with every puff released, and it was a redemptive, liberating release. He had held it all in for too long; his anger over his father, his mother, and Wayne and what had really happened that night. He needed to say it all and he spared no feelings, certainly not Deb's. He didn't stop until he was out of breath and his entire story came out, leaving Deb stunned and speechless.

Thankfully Howie was a seasoned pro. He was neither stunned nor speechless. He talked to them for a long while about their options, what he advised them to do and what may or may not happen. Howie placed a reassuring arm around Landon's shoulder. "So what do you think? Are you ready?"

Landon hesitated but nodded.

"Okay, good." He squeezed his arm in support.

"So, we just go there?" Deb asked, terrified.

"Yeah, the judge may not even allow us the interruption, but we need to get down there and try. One way or another, the truth will come out. Better it be on our terms."

Dan was brought into the court for his first day and immediately saw Louis sitting there waiting for him. He had known what to expect since they had talked the evening before when Louis came to greet him in their usual small conference room reeking of greasy burgers and fries. Even in his precarious position, this tense, fearful place where the unknown loomed large and scary, his mouth watered. Louis smiled and pulled out a large bag from Five Guys® and placed it on the table. "Compliments of Faith," he said, and Dan immediately relaxed.

He spent the next hour and a half explaining one last time what today would be like and where he thought they stood, which was not in a bad place. The prosecution had structured their case largely around the DNA evidence found under Wayne's fingernails, which Louis said could easily be explained when Dan, in front of many witnesses, tried to break up a fight between Wayne and Johnny. The rest went to circumstance and motive. They had a really good shot, he said. In his opinion, the DA had rushed for a conviction under the pressure of the small town pitchforks and high profile publicity.

Still Dan couldn't prepare him for the terror he felt at that moment taking a seat at the defense table. Trying to control his hands, which had started to tremble, he clasped them together and sat down next to Louis, who smiled warmly and patted him on the shoulder reassuringly. Dan turned around and found the faces he was looking for, Jake and Lola, and gave them a goofy grin. Jake, who sat like a wooden soldier, momentarily relaxed and smiled and Lola, who looked like a baby doll with wide tentative curious eyes, grinned and waved frenetically. He scrunched up his face at them and then looked over at the two women they were nestled between, Nicole and his mom. He gave them eyes, and they sent back support and love to him with theirs. His mom blew him a kiss.

His view broadened and he studied the prosecutor, Jean Gibbs. She was about his age with strawberry colored hair pulled back in a tight bun, which drew attention to her thin arched brows and her matching colored lips. She wore a sleek dark pantsuit with an antique diamond and opal brooch of a star on her lapel. Behind her sat rows filled with people. In the front, he recognized some of Wayne's family, especially his parents and brother who had occasionally shown up at games over the years. A few rows behind him were the people who made him catch his breath with sadness. Sitting there were people from their town who he recognized from FYO, or from the schools or the supermarket who had come out to support Wayne, and behind them sat a few of the boys from his team, sitting there awestruck in their uniforms with their golden belts and special hats that they would soon remove for the judge. They were all looking at him and looking away, unable to meet his eye. They wouldn't have found any hostility there. Dan understood and wanted them to know that it was okay. Their parents were, of course, there as well—Mikey, Robin and Nick, Matt and Barb and Sean who gave him a sad, small wave, all wearing memorial pins attached to their shirts. He was happy not to see Deb among them, maybe she had come around, maybe she was no longer, as Nicole had conveyed, leading the charge against him.

His eyes moved around toward the back and that's where he found her. Faith. She was sitting on his side of the courtroom next to Marie and Rich. Overwhelming relief filled him. It had been so long and just the sight of her gave him renewed strength. He knew she supported him, but to see her sitting on his side made a statement in his heart. They locked eyes, and neither could communicate all that needed to be said. He acknowledged Maria and Rich and then there was a slight commotion as everyone started to rise for the judge entering the courtroom as the bailiff announced, "Please rise for the honorable Judge Andrews."

Louis leaned in. "The judge will say a few words and then swear in the jury." Dan nodded. He was ready.

The judge had just begun addressing the court when another commotion disrupted the opening proceedings. A stocky man charged into the courtroom and walked directly to the prosecution's table. Behind him walked Deb and Landon, who moved far less assuredly, stopping in the middle of the aisles for everyone to stare while Howie spoke in heated whispers to Jean.

"Don't let us disturb you, Ms. Gibbs," the judge snapped. "We'll just sit here while you and Mr. Wynn here have your meeting."

Jean stood, full of apology and looking uncertain. "Your honor, I am sorry. It's just that some new information on the case has just been brought to my attention." The judge and Louis looked over to her and Howie skeptically.

"I apologize, your honor, this information was just relayed to me this morning. I tried to call Ms. Gibbs on the way, but, of course, she was a little busy. And I don't take this interruption lightly. I was thinking in the best interest of your time and your court's time."

"Yes, Mr. Wynn, I am well aware of your solicitous nature. Thank you." Howard controlled his grin. He had been in Judge Andrews courtroom many times. "Please, all of you approach the bench."

Louis, Jean and Howard all moved forward, and the entire courtroom leaned in hoping to catch a thread of their whispers. After some heated back and forth and snipes between the attorneys—Louis said, "Well, maybe if you hadn't rushed to trial!" Jean, hissing back, said, "You can't brush over DNA and motive!" Louis again said, "How about real evidence and truth." Jean rolled her eyes and said, "Oh please!" And the judge shut them both up. "In my chambers, all of you now!" Howard, Louis and Jean went back to quickly gather some of their papers, and Louis put a reassuring hand on Dan's. "This could be good for us," he said and hurried off.

The court broke into disorder. Everyone was talking over each other trying to figure out what was going on. Faith kept her eyes on Dan, who remained in his prescribed seat twisted around to talk with his kids. He looked so engaged and animated, it warmed her heart to see them together. It made her wistful for her own boys, who she had shipped off to her parents over the weekend. Wayne's family had given her a hard time about it, but she was happy they weren't here. All the ugly that would come out was not for their ears. They would hear enough without having a front row seat. She looked over to the boys of Wayne's baseball team sitting on the benches supporting his memory, and it made her happy for him. Yes, his goal was, first and foremost, winning but he wanted to mean something to his team. He would be pleased that they were here dressed in uniform honoring him. She understood the need for justice, and for closure. That something horrible had happened and someone had to pay. If only it weren't Dan sitting there on the other side.

Faith never for one minute thought him capable of such an act. That, of course, wasn't exactly true. She absolutely believed in him but that didn't mean she hadn't had moments of doubt, where she contemplated the possibility, the what if's that you can't help but consider. As if he sensed her thinking about him, Dan lifted his eyes across the crazy and found hers. They held together, and her heart and her body connected to his on impact. Immediately, she was drawn to him and desperately wanted to run over to be by his side, if not on his lap and definitely in his bed. She wanted this man with her. She wanted time to find out if they were meant to be. She wanted him. In every way, she wanted him. Except, of course, if he murdered her husband, she thought sardonically, almost laughing at the ridiculousness of it all because clearly none of it was funny.

Both of their attention was drawn to the short lawyer who emerged from the judge's private chambers, moving with purpose. He found Deb in the center of the a swarm of Rockets, Matt and Barb and the other parents of the team with Landon sitting quietly as his teammates lobbed him question after question. Howie plucked them from the crowd to follow him as Dan stared with rapt attention.

Jean knew they had rushed a bit, caved to community pressures. Not that Dan wasn't a strong case. It could go either way, and she could definitely win it. She listened to what Howard had to say, the new evidence and testimony that he offered to the case. She objected because she had to, but honestly was fine when the judge decided that he would hear what Landon had to say in chambers and then decide on relevance. It was fair and Jean, although she liked to win, valued true justice more. She wasn't interested in prosecuting an innocent man. She had done that once before unknowingly in her career, and the years that man spent in jail haunted her. She did wish she had connected with Howard earlier so that she would have more control over the situation, but like her grandmother used to say, "What will be, will be."

Howard strode back to judges chambers with Deb and Landon nervously following like little ducks behind. The judge gestured for them to sit before him. "Hello, I'm Judge Andrews," he addressed himself mainly to Landon. "And I hear you have some information you'd like me to hear." Landon shrank in the chair. "Just tell me the truth, young man, and it'll all work out."

"Just the way you did in my office," Howard encouraged.

After glancing quickly over to his mom for reassurance, he cleared his throat loudly and began.

CHAPTER 22
(Wayne Gets Tagged Out)

It took him fifteen minutes to get to Tigers Turf, about eight minutes longer than it should have, but Wayne kept stumbling, using a bush, a fire hydrant and on one unfortunate occasion, the sidewalk, to assist him on his journey. Maybe he'd get lucky, he thought, and the field house office would be left open. He could lay down on one of the couches and drop that check on Joe's desk. He had forgot in all the celebration and commotion to give it to him. He didn't want that over his head. He had made a mistake that he hadn't thought through clearly but didn't want his name, Joe, the Rockets team or the Fort Jefferson Youth Organization to have any negative impact from his actions. He loved FYO and everything it stood for. He just fucked up a bit. He should have known better, but he was prepared to make amends. If it wasn't open, first thing tomorrow he would bring it over to Joe personally.

He was only two blocks away when someone opened their door to shout at him. "Hey, buddy, get out of here or I'm calling the police!" Wayne saluted him and wobbled forward. "On my way, Captain."

Once he arrived at TT, he went straight up to the field house but, of course, it was locked. He gazed out appreciatively into the beautiful sleeping complex; the fields, as always, calling to him. He opened his flashlight on his smart phone to guide him to the only place that felt almost like home, Field 2.

With nothing to do at the moment but wait for Dan to hopefully come pick him up, he set the trophy on the ground, placing Landon's cap over the central figure on top. He hooked it on using the back hole created by the size adjusting snaps where a girl would typically pull a ponytail through so that all you could see of the player was a golden bat sticking out. Then he sat down, relaxing in the center of the pitcher's mound and played with the flashlight on his phone, shining it around the bases and recreating plays. "The Rockets go to work at the top of the fifth as darkness settles into the Fort Jefferson night. Josh starts off the inning smacking a single, finding the hole in between short and third and running to first." Wayne shined the light from first to second, then put it back on home plate and continued his commentary. "Reggie is up next, he wipes the sweat from his brow and steps to the plate. He takes the first pitch for a strike. He fouls off the second. He steps out of the box and takes a practice swing and when he steps back in, he's focused and ready. The next pitch is low and outside and he takes it for a ball. He's waiting for his pitch. Finally, it comes and he smacks a blast straight to center for a double. The crowd is up. Josh is on his horse and scores. Reggie takes off as well." Wayne tracked the light to bases. "Now Derek is up at the plate with the winning run on second. The crowd is tense. The defense ready. They know this kid can really hit. The pitcher throws a blazing fast ball down the middle for a strike. The last breath of light whispers on the horizon as Derek raises his bat, twirling it a little, ready, intense. He's got this. The pitch is on its way and Derek swings and connects sending a cannon like blast deep into the outfield. Wait! It's a home run! Reggie comes home! Derek comes home! The crowd is wild! And the Rockets win! The Rockets win!!!"

The sound of clapping hands scared him. "Who's there?" he called out, shuffling backward and rising as quickly as he could to his feet. The person made no sound, but Wayne heard his feet shuffling and heard him circling around. "I'm not kidding!" he yelled. "Who is that?" He remembered the trophy on the floor next to him and leaned down to grab it. Hearing movement near him, he whipped his flashlight over trying to capture his mystery assailant but kept missing him. He felt like a cornered animal, his heart racing beyond acceptable limits. If this person didn't kill him, it was possible he would have a heart attack. He turned in circles, guarding himself, using the trophy as his weapon. He heard footsteps coming toward him and he backpedaled, spinning his head left and right in terror.

"Don't you come near me! Do you hear me!" his voice echoed into the dead of night, the bleachers empty, the dugout void of players. The sound of footsteps came closer and Wayne swung the trophy around wildly, slicing through the air, striking nothing but sending Landon's hat flying. He moved backward, winding up on home plate, at once holding the trophy high and ready to strike, then whipping the flashlight frantically from first to second to third.

"You made it all the way home," a voice whispered from behind, scaring the shit out of him and causing him to scream out as he tripped and fell.

The night grew even quieter as Landon shone his own light down to see Coach Savage, his head up knocked against the base of the trophy, little spots of blood splattered against the white of the bag.

He shut off his light and ran as fast as he could back home.

CHAPTER 23

Landon finished his story to the audible, slow intake and outtake of breath in the room. "Well that's some story, Landon," the judge said. "Why didn't you come forward sooner?"

"I was scared," Landon admitted, not much of an excuse but an appropriate one for a thirteen-year-old boy.

The judge nodded. He turned to Louis. "So I assume you're looking to make a motion for dismissal?" Before Louis could say anything, he turned to Jean. "Are you going to object?" Jean flustered. As prosecutor, she didn't know if she was going to object or not. She needed to call her boss, the district attorney. "I would like the night to go over Landon's testimony and align it with the narrative I have for that evening."

"You have until after lunch. Then I will hear any arguments from both of you. I am going to dismiss the jury for the day. No need to waste everyone's time here."

When Louis emerged, Dan could tell the news was positive and he sat up straighter in his seat filled with hope. Louis slid next to him and gave him an encouraging nod as they waited for the judge to speak. He banged his gavel for complete attention. "New evidence has come to the court for consideration and may have a deep impact on this case. I will be hearing arguments for dismissal from both sides later this afternoon. Jurors, you are released for the day. We will make you aware with a phone call later this evening if that release becomes permanent. He banged down the mallet again and the silence broke into uproar.

"This is all good," Louis said to Dan. "Even if he doesn't dismiss, we have more than enough evidence for probable cause. I think you can start packing your bag, buddy. It's time to go home."

Dan nodded but was too afraid to open his mouth to speak. He was so filled with emotion, it was already leaking a little bit from his eyes and he worried his voice might break. Louis gave him a quick hug. "Hang tight, buddy," he said comfortingly. Then the bailiff came and took him back to his cell, for what would hopefully be the last time. He caught Faith watching him go, wiping away tears of her own.

Before leaving the courtroom for an intense two hours of analysis, dissection and back and forth with the DA, Jean Gibbs pulled Faith aside for a private moment.

"Can we talk for a moment?" Jean asked, assessing her through chestnut brown eyes under plucked brows; her lips a serious, thin line as well. "I know we haven't spoken much since you made it clear straight from the beginning that you didn't believe we had the right guy and wanted to be kept out of the case. And I know I gave you a bit of attitude and suggested that your opinion maybe be clouded by certain feelings." Up close, Faith could see the small pores that from any distance her foundation smoothed over. She opened her mouth to respond, but Jean wasn't interested and waved it off. "Now I'm not here to judge or ask about your relationship with Dan, but I would like to know if you still feel as though we have the wrong guy. If the victim's widow is still in favor of the case being dropped?"

Faith tried to keep a straight face and not jump up and down. "I am. I don't believe Dan did it. And although I don't want to speak to my current feelings, I know you're aware of certain rumors about Dan and me." She was babbling and couldn't stop. "And I just want to say, since you never asked outright, that although Wayne and I did not have a good marriage. He was a serial cheater. Dan and I did not have an affair."

"You don't have to say that," Jean said.

"I needed to because it's true."

Jean nodded. "Maybe, but if the feelings were there, regardless of physicality, it still speaks to motivation. Especially with the other circumstances."

"It's thin," Faith said firmly. "You have a confession. And if having a crush on someone you shouldn't or feeling underappreciated are motivations for murder then there are a whole lot of potential murderers around. Including me." Her mouth turned up just a little, pleased with her response until the prosecution shot her down.

"Oh," Jean said, her brow straining at the arch, "don't think you weren't near the top of the list."

After Jean left her, Faith sought out Louis. She found him with his assistant, still at the defense table, just finishing gathering up his papers and shoving them in his briefcase and getting ready to head out. He needed the next couple of hours to prepare his motion and arguments for the judge. "Just give me two minutes, please," Faith pleaded with him. "Please."

Louis looked down at her and sighed, but he stopped his hustle and bustle. "Anthony, I'll meet you outside," he said to the man next to him, then turned to her. "I have two minutes to fill you in. Sit."

After lunch, most of the courtroom had cleared out with the exception of Faith and Deb. Dan's mother and Nicole had taken the kids back to her house, and Faith promised to let them know the minute they came out of chambers. Deb had asked Howie if it was okay for Landon to go home with one of his teammates instead of waiting around, but Howie had said it was better if he stayed. Thankfully, Sean had given the okay for Chris to stay to keep him company. They were out in the hall, hopefully playing with their phones and not calling any attention to themselves.

Faith and Deb sat on opposite sides of the aisle hyper aware of the other's presence and doing their best to ignore each other. An hour passed and then two. Besides a furtive glance, neither acknowledged the other. Faith spent half the time sitting there fantasizing about going over to confront her in a way that she wasn't prepared to do when they had met at Blue Finn. Now she was ready and could visualize the whole thing. Everything she would say and everything Deb could say back. It was taking all her patience to maintain her reserve and try to be the bigger person. Occasionally, she would almost cave and turn toward her to speak but then shut her mouth. Why did she need to talk to her, what benefit would it bring her, what validation? It wasn't going to change anything. It wasn't going to have changed the years she slept with her husband. It wasn't going to change the fact that she deserted her friend in a time of need. It wasn't going to change anything.

But, it would probably make her feel better. Without thinking any more, she stood abruptly. Deb turned at the sound and they looked at each other boldly, eyes alert and aggressive. Now that she was up and had literally taken a stand, she realized that everything in her brain was judgmental and self-righteous. She changed her mind. There was nothing to say to this woman. She shook her head a little and sat back down.

"What?" Deb challenged. "Just say it! Go ahead. This is your chance. You've wanted to call me out for years. Here I am!" She was manic, shouting and aggressive in her emotional desperation. "Come on!" she yelled, practically begging.

"I realized I have nothing to say to you," Faith said calmly, although she was shaking and trying hard to keep the nerves out of her voice. "You know what you did and who you are. You have to live with yourself. I'm sorry for you, Deb, but I don't feel bad for you one bit. You made your bed and you slept with my husband in it. You should have been paying more attention to your son. He's the one I feel bad for."

Deb's face burned with shame and rage. "Don't talk to me about Landon!" Her voice edged up dangerously. As if on cue, Landon and Chris walked in.

"Ma," he asked and upon seeing Faith both he and Chris stopped. Chris waved to her. "Hi, Mrs. Savage."

"Hi Chris," she said. "How are you doing?"

"Fine."

"Good." She turned to Landon who looked frozen with mortification. He had, in essence, killed her husband. "Landon, come here. I'd like to talk to you a minute." He nodded as Deb looked ready to pounce.

He sat down stiffly near Faith, practically holding his breath and wincing as if she were about to slap him. His leg jumped up and down nervously. She put her hand on his knee to calm him. "Listen, Landon. I know what happened and although I can't be inside your head, I imagine you've got a lot of guilt and sadness and confusion and a whole mix of feelings. I want you to know, and I really want you to hear me here, that this was an tragic accident. I don't want you carrying the weight of this around your whole life. It was an accident."

"But," Landon stammered, tears falling from his eyes. "It is my fault. The whole thing is my fault. And I did hate him. I wanted him dead." He cried more openly, leaning over and Faith rubbed his back until he pulled himself together.

"Feelings of anger are not the same. A lot of people wanted him dead in theory, but you didn't kill him. It was a tragedy, a horrible thing that happened. But Wayne played a huge part in why it did. He was an adult and there was a lot of unfortunate things that night and so many nights before that ultimately put him at Tigers Turf that night. You reacted to a bad situation, but you're not a killer."

"Derek and Reggie are going to hate me. The whole team is going to hate me." He sniffled, the tears still running down his maturing face, right at the cusp of the transition from boy to man. He really looked a lot like his mom, Faith realized.

"I can't say any of this will be easy, not for my boys or you, but in time it will all get just a tiniest bit better and you will keep going from there."

He nodded, wiping his snotty nose with the sleeve of his uniform, and Faith almost smiled because Wayne would turn over in his grave seeing that. "Thank you," he said.

"Yes, thank you," Deb agreed, now standing right near them. She looked as though getting those words out were an effort. She may have meant them, but it was not easy for her to say them.

Faith didn't answer. She didn't want her thanks. She wanted her to step back and allow her this moment with her son. "You're welcome," she said, directing her words straight to Landon, who just nodded blankly. There was nothing more to say, and they shared an uncomfortable minute where Landon still sat, sniffling, dripping and wiping with Deb standing stoic next him and Faith now trapped in and trying to figure out how to remove herself from their presence. She stood to excuse herself and as she did, Louis, Jean and Howie walked back into the courtroom, all of them looking grim.

Deb immediately made a move toward Howie, gently pulling at Landon's arm for him to follow as he made the same move toward her. They slid into the empty benches, and Deb stared at him with a frenzied anticipation unable to stomach what Howie might possibly reveal.

"The prosecution is not going to press charges against you, Landon," he said, and Deb immediately broke out into tears. She had sucked up and sucked in and pushed away and down all of her feelings and fears, and now all at once her relief flooded her, emotion cracking through those walls of reserve and composure until it broke them down entirely and she sobbed as Howie pat her shoulders awkwardly.

Faith watched the scene, momentarily distracted before moving toward Louis. As she walked the aisle, she bumped past Jean, who assumed she had been looking for her. "The judge ruled to dismiss the charges," she said, matter of fact. "I'll be honest, there was enough evidence to convict and I'm not a hundred percent sold on Dan's innocence. But Landon's testimony certainly creates reasonable doubt."

"Okay," Faith said hurriedly, about to break apart at the seams, not really hearing anything except 'dismiss the charges.' "Thank you, I'll let the rest of the family know." She waited for Jean to continue on out of the courtroom before running over to Louis. She stood before him, eyes raised in question. "Is it true? Is he cleared?"

He smiled broadly, and his large hands opened wide expressively. "It is true. The papers are being drawn up as we speak."

"Thank you," she said. "I can't believe it."

"Believe it. Dan should be out in a couple of hours."

"I'll call Nicole."

"No need. My assistant already has."

"Does he know?" Faith asked.

Louis shook his head. "Not yet. But he will shortly."

"Can I tell him?" she asked.

Dan paced back and forth in his cell going through every emotion, from hopeful and excited when he first got back, to questioning and concerned as the hours ticked by, to finally negative and disbelieving. Now, he was certain that it had all gone wrong and he was bracing for the news. Would he spend his life in jail? Would he not be around to watch his kids grow? He had managed as well as could be expected this last month but now that they neared the end, he felt like he was at his breaking point. He simply could not handle one more thing. He held onto the bars of the cell and leaned his head down on them, his eyes closed, lost in a meditation of sorts, trying to stay calm and in control. He used different methods different days, sometimes he went back through his life and picked out a day, the birth of his kids, his first kiss, the game in high school when he pitched a no hitter. He often lost himself in baseball, the steadiness and the stats. Right now, he was back in college at a nail-biter of a game. He'd start at the beginning and to the best of his memory, recreated the entire game. Every at bat, every pitch, and every play. It was a mind consuming exercise that kept him away from the spiral his brain tended down if left unoccupied.

"Williams!" a guard yelled jarring him from his thoughts. He lifted his head. He had no idea what time it was, especially without a watch or a phone in the constantly dimly lit cell area, but it was late. "Attorney visitation room, now."

Dan nodded and stepped back as was the formality when a guard opened the cell. Once the door was opened, Dan walked in front with the guard behind. They moved outside of the cell block and down a hall into an area where the visiting rooms, offices, and some private attorney meeting rooms were located. By the door, Dan again stepped aside allowing the guard to unlock it. When he finished, the guard then stepped aside and motioned for him to enter.

Dan walked in expecting to see Louis' hulking form occupying the table, his presence overwhelming the small space but the table was empty. The door clicked closed behind him. He turned his head the other way and saw her, standing small and quiet, hands neatly clasped in front of her, misty eyes lifted to his.

"Faith," he croaked out, choked with feeling, emotion clogging his throat and dripping out his eyes.

She moved toward him, throwing herself on him and wrapping him in a hug. He held her tightly, crushing her to him, too overwhelmed to do anything but squeeze. She stayed pressed against him for minutes, neither of them willing to move or break or capable of speech. For Dan, she represented hope for the future, and for Faith, he represented the same. He lost himself in her hair and her neck while she buried her face in his chest. Finally, they pulled back enough to look at one another. Faith's hair stuck to the dampness of her cheek, and Dan gently pushed it aside. "It's so good to see you," he said. Words were completely inadequate at a moment like this. She blushed, and her eyes smiled at him. "Please tell me it's for a good reason and you're not here to soften the blow."

She touched his face, and rose up on her tippy toes bringing her mouth to his for a soft light kiss, then moving across his check before reaching his ear. Dan's knees almost buckled. He was weak with tension, hope, and anxiety. He closed his eyes, wanting to remember this feeling, this moment, just in case he needed it in reserve as she placed her lips on his lobe for a last kiss then whispered, "It's all good."

He crushed her to him, immediately sweeping her up and whooping her around. She giggled blissfully as they swirled together around and around in a circle of joy and relief. When they had twirled enough to make them both dizzy, their faces almost breaking from the strain of happiness, Dan slowed down and placed his mouth on hers. They spun out their last turn, bodies and lips locked together in a tight, deep and meaningful embrace. When they separated it was as though the world had brightened. Not even the dull, dirty gray room they were in seemed as small and dim. He hugged her to him again securely, refusing to let her go for even a second. She looked at him, scrutinizing his face and reached up and placed a hand on his cheek. He looked beaten down, thin, unshaven, exhausted; his rugged healthy good looks transformed by lines and cheekbones.

"You look really bad," she said and he laughed, the softness and sparkle in his eyes returned.

"Thanks a lot." He dipped his head, nestling in her hair and in her neck. "You look even better than in my dreams."

She leaned into him, feeling him grow stronger with every moment passed. They rocked back and forth in each other's arms until a quick knock on the door gave them a moment's warning before it swung open. Louis practically had to duck to get into the room from the hallway. "Kids!" he boomed. "Daddy's here to take you home."

It was after midnight before Dan finally had his official release in hand and sat in Faith's car on the ride back to his house. They barely spoke. Dan spent most of the journey looking out of the passenger window quietly lost in thought. He had spoken with his mother, Nicole and the kids about an hour or so before. Of course, they knew the good news but he hadn't been able to speak with them until then. For Faith, listening in had felt like an invasion of privacy, their love and joy so overwhelmingly intimate and pure. He promised his kids he would be there when they woke up in the morning, to make them breakfast and do whatever they wanted with the day. He would be there, he said, his voice breaking with emotion. He hung up, and Faith reached over and placed her hand on his and squeezed. He squeezed back and focused on the view outside the window.

They pulled up to his house, and she unlocked the door for him. He stepped out into the cool night air, breathing deeply, taking in the trees and leaves moving in the light breeze; the dark black summer night sky full of brightness and a million stars. It was a beauty that he hadn't seen in some time and worried that he might never see again.

"Faith," he said, wanting to share it with her but then realized she hadn't left her seat in the car and sat watching him through the window. He walked around, bent down, and leaned into the open window. "Hi," he said softly. "Of all the driveways in the world, here you are in mine."

She smiled at him and he bent in farther and kissed her. She accepted greedily, almost too greedily, her body practically weeping with longing. Her desire which had been shut down for so long, he had reopened that month before, however briefly, but enough for her to remember the exquisiteness of pleasure. And once the body remembers, it can't forget. It waits on low burn until reignited again. Now after over month without his warm mouth on hers, the cool air in her face, his house like heaven's gate before her, she had to hold herself back from pulling him into the car.

"Are you gonna come out?" he asked.

She shook her head. "I don't think I should." He looked at her quizzically, and she babbled on. "It's just late, and you must be so tired.

I'm sure you want the night to sleep in your own bed and just relax and appreciate the fact that you're finally home and alone in your house. I don't want to invade your space. This has all been a lot to process."

He looked at her thoughtfully. "Faith, I've been in that cell for twenty-nine days. And one of the only things that got me through each and every night was thinking of you. I've spent all those nights alone with only the dream of you. I don't want to think about you tonight. I want to have you. Please stay." He pulled up the door handle, opened the car door, and held out his hand to her. "Please."

She placed her hand in his, and he gently pulled her from the car into his arms. The night wrapped around them and they lost themselves for a moment in each other like teenagers until finally he lifted her up and carried her to his doorstep. He placed her down while he worked the keys in the door and Faith almost couldn't wait to get inside, but didn't want to rush him. "After you," he said and gestured her in, pushing closed the door behind them.

She couldn't even wait another step and reached her arms around his neck, pulling him close. They stayed by the door for a while, slowly kissing and enjoying the sensation of being pressed together, the heat rising between them. Faith slid her hands underneath his shirt unable to control her deep need to feel him. He pulled back slightly, which made her pull back considerably. "What's wrong?" she asked, already self-conscious.

"Nothing is wrong."

"I know. It's too much too fast." She stepped away from him. "I'm sorry. I knew you needed some time."

"Faith," he said evenly, moving toward her. "I don't need time." He smiled. "I need a shower. Interested?" She blushed and nodded, and they walked up the stairs together.

By 7:30 a.m. the next morning, Dan left his house like an excited pup to go see his kids, leaving Faith at his kitchen table with a cup of coffee, a kiss and a contagious smile. "Dinner tomorrow?" he had asked and she nodded. "Honey Wild? 7:30?" She nodded again. He had beamed at her and bounded out. Now she sat at his table, luxuriating in the lingering effects of last night's loving, she felt both energized and lazy, flush and girlish, sober and giddy. It was so good. The shower where they washed each other from their hair to their toes and the bed where they explored each other again. It was quicker, filled with an urgent, pent up need and afterward, exhausted, they went right to sleep, nestled in soft blankets and each other.

Faith was so happy her boys were at her parents and at the very least they would be spending the week there. It gave her some time to spend with Dan and also to think. Being with Dan wasn't exactly a simple matter. Now that they'd gotten through the unbelievable nightmare of the last month, the idea that they could just be together was as comforting as it was unsettling. Wayne's death and her awakening with Dan had happened in the same breath of time. It was all so fast that it was almost simultaneous. There was no time to dissect any feelings or figure out any logistics. She and Dan weren't a typical new couple by any means. They had gone from zero, well, almost zero, to a hundred in a the beat of their fluttering hearts, overwhelmed emotions and unbelievable circumstances. The outside world exploded and now even though the main damage had been done, there was wreckage and they would need to figure out how not to hurt others and get burned themselves. It unfortunately wouldn't be as easy as a kiss and a cup coffee and on with our days.

She relaxed, slowly sipping, in no rush and completely unaware of the tropical storm brewing outside. The heated whispers already floating down the street like butterflies, sighing like the breeze into open windows, being left on doorsteps like the morning paper. From one street to the next and all through Fort Jefferson, the hushed voices circled and swirled carrying curiosity, judgement and speculation, picking up speed as it churned. It began as a simple observation and a raised brow when Marni Kingston, who lives across the street from Dan and has a son the same age as Derek, Reggie and Jake, opened her door early that morning to put her younger kids on the bus for camp and happened to notice Faith's car parked in his driveway.

Rockets Team Chat
(Chris, Max, Dylan, Balls (Josh), Ryan, Money (Manny), Tyler, Jimmy, Carlos, Benji, Sam) Landon – Off chat

Chris – Dudes!!!

Jimmy – Brain exploding!

Tyler – I know!

Chris – Kapow!

Money (Manny) – So Coach Dan, huh?

Balls (Josh) – I really didn't think he did it

Chris – Big talker now, huh?

Balls (Josh) – I didn't

Tyler – I didn't either

Money (Manny) – Did you hear about Landon?

Ryan – What about him?

Max – I don't think you should share any of that here

Chris – What? I didn't hear!!

Dylan – My parents don't tell me nothing!

Carlos – You guys are scaring the rookies

Money (Manny) – Sidebar me

Ryan – Benji? Sam? You afraid?

Chris – Boo!

Balls (Josh) – Not helping

To: Rockets Families
From: Robin
CC: Matt, Mikey
BCC: Deb
Subject: Changes

Hi there everyone,

Just wanted to let you all know that I will be taking over Deb's responsibilities as team manager. Deb has some personal issues that need her full attention and our thoughts are with her. I know most of you know me, but I want to introduce myself to the newer parents. I'm Robin, Dylan's mom, and Nick is my husband. We've been with the team for three years. I'm always on the sidelines so if I haven't met you already, I will be sure to say hello at our next game or practice. (Got to get to know the people I'll be asking to bake for our next Cooperstown FunRaiser, right? ☺ But that's for another email.)

Deb has always had us prepared for our games (Thank you, Deb!) and I plan to follow in her footsteps while also taking things in a new direction. (Hint: We're also going to sell coffee now at our bake sales!) I have so many ideas I can't wait to share with you! Like new uniforms!! I've always favored those tie dye camouflage jerseys! And a snack rotation where different parents bring snacks for the kids each practice!

But back to business! There have been a lot of changes these past months. We have a new head coach (Yay Coach Matt!) and assistant coach (Yay Coach Mikey). We have three new players (Welcome Carlos, Sam, and Benji!) with the possibility of a fourth on the horizon. Coach Matt has his eye on an great new player to bring to our team. We have Cooperstown just weeks away, and there's so much to do. (I will send out a detailed email later this week on our hotel reservations, dinner reservations, and the list of necessities you will need to pack for your children.)

Also, some business. There will be a practice tomorrow at 6 p.m. Kids can wear shorts.

As a final note, I just think we should acknowledge the fact that our former coach, Dan Williams, has been released and cleared of all charges. We wish him well. I, for one, have already dropped a tuna casserole at his house welcoming him home. It would be nice for some of you to make a similar gesture. We are the Golden Rockets. We have an example to set!

To the stars, Rockets!!

Your faithful and eager new admin,

Robin

Deb sat in her kitchen reading the email she just received from Robin, effectively firing her from the team. It was passive aggressive and disgusting. Five years she had worked with the golden Rockets giving everything she had to Wayne and the team. She lived and breathed them. She put them before herself. She loved them. And Matt didn't even have the balls to tell her himself. What a coward. Not even a heads-up from her friend Barb. And Robin? Just usurping her with such glee. Ugh. She wondered if she'd receive a bcc email similar telling her that Landon had been cut as well. She wouldn't be surprised. Not that she should really care about any of it. She needed to pick up the pieces of her life and put them back together. She needed to get her priorities back in order. She had been consumed with Wayne to the point where she lost perspective on Landon. She didn't realize what she was doing to him. She hadn't even considered him. It was all about her, and now it was time to be all about him. Not that that was good enough. She had a lot of making up to do. And therapy. A lot of therapy both separately and together. Her emailed dinged, and she clicked on it.

From: Matt
To: Deb
Subject: Season's change

Deb, I hope you're not in shock as I'm sure you just saw Robin's email. I'm thinking you're savvy enough to have expected it. I probably should have told you first. Okay, I know I should have. But you know how it works, and you know that you can't be an effective admin for the Rockets anymore. Wayne is gone. You were a part of his reign, and there is no question that you did a great job. But I need a fresh start. Too much has gone on. It's time for you, and unfortunately (as the team will sorely miss his competitive spirit as well as his strong arm and his bat), it is also time for Landon to go. I've always enjoyed working with you and being side by side in the trenches. I wish you luck.
Matt
Oh, and if you wouldn't mind, please gather up all the Cooperstown essentials and any other team information you have and leave it with either Joe at Tigers Turf or you can leave it in my mailbox or Robin's. Thanks.

Well, he's right. No shocker here. She saw that one coming. She probably would have advised Wayne to do the same thing. Dump the deadweight dragging the team down. But Landon might not see it that way. Landon was going to struggle. They might have to switch schools just to give him a fresh start with some new friends. Maybe it was a good thing being let go. Yes, it was a good thing. She knew it. Too much had happened. Still, fuck them those fuckers. Thanks for your years of service, but you are no longer necessary. No one was going to run that team like she and Wayne did. Together they were the fucking King and Queen of FYO. They ruled. Dunk that in your coffee, Robin. And enjoy it with your piece of shit new head coach! Fuck you all very much.

Honey Wild was an intimate and understated restaurant hidden in the center of Main Street, nestled between Lee Lee's Ice cream and the Blooming flower shop. With a dark store front and just a small framed menu sign, it was the kind of place you could pass a hundred times and never notice.

Inside was dimly lit, just one shade above dark but so cozy. Open brick walls and rustic tapestry draped over the windows added warmth, making you feel like there was a fire roaring, even though there were only the small candles glowing on each of the twelve tables. Even though it was Wednesday, the restaurant was full but they got lucky with a last minute cancelation. They sat at one of four tables for two, against the wall, the candle flickering between them, making their wine and their eyes sparkle. Dan was happy. Faith could see that right away. He was home two days and had spent almost all that time with his children. Yesterday, he had taken them to Splish Splash, a waterpark about an hour away, and today they had gone bowling. Tomorrow, Jake wanted to see a Mets game and the next day Lola had them scheduled for Chuck E. Cheese®. He was on a leave of absence from work and decided that he wouldn't return to the office for at least another week. He said he hoped to spend his days with his kids and his nights with her. She couldn't think of anything better but sitting here in town having dinner together made her feel on display. She could already see a few of the tables staring over at them. She tried to ignore it, but when Dan put his hand over hers she automatically pulled away. He looked at her curiously. "Did I do something wrong?"

"No, not at all." She leaned in closer. The restaurant was so small you could practically eat the food off the table next to you. "I feel like everyone is looking at us."

Dan glanced surreptitiously around, smirking a little. "I don't see anyone I know and everyone kind of seemed absorbed in their own conversations." Faith looked around self-consciously.

"You're right. Maybe I'm being paranoid."

"Should we put on dark glasses?" he teased.

She gave a small laugh. "Then we wouldn't be able to see anything."

"We can leave," Dan said. "Really. I've got like four casseroles in my fridge that some of the moms from the Rockets dropped off. We can just eat that."

"Seriously?" Faith looked both amused and appalled. "I can't believe they dropped off casseroles. Sorry I didn't support you when you were in the fight for your life, but here's a nice lasagna. No hard feelings." She couldn't stifle her giggle.

"We can leave," Dan reiterated. "I don't want you uncomfortable."

"No, it's okay. I've got to get used to it, right? I'm just so used to hiding."

"If anything," he said, "they can't help but stare because you're beautiful."

She shook her head, unable not to smile. "Stop it.

"It's true."

"I'll bet you say that to all girls at Tigers Turf."

"Only the ones who pick me up from jail and let me..." He gestured for her to move toward him and he whispered dirty sentiments in her ear, ending with a nibble. She sat back, flushed with heat.

It took a second for her to collect her thoughts; his smug smile completely distracting. She needed to turn down the thermostat in here and took a sip of cold water. "It's just that, we've started a little backward and I'm just trying to find the balance."

"Oh, serious stuff. Yeah. Okay." He stayed quiet for a minute, looking at her carefully, and Faith tried to wait patiently, biting her lip to keep from tapping her foot. Finally, he spoke. "What do you say we don't talk serious for at least the week? I know we're all backward, and I know we've got some figuring out to do, but right now can we just forget and pretend? Can we just enjoy each other and this moment? It's been so bad and this is so good. Soon enough your boys will be home and I'll go back to work and life will move on and we're going to have to deal with reality, which will be messy and uncertain. I'm hoping we can figure it out but right now while we can, I want to just pretend that we don't have any baggage or history. That it is just you and me, and we are falling in love." He put his open hand back on the table and offered it to her.

Her eyes wanted to look around the restaurant but remained fixed on his. They smiled at her. She couldn't resist his words or his gesture and placed her hand in his. He squeezed and then let her go. The waiter took their order and they spent the next hour and a half eating, drinking, and talking. She relaxed and they had a wonderful evening, so happy to just pretend and be normal and fall in love.

They were waiting for their check when a woman, with her husband standing next to her and a couple behind them, stopped on their way out the door. "Hi, Faith. I don't know if you remember me but my son Harry played basketball with your boys a few years back."

"Oh, hi," Faith said, clearly uncomfortable.

"Yeah," the woman continued paying no attention. "And Dan we see you all the time at Tigers Turf. My younger son plays on Bill Segal's team."

"Oh, that's nice."

"Anyway, just wanted to stop and say glad your home, Dan. We never thought you did it." She turned her attention to Faith. "And we had heard some buzz about you two, but I didn't believe that one either. That one was too much to believe." She cackled. "Guess I'm one for two!"

Faith looked horrified. So did the woman's husband. He looked at her with eyes filled with apology. No one knew what to say after that so Dan just stared at her until she flustered. "Okay then, have a good night." They shuffled past.

Dan paid the check and they left in silence, taking the eyes of most of the rest of the patrons with them.

They drove in silence back to Dan's house where Faith had left her car so that she could leave in the morning and go do what she needed to when he left to spend the day with his kids. Now, every second she was sure she would just take it and go home. She had deluded herself into thinking they could have a chance, and he had reinforced it by asking her to pretend. But there was no pretending in a small town. Dan pulled into his driveway and turned off the ignition. They sat for a while staring straight ahead, the emotion of the situation still raw and tense between them.

Finally Faith turned to him, her eyes sad but when she opened her mouth to speak he stopped her. "Please don't go," he said. "Please don't let them define us." Faith closed her mouth and turned back to the window. Staying would only add fuel to the fire. But the fire was already burning.

"They're right. What kind of person am I?" she asked low and quiet. "My husband has barely been dead two months." Tears dripped down her face, and she turned toward the window.

"Faith," he said, not touching her. "look at me." She sniffled and shook her head. "Look at me," he insisted. Slowly she turned, her faced, damp and streaked. "I know this is hard. But you are a wonderful person. There is nothing normal about any of this. We both know that even though Wayne may only be dead a short time, your marriage has been dead for much longer."

"I know that. But it still feels wrong."

"What feels wrong? Me?"

"No." Her tears fell harder now. "No," she managed. "You couldn't feel more right. But our timing is wrong."

"Timing has not been our friend," he agreed.

"I have to go," she said and he looked at her heartbroken. "If I don't go now, I'm going to follow you right into your house and even though it's what I desperately want, I can't. I have to think."

"Okay. If that's what you feel like you have to do. I can't stop you."

She smiled. "You probably could, but don't." She reached out and touched his face. He grabbed hold of her palm and kissed it softly. She shifted a little closer and tilted her face to his. Gently, he kissed her mouth which parted with want, first softly then deepening with building need. Faith desperately wanted to move from her seat onto his lap. She ached with such hunger that the only thing she could do was pull back. "Coach Dan," she said sounding throaty with desire, "I am almost afraid of the way you make me feel."

"Sweet Faith, I'm completely falling for you."

With a sigh deeper than a nice shot to centerfield, she unlocked her door, got out and got into her car. With a little wave, she left.

Text from Landon to Reggie and Derek
I'm sorry.

Text from Landon to Jake
I'm sorry.

From: Bob Stanley
To: Joe
Subject: Fields

Joe, enough already with the crappy times. Give lacrosse its due.

From: Joe
To: Matt
Subject: Fields

Lacrosse is up my ass about the fields. Talk to Bob and figure it out.

From: Barb
To: Robin
Subject: Moving on

Did you hear about Faith and Dan?

From: Robin
To: Barb and Marie

Disgusting. Wayne's been dead a minute.

From: Marie
To: Barb and Robin

Whatever is going on or not, don't you guys think they've both had a tough enough time that they don't need your judgement.

From: Robin
To: Barb and Marie

Oh, it's going on. I heard it from reliable sources. And I'm not judging Dan.

From: Barb
To: Marie and Robin

Snort.

From: Marie
To: Dan
Subject: You

Just checking in. I hope you're settling back in and doing okay. Rich and I would love to meet you one night for dinner/drinks. We're so glad you're back. If there's anything you need (I'm sure it's not another casserole!) please call us.

From: Dan
To: Marie and Rich

Thank you. I appreciate your unwavering support and would love to meet up one of these days. Or you could come on over for some casserole!

From: Marie
To: Faith
Subject: Just hi

I know you've been overwhelmed with everything, and we don't typically do this but let's maybe make a plan for lunch one of these days.

From: Faith
To: Marie

I'd love to.

Dan parked his car at Tigers Turf and cut the engine. It was the first time he had been there since being led off in handcuffs about a month and a half ago. Initially, he hadn't wanted to come back but today both kids had plans. After spending over a week together every day they finally became comfortable with the idea that he really was home. Now their full days of quality time might be half days. Today Lola was asked to a friend's house to play dress-up, and Jake was meeting a few of his buddies to hang out at the park for basketball and to walk around town and get a slice of pizza. It was the way it should be.

He was beginning to feel somewhat normal as well, to think of the last two months as a nightmare that happened to someone else. Dan tried not to think of it at all. It had been a lynch mob and almost all the people he thought were his friends had deserted him. But it strengthened his relationship with his ex-wife and he knew who his real friends were, regardless of how many casseroles filled his freezer.

Getting out of his car, he rested against the back bumper and enjoyed the late afternoon summer day. The last week's humidity had broken and today was finally a day where being outside was enjoyable, where he didn't crave a cool shower every few hours, not that the kids ever cared if they dripped in sweat. In fact, the more sweat to drip in and dirt to roll in, the better.

He breathed easy, taking in the scene. It was around 5 p.m. on a Friday, and the fields were all full. He could see Jeff Blum from Rockets White playing over on Field 3 while Matt commandeered on Field 2. The other fields were filled as well with younger teams, and over on the side, lacrosse was holding a practice. Dan saw Bob Stanley walking toward him. Bob was immediately recognizable with his strong stocky frame and short buzz of blond hair. He and Bob weren't friends, but they weren't not friends. They interacted occasionally at FYO events, and he saw him around town. But mainly to Dan, Bob was just a huge lacrosse guy and his wife Erika had been sleeping with Wayne.

"Hey, Dan," he greeted, stopping in front of him. They shook hands.

"Hey, Bob."

"Glad to see it all worked out."

"Thanks." They really didn't have anything to say to one another but coming to Tigers Turf, Dan knew he was coming to the most public place he could. It was where all sports congregated and he knew almost everyone, and now for sure everyone would know him. He had to get it over with sometime. "So how's the team looking?" he asked.

"Pretty good," Bob said, happy to be on less awkward ground. "We're pretty strong. So, how about you? Coming back to baseball?"

Dan shrugged. "I don't know. I'm not there yet."

"Sure, I get it," Bob said. "Well good seeing you, man." They shook again and Dan watched him continue on and head into the field house, probably to meet with Joe.

He stayed put for a while, just watching the scene, the children exerting themselves, running and fielding out in the fresh air, the coaches lording over them, shouting encouragement and order, Donny zipping around in the background bringing a bat bag over to Field 5 or an emergency ice pack for a kid on Field 3. Parents filtered around, moms half-heartedly watching the play, more interested in chatting with their friends, hopefully paying attention at the right time when their kid was up or made a play and then clapping and hooting wildly. The hyper-attentive dads, annoying their children, following them from the batter's box back to the dugout, commentating on what they did wrong or right. The younger siblings stuck at the field, complaining but having fun with other captive sibs, throwing balls against the wall, having catches, running around wild, sipping Slushies, ripping off bites of pretzel or trying to blow bubbles with giant gobs of Big League Chew after coaxing money from their parents for the snack bar. It was a picture of everything good about youth sports without any of the politics; the fighting for fields, the alpha coaches and nepotism, the rigged evaluations, the lacrosse vs. baseball, the cuts, the crazy parents, the annoying, difficult kids, the 8 a.m. games an hour away that you have to be at an hour early, the in-team fighting...

But even with all the nonsense there was still so much comradery and community, excitement, and team spirit. There was fun and play, hard work, discipline and focus, filled with life lessons about winning and losing, friendships and bonds, rivalries and respect. It was everything he loved about the game.

He just watched, nodding occasionally at a local parent who he could tell wanted to approach but was uncomfortable. He'd wave, they'd smile, wave back and move on, the ice broken without any uncomfortable interaction. After about fifteen minutes, he saw Bob leave the field house office, walk to his car and leave. Two minutes later, Joe was by his side, welcoming him warmly with a quick hug accompanied by a bunch of rapid back pats. "So good to see you, man."

"So good to be here," Dan said, returning the embrace. "Thanks for checking in with Faith. I really appreciate that."

"Of course. That must have been some nightmare for you."

"It's in the past," Dan said.

"I'm a little shocked about how the whole thing turned out."

"Has Deb or Landon been back?"

Joe shook his head. "Not since it all came out. And did you hear? Matt dumped her."

"That's a shame," Dan said. "But I'm not surprised. I know a thing or two about team loyalty on the Rockets."

"I don't blame you your bitterness," Joe said. "I'd be one pissed mother fucker. They were all, well almost all, a bunch of assholes."

"No argument here. But I'm not holding on to it. It was a difficult situation."

"You're a better man than me."

Dan smiled. "I don't know about that. I'm just trying to go with the program." He changed the subject. "So how's things with lacrosse? You had a meeting with Bob?"

"Fucked up as always. Matt's trying to be Wayne and bully Bob off the fields, but Matt's no Wayne. Baseball and lacrosse might never be best friends, but we're working on respecting the boundaries and each other. Bob's up for a board position. We need a better balance to soothe the natives. It's gonna work out better."

"Oh, Bob on the board and not Matt? He's gonna be pissed." Dan smirked, enjoying the small spiteful pleasure.

"He'll get over. He has no choice. He's gonna be even more pissed when he finds out who else is being considered for a place on the board," Joe said, eyeing him shrewdly.

Dan raised a questioning brow and looked at him with surprise. "You're kidding."

"I'm not. We had a meeting last night. You were nominated and quickly seconded. I think the reign of bullies is over. You've had quite a time of it, and I think now everyone wants to see you succeed. Plus, no one knows baseball like you. If it weren't for Wayne, you would have been on the board years ago. Actually, Bob too. It's really a no-brainer."

"Thanks, Joe. I'll think about it." It was surreal that just weeks ago he was the pariah of the town. His team had turned against him. His friends had turned on him as well. And now, he was being coaxed back into the fold, being brought casseroles and sought out for handshakes and smiles, redeemed at FYO and offered a new distinguished position.

"Think about this as well," Joe continued. "Jeff Blum has mentioned to me more than once that he would love to coach with you. If you're interested in taking the white Rockets to the next level. They're not a bad team and Jake has a few friends on there." Dan nodded, thinking. "And let me just say, about the whole ball throwing through the window, I really tried to get to the bottom of it, but there was just a lot of rumor. Some people said it was a couple of your Rockets, with Manny as the ring leader. But I also heard it was a bunch of older boys already out of the FYO system just being assholes. So I'm sorry about that. I really wanted to be able to hold someone accountable."

"Thanks." They stood together in silence for a minute watching the teams play.

"Okay, I've got to get back to the grind. I'm glad you're back, Dan. And think about what I said."

"Definitely will," he replied.

Dan stayed for another minute before taking his time walking toward Field 2. He needed to see everyone and get it over with. Donny zoomed by in his cart and slowed next to him. "Danny!" he said, as much of a smile as the thin lines of his mouth was capable of stretching. "So good to see you. I was worried there for a while."

Dan smiled. He always liked the stiff, serious groundskeeper who was the eyes and ears of TT. "Me too, Don."

"And how's that pretty little Faith?" he asked, and Dan immediately bristled until he took in Donny's easy manner and genuine curiosity and realized there's was no judgement lurking behind Don's words.

"She's good," he said, all of a sudden feeling a wave of melancholy. It had been a week since he had seen her. And she had cut short their usual email play. He wasn't at all sure what was going through her head and it was driving him crazy, but he resolved to be patient and give her some time.

"Don't tell anyone I said this," Donny said conspiringly, "but I always thought the two of you would make a nice couple."

"Me too, Donny."

"Did you see the banner?" Donny asked, gesturing over to the outfield fence. Dan looked over and saw that it a was tribute to Wayne. It read, "Hit one for Coach Savage. In loving memory of a winning coach and dad."

"Really nice. Wayne would definitely appreciate."

"Oh, and he'd love this. They've made up a new sign renaming Field 2 as Wayne's Field. They're waiting till Fall season to have a little dedication before putting it up. And there's talk now of creating a special 'winners tournament' in his honor. Only the best ranked teams and all that."

"Of course." Wayne was almost bigger at FYO in death, just not as loud.

Donny left him by the field, and Dan wished the walk was longer. For some reason, pretty much everyone was in attendance. He noticed a new bench a little off to the side and sat down to watch the boys practicing rundowns, not even noticing the small gold bar with the inscription, 'For Coach Wayne Savage. To the stars. Love, your Golden Rockets.' He observed Matt and Mikey having a deep discussion in the dugout. Matt caught his eye, acknowledged his presence and returned to what he was sure was a lecture to Mikey on what he needed to be doing. Dan turned his attention to the players and realized he didn't recognize almost half the boys. He looked over to the bleachers and saw Marie and Rich, Nick and Robin, and Barb and Sean sitting with four other sets of parents he didn't recognize. Things really had changed. This looked and felt like a completely different team. Except there was Matt, barking some disappointment out to Dylan, who had just overthrown to Chris. "Come on, man, is that how you throw?" And, of course, Mikey was hopping around unable to control his energy.

"Dan!" Marie said, noticing him. "Hey there!" He stood, and they hugged. When they pulled back, she looked at him searchingly. "How are you?"

"I'm hanging in there."

"I'm so glad to see you." Her eyes were as sincere as her words. All of a sudden, they were flanked by the rest of the parents on the team greeting him and patting him on the back, welcoming him with vigor. You would never know they sat on the opposite end of the courtroom refusing to look at him. "Did you get the brownies I dropped off?" Barb asked. "Are you coming back to the team," Nick wanted to know. "Really good to see you," Sean said. "Hey, we've got coffee, want some?"

He shook his head. "Thanks, I'm good." He stayed pleasant but distant. This wasn't his team any longer, nor were they his friends. Robin started telling him about the Cooperstown tournament that they were leaving for in three days and most of the others jumped in with last minute questions about reservations, logistics of rides, and things to bring.

"It was good seeing you guys," he said and walked away from the group feeling good about not being a part of them anymore. He and Jake had talked a lot about baseball and his feelings on the matter. Jake loved the game and would try out for the middle school team this year. Whether Dan would coach or he would play travel was still up in the air. They were taking everything slow. There was no urgency at the moment, except to get back to his car and leave Tigers Turf. He had enough of being the local celebrity. It was exhausting interacting with so many disingenuous people. He wasn't one to play games before but since everything that had happened, his patience in dealing with phoniness was very short. He wasn't looking to make enemies, but he wasn't interested in friends like that either. He wanted his life to be focused on appreciating every day and the important people in it. Corny? Yes. Although true. He hoped the feeling would stay with him and not fade over time into business as usual.

He was almost at his car when he saw her, carrying a large box and struggling a bit as she walked up to the field house. He immediately changed direction and headed toward her.

"Can I help you with that?" he asked and took the box from her hands.

Relieved of her burden, he could tell that seeing him had unsettled her and that unsettled him.

"Thanks," she said and looked away.

"Faith?" he questioned with concern, trying to get her to meet his eye, but she wouldn't. "What is it?" It was a plea, but Faith ignored it and answered a totally different question.

"I was going through Wayne's things while the boys were still away and found all this stuff from FYO. I didn't know if any of it was important so I figured I'd just leave it with Joe."

Dan didn't care at all about the box or what was in it. "Faith, why won't you look at me?"

She looked beyond him, refusing. "I have to go."

"Faith!" he said stronger, louder, and two random people walking with their kids turned. "Please," he said more quietly, more desperately. "What is it?"

She finally looked at him and the pain in her face was tough to see. Tears floated in her eyes and when she blinked, one swelled over and ran down her cheek. He reached out to wipe it away, but she stepped back. "Don't." Her voice quivered, and she looked around nervously. She saw two woman walking together with their sons glancing at them and whispering.

Dan followed her eye and saw what she saw. "Don't pay any attention to people like that," Dan said. "Ignore them."

"I can't." Faith said softly. "It's not just them. It's the whole town. I'm getting hate mail," she said even more softly. "I'm afraid to let my boys come back from my parents. I'm having them stay there for the rest of the summer."

She was so fragile, Dan almost wrapped her up in his arms despite what she said, but he didn't. "Is it really that bad?" he asked, reaching out to her with the tenderness of his voice and the appeal in his eyes.

For a moment, her control dissolved and she stared back, drawn to him as always, wanting him as always. All she had to do was to reach out and touch him, slide her hands under his shirt, get lost in the soft, demand of his lips. If only she could pretend the hushed voices and finger pointing didn't matter. Shutting her eyes, she blocked him out and regained her composure. "I have to go," she said, refusing to look at him once again. "Please leave that with Joe for me." She turned around and walked back to her car and left without turning back.

"Did you hear about Faith and Dan?"

"She's disgusting."

"But he's kind of dreamy."

"Still disgusting."

"I heard they were at Tigers Turf together."

"I heard Don caught them making out by the field house."

"I heard they were having sex behind the field house."

"She has no shame."

"Her poor boys."

"What does he see in her?"

"Baseball royalty."

"Her husband is barely cold."

"He wasn't too bad, either."

"All the women he was sleeping with would agree."

"Fucked up people."

"She's disgusting."

It was after dark when Faith heard a light rap on the back door of her house. At first she thought it was nothing, but then it happened again. She grabbed a bat—there was always a bat lying around in her house—and padded toward the kitchen to investigate. She had been living alone without the boys for a couple of weeks and without Wayne in the house for over two months. She didn't mind being alone. In fact, she really enjoyed it except when it was dark and there was hate mail stacked in her office and mysterious sounds coming from her backyard. She considered calling Detective Jonas. They had been speaking over the last few days regarding the mail. She knew he couldn't really do anything but wanted it on record, anyway. Most of the letters were anonymous, although not all, and almost all of them were non-threatening reprimands. It seemed Fort Jefferson was filled with morally perfect people who could stand on their sanctimonious platforms and judge her. There were a few though that seemed like they would relish a good old fashioned stoning, and they already had their rocks picked out.

She turned on the backyard lights and immediately saw a figure standing up against her window. She dropped the bat and screamed. Dan gave a small wave and mouthed, 'I'm sorry.' After taking a deep breath and disarming the alarm, she slid the glass door open and let him in, giving him a half-serious dirty look.

"Were you trying to kill me?" She locked the door behind him.

"Sorry," he winced. "I was trying to be covert."

"Mission accomplished," she said, and they lapsed into silence.

"You shouldn't be here," she said.

"I took a cab that dropped me two blocks away and then I walked here."

She smiled. "Very secret agent."

Her smile brightened his face. "Williams. Dan, Williams. But you can just call me Double O."

She looked at him amused. "No 7?"

"Nah. I'm just double O. Want me to take you upstairs and show you why?"

She blushed immediately and laughed. "Stop it."

He moved toward her, capitalizing on the light moment and drawing her into his arms. She let him, knowing she shouldn't but wanting to be there anyway. They stayed like that for a while before Dan pulled back. "How could you shut me out?" he asked, hurt.

"Come," she said and he followed her into her office. She motioned to the desk and Dan saw what looked like about a dozen letters scattered. He picked one up and read it to himself. 'Faith, You're a dirty disgusting whore. It's a good thing your husband isn't alive to see you embarrass him like this.' He winced. He picked up another. 'How dare you tarnish your husband's memory like this? What kind of a person are you. I feel bad for your children.'

"Are they all like this?" he asked, shocked.

"Various versions of the same theme."

"Wow."

"Yeah."

"How did I become the accepted one and you vilified?" He remembered the hate mail that he received. Somehow, it didn't feel nearly as threatening.

"Small towns work in mysterious and sinister ways," she said sadly. "I am most concerned for my boys. There's only three weeks before school."

"Can we call the police?"

"Did that."

Dan began to pace. "Detective Jonas?"

"Did that too."

He looked at her frantic. "There must be something we can do."

She returned his gaze soberly. "We cannot sleep together."

He dropped the papers and moved toward her, sweeping her up in his arms. "Not an option," he said and kissed her deeply.

"Dan," she breathed, making a half-hearted attempt to stop him, but there was no way she could stop him; she couldn't even stop herself. She was melting from the brain down.

He kissed her slow and long, pulling her against him, making her body ache with need. "Too long," he said and lifted the soft tee shirt she was wearing from her body. She tugged his shirt up, and he pulled it off as well. Skin to skin, they rocked together as the rest of their clothing disappeared from their bodies and the world outside disappeared along with it.

"Well that wasn't supposed to happen," Faith said afterward.

"Of course, it was," Dan said gruffly and pulled her to him.

She sighed and kissed his cheek. "I really don't know where to go from here. This is bigger than us. I can't fight people like this."

"We'll figure it out together." She looked at him skeptically. "We'll just do it in a secret super spy way for a while. But together. Okay?" He searched her eyes earnestly and she nodded, half wishing she was stronger and could suffer this nightmare alone, but she needed to share this difficult time and have his love and steadiness to support her.

"Between sunset and sunrise," she agreed.

"It's going to die down," he said. "I promise it will."

"Hopefully, it doesn't kill me first."

CHAPTER 24
(Wayne – Game Over)

Wayne lifted his head from the cushion of home plate and slowly sat up. He gingerly felt around under his hair for damage, his fingers coming away damp with blood. He really needed to cut back on the drinking. He took a breath, stretched round his neck, cracking it, then rolling back his shoulders. The whole scene that just happened was really fucked up. He needed to have some strong words with Landon. He had seen him right as he was falling, the light of the phone casting a stray beam over in his direction. He saw the kid clear as day. His terrified, confused face.

He was angry but not that angry, the alcohol blurred his temper. Landon meant no real harm. He was fucking with him a bit, but he had been fucking with his mom for years. So they were even. He was over Deb. She was a great gal, but he wasn't really that into her to begin with. Still, they were a team and teams looked out for one another. He would sit down and talk to the boy. It wasn't like he had much of a father's influence anymore. It would be okay. They would be back to business as usual in no time and start their concentrated focus on preparing for Cooperstown. He needed to have a serious talk with Deb as well. She had to understand that she was important to him and to the team but that they were not anything and would never be anything more than casual, and that for her sake, they shouldn't ever be that again either. It was Erika who he needed, that sexy bitch who surprised him and drove him wild; a tiger and a kitten with a great pussy. She had him whipped good. He couldn't get her off his mind. He pressed her number again, but it just rang and she never picked up.

"Calling my wife?" The voice came from darkness and Wayne literally jumped out of his skin.

Bob Stanley.

"What are you doing here?" He tried to sound imposing when really he was just a shock full of nerves.

Bob laughed. "I could ask you the same. Johnny told me about the fight at Flynn's, then you called Erika, who told me where you were. I came to kick your ass. But apparently, there was a line."

Wayne didn't know how to play this guy. He wasn't a teenager or a dumb ass tool like Johnny Smith. Bob was formidable, and he was fucking his wife. He went with his usual charm. "Yeah, I'm a popular guy."

"Who's running his mouth off about my wife."

Wayne couldn't help himself. He poked the bear. "Maybe you should be more worried about your wife's mouth."

Bob charged Wayne, shoving him back from home plate into the fence around the batter box. They lashed out at each other, Wayne clocking Bob in the stomach. Bob missing his face and connecting with this shoulder. It was dark and hard to see so they grabbed at each other wildly, missing more than hitting.

"Stay away from my wife!" Bob shoved Wayne, and they both fell back.

"Your wife can't stay away from me! She likes my big balls better than your hard little ones!" Bob lunged at him. Wayne lunged back. They wrestled against one another, two testosterone driven animals, rivals in every way, until Wayne kneed Bob in the groin and he fell back in pain, stumbling over the trophy laying on the floor.

"How's your stick feel now?" Wayne taunted. "Lacrosse is for pussies, man." He spat on the ground as Bob rolled over onto himself, roiling in pain. "Don't worry, I keep Erika real satisfied. My stick is nice and thick." He kicked at Bob. "Fucking loser. Good luck getting any field time now."

He turned away, bending down and grabbing his phone but it was a mistake. Bob was on him and knocked him to the ground. He landed a blow to his gut that knocked the wind out of him. Then it was Bob's turn to lord over Wayne. He kicked him in the side. "How's that feel, asshole?" Wayne moaned, unable to catch his breath. "Yeah, that's what I thought. And if you fuck with my wife or lacrosse anymore, I swear you'll pay." Bob stared down enjoying watching his pain.

Slowly Wayne got to his knees, somewhat recovered but exhausted. He really needed to drink less and maybe fuck less. Looking at Bob glaring at him with such hate, he almost felt bad. It wasn't easy coming in second.

"I'm out of here," Bob said and turned away; his rage dissolved, already feeling defeated even in his victory. He really loved his stupid, cheating wife right down to her Gucci underwear, and now they probably would have to divorce. It was going to be a mess.

"Hey, Bob," Wayne called, stopping him.

There was no aggression in his voice, and Bob almost thought he might apologize. "Yeah?"

"So you think you could give me a ride home?"

"You are such an asshole," Bob said and continued walking off. He really hated that fucker.

CHAPTER 25

From: Nicole
To: Faith
Subject: Support

Dinner again soon?

From: Faith
To: Nicole

Next week. Don't forget the drinks.

From: Dan
To: Faith
Subject: Things that go bump in the night

I hear there are intruders in your area. They tend to break in after dark.

From: Faith
To: Dan

I've heard about that, and I really hope no one tries to break in to my house tonight because, silly me, I've forgotten to lock the back door.

***

Detective Jonas sat at his desk, going over the file of a new case when Erika Stanley sashayed into his office on white kitten heels and a pink tank dress skimming her shapely body. "Good morning, Detective," she cooed.

"Mrs. Stanley," he greeted. "What do I owe the pleasure?"

"You're quite the sweet talker, aren't you," she said. "But believe me, Detective, this isn't a pleasure call."

This woman was something else, Detective Jonas thought. The most interesting part of his job weren't the cases. It was the people. There were no uninteresting people. They all had a story and a history. He was fascinated by them all.

He gave Erika the once over. But some were even more fascinating than others. "Well, I'm sorry to hear that," he said, and Erika smiled a sexy little smile.

"I appreciate the sentiment, Detective. Maybe another time." She sighed like she was Scarlett O'Hara.

Detective Jonas kept a straight face but cleared his throat. "So what is it that I can do..." He changed his mind midsentence. "How can I help..." There was too much word play with this woman. Finally, he decided on, "What are you doing here, Mrs. Stanley?"

She leaned forward, giving Detective Jonas a nice view of her cleavage before pausing for seductive drama. "It really is some serious business. I have something very private to disclose to you."

Detective Jonas raised his brow. This woman could talk a priest out of his celibacy. "What is this about, Mrs. Stanley?"

"The Wayne Savage murder," she whispered. "I may have some new evidence."

"That case has already been put to bed," he said matter of fact, instantly regretting his choice of words.

"Now you're talking my language," she said.

If the detective were any less seasoned, he would have rolled his eyes and also smiled. He walked right into that one.

***

From: Robin
To: Golden Rockets Parents
CC: Matt and Mikey
Subject: Cooperstown and Summer Wrap up

What a week at Cooperstown! How can I even begin to wrap it up!

The frantic competitive pin trading, the nail biter games, the come from behind victories. Carlos' unexpected fractured finger and his determined, 'I will not quit' spirit! The amazing play and team work by everyone! Will we ever forget that wing eating contest! The siblings running wild retrieving foul balls! The painted gold nails for all the moms, compliments of Josh's little sister Fanny! The Ice creamery! Max's game winning, jump to our feet home run! All the Advil poor Coach Mikey had to pop for his back so he could sleep in the bunks with the boys! The opening ceremony—Skydivers! The closing ceremony—Fireworks! The millions of moments between. We won, we lost, we won some more! Ultimately finishing in the top ten—the highest level ever reached as a team in all the years of FYO!!! I mean, that is such a testament to our coaches and our team's talent and determination!! We were gold out there, and we took it to the stars! The most poignant moment, the team picture (see attached) where everyone cheered. "For Coach Wayne!" Thank you all for your commitment and support!! For the carpooling and the snacks. For showing up with the mosquitos and the heat, ready to cheer! It was quite a run!

Now for more official business. The Cooperstown tournament marks the end of the summer season. Congratulations, you have earned two weeks of no baseball. But get ready. Fall is just around the corner and this is no longer the little leagues boys and girls. We are stepping it up. Coach Matt is holding tryouts for the new travel team. Whether you've been part of the Rockets for years or are brand new, it's a level playing field. Your child will make the team or not on their merits. I will be sending out dates in the near future. Keep a look out.

Again, thank you all for your support. See you at the fields. I'll be in touch.

Your loyal admin,
Robin

Oh, and I am still in possession of a blue hoodie, a red water bottle, Oakley sunglasses and a pair of orange batting gloves that were left behind. Please email me to claim them.

For the next few weeks, Tigers Turf briefly hibernated; officially closed, except to Donny and the crew who worked the fields, reseeding and doing a general cleanup for fall. Joe, of course, still held court at the field house and had a never ending string of coaches, board members and disgruntled parents with whom to contend. There were always complaints of favoritism, that coaches handpicked their teams, paying little attention to the evaluations, and yet, ironically it was always those same parents that had no problem driving him nuts requesting to be with this one, but not with that one and to have this coach but definitely not that coach. It was an insane tightrope to walk season in and season out. But youth sports never stopped, so neither did FYO or Joe. There were applications to file, schedules to make, fields to divvy up, evaluations to hold, uniforms to order and a hundred other details for the upcoming season of intramural baseball, lacrosse clinics and flag football that ran from grades K-8. There were new coaches to approve, and background checks to run. There were internal politics to navigate through. Joe tried to play straight with everyone, but it didn't always work out. Sometimes teams had to roll over, sometimes they got crushed, but this was a machine that needed to keep turning.

Both Dan Williams and Bob Stanley were formally nominated to the board, but it would not be official until the board met next in September. With the two of them working together on the inside, it seemed a more promising future for FYO to support and promote both lacrosse and baseball more evenly than in the past. Joe hoped for less in-house competition between the two sports. There was enough to deal with on their own turfs.

Matt was pissed to be overlooked for a board seat, but his time would come, and right now he had everything he wanted. He was head coach for the Golden Rockets, something he had been pining over for years, and he wasn't doing a half bad job. He had clearly apprenticed under the school of Wayne but he was more tempered, and slightly less polarizing, probably because he was more tempered. It was a whole new team out there, but that was how it went. Teams morphed and changed, they grew up and out of their old uniforms; what fit perfect in the fall rode short and tight on the all the boys by spring. It was bittersweet, but youths didn't stay youths forever and the seasons and the boys continued to change while the coaches and parents held on for as long as their kids still allowed them to play with them.

Joe had the privilege of seeing them all; the young dads full of excitement strutting on to the fields with geared up, gung-ho five year olds or dragging tentative weepy first timers, hoping to coax them into a love of sports. They played side by side with the older, more seasoned kids, some with talent and some with good old fashioned effort; both barreled through the program year after year with their friends and their teammates, snapping gum, spitting seeds, swinging bats and balls, dads hanging on every pitch and moms on the sidelines bringing snacks and spirit, all of them cheering and complaining, backing down and stepping up and loving it, even when they hate it because in the blink of a season this time in their lives will be gone, their children grown and flown, the carpools and schlepping done, the balls, sticks and helmets retired and the bleachers filled with all new parents.

This will all be just a moment in time wistfully remembered, when life was good, the sun shone over green fields, children's smiles and friendly faces, where they won some and lost some, struck out and hit some out, but enjoyed the best of life and the game when they were still young and lucky and had their children by their sides.

In less than three weeks, FYO would reopen the gates and a new season would begin. Joe was overwhelmed, overextended and looking damn forward to it.

CHAPTER 26
(Wayne – Dead at Home)

Wayne kicked the dirt, cursing. It was getting later now, well after midnight. His drunken buzz was coming down to a low exhausted hum that left him feeling a little sick and disoriented. He just wanted to be home now. For the first time, he considered calling Faith. She would, of course, just pick him up, no questions, just silent judgement radiating from her. They never discussed what he did on his many nights out, and she didn't ask. Reaching out to her was a breach of their unspoken agreement, and he didn't relish doing it now. "Fucking Dan!" he cursed out loud to the silent night air. If he would have just picked him up, none of this would have happened.

He searched around a bit in the dark for his phone, finally finding it back by home plate lying next to the trophy. He started tapping at the key pad, but even before he finished he heard steps approaching.

"You forgot your dignity, huh?" He laughed. "Sorry, I don't know if I can get that back for you." But the voice that answered was not Bob.

"You have something to say to me, Wayne?"

Again, Wayne startled. He squinted into the night, his eyes having adjusted to the darkness. "Dan? Is that you?"

"Yeah, it's me Wayne. I got your message."

"Well, shit, this night is going to give me a fucking heart attack!" He started to stand. "Let's get the fuck out of here."

"I didn't come here to give you a ride."

"Of course, you did. Now let's go."

"No. I came here because I needed to tell that I'm done. I'm stepping down from the Rockets. I don't want to coach for you, and I don't want my son playing for you. And I'm not your fucking driver. Call yourself a cab, asshole."

"You're fucking kidding me? You came here to tell me that?"

"Yup." Dan turned to walk away. "See you round."

"Fuck you!" He spat. "You don't walk away from me. I'm in charge here! Don't take it out on me if you never had the balls to stand up for yourself or Jake." He taunted him, but Dan kept walking. "You just took my shit day after day. You sat in that dugout being my bitch." Desperate, Wayne continued yelling, but Dan kept moving farther away, taking his life in a new direction and Wayne wasn't in the picture. "And don't think I don't know the hard-on you have for my wife! But she's mine, not yours. I'm head coach and you're my assistant. I've got it. You don't. Deal with it! And give me a fucking ride home, bitch!" He huffed with anger like a ten-year-old having a tantrum.

Dan slowed. "Bye, Wayne," he said. "Have a good—" He didn't finish his sentence because Wayne charged him.

Dan didn't move fast enough, and Wayne knocked him to the ground. They scuffled a bit, rolling around in the grass, landing jabs both verbal and physical, but it only lasted a minute before Dan pushed him off. They both stood panting.

"All these years, I tried to be patient with your alpha male bullshit. I tried to stay even for my kid and because I thought it was easier, even though it wasn't easy for me." Dan brushed himself off. "But I realize now it was harder for you. I'm a better coach and you know it and you can't stand it, but you needed me if you wanted to stay a winner, right? You need me, asshole. I don't need you. Good luck without me, buddy. I'm gonna start my own team just to kick your ass." He spit in the dirt and once again turned his back to walk away.

"You don't walk out on me!" Wayne yelled. "You're not in charge. I'm in charge! I am FYO! FYO does what I want! You will never have your own team, and Jake will never play there again!"

Dan stopped. He knew he should continue to walk away. He had the upper hand, but he had walked away too many times. "You just never know when to quit, Wayne."

"And that's all you know how to do." Wayne laughed.

This time, Dan lunged at him and Wayne was ready. They shoved each other against the fence. Wayne's foot knocked against the oversized trophy. He picked the heavy ornament up and jabbed at Dan who side stepped away from it. Wayne swiped at him again but this time Dan grabbed at it, tugging it from his grasp.

The next minute happened so fast and in slow motion. Dan took the trophy in both hands, gave one wild swing in the dark and connected with Wayne's head. Wayne dropped to the ground, almost in the exact spot at home plate where he fell with Landon. This time he didn't get up.

CHAPTER 27

It happened slowly and then all at once. People started moving on from her. There were new and more exciting dramas to focus on: another local affair, a botched plastic surgery, a hot new yoga instructor—male. Well, maybe not more exciting but yesterday's news was still yesterday's news. There was a small blip and some renewed excitement when gossip started swirling around Bob Stanley as the real possible murderer. She herself had heard it through the rumor mill. People were saying that Erika Stanley had gone to the detective and revealed that not only did Bob hate Wayne for a number of reasons, but the night of his death, after a fight a Flynn's where Wayne told a bar full of people she was sleeping with him, Bob had pressured her into revealing his whereabouts, and she had told him where he would be.

Faith didn't want to listen to rumors and tried to ignore them, but ultimately she couldn't help herself and called the detective to see if there was any truth to the story. The detective came by the house later that day.

"Faith, I cannot prove a thing that Mrs. Stanley has alleged," he had said.

"But what do you think?" Faith had asked. "Do you think he did it?"

Detective Jonas seemed to be considering what to share and what to keep to himself. "I'll say her story is somewhat credible, given the triangle between them, but after doing a little digging I also discovered that Mr. Stanley is in the process of divorcing Mrs. Stanley and that with her public affairs she has a lot to lose. Given that there are no eye witnesses or hard evidence, and the state already has a closed case with a confession, I don't see this matter being reopened without a lot of pressure."

She nodded. She didn't even know if she would want it reopened. She and her boys had been through enough. Wayne had been gone for three months now and they were slowly moving on with life. She didn't want them to deal with the talk and rumors all over again; the newspapers hounding them and becoming pariahs for the 'possibility' that the husband of someone who Wayne was sleeping with, in the heat of the moment, may or may not have killed him. No. They needed to move on and get away from all of the ugliness, so anytime anyone mentioned Bob's name or the possibility, Faith shut it down. Wayne's death was a tragic accident and that was that.

That was what the courts thought and her boys thought and that was the story she wanted them to have. She had a momentary flash of worry for Landon, who if this were true would spend his whole life potentially blaming himself for something that he didn't do, but she couldn't worry about him now. Her boys were her main concern.

They seemed to be doing okay, but grieving teens are tricky. You never know what's really going on in their heads. Faith vowed to be super vigilant and connected, especially with Derek who was typically more closed off.

She was careful to speak highly of Wayne, to highlight all the wonderful qualities about him, his devotion to them and to reinforce his expectations and the hopes he had for their futures. He had done right by them financially. Her boys were set up for college and he had put enough away for them to be secure for a long time, and if she sold the house and downsized, possibly forever. Wayne always lived large. Faith could live a lot smaller if she needed to, but right now she was lucky enough to not have to think about that.

She could finally walk around town or go to the supermarket like she had the year before. Once again, people sought her out to smile and say hello. The hate mail had stopped and if people were still whispering about her, she didn't see it, which was good enough. Honestly, she was used to a little gossip. She had been married to a serial cheater for years.

It was all starting to settle, she thought hesitantly optimistic, and dropped a few quarters in the meter. She was meeting Nicole and Maria at Hara's for sushi and drinks, just like they had every Wednesday night for the last three weeks. It had become a standing date from the first, when they all gathered together and realized that they all truly connected and liked one another. It was almost amazing considering all the long term friends she had that she had avoided for months now and had no interest in having lunch with. These woman were her support group that she trusted and relied on. They had not only become indispensable to her in the short period of time since Derek and Reggie had come home from her parents', they had also become essential to them as well.

Faith easily reinforced their friendships with Jake and Max, and the four boys rotated between her house, Nicole's, Marie's or Dan's. She knew they would always be in safe homes with people looking out for them.

When she got in the restaurant, Nicole and Marie were already sitting there engaged in an animated conversation. They looked up when she walked in and smiled brightly. Nicole hurried over. She had finally found her team.

***

(Group Text between Derek, Reggie, Max and Jake)

Reggie - Dudes, our moms are out again

Jake – They go out more than we do!

Max – I told my mom to bring me home sushi

Derek – Reg, let's put in an order!

Jake – Maybe we should just show up and surprise them

Max – Yeah, snort, they'd just love that

Derek – It would be funny

Jake – My dad can drive us!

Reggie – Well, my mom would love that

Jake – That's not what I meant

Reggie – Damn. Sensitive much?

Jake – You know I'm cool.

Reggie – Aw! Brother!

Max – I feel so left out!

Jake – You can be our weird cousin!

Max- Luv u too man!

Reggie – Der? Don't make me get up and come find u

Derek – I'm here

Reggie – You ok?

Derek – U know I love your dad, Jake. Just working thru it

Jake – We all love u, dude. It's not easy

Max – We're here for you.

Reggie – We'll get thru, brother.

Derek – I know. Thx guys.

Max – So should we go?

Jake – Nah. Too lazy now.

Reggie – Totally texting her our order

CHAPTER 28
(Wayne – Post Season)

Deb sat in her room reeling from the nights events. Was she really that desperate? Apparently she was. She allowed a man—granted one that she loved—to use her regularly. Landon was right, she actually begged him to. She was a slut, whore. She was disgusting and pathetic. He didn't say one wrong thing. She convinced herself that Landon wasn't interested in her or what she was doing, and was just horrified and amazed at the close attention he had been taking.

She took a bite of the large hunk of pie she had taken into her bedroom. If she didn't have a man, she might as well get a little fat. What was the difference? She knew she was moping, but she also knew it was time to take a stand. She couldn't be having sex on her front lawn. She couldn't pretend anymore that her teenage son was oblivious. She had avoided hard conversations with her ex because she was so damaged from his abrupt departure. She hadn't expected his betrayal, and she had a hard time even speaking with him. He totally shocked her by le aving and then devastated her even further by proving to be a shitty father. She needed to step up and make him man up, for Landon's sake. She took another bite of pie and even though it was so late and time for bed, she was wired and realized she would love a cup of hot tea to go with it. She put on her pajamas, wrapped herself in a comfortable robe, and headed back to the kitchen. When she passed Landon's room, she knocked and when no one answered she slowly opened it and walked in.

The room was empty. She looked around, even opening his closet as if he'd be sitting there on the floor like he did when they played hide and seek when he was a kid. Fuck. She walked downstairs calling his name. "Landon? Are you down here? Landon?"

He wasn't downstairs either, and Deb started to panic. She knew where he must have gone. She pulled the strings of her robe tighter and grabbed the keys to her car. She pulled the door open just as Landon was pushing it and they practically bumped into each other.

"Landon!" Deb said in surprise, and he looked at her just as stunned. "I was just coming to find you." He trembled slightly and his shoulders hunched high and tight as if he were trying to hide his face in them. "Are you okay?" she asked softly and reached out to touch him.

He flinched. "Fine."

"Where did you go?" she asked, keeping her voice light and undemanding. She could feel the anxiety radiating off of him.

Impossibly, he lifted his shoulders a little higher and sunk his head even lower. "Nowhere. I needed air."

He didn't meet her eye but she already knew that he was lying. "Okay, and you're all right?" she asked, almost touching him again but checking herself and pulling back.

"Yeah. I'm going to bed."

He still stood there for an extra beat. Giving her a moment to try to hug him with her words. "It's going to be okay, Landon. I love you, and we're in this together. Just you and me. Okay?"

He still wouldn't look at her but nodded and brushed past. She watched him slowly slump up the stairs. Before she closed the door, she looked out into the cool night, looking left and right, up and down her quiet street, wondering about all that had happened and what the next day would bring.

When Johnny had called Bob and told him that Wayne was shooting his mouth off for all of Flynn's amusement, he had slightly lost his fucking mind. He raced home and confronted Erika, who tried to purr her way out of it as usual. In the back of his head, he knew not to trust her, knew deep down who she was, but she had him and she knew it. He wanted to believe her and almost bought it until he went back through her cell and found Wayne's number not twenty minutes before.

Then he lost his fucking mind all over again and forced her to fess up. She did, revealing where he was and admitting between hiccups and tears how Wayne had pursued and seduced her. Of course, he didn't believe her but he accepted it enough to take it as reason to go and confront Wayne, to have a place to release his fury. In fact, he was happy for the excuse. He hated Wayne. The two had been circling each other for years, the two top dogs of their competing sports. Wayne was an asshole who was fucking his wife. He had kept lacrosse as the black sheep of FYO and Joe, sympathetic to baseball, had allowed it. He was tired of the shitty times and the shitty fields. He was tired of taking a back seat to Wayne. The thought disgusted him. He was superior to that man in every way. He had looked forward to bashing his fucking smug ugly mug.

It didn't go exactly as planned but he was glad to have bested him to some degree, although now that the adrenaline had dissolved, he knew it was just a distraction from reality. He needed to confront him for his own pride, but it didn't change anything really. He was going to go home now to his beautiful, sexy wife who would get down on her knees and lick his balls for forgiveness. Tomorrow, he would go about finding a divorce lawyer.

From the minute Dan had received Wayne's message, the blood that had barely settled to a simmer rose to full boil. Why did he always have to make that extra stir of the pot? Why couldn't he just leave it alone? Hadn't they had a difficult enough night? He didn't play his kid on purpose just to fuck with him. He already got in the middle of one fight because of him. They had words which had escalated. He had felt marginalized by him for far too long. And now this. On top of everything, Wayne thought he could call him up for a ride? That he was really just his bitch who would come when he called.

Dan had paced his kitchen, completely agitated. He knew he should just go to bed. If he had a wife and his kids at home, instead of living alone, he probably would have. Instead, he had grabbed his keys.

The whole way to Tigers Turf he thought about the kiss he and Faith had shared earlier. It warmed him and calmed him, and also riled him up. There was that fuck you to Wayne that he reveled in, but mostly he knew it was awful because it had been so perfect. His fantasies had been pretty impressive over the years but it could never compete with the reality of having his hands in her hair, tracing his fingers down the smoothness of her face, the soft wetness of her lips and the desire in her eyes. His stomach dipped just from the memory of the weakness in his chest and the urgent, almost painful hardness of his groin. Imagination was child's play.

The truth was that he wanted Wayne out of the picture for years and now driving on his way back from the field, he realized he had his wish. Whether he meant to or not, he had killed Faith's husband, the father of her kids. Another human being. A dad.

A strong wave of sickness rolled through him and he pulled over, and opened the car door thinking he might vomit, but only retched a little. He needed to keep it together, he told himself, breathing deeply in and out.

He didn't know if it was a smart idea to leave him and run. It very likely wasn't, but he watched enough Law and Order to know that he had motive and opportunity. It might be deemed an accident or it might not. It wasn't a chance Dan wanted to take. He was man of the community. He had kids. He just needed to let this all just blow over as an unfortunate, drunken accident, which it kind of was. He hadn't meant for it happen. He had meant to walk away or to beat the living shit out of him. And, yeah, he wanted to kill him. But not really.

Standing over Wayne and realizing what had happened, Dan was horrified and numb. But after a moment of brain exploding paralysis, he immediately stopped thinking and started to move. His first instinct had been to wipe down the trophy with his shirt and then run for the hills. He had some scratches on his arms, and maybe a few black and blue marks, but nothing that couldn't be written off from the brawl at Flynn's.

He pulled into his driveway for the second time that evening, talking himself through it. Bottom line was he could not change anything now. He should have been more in control and not so reactive. He wasn't an animal like Wayne, and yet, now he was worse. His brain traveled back to the kiss he and Faith's shared. It was so much better to think about, but that kiss might be the last he ever has. He could still call the police, he thought. He could. They might believe him. But they also might not.

No, he decided and right at that moment committed to his fate. There was no going back now. He wasn't going to let Wayne ruin him and have the last word. He had sat quiet in his dugout for too many years. Tomorrow, he would be calm and cool and go on like nothing happened. He was the good guy. He could pull this off.

CHAPTER 29

School had already been in session for about a week on the Friday before the first day that Tigers Turf officially reopened. The infields had been raked, dragged and consistently watered; any patches in the grass reseeded. Before the spring season, they would hire someone to laser grade.

Of course, today, like most days, parts of the complex were already in use. Football and Lacrosse had held an area for the weeks of August alternating times for their summer camps. And now Matt was holding an unofficial 'open' practice over on Wayne's Field. They hadn't even formally put up the new sign yet, but everyone had already easily shifted to calling Field 2, Wayne's Field.

Dan saw a multitude of new kids mixing in with the few he knew.

"How's it going?" Dan said to Matt who was conversing with Mikey over a list of new potential players. "Hey, Mikey," he said, acknowledging him.

"Hey, Dan. Good to see you."

"Mikey," Matt ordered. "Get 'em all lined up for a timed run down first and then around the bases. Let's see what we've got."

"Got it, Coach." He walked off to get things started.

"So," Matt said. "Long time no chat."

"Yeah, well in my defense part of that time I was in jail." He didn't say it with malice. He was over that. He was over all of it. He didn't want to be friends. He just want to live peacefully in the community.

"Touché." Matt tipped his hat. "And congrats. I hear you've been nominated to the board." Matt cast him a calculating glance but matched it with a smile.

He shrugged, brushing it off. He didn't want to get into it. "So looks like a lot of players have come out for your team."

Matt turned and looked out to the field—the kids running full speed to first, Mikey punching the stop watch as they hit the bag. "We'll see what we've got."

"So you and Jeff, huh?"

"Yeah, we're just going to run a few tournaments together and see how it goes."

"As long as you don't steal any more of my talent." He was referring to Max, who had switched teams to join him.

"Wasn't my call, talk to the parents. But I'm not poaching. We've got our own talent."

"I know. Just needed to say it. I'm sure you and Jeff will get along. You both have similar styles."

Dan wasn't sure if he was being insulted but decided to ignore it and continue watching the kids. "That big kid moves fast for someone of his size. Get him to keep his head down and he may beat some out."

"I know that." Matt scoffed a little.

"I know you do." Dan stood back from the fence. It was time to go. "Okay, see you around. Good luck with your team."

"Thanks. You too," Matt said and extended his hand. "No hard feelings."

Dan almost hesitated but took it, his lips curled up into an almost grin. "There's no crying in baseball, right?"

"Damn straight," Matt agreed.

He went into the field house to see Joe and tie up a few loose ends before he and Jeff met with their team the next day. He found Bob instead. "Hey," Bob greeted with a smile broad as his chest.

"Hey, man." They shook hands. "So I'm sorry to hear about your divorce." Dan never would have said anything, but it was all over town. Not mentioning it would be even more awkward.

Bob shrugged it off. "Yeah, thanks. It sucks." There was nothing more on the topic to discuss. Bob had filed immediately after Wayne's death was judged accidental and the case closed. Also, after he found out about Erika sucking another guy's cock. He had no choice but to cut her loose. It was a delicate situation that brought him much sadness.

Bob had no idea what had actually happened that night. He had seen the kid run off right before he came. All he knew was that he left with Wayne very much alive. Who knew, maybe the kid came back, maybe he had a heart attack, maybe Dan actually did kill him. He didn't know, and he didn't care. He wanted nothing more than to be done with the whole ugly business.

"Been there," Dan said. "I hear ya."

"And I'm sorry about all you went through as well," Bob said tentatively, sounding somewhat uncomfortable with the sentiment.

Dan had heard the rumors regarding Bob's potential involvement. They were nonsense, of course, but it still helped sway the tide in a direction away from him. It was all water under the bridge as far as he was concerned, and he hoped this would be the only time either of them would ever bring it up.

"Thank you," he said simply.

Bob quickly changed the subject. "So it looks like the two of us will be seeing a lot more of each other."

"It does seem that way," Dan agreed, happy to be on safer ground. "And I want you to know I'm not for any of the one sport over another crap. We'll all figure the fields and times out so that it's fair, or at least fair enough for everyone."

"I appreciate that. Lacrosse has been sloppy seconds for too long."

"I agree." They looked at each other for an extended, slightly uncomfortable beat when they realized they had nothing more to say to one another. "So, you know where Joe is?" Dan asked.

"Nah. I came in to drop off a bunch of applications for some players that parents had left with me. They're always leaving shit in my mailbox. Don't they realize it's easier to just drop it here."

Dan gave a small chuckle at the expense of 'parents,' common ground for coaches of all youth sports. "Okay, I'll catch up with him tomorrow. See ya round." Dan walked out and headed to his car. The two minute walk took fifteen minutes. It seemed everyone he passed wanted to stop and say hello. Finally he exited the field. He needed to get home and shower. It was already almost 6 p.m., and he had to get ready for a hot date.

Since Derek and Reggie had returned from Faith's parents a few weeks back, Dan and Faith had to modify their dusk to dawn romance into something more appropriate. It was all still new, and they were figuring out how to balance real life with the clandestine overnights they had been sharing.

Faith had a long talk with her boys. They needed to know the rumors and the truth, at least the basics of truth, before she let them back out into the arms of the town. Thirteen year olds weren't babies, but they weren't adults either. They were still immature boys who had recently lost their father, and she needed to be extremely sensitive. They listened carefully to the selected information she offered. She said only that people were talking about her and Dan's friendship, questioning if it were more than just a friendship, and she needed them to know. She had decided to try to answer any of their questions honestly. She wanted them to trust her and feel safe.

"Is it?" Reggie had asked point blank.

"Maybe," Faith said thoughtfully. "We're figuring it out."

"You're dating Coach Dan?" Derek asked. He didn't sound as angry as he sounded surprised or maybe shocked. The whole time, he had seemed to be half-listening staring off into space but all of a sudden the clouds parted and he seemed to be getting it. At thirteen, many kids had an amazing ability to see only themselves. Derek probably never noticed the strain in his parent's marriage while Reggie watched it all with alert attention.

"I don't know if you'd call it dating at the moment," she said carefully, "but there are… feelings there."

"What about Dad?" he asked earnestly.

She took a breath, hoping to not screw this up. "Your dad and I were married a long time, and we had you guys and were committed to doing the best we could for you. Sometimes, the love you feel for your husband or wife can change through the years. Sometimes, it just happens and you grow apart. It happened to Daddy and me. We were more like partners who were united in our love for you guys. No matter what happened in our marriage, we would always be there for you."

They listened to her carefully. Reggie immediately understanding, Derek's gaze returning to that far off place, probably because he understood as well.

"It's cool with me, Mom," Reggie said. "We want you to be happy." He nudged Derek, who seemed startled but nodded.

Faith breathed, happy to have the first conversation out there. Hopefully, it would get easy. "We're all going to take this very slow. You guys come first with me. It is us and then we'll see. Okay? But seriously, you are first."

"But I'm really first," Derek said, and Faith couldn't have been more relieved by his hint of a smile.

"By three minutes, dude!" Reggie countered.

They started playfully shoving each other, and Faith knew that the serious talk was tabled for the moment.

Even though the boys sort of knew, and even though much of the town sort of knew, Dan and Faith avoided being seen together so as not to exacerbate an already delicate situation. It was just too soon. Maybe once baseball started and they all started seeing more of each other it would just naturally happen, but right now they took whatever time fell in their laps.

Tonight, like last Friday night, their boys made plans together to hang out with a new group of kids. Faith liked that they had separated themselves from their old Rockets team. It had gotten too toxic. She would never encourage them to drop friends but it had happened automatically, both the boys and the Rockets moving on. This new group of friends included some of the boys from the White Rockets who they would be playing with, at least for the near future, including Jeff Blum's son Jordan. They seemed like good kids and she was slowly getting to know the parents.

She had a wall up now that hadn't been there before. After all that happened, it was hard to trust people. Yet, it seemed as though the town's outrage, at first at Dan and then at her, hadn't even happened. Everyone she met had been nothing but nice, if not warm and welcoming. She even had two casseroles in her fridge to prove it. It amazed her every time she opened the fridge and saw them. They had moved on, and she was trying to as well.

It was funny that through everything she and Dan had gone through, Wayne's transgressions in life had disappeared and he somehow managed saint status. Not that she was interested in knocking that down. She would much prefer her late husband to be considered a hero for her children's benefit. It was just ironic.

Last week, Derek, Reggie, Max and Jake had all gone with their new group of friends to the house of one of boys, a friendly good natured kid named Jayden. They spent the evening jumping in their pool, running round their massive lawn, playing soccer and touch football and snacking on chips and pizza that the boy's parents generously provided. Her boys had come home happy and chatty, talking about the fabulous house and everything they had done. It was so good to see them acting like normal boys.

Tonight they had plans with the same group to go see a movie in town and maybe get some ice cream afterward. Nicole was not only on pick up duty for Reggie, Derek, Jake and Max, she had invited them all to sleep over at her house, an intentional and appreciated gift to her and Dan, allowing them some undisturbed quality time. After what they had been through, they couldn't have appreciated the gift or the gift giver more.

At 7:29 p.m., the sun officially retired for the evening. Seven minutes later, the alarm chimes alerted Faith that someone had opened the back door. She smiled in anticipation and waited. Right now, there was no way she would trade their secret dates for real ones. The bubble of just the two of them against the world was too magical to pop. She hadn't been this happy since ever.

The house was dark with only a few of the dimmers set on low to guide him. He gently placed a large bag of takeout Chinese on the table and slowly and quietly made his way through the house, taking off his shoes at the bottom of the stairs and padding up. He reached her bedroom and stood in the entranceway, gazing at her standing there in a soft, silky pink robe loosely tied.

"Hey, Coach," she said, her eyes twinkling in the light of one of the two candles she had lit.

He moved toward her and she stepped to meet him. It had been a week since they had seen each other, and he couldn't take his eyes from her. She was so beautiful and he truly loved her, not that he would say that out loud. Not yet. He didn't want to frighten her, to make her question their connection with labels or any nonsense. He was just so happy to hold her. He kissed her lips gently. "I missed you," he said.

She sighed, feeling the heat of his body, melting her insides and igniting a fire of her own.

"I'd like to schedule a midweek practice as well, if possible," she said, her voice throaty, tugging at the button of his jeans. "There's a lot of work to be done."

"I'll check the schedule," he said, running kisses down her neck, loosening the sash of her robe, touching her everywhere until she groaned with need, and pushed him on the bed.

She straddled him, biting his lips, rubbing herself against him. "Looks like someone is up at the plate," she teased.

He flipped her so that now he was on top. "I'm looking to put a hard line deep into centerfield." He ran a finger under the rim of her underwear and she lost her words, her breath and herself. Playtime was over.

"Homerun," she purred contentedly when they had finished, smiling and nuzzling up against him.

He smiled sideways at her. It had all worked out. Wayne truly had been the only thing in his way. Now he had the girl, his own team and the support of the community. Sometimes, good guys do win. Or sort of good guys.

Landon was a real regret. He worried for the boy going through his life thinking he had accidentally killed Wayne. In some way, he didn't know how yet, but he would try to be there for him. Just as he hoped to be there for Derek and Reggie. And, of course, Faith. He would do his best to take care of them all.

He felt bad about Wayne but not as bad as he thought he might. It wasn't what he had expected or wanted to happen. It just had. And now what was done was done. If Wayne taught him anything it was that you had to take the opportunities that were given to you.

Content, he kissed Faith softly and repeated back the first words she had ever said to him. "Welcome to the big leagues."

***

Rockets (White) team chat (Derek, Reggie, Jake, Max, Jordan, Jayden, Henry, Lucas, Jesse, Jack, Owen, Leo)

Jayden – Official first team chat!

Henry – Here! Here!

Lucas – Hear? Or Here?

Jack – It's here!

Owen – Our team is awesome

Henry – Here! Here!

Jack – Okay now you have to go over there.

Jesse - LOL

Leo – We have awesome coaches

Lucas – Suck up!

Jordan – Totally agree

Max – Bahahaha!!

Derek – It's true

Jake – Thx guys. Thx Der

Jordan – Yeah thx

Henry – Practice later! First tourney together in three weeks!

Jayden – We are going to rock it!

Reggie – Hells yeah!

Jake - Feels so good to be back in the game!

Derek – It's baseball, man!

Reggie – Best game in the world

Jack – Unless you play lacrosse

Owen – Well, duh.

Leo – Why would anyone want to play lacrosse?

Max – True dat.

Jake – Don't ask my dad

Reggie – I love all you guys! Even though I just met some of you!

Owen – Love is the most important thing in the world but baseball's pretty good too.

Jordan – Yogi Berra!!

Owen - Nice

Henry – We're a team now. We stick together.

Jake – We'll lift each other up

Jayden – Except Henry, he eats too much

Leo - ROFL

Derek – Your dad always said that

Jake – And yours always said, play like the winners we are

Max – My dad says, listen to your coaches

Derek – Unless they're freaking crazy

Reggie – Here, here!

ABOUT THE AUTHOR

Alisa Schindler lives in the wild, wild suburbs doing extremely exciting things like picking up her children from school, schlepping to baseball practice and burning cupcakes. She lives dangerously by rollerblading on her street and eating far more ice cream than any middle-aged person should. Her free time is spent at the computer writing, which makes her husband happy because it keeps her from shopping and her kids happy because they're eating chocolate bars while running with scissors. She loves and truly appreciates her three boys, her husband and her friends who keep her sane and smiling.

Catch up with her on at Facebook.com/authoralisaschindler/ at Twitter.com/icescreammama, or on her blog at Icescreammama.com where she occasionally hangs out.

OTHER TITLES BY ALISA SCHINDLER

Secrets of the Suburbs
Murder Across the Street